Colorado Dream

THE FRONT RANGE SERIES

CHARLENE WHITMAN

UBIQUITOUS PRESS

Morgan Hill, CA

Colorado Dream by Charlene Whitman

Cover and interior designed by Ellie Searl, Publishista®

ISBN-10: 0986134724
ISBN-13: 9780986134722
LCCN: 2016959690

Be sure to join Charlene Whitman's readers' list to get free books,
special offers, giveaways, and sneak peeks
of chapters and covers.
Sign up at www.charlenewhitman.com

UBIQUITOUS PRESS

Morgan Hill, CA

Praise for COLORADO PROMISE
Book 1 in The Front Range Series

"A fresh new voice in Historical Romance, Charlene Whitman captured me from the beginning with characters I won't soon forget, a sizzling-sweet romance, a love triangle, spiteful villains, heart-throbbing heroes, and a plot full of intrigue that kept me guessing. Ms. Whitman's magnificent research transported me to the Colorado plains and left me longing to join the characters amidst the wildflower-dotted fields, rushing rivers, and panoramic Rocky Mountains. Fans of Historical Western Romance will not soon forget *Colorado Promise*."

— MaryLu Tyndall, best-selling romance author

"An adequate writer of historical fiction will include minor bits and pieces about the setting of their story. A good writer will do a bit of research to make sure there are historical facts included in the pages of their novel. A superb writer will create characters that could have actually lived during the time in which the story takes place and allows them to act as people in that time period would have really acted. Charlene Whitman is a superb writer."

— Examiner.com

"Ms. Whitman's voice is honest and true to the times. Not only in the way her characters spoke but also in the narrative. I lost sleep because I wanted to know what happened next. It's one of those stories you become invested in the characters. Five stars and 3 'YEEHAWs' to Charlene Whitman and *Colorado Promise*!"

— author Su Barton

"I was so utterly thrilled to have a story hold my attention this completely. It is the second in The Front Range series, but the story was complete within itself. Monty's and Grace's faith in God was strong as they met with many disastrous situations. It was also a story of holding onto hope when there appeared to be no hope. To me, this is the perfect story to 'cocoon' yourself in to your favorite reading spot, and try not to come out 'til you're done."

— D. Coto

Also in The Front Range Series by Charlene Whitman

COLORADO PROMISE
COLORADO HOPE
WILD SECRET, WILD LONGING
WILD HORSES, WILD HEARTS

$$Chapter\ 1$$

September 9, 1877
New York City, New York

THE SLAP ON ANGELA BELLINI'S cheek burned, but not as fiercely as the hurt in her heart. The pain and disappointment smoldering there sizzled like hot embers, threatening to reduce her to a pile of ash. She glared at her father's back as he stomped out of the room.

Why couldn't her papá understand? She would not marry Pietro, no matter how wealthy his family was, no matter how many years her papá and his had planned such an arrangement. "It is our way, Angela," he had told her again, his face hard and eyes dark and menacing, leaving no room for debate. "And you will marry him. You are twenty years of age—you are lucky he is still willing. You've made him wait long enough."

When she forced her objections past the rock lodged in her aching throat, she knew what would follow. What always followed.

Her papá's rage erupted in a torrent of Italian curses that ended with a slap that knocked her nearly senseless against the foyer wall.

As she slid down in a heap by the front door, she had caught a glimpse of her mamá in the kitchen, her back turned to her in unspoken submission. Angela huffed. *I will never marry and become like you, Mamá—squashed under the thumb of some man who wants only subservience and a crowded apartment full of squalling babies.*

She swallowed back tears. She would not cry—not today. Today she would take the first steps—real steps—toward her dream. And no one, not even the powerful and prominent Giusepe Bellini could stop her.

Their tiny stuffy apartment rumbled—as it always did six times a day and twice each night—from the Third Avenue El Train fifty feet away. The noise of the wheels clacking and the platform rattling mingled with the loud voices of her downstairs neighbors arguing— Mr. Paolino's tenor to his wife's shrill soprano. Outside her window, carriages clattered on cobblestones in sharp staccato, and shoppers and merchants carried on in boisterous conversation, sounding no more pacifying than an orchestra tuning their instruments.

On most days Angela could drown out the suffocating symphony of Mulberry Bend by rehearsing violin caprices in her head, imagining her fingers flying over the fingerboard, her right hand bowing the strings, eliciting the sweet and sonorous timbre of her instrument.

But on this stifling, humid September afternoon, the many pieces she'd memorized—no, absorbed into her very soul, as if food that nourished her—flitted away, out of reach, as she pulled down the heavy carpetbag from the hall closet—a bag that she'd found months ago stuffed behind a stack of wool blankets.

She stopped and listened. Her mama was humming in the back room as she folded laundry. Her two younger siblings were off playing with neighborhood children—in the street, no doubt, as the sweltering heat was worse indoors.

Angela's hands shook as she dabbed her perspiring forehead and neck with a handkerchief and went through her mental list of all she would need on her trip. Not much—she'd only be gone ten, perhaps, twelve days, if all went as planned. She pushed from her thoughts her papá's impending fury at her insolence and the resulting punishments that would await her upon her return. But she had made her decision, and there was no turning back.

Hurry, she told herself. Her papá had gone downstairs to the corner market, and while he often spent an hour or more on Sunday afternoons smoking cigars with the men of the neighborhood, discussing the politics of her close-knit Italian community and their various business ventures—*and arranging their daughters' marriages*, she thought bitterly—he could return at any time.

In her bedroom, she gathered the neat stack of clothes she had put in her bottom dresser drawer, then stuffed them into the traveling bag along with her few womanly items, her prayer book, some sheets of music, and a spare pair of shoes. She checked her reticule and found the roll of bills—the money she'd earned over the last two years from babysitting and teaching music lessons through Signore Bianchi's instrument shop on Second Avenue. She hoped it would be enough for the quality of violin she planned to buy.

Mr. Fisk hadn't answered her inquiry regarding pricing in his letter. He merely assured her he would provide her with an exceptional instrument and that they would work out the financial details once she arrived in Greeley, Colorado.

Would her meager savings be enough? It had to be, for she couldn't return to New York and face the audition committee without a proper instrument.

The director's words still stung. "You're a talented musician, Miss Bellini. But you bring shame to your craft by playing on such an inferior violin. Come back when you have an appropriate instrument." The three committee members had politely frowned when she flustered an apology and hurried to the exit of the symphony hall, pressing down her humiliation and frustration as tears welled in her eyes.

Her papá could well afford to buy her a violin of exceptional quality, and every year at Christmas she begged him to indulge her love of playing with the purchase of a new one, but he only laughed in cool disdain and waved her away. *"Give up your foolish dreams, Angela. Your place is in the home, with a husband and children. Not on the stage."* Her papá regarded music appropriate only at holidays and festivals and family gatherings, and only traditional song and instrumentation. He didn't—couldn't—understand this dream she nursed. The dream to play in the New York Philharmonic, to play on stage before an audience, to be a part of the creation of ethereal music that filled a great performance hall and moved listeners to tears.

To make matters worse, her older brother, Bartolomeo, sided with their papá, constantly nagging her to "get married already and stop being a burden on the family." Although he was but two years older, he and Dora had three children. And Dora—and most of Angela's other girlfriends from her school days, who were also married—gave her constant looks of pity, as if Angela was missing out on life's greatest joy. But they just didn't understand.

She had to fan the tiny spark of her dream to keep it alive, to prevent it from being snuffed out by her papá's stern expectations and society's demands. And it had nearly been extinguished a month ago, upon her papá's brash public announcement of her engagement to Pietro—an arrogant youngest son of a successful wine merchant who had no love for music—none whatsoever. She harbored no hope that he would ever understand her passionate need to play the violin, and no doubt he'd forbid her pursuit of her dream.

And then she'd read an article in the *Times* about one George Fisk, a master violin maker in a newly founded town in the West— a place called Greeley. On a whim she'd written him. Why? She didn't know. She could purchase a violin in Manhattan—one of sufficient quality. But there was something about the description of this man, Fisk. The way he spoke about the instruments he made. The care and time and love he put into each one. He built his instruments with a passion and love for beauty and music that resonated with her. For, she wanted more than a good violin. She wanted one that spoke to her soul, one made just for her. George Fisk promised he could provide just that. But she had to travel halfway across the continent. Was she willing? he'd asked her.

Yes, she wrote him. *Yes, more than willing.* Although, she'd never traveled outside of the city, and the thought of venturing into wild country, alone, made her stomach twist. But Fisk had told her not to worry. He would see to her accommodations and show her around his "wonderful little Western town." And she had to admit— she was ready for an adventure.

She looked around her cramped tiny bedroom situated in a crowded apartment in a busy, noisy city. I'm more than ready for peace and quiet, and to get away from Papá's mean spirit and violent temper.

What must it be like to stand under a wide-open sky spattered with stars, with no neighbors quarreling or trains rattling or horses' hooves clacking on stones? Her heart yearned for such open space, for such silence. Silence that longed to be filled with beautiful music. She imagined nature itself performing a symphony of birdsong and coyote howls and water cascading over rocks. Those were some of the images her mind drifted to as she played, and she longed to merge her own musical voice to that of creation, if even just for a day or two.

She smoothed out her counterpane and plumped her pillows, careful to leave her room clean and neat, though that would hardly diffuse her papá's wrath or her mamá's fretting. After taking a last look around and assuring herself she had all she needed, she put her summer bonnet on her head and tied the strings under her chin. Then she put her leather purse inside the cumbersome carpetbag and hefted it with one hand. But when she reached for her violin case sitting on her dresser, she hesitated.

The peeling black leather case had been opened and closed hundreds of times over the years, and while she had a special place in her heart for this little violin that her aunt had given her ten years ago—a present that changed her life and ignited the dream in her heart—she would never play it again. It had outlived its purpose in her dream.

She slung her wool coat over her arm, though why she thought she needed it in the heat of summer, she couldn't say. But she had no idea what the weather might be like in Colorado, so close to the mountains called the Rockies. Then she checked her timepiece—a family heirloom given her by her grandmother. It faithfully kept the time so long as she wound it each day, and it now told her it was 3:10. She had twenty minutes to catch the El to the Grand Station in Midtown.

She drew in a long breath and let out a sigh. No more stalling— she must not miss this train if she meant to board the five o'clock railway heading west.

Five days on a train—how would she manage? She couldn't afford a sleeper car, so she would have to sleep sitting up in her seat, among so many strangers and subjected to the dust and smoke and grime. She stiffened at the thought of such cramped quarters and lack of privacy. But it was worth it, to get the violin of her dreams. *Be brave,* she told herself. *You've endured worse.*

She peeked into the narrow hallway and heard her mother still humming in the back room. Taking quiet, cautious steps, she tiptoed to the front door and cringed when the wood creaked on the hinges as she opened it. A glance down the hallway and a moment's silence told her no one was nearby or ascending the stairs to the third floor.

But her breath of relief hitched in her throat upon hearing her mamá's voice behind her.

"Angela, *mi cara,* where are you going?"

Angela spun around and dropped the bag to the floor at the landing. Her heart sank at the look on her mamá's face. She only then remembered that she'd forgotten to set out the note she'd written and hidden in her desk drawer.

"Oh, Mamá, *mi dispiace.* I . . . I am taking a trip." She gulped, not knowing any soft way to say this and fearing her mamá might try to stop her. Or worse—go fetch her papá.

Her mamá hurried over to her and took her hands, then squeezed them again and again. Her tired pleading eyes stabbed at Angela's heart. *"Non capisco*—I don't understand. Where, why . . . ?"

Urgency pressed Angela; if she missed this train, she would have to buy a new ticket another day. And she would no doubt lose the money spent on the first ticket—something she could ill afford.

She picked up her bag and lugged it down the stairs, her mamá trailing behind.

"Please, *mi cara,* tell me you are not running away. My heart would break."

Angela stopped midflight and turned to her mamá. She reached out and grasped her hands. "Oh no, Mamá. I am only taking a short trip. I've arranged to purchase a violin—"

"But your bag! What trip? How far are you going?" Her mamá seemed about to swoon, and the hot stairwell with its cloying sooty air was no doubt making her mamá feel worse.

"Come walk with me," Angela said in a soft, loving voice, hoping to dispel her mamá's rising agitation, all the while sensing time marching to a quick metronome in her head. "I'll explain." *You must hurry!*

And while she tried to tell her mamá how she was traveling to a town called Greeley in the state of Colorado to buy a violin, she could see the questions and confusion rising to hysterical proportions in her mamá's eyes.

"No, you mustn't go, Angela. You know what your papá will do when he finds out! Just come back with me, back to the *appartamento, per favore. Per la tua sicurezza.*"

Angela scowled as she practically dragged her mamá across the busy street, weaving through coaches and hansom cabs and horse-drawn buggies, and dodging the piles of animal refuse adding stench to the heat rising from the cobblestones. *My safety? How could she think of our home as a safe place?* Papá thought nothing of striking her mamá for the least infraction—a lukewarm supper, taking too long to bring him his slippers, or failing to fetch the day's newspaper. Her mamá still sported a swollen eye surrounded by black and green bruising. Punishment for undercooked veal picatta. Yet, her mamá took her blows without a word of complaint.

Angela's normally sympathetic feelings took a hard edge as she spun to a stop at the base of the El Train's wooden staircase and studied her mamá's distraught face. Instead of compassion, she only felt pity for this woman for tolerating so many years of undeserved mistreatment. She thought of her seven-year-old sister, Rosalia, who already mimicked her mamá's subservience and cowering, despite Angela's attempts to instill autonomy in her and get her to voice her own opinion on matters.

She shook her head and pried her mamá's fingers from her arm. *Maybe I should run away and never come back.* But she knew that was foolish to consider. She loved her family, despite their flaws. And though her papá had a temper and a mean streak, he provided for them all dutifully. Which was more than many living on the streets of New York had.

In the distance she heard the blast of the train's horn, announcing the arrival of the three-thirty train north.

"Promise me you'll come home as soon as you get your violin," her mamá begged, tears leaking from her eyes.

"I promise, Mamá. You know how important this is to me."

Her mamá's eyes warmed with love. "Of course. You have a gift, and you must use it." She lowered her voice and stroked Angela's cheek. "You must chase after your dream. For if you give it up . . ." Her throat choked up, and she pursed her lips and said no more.

Suddenly Angela understood. Her mamá had always encouraged her to play. She was the one who'd arranged Angela's music lessons and risked Papá's anger by secretly slipping coins from the household jar to pay for those lessons and replacement strings for her violin. Her mamá had never shared much about her own childhood, but Angela sensed a broken dream in her mamá's voice.

"Go, then," her mamá whispered when they got to the top of the stairs, as the massive hulking steam engine came to a grinding, shuddering, and screeching halt at the station.

She reached into a pocket of her skirt and emptied a handful of coins into Angela's hand. "If you need more, send me a telegram. I can ask your zia Sofia —"

"I'll be fine, Mamá. *Grazie.*"

A conductor yelled for passengers to board as the heavy metal doors slid open. Dozens stepped down off the train while others waited to board.

Angela threw her arms around her mamá, and they stood on the platform in a long embrace, until Angela broke away, tears dribbling down her cheeks.

"Ti amo, Angela." Her mamá stroked Angela's hair and rested her hand on her cheek. *"Stai attento.* Watch out for strangers. Guard your purse. Don't —"

The last few waiting passengers stepped into the train car as the conductor announced the final call to board.

"I will, Mamá. I will send a telegram when I arrive, and I'll let you know when I'll be returning —"

"Angela Bellini!"

Angela heard a gruff voice yelling her name from the street below. A pang of fear stabbed her chest. *Papá!* She looked at her mamá's horrified face.

"Hurry, *mi cara.* Get on the train."

Her mamá pushed her toward the train car. Angela hesitated and held on to her mamá's arm. She feared what Papá would do to her mamá upon learning she'd let his daughter leave without telling him. *Without warning him.*

Her mamá's urgent words left her no time to waver further. Two blasts from the train's whistle indicated its imminent departure from the station.

The stout conductor in his dark-blue uniform gestured to her. "It's now or never, lass," he said with an Irish brogue.

"Go," her mamá urged, a surprising hint of courage shining on her face. "Get your violin." She gave Angela a smile that gleamed with pride and approval. That was all Angela needed.

She gave her mamá a quick peck on the cheeks, then rushed inside the train car that was only half full this hot Sunday afternoon. She plopped onto the wooden bench as the door slid shut and clicked into the lock. With another blast of the whistle, the train lurched forward and began chugging along the rails at a snail's crawl.

To her shock, she spotted her papá running along the platform.

"Angela, get off this minute!" he yelled as he chased after the train, panting and waving his arms.

Angela, horrified and embarrassed, sank lower on the bench and turned to face the windows that looked out upon the rows of crowded multistoried brownstone buildings. She knew if he could, he would drag her off the train. She gulped thinking he might follow her somehow to Grand Station. But he didn't know where exactly she planned to go. *And Mamá will never tell him.*

A frisson of fear shuddered through her body at the thought of her papá interrogating her mamá, demanding to know where his daughter was heading. Blaming her for his daughter's obstinacy and misbehavior. For her rebellious nature.

Angela let the tears fall as she snuck a glimpse back at the receding station and watched her papá forcefully grab her mamá's arm and drag her toward the stairs, as if she were one of his children who needed a spanking. Though, she knew Papá would do worse. *And it's all my fault. But it's too late to make amends. The damage has been done.*

Angela pulled her carpetbag close to her feet and buried her head in her hands. What would she return to in two weeks? She dared not imagine. Was this violin worth the price? Worth her mother's suffering and her own possible banishment from her family?

She supposed she would find out—once she arrived in Greeley five days hence.

Chapter 2

BRETT HENDRICKS SMACKED HIS PINTO on the rump with his quirt while kicking hard with his spurs into the flanks of the distraught horse. Pressing in all around him, wild range cattle lowed and snorted, eyes ablaze and horns shaking in threatening fashion, surging across the corral like an irresistible tide. The mass of hot bodies, their hides shimmering brown and white in the late-morning sun, crushed Brett as he waded his way through, sweat streaming down his neck and soaking his shirt.

The first shot missed by a long chalk, but the second ball whistled by his ear. Brett let out a string of curses. Steers reared up, paddling in panic with hooves dangerously close to his horse's muzzle. His little stallion reared back, nearly dumping him onto a frightened passel of blattering calves near the pen's railing. Brett gathered the horse, mouthing soothing words, then pressed ahead, leaning hard into the withers and half-burying his face in the mane.

Dang fool, cowboys. These beeves are gonna stampede, break down the fence. But Brett didn't regret the what for he'd given the arrogant kid. Though he doubted it'd do any good. Fellas spoilt like that—they weren't likely to see the wrong of their ways.

With renewed determination—fueled partly by anger at Orlander's kid and partly at himself by his stupidity for thinking he could make his escape through the cattle pens unscathed—he pressed harder. He hadn't figured that beef-headed son of a rich rancher and his cowpunchers would set in pursuit. But, come to think of it, he wasn't surprised the fella had a hankering to shoot him.

Well, he *had* about broken the kid's nose. And humiliated him in front of his pals. But he deserved it—and worse—and that was the God's honest truth. One thing Brett couldn't cotton to, and that was the mean treatment of women. In a flash, he saw in his mind's eye his pa's big, rough hands around his ma's soft neck. He squeezed his eyes to force away the image, then blew out a breath and kicked harder, letting anger spur him like a whip to his back.

Somehow he made it to the gate, worked the cattle back, then jiggled the heavy beam and slid it across. One thing about Dakota—you couldn't find a better cutting horse that eager to take direction or as nimble and quick on the feet. Brett couldn't blame the small stallion for his fearful prancing. A crush of cattle was a danger to man and beast alike.

But they'd gotten out of the pen unscathed, for the most part, and the open range spread out north before him.

A quick glance back as Brett secured the gate showed the three riders working their way back out the entrance to the corral, cows flinching at the thrashing of their quirts to make room. Brett grunted. Orlander's men would circle around and catch up to him in a few shakes of a rooster's tail.

"Come on, fella—let's get a move-on," he told Dakota, pulling his slouch hat over his ears and securing his neckerchief that had slipped down in all that tussle. With a hard kick, they set off galloping north, billows of gritty dust swirling like devils in the wind, like cactus needles biting his cheeks.

He tried to recall the lay of the towns to the north of Denver. Not much for miles. Some settlements along the Platte. He'd never ridden for any ranches in Colorado, but heard about some of the big ones. At least five or six had been at the cowboy contest.

He grinned, thinking about the get-away money rolled up inside that blue ribbon in his saddlebag. Now that he was on the drift—again—that would tie him over until he landed in another cow-punch outfit. He hadn't meant to get in that fight with Humphrey's foreman, but he couldn't abide the man's mean, ill-tempered ways of picking on the tenderfoots a minute longer. And none of the other cowboys were sad to see the brute go—he was cordially hated by all. He'd done 'em all a favor—even though the prank had cost him his job. He couldn't help but grin.

With wide-open space to run, Dakota chewed up the hard thirsty ground peppered with sage brush and patches of buffalo grass. The horizon wavered in the heat like ripples on a lake off in the distance. Brett reckoned it was nearing noon, and the day would only get hotter. With a frown, he took a mental assessment of the gear in his saddlebags, and while glad he had his bedroll and war bag with his gear, he'd not bothered to refill his canteen or rustle up some hard tack or even biscuits. Well, he hadn't planned on making such a hasty run for it. At least he'd been saddled up when he'd come upon young Orlander and that Mexican girl.

Brett gritted his teeth, thinking how he'd nearly killed the kid. He'd wanted to—badly. Good thing those three cowpunchers had been standing outside the barn—seeing 'em had made him rein in his rage. But they'd recognized him—he was sure of it. Prob'ly got a good look at his face, seeing as he'd beaten 'em all in the contest. Some cowboys were poor sports, and they'd think nothing of throwing a few punches just out of spite and jealousy. He'd been beaten up before. And this wasn't the first time he'd been shot at either.

When he came upon an old wagon road scrambled with ruts, he pulled Dakota to a stop and let the lathered, heaving horse rest a moment. Quiet settled on the prairie, punctuated by Dakota's huffing and the swishing of his tail. Nothing moved in the stifling dry heat but a couple of long-eared jackrabbits foraging.

Brett threw a hand over his eyes in the glaring sunlight and looked south, then grimaced. A plume of dust trailed in his direction, and he figured his pursuers would be upon him inside of an hour. His tongue stuck in his mouth like a boll of cotton, and he could hardly swallow past the dust in his throat. As far as he could see, there was no water to be had. No stand of cottonwoods indicating a spring or creek. Nothing.

He checked his Colt .45 and his Springfield rifle. They were loaded and ready, but he hoped he wouldn't have to use 'em. He'd never killed a man, and he didn't cotton to the notion, but he would if he had no other choice. Why in tarnation were those fellas still after him? He figured they'd have given up the chase by now. Go back to their outfit, have some chow, start back to their ranch. It made no sense to go that far a stretch just to even a score.

Mumbling under his breath, he chastised himself for getting in yet another fix. But that appeared to be his lot in life. Always on the move, never staying long in one place or t'other. Trouble seemed to find him wherever he went. Or maybe he just looked for it. Didn't matter. He'd just keep moving.

He urged Dakota back into a gallop and thought on the way those cowpunchers had stared with wide eyes when he'd eared down that wild mare and got her under his legs in record time. He'd overheard a group of 'em talking before the event. From all appearances, his reputation had preceded him. Though he'd only competed down in Texas over the last couple of years, somehow the cowboys in Colorado must have learned about the wrangler—the one they called Bronco Brett—that could break any horse, no matter how ornery. Seemed like word traveled far and wide as cowboys went from ranch to ranch and met up at the spring and fall roundups.

Brett had won firsts in every contest, though he shied away from the roping and bull busting. Sure, he was plenty strong and good with a lariat, but so were a lot of other cowboys. But no one could come close to beating him in the wild-horse-breaking events— not a one. He loved nothing more than meeting eyes with an animal that had never been touched by human hand and working 'em into submission to a place of trust. Many had asked him how he did it— as if he had some kind of magic ability. But he'd only give a shrug for an answer. For he didn't rightly know. A God-given gift, he reckoned.

Hot wind abraded his cheeks, and his hair kept falling into his eyes as he rode the stallion hard. Another glance showed his pursuers within a quarter mile. He shook his head and clenched his jaw. *Crimany, why aren't they quittin'?*

Suddenly, wind gusting from the west nearly toppled him off his horse. Dust erupted from the ground and clogged the air, wrenching his hat from his head and sending it flying from the strings behind his head. He pulled the neckerchief up over his nose and stuffed his hat down, then tightened the strings. Dakota slowed, showing distress and an abiding reluctance to press forward in the dust-choked air that turned the prairie into a gloomy brown soup.

Wind screamed across the plains, and Brett lost his bearings. He slowed to a walk, worried his horse would stumble. But his pursuers didn't seem to share the same concerns. He felt the ground shake before he heard the pounding of hooves through the roar of the dust storm. They were nearly upon him. His right hand fell to rest on the butt of his Colt that was fixed in a loose cross draw holster on his left hip.

He spun Dakota around. Through the oppressive haze he made out three riders, all wearing wide-brimmed hats, their faces half hidden by their bandanas. But Brett recognized Orlander's kid by his slight build and the manner in which he rode. Brett had watched him—and those two cowpunchers—in the team roping event. Orlander was maybe seventeen, but the two swarthy types had about ten years on the kid. Maybe two or three years older than Brett was.

Dakota's flanks heaved. The stallion was nearly played out, and the air was clogged with dirt that kept churning up from the ground in geysers of wind. His prospects were bleak if not downright irritating.

"Hold it right there, Hendricks," one of the men yelled over the gusts. "Git down off y'r horse and come on back to the ranch with us, peaceful-like."

Brett scoffed. *Not likely.* He knew they wanted a clean shot and would leave his body for the coyotes and buzzards to feed on.

The three men sat their horses about a hundred feet away, waiting. He doubted they could hit him if they fired their guns from that distance. But then, he didn't want to gamble on the chance that one of 'em might be a good shot. Three to one. If he fired, what were his chances?

He weighed his options. Dakota was spent, but he couldn't see any other recourse.

He made to swing down from his horse, watching out of the corner of his eye as the men walked their horses over to him in a cautious manner, guns at the ready.

But just as his right leg touched the ground, two shots sliced through the air, and Brett's right thigh detonated in a flare of hot pain. He squelched a scream as he gritted his teeth against the pain.

He caught Orlander's smug grin through the haze, his rifle smoking.

Why, that no-good . . .

Brett, in a sudden reversal, swung back up onto the saddle, pulled out his Colt, and fired back over his shoulder, the ball exploding from the gun and the weapon recoiling against his cheek.

The man to Brett's left yelped as the ball grazed his shoulder. In that moment of surprise, Brett wheeled back north and kicked Dakota hard.

Shots fired in the gloom as wind lashed whips of dirt into Brett's face. Hearing the horses approach, Brett leveled the Colt against his left shoulder and fired off three more rounds, hoping more to discourage and slow down the men rather than kill 'em. If he could just get enough distance, he might be able to lose 'em in this dust storm. Or so he hoped. He clenched his teeth so hard, his jaw ached. *Hurts like the dickens—and then some.*

He couldn't hear a thing over the ruckus of the wind as he yanked the reins sharply to the right and urged Dakota on blindly across the prairie.

"Go go go!" he yelled, leaning all his weight against the horse's neck, keeping his head down in case more lead was heading his way. He was grateful they hadn't shot his horse. At least they'd had enough decency to aim for him—or so he reckoned.

As the pain turned his leg into a wad of searing heat, Brett gave the horse his head, lightening up on the reins and praying Dakota would just keep running. Brett strained to listen through the maelstrom of dust, grit, and pebbles flinging into his face and body, but he no longer heard shots or horse hooves or the voices of men.

Brett lost track of time, his head hot, his mouth dry, sweat drenching his clothes and yet drying almost instantly in the hot wind. The pain in his leg subsided to a dull ache, but his trousers were wet with blood. He knew he had to stop and tend to his wound or he'd lose too much blood.

Presently, the wind fluttered to a stall, and blinding sunlight streaked through the settling dust. A calm settled upon the prairie like a thick smothering blanket, and Brett pulled Dakota to a stop. While the horse heaved heavy, troubled breaths, Brett pulled down his dirt-caked handkerchief and loosened his stuck tongue. What he'd give for a glass of water right now.

And his horse sorely needed water too.

He surveyed the desert around him in all directions. No sign of Orlander and his men. No sign of water either, or a road. The Rockies lay to the west, and the sun dangled just above Pikes Peak. He had maybe two hours before darkness erased the world.

He wiped the grime and sweat out of his eyes and slid off his horse, careful not to put weight on his right leg. Every muscle ached, but his thigh screamed in renewed pain at his movement. No denying it — he was bad hurt.

"Arrrgh," he ground out as he gingerly pulled the stuck cotton of his trouser away from his wound. There wasn't much he could do about the ball in his thigh — not without water. He pulled down his saddlebags, rummaged through, and took stock of the contents. Just as he figured — not a drop in his canteen and not a crumb of food. At least Dakota found the spare tufts of buffalo grass appealing.

May as well rest a spell. He hobbled over to his straying horse, undid the cinch, threw the stirrup over the seat, and pulled the saddle down to the ground in an explosion of dust. He slid the headstall off his mount and set it next to the saddle. He knew his horse wouldn't wander far. Brett was hungrier than sin, but the thought of expending an ounce of effort to hunt down some game on this godforsaken prairie wearied him. Afar off he thought he could make out some prickly pear. That'd give him something to wet his throat. But first he had to do something about his leg.

He ripped an old nightshirt into strips, then tore away the bloodied section of his trouser leg, exposing the wound. It was festering something bad with all the sweat and dirt and blood making an ugly paste two inches from his knee.

Shadows crawled along the ground as the sun snagged in the peaks of the Rockies. Ground owls hooted in their holes, and the air droned with insects. Brett blew out a frustrated breath. He didn't dare chance an infection that would cost him his leg. He'd seen a man with a gangrened foot once. It was uglier than sin, and the poor fella died before he could get the foot cut off.

Crimany. I don't want to end up short a leg. He bit down on his lip as he limped over to the saddlebags and pulled out his cartridge belt. He found his knife and flint box and set to work. It took him only moments to get a small fire going of tinder and dried tumbleweed branches. He held the knife tip in the flames for a minute, then searched around until he found his leather quirt.

Dakota lifted his head at Brett's activity, then, with a snuffle, went back to foraging, content for the moment.

He hoped the horse wouldn't bolt when he screamed.

Brett plopped down in an ungainly fashion next to his little fire, then positioned himself, knowing nothing he did would prepare him for the pain. He stuffed the wooden end of the quirt between his teeth and clamped down. Then, sucking in a breath, he poked the tip of his knife into the hole in his leg.

His shriek was muffled by the mouthful of leather as he fished around in the pulpy mass of flesh until he located the lead. Salty sweat poured into his eyes as he choked back the bile erupting in his throat. Not wanting to prolong the agony, he dug in and popped out the ball, then arched back in a grimace of new pain that shot through his thigh.

He spit out the quirt and panted hard, snorting out breaths as his shaky hands loosened the strings on his pouch of gunpowder. Stretching out his shaking leg, he dabbed at the blood oozing from the hole, then, when it abated, he sprinkled a thin layer of the black powder on the wound.

He clenched his eyes as ripples of pain washed over him, then, when he'd caught his breath, he pulled out a glowing piece of tumbleweed branch and touched it to the powder.

It flamed up in a hiss, and Brett screamed at the new eruption of pain as the wound was cauterized. He spit into his bandana—on the end that had the least grime—and used that to snuff out the fire on his leg, though it did nothing to soothe. He wished he'd brought along a bottle of whiskey. But this would have to do until he could get to a town.

He'd spent many a night on open rangeland. And many a night alone. The Front Range didn't scare him, and there was nothing around he couldn't handle, now that the threat of Injuns was mostly gone.

Times sure had changed. Weren't all that many years ago when a body might ride in any of the cardinal directions across the plains and end up getting scalped or killed. But now they were gone—like the buffalo—herded off to Oklahoma, he supposed—the Pawnee and Sioux and Cheyenne. The big complaint among ranchers now were the "grangers"—the emigrant farmers coming from the east and south, homesteading and crowding out the wide-open spaces such that the large cattle herds could no longer roam. That newfangled barbed wire was a pox on the freedom of ranchers who'd once ruled the West.

Brett had spent most of his life as a cowpuncher, riding on the open range in Texas and down to Mexico territory. He wondered if the life he led would vanish presently along with the buffalo. Then what was a fella to do?

His long-held dream of owning his own horse ranch wavered like a mirage on the horizon, always out of reach. An impossible dream.

Well, at the moment, his worries and dreams seemed a mite insignificant. With darkness collapsing on the plains, and his leg throbbing and swollen, he brooked no hope of heading over to that patch of prickly pear. He hoped the buffalo grass would slake Dakota's thirst for now.

By the time he fetched his bedroll and fed the fire, which sent sparks sputtering into the dusky sky, exhaustion hit him like the flat edge of a frying pan. He thought about hobbling the horse, but just the idea made his eyelids heavy. With a rumbling stomach and mouth as dry as chalk, he pulled his wool blanket around him as the cool of night drifted across the Front Range and fell into a hard sleep.

Brett threw off his blanket, feeling as if someone had set him afire. An angry sun blazed overhead, scorching his face and neck. He moaned at the slightest movement, his leg also aflame. After struggling to sit upright, he winced at his swollen thigh, red and ugly, but was relieved to see it wasn't discolored much or festering with pus. His head spun madly as he lifted it with some effort and looked around.

Dakota nickered at his movement and walked over to him with his head hanging and eyes imploring.

"Yeah, yeah, I know, fella. Time to go. We need to find water." He reached up and stroked the stallion's muzzle, then rose to his feet. A streak of blinding white light seared his eyes for a moment, but then the pain was manageable. He could hardly put any weight on his leg. Worse though was the pounding in his head. He'd been lying in the sun too long, he thought, then felt his forehead—hot as a furnace, and sweat trickled down his neck. In the glaring sunlight he could just make out the mountains to the west. At least he had a general notion which way was north.

It took all his strength to get the saddle and gear back up on Dakota's back. After tightening the cinch, he managed to swing up in the saddle, though he was glad no one was around to see his sorry effort. He nearly tumbled over the off side of the animal, then had enough presence of mind to straighten before falling to the ground. Why'd he slept so long, he couldn't figure—unless he had a fever. His head sure felt like someone squeezed it in a vise.

With reins loosely in hand, he urged Dakota forward, but the horse resisted moving faster than a snail. Heat bore down on man and beast alike, and the ground sweltered and seemed to undulate under the oppressive ball of fire overhead.

Rattle your hooks, Cowboy, or you're gonna die out here. He kept straining to see across the miles of high desert, searching for some sign of water. Those prickly pears he thought he'd seen eluded him. The only vegetation around was creosote, and while the stems and leaves made a good tea for cramps and colds, the plant was worthless as a source of food.

Dakota stumbled along in the blazing heat, and Brett nodded off over the saddle horn. He tried to keep his eyes open but grew languorous as the day dragged on. Every so often he heard a hawk

24

cry, but aside from the occasional moan of the wind, the desert was silent and bleak. He knew if he kept north he'd bisect a river. The Big Thompson ran down from the hills across the plains, and above that the Platte. There was no chance he'd miss some piece of water if he kept north.

But when he lifted his head after dozing off again, he craned to see around him and get his bearings, only to have his breath hitch when he realized the Rockies were dead set behind him. How long his horse had been wandering east, Brett had no clue. But the day was fast slipping away, and water seemed no closer than it had yesterday, when he'd been shot.

He could hardly swallow, and his lips were chapped and swollen. His head now felt like a ball of fire as hot as the sun. Dakota, feeling him stir, came to a stop and refused to take another step. He felt bad for the horse but worse for himself. He could barely open his eyes, and his leg sent sharp pangs up into his stomach with every slight movement.

He toppled from the saddle to the ground, landing on his back. *Rest. Just a bit of shut-eye, and I'll be right as rain.*

He pulled the brim of his hat down over his eyes to block the sun and fell into a hard, deep sleep. When he next woke, the sun was peeking over the eastern horizon, bleeding colors of peach and pink across the flat land.

The sight confounded him. What was the sun doing in the east? Had he somehow slept through another night? What day was it? He'd lost track of the time, and hardly recalled where he was. Colorado, he thought. Where was his horse?

He stumbled to his feet, his head as heavy as an anvil, and hot and throbbing with searing pain. He could barely stand on his wobbling legs, weak as he felt and in desperate need of water. There—he spotted the stallion over by a dry gulley, his head hanging in misery. Brett felt like an utter fool for getting 'em both in this predicament.

With renewed anger — at himself and at that Orlander kid — he stumbled over to the horse and pulled the reins down over his head. He'd left the poor animal saddled all night. How could he have done such a thing? Dakota turned his head and gave Brett a half-pleading, half-surrendered look.

"I know, but we gotta keep moving, fella." Brett clucked his tongue and got the horse walking alongside him, and together they headed north once more, a cool morning breeze tickling at Brett's ears. He knew, though, as soon as the sun lifted off the horizon, the day would turn hot once more. They needed to make good time before too long. Still, there was nothing promising to the north — or in any direction. No sign of a road or trail, no buildings or copses of trees. No water.

Suddenly, Brett saw movement out of the corner of his eye and spun left. He'd nearly stepped on a rattler. Now that would make good eating. He could just crush the thing with a rock, skin it, and cook it over a fire. Just the thought made his mouth water something fierce.

But as Brett pulled Dakota back away from the snake, the horse sidestepped and faltered, then went crashing to the ground with a wild and frantic screech of pain.

Brett lunged to the dirt, reins still in hand, and met his eyes with the horse's wide, terrified ones. Dakota thrashed and squealed, trying to get upright, flailing legs and hooves. Brett scrambled to get out of his way, figuring the horse's panic was due to his dehydration and unsteadiness.

But then he saw Dakota's left rear leg.

Anguish strangled Brett's throat. The cannon bone was snapped clean in half, the sharp bone protruding through the brown hide. The horse must have stepped into an owl hole or prairie dog burrow when he backed up.

Oh, Dakota. Oh, no. Brett couldn't help himself. Tears poured down his face as he watched the pinto scream and kick. His pal, his loyal pal. It wasn't fair. It was all his fault.

He kicked hard at the ground, cursing the day he was born. Cursing the desert and his rotten luck. Maybe he was getting his just deserts. But why did Dakota have to be the one to pay the piper?

Swallowing back tears and swiping the dirt from his eyes, he made his way carefully over to Dakota's flank, muttering soft, comforting words. All lies.

"That's all right, you'll be fine, I'll take care of you, just take it easy, quiet now. Easy, fella."

His faithful trusting horse panted in short bursts of pain but eased off his squirming as Brett laid a hand on his shoulder and pulled out his Colt pistol from its holster.

Taking a deep breath, Brett hardened his face against the sorry duty now laid upon him and cocked the trigger. He met Dakota's pained gaze.

His aim was steady and true — he at least owed that to his horse. The ball of lead shot straight into the side of Dakota's head, below the ear, killing him without delay. Smoke from Brett's gun rose into his nose, the acrid smell making him choke up. His ears rang.

Brett stood still, unblinking, staring at his lifeless horse, his heart empty and his soul numb. Then he wiped his face with the back of his hand and set about the task at hand. He worked efficiently, his head pounding and his leg screaming in pain, and managed to slide the saddle off Dakota. The bridle he placed inside the saddlebag, which he slung over his shoulder. Why he thought he could haul the thing across the desert, he had 'airy a clue. But he didn't cotton to the notion of leaving it here alongside his horse. And he sure wasn't going to leave his saddle for some no-good granger to find.

With a lump aching in his throat, Brett heaved the saddle into his arms and shifted the weight until he could stand. On a good day, hauling a saddle and toting saddlebags full of gear and a rifle would stretch a man's strength. But this was far from being a good day. In fact, it was turning out to be one of the worst days of Brett's life. *And that don't say it by half.*

Brett flashed on his ma's pretty face, all bruised and swollen.

Well, this wasn't the worst day, not by a long chalk. But it sure as heck wasn't the best either. He sent a silent good-bye to Dakota, thinking on how the animal had deserved better—much better. Brett wanted to scream, but he'd lost his words in the dust and heat.

He took a look-see around him. The Rockies lay to the west, mocking him with their peaks of white snow, promising waters flowing in cascades down the sides of the mountain. To the north and east lay more desert. To the south, nothing but trouble.

The sun was warming the land. Already sweat beaded on Brett's forehead. With a heart as heavy as his load, he set off, one foot after the other, keeping his hat brim down to block out the glare, keeping his thoughts few and corralled so his eyes didn't well up with tears. Weak, weary, thirsty, peckish, and in pain, he trudged on—because there weren't no other choice afore him.

Chapter 3

ANGELA DROPPED THE HEAVY CARPETBAG at her feet and looked around her in the late-afternoon glare. A few other travelers exited the train car behind her at this small, unassuming station that shared no resemblance to Grand Station in New York. A simple wooden sign with "Greeley" painted in large green block letters nailed to the railway station house greeted her. She'd caught glimpses of the modest wood-sided houses as the train pulled into town, many whitewashed with planked porches and garden plots hugging the structures, jumbles of colorful blooms trailing up railings and spilling out of earthen pots on porch steps.

Five days sitting in a rocking, jostling, smoke-filled railcar left her grimy and sticky and in need of a hot bath. Every muscle felt stiff and sore, and though the thin dry air invigorated her as she breathed deeply, her heart still weighed heavy from her worries and misgivings.

At each stop along the route she'd considered turning back and catching the next train east. But then she'd reminded herself that whether she returned with or without a violin, the same fate awaited her. She'd come to one clear conclusion, though. Before journeying back to New York, she would inquire of her zia Sofia if she could live with her. Temporarily—until she could assess whether it would be safe to return to her apartment under her father's harsh hand. If she could pass that audition with the philharmonic, she might be able to afford her own small apartment and see her dream realized. Oh, how she longed to play alongside such masterful musicians as Joseph White and Eugenia Pappenheim. The thought sent a shiver of yearning through her.

The first time she'd seen Miss Pappenheim play, Angela had been thirteen. Her widowed aunt, after giving her the violin for her birthday, had surprised her the next day by showing up in her fancy carriage and carrying a beribboned box that held the most beautiful dress Angela had ever seen. On their evening out, the two of them had sat in a private box and watched the orchestra play Haydn's Symphony in E Flat Major, with the conductor punctuating the music with his white baton held in his gloved hand. And while the swell of all the instruments had transported her to some heavenly realm, it was the solo violinist's bowing that sliced open her world as if with a shimmering knife.

Angela had never heard such divine music. From that moment forward, she knew that nothing else would ever come close to bringing such deep-seated joy and peace to her heart. She determined she would devote all her time, energy, and heart to mastering the violin so that one day she could coax such ethereal music from an instrument in her hands.

As Angela stood on the splintered and weathered planks of the railway station, she closed her eyes and let her resolve and the memory of the melodic cadences of the Haydn symphony envelope her. Calm seeped in and filled her every pore, and a smile lifted her lips.

She had arrived, and a violin—and her future—awaited her here, in this unremarkable Western town. She had come this far— taken this hard step. Best to push aside thoughts of her parents and New York and take another step.

Yet, another concern rose in her mind—how far her savings would stretch. Mr. Fisk had assured her she would be able to purchase a quality instrument with the money she'd budgeted, but that left little for accommodations and food. She hadn't expected such high prices for meals on the train and so had subsisted on mostly toast and eggs, skipping the more pricey dinners. Her unappeased stomach grumbled in complaint even now as she took bag in hand and walked over to the street. Surely, if she purchased food from a grocer's and conducted her business expeditiously with Mr. Fisk, she could soon be on her way back to New York with a few coins left in her purse.

Small rickety shops lined wide Eighth Avenue—a general store, a blacksmith's, a haberdashery, and a mercantile—many with flat wooden awnings covering wide boardwalks. Along the next block of mostly one-story shabby buildings she noted a druggist's, and then her eye caught on a larger corner building bordering a church sporting a bell tower at its peak—The Greeley Opera House.

Opera? In a fledgling town such as this? She smiled to think that the inhabitants of such a remote place would appreciate and support opera. She'd imagined gunslingers and cowboys galloping down the center of the town. But instead, the townspeople were modestly but nicely dressed. Perhaps not in the fashions one saw in Midtown New York, but Angela noted something akin to pride in these residents' steps and manner, though the town was bare and unimpressive, to say the least.

Dirt blew up from the dry street in gusts and seemed to coat everything around her. But mostly the town seemed clean and tidy, and the wooden storefronts painted in clashing colors added a touch of luster and personality. Young maple trees lined the dirt street's edge, which Angela imagined would quickly grow into tall, stately trees offering shade to strollers on hot summer days such as this one.

Plenty of people were about on this Thursday afternoon — shopping, conversing in front of shops, driving wagons loaded with hay and bags of what she guessed might be seed or potatoes. A few carriages like the ones in New York wheeled along pulled by pairs of horses, which made Angela wonder where all these people had come from and what dreams they were chasing. She imagined each and every one of them had left some former life behind — a very different life — to take a chance on a Colorado dream.

Had they found their dream in this simple, unassuming place? Surely there were hardships in such a remote, wild corner of the country.

She'd heard the West had been tamed and the Indians subdued and no longer a threat, but was that true? Her eyes caught on a few cowboys in their brimmed hats, dusty boots, and heavy canvas brown trousers chatting in front of the mercantile, gun belts strapped around their waists. Three horses loaded with packs behind their saddles snuffled at the post they were tied to, their tails flicking at flies. Angela noticed rifles tied to the sides of the saddles. One cowboy caught sight of her staring and cocked his head and grinned at her.

Her face flushed with heat, and she promptly turned away, not wanting to encourage his attendance upon her. He seemed wholly uncultured and uncouth, and she could only imagine his intentions. No doubt men like him — like these cowboys — lived a wild and carefree life, with reckless abandon and lacking all decency and fear of God. And she imagined they hardly ever bathed.

New York was a meld of cultures and peoples, but she'd never seen a cowboy before—except on the cover of dime novels in the library. She'd hardly believed they were real—until she'd noticed hordes of them milling around the Denver depot. The young men before her looked every bit like the drawings she'd seen—rough and intimidating. Unruly hair poked out from under hats, and all had moustaches and ragged beards. They stood joking and laughing, unhindered and unconcerned over who might be watching them, as if they hadn't a care in the world.

But . . . what would it be like to have such freedom? she wondered. She imagined they worked at some local ranch, herding cattle to market. She recalled a newspaper article she'd read somewhere about cowboys who lived out under the stars, sleeping on a blanket on the dirt, only going into a town every few months. What a lonely life that would be. Yet, the picture was also an idyllic one, so far removed from the noise and shouting and crowding of a city. It was a rare moment indeed when she could make out the stars at night in New York City with all the lights and buildings in the way. She longed to see the wide expanse of night sky. Maybe now she would—without having to walk more than a few steps outside her hotel.

She chided herself. *How easy to romanticize such a life.* She knew the West was beset by harsh winter storms, drought, and tornadoes. *And don't forget snakes!* If there was anything Angela feared, it was snakes. She knew her fear was unfounded—the only snakes she'd ever seen were at the Central Park menagerie on East 64th Street—safely contained in glass enclosures. But even the thought of one underfoot utterly unhinged her. Well, she imagined the town of Greeley had few, if any, snakes slithering down their streets.

Stepping carefully along the rutted dirt road in her ankle-high traveling shoes, her heavy coat slung over her arm, Angela made her way to the glass-doored entrance to the Greeley Hotel. Thoughts of that hot bath tickled her as she waited until the older gentleman at the reception desk attended her. But those enticing thoughts flitted away when she learned a room for the night would cost $1.45. She hadn't imagined she'd have to pay that much. She might be able to indulge for one night, but not more.

Well, take the room for now. You can freshen up, get a good night's sleep, pay Mr. Fisk a visit, purchase your violin, then head home on the next train back to Denver.

With that resolved, Angela dug her purse out of her bag and paid the clerk for a one night's stay in their cheapest room.

Angela couldn't help herself. Not an hour later, after bathing and donning the only set of clean clothes she had, she meandered down Eighth Avenue and stopped in front of the opera house. To her surprise, she heard music filtering through the closed doors and windows. A woman was singing, accompanied by what sounded like a small orchestra. Were they rehearsing for a performance? She saw no posted notices on the side of the building.

She walked over to the entrance and quietly pushed open the heavy wood door. A blending of strings and woodwinds washed over her; the musicians were not half bad. Angela didn't recognize the music; however, she knew little about opera. Most of her musical training had come from the sweet old instrument maker at the shop on Second Avenue in Mulberry Bend, who often dropped sheets of Paganini caprices or Vieuxtemps etudes in her waiting arms and gave her weekly lessons that consisted mostly of scales and fingering technique.

Without warning, the music stopped, and she heard a muffled voice through the closed doors separating her from the auditorium, along with the shuffling of feet and chairs. Before she thought to return outside, the door before her flew open, and a young woman with dark hair and large brown eyes nearly bumped into her.

"Oh, my apologies," the woman said, her smile warm and friendly. "Who are you?"

Angela was a bit taken aback by her forwardness and fumbled with an answer. "I . . . my name is Angela Bellini." She stepped to the side as men and women of various ages and in casual attire filed past her and this curious woman, carrying instrument cases. Her inquisitor wore a simple calico dress with lace edging and carried a flute case and a folder of music in one hand. Angela guessed she was close to her age. A glance down to the woman's hands revealed the lack of a wedding ring.

"I'm Violet Edwards. Are you new in town? I've not seen you before. I play flute." She lifted a cotton bonnet from the bench and wiggled it onto her head, wayward strands of hair slipping down past her shoulders.

Angela couldn't help but smile at Violet's infectious enthusiasm. "I can see that," she said, nodding at her flute case. "I'm a violinist. And yes, I actually just arrived on the train today."

Violet's eyes lit up. "I'll bet you're here to meet George."

"George?" Angela felt flustered, standing in the narrow foyer. Perhaps Violet had her confused with someone else.

To Angela's surprise, Violet linked her arm through hers and led her out the front door. A stern-looking woman in her thirties, wearing a dark, drab dress with pearl buttons, came striding out behind them, gave Angela a cursory glance, then looked at Violet.

"Wonderful playing, Violet," she said with a smile that looked about to crack her face.

"Thank you, Mrs. Green. I do love that opening movement."

Mrs. Green gave Violet a curt nod and hurried on her way, a large canvas bag bulging with sheet music slung over her shoulder.

Violet giggled as she watched the woman stride away purposefully. "That's Annie Green. She teaches school and also gives music lessons. Charitable and dedicated, to a fault. But she'll never stop reminding you how much she hates living here and longs to return to her home in Pennsylvania."

"Then why doesn't she leave?" Angela asked.

Violet grinned and shook her head. "Her husband dragged her here. Like so many other men struck with *the fever*, he wanted a new start in the West. Not a whole lot of women like being transplanted from a comfortable life to a place full of dirt and dust and hardship. Every year it's something else—locusts eating all the crops, months of howling winter winds. It makes some people crazy."

Angela studied this curious woman. She exuded contentment and happiness. How was she different? "And what about you—how did you land in Greeley, Colorado?"

Violet started walking down the street—where she was headed, Angela had no idea, but she kept pace with her. "Oh, my father is an architect, and he's designed many of the prominent homes in town. We've came five years ago, when it was Union Colony. It was quite a shock, truth be told. Mostly just . . . dirt, everywhere the eye could see. Shacks and shanties. A wholly depressing place. Believe me—I wanted nothing more than to go back to New York—"

Angela's eyes widened in surprise. "That's where I live—in Mulberry Bend."

Violet's countenance took on a perky look as they turned a corner onto a narrower street lined with simple homes. "You're Italian, then? I love Italian food."

Angela couldn't help but laugh. Violet's shape testified to her love of food, though she wasn't fat. But she filled out her dress the way her aunt did. Zia Sofia was always cooking or eating something when Angela visited her Uptown apartment, and she'd taught her favorite *nipote* how to prepare some of the traditional dishes of Abruzzu, the coastal region her family hailed from. "Yes," she said. "And I've come to purchase a violin."

"From Mr. George Fisk," she announced rather than asked. "He's famous for his violins. People come from all over the country to buy his instruments. They're truly magnificent." She stopped abruptly and turned to face Angela. Her expression grew serious.

"You may not know this, but George's wife recently passed away in June after a long bout of illness. Lucy, poor thing, suffered from epileptic fits. George loved her so much." She sighed and looked over at a simple pale-yellow house they now stood in front of. A gravel walkway led to a wide porch that featured a cushioned swing, two wooden chairs, and two large pots with wilted flowers in them. The sweltering heat and dry air made Angela dizzy.

"Lucy was a wonderful, sweet woman, and she rarely ventured outside. But everyone loved her. She had a big heart. The local band played at her funeral—here, in the backyard. It was a sad service, and George . . . well, he's having a hard time of it." She paused, her voice quiet, in sharp contrast to her earlier exuberance. "I just thought you should know."

"Do they . . . does he have any children?" Angela asked, wondering if she would ever love someone so truly. What she'd seen of her parents' loveless marriage was the reason she'd resolved not to marry Pietro. Theirs, like the one they planned for her, had been an arranged marriage to benefit the families involved. But she hardly saw how it had benefited her poor mamá, who felt the blows from Papá's hand all too often.

Angela gulped down the tears threatening to make a curtain call. *No, I won't marry*, she told herself, though she longed for the tender affection of a man who adored her. But what man would ever want to marry a woman who loved music above all else? She was already too old to marry, anyway. And she'd seen few men who treated women with the respect and love she'd fantasized about in her thoughts late at night in her bed. Her perfect man would be gentle and soft-spoken, kind and generous, gracious and polite. But more than that, he would encourage her dreams and love music. She imagined only another musician could ever understand and share her passion. Perhaps if she got that position with the New York Phil—

"No. I imagine Lucy's health hadn't permitted it," Violet said, jarring Angela from her thoughts. Then she remembered she'd asked if Mr. Fisk had any children.

Violet brightened. "But he's like a second father to me. We sometimes play duets together, and in the past, he played in the town band at special events, like the Fourth of July celebrations at Island Grove Park. You won't regret buying a violin from him. They have the sweetest, warmest sound." She made a little noise in her throat and smiled. "Makes me think twice about wanting to be a professional flautist."

She turned suddenly with wide eyes. "I'd love to hear you play! Let's get together soon, once you have your violin. Just come on over—I live on 18th Street. You'll find your way around town with ease. Avenues run north-south and streets run east-west. They're all numbered, and the town is laid out basically in a square. Hard to get lost."

Angela chuckled. "I imagine so. Not unlike New York."

"Most of the first members of Union Colony were from New York. That's where our founder, Nathan Meeker, came from. He was a newspaper publisher there, and he puts out the *Greeley Tribune*—our local newspaper."

Angela's eyebrows rose. What a strange coincidence to come all this way to a remote corner of the West, only to find this tiny town was made up of people from her city.

"Well, I have to get home," Violet said suddenly. "Mom is at a charity meeting of some such, and I have to feed my brothers and my dad. Do you like to ride horses?"

Angela wasn't sure what to make of this whirlwind of a woman. She jumped from topic to topic as if running through scales in every key. "Well, no. I've never ever seen a horse up close. Other than those pulling carriages."

Violet shook her head as if she couldn't believe her ears. "Hey, you're in the West! You have to ride a horse sometime before you go back to New York."

Angela wasn't so sure about that, but she nodded politely. "Well," she said, looking around and wondering why Violet had taken her partway down this street, only to leave her here. "It was a pleasure meeting you—"

Violet seemed to ignore her and instead took her arm again and practically marched her up to the porch of the yellow house. Before Angela could protest, Violet rapped three times on the door.

Presently, Angela heard slow, muffled footsteps approach, and then the door opened to a tall brown-haired man with a shaved face and long side whiskers, wearing a crumpled white shirt that hadn't seen an iron in a while. His gray trousers hung loose on his narrow frame, and he shuffled in leather slippers. His hair also looked as if a comb hadn't paid a visit in a long while. *This must be George Fisk,* she suddenly realized.

Angela's hands grew clammy. She'd hoped to prepare what she would say to this master instrument maker. Would he feel she was worthy of one of his violins?

His drawn, tired face lit up upon seeing Violet.

"My sweet girl — so nice to see you." He took Violet's hands in his and showered her with a loving smile. Then he turned and looked at Angela. His eyes studied her, assessing her, and Angela grew uncomfortable at his scrutiny.

"And whom do we have here? I've not seen you in town before," he said sweetly, then added, "and I'm sure I would have noticed such a refined young lady."

Angela's cheeks heated at his remark. His manner was unabashed yet respectful. "I'm Angela Bellini, Mr. Fisk — pleased to make your acquaintance." She tipped her head at the introduction. "We corresponded recently. I've just arrived by train — "

"Ah yes," he said, a tinge of weariness lifting from his face. "Come in, come in, my dears." He gestured Angela inside with a wide sweep of his arm.

Violet stepped back. "I'm afraid I can't stay, George. I have to feed Henry and Thomas tonight."

Mr. Fisk frowned in disappointment. "I understand. Well, don't be a stranger. We have that Hoffmeister duet to work on for the hospital dedication."

Violet nodded. "I'm still struggling with the allegro movement."

"It's not an easy piece, my dear, but I have utter confidence in your ability to master it."

Violet beamed at his words, and Angela got the impression that Mr. Fisk didn't heap praise lightly. There was an air of perfectionism about him, and the glimpse she caught of the inside of his simply appointed home attested to a fastidious and neat nature. Though, his personal grooming belied such standards. She could hardly imagine how debilitating and abiding his grief must be. And a man having long been married would most likely be unaccustomed to washing and ironing his clothes.

"I'll be off then," Violet said. "And I'll come over Wednesday after lunch," she told the violin maker. Then she looked at Angela. "Once you have your violin, come show me. And we could use you in the orchestra." Her smile teased.

"Thank you," Angela told her. "I'm happy to have made your acquaintance."

Violet skipped off with a wave, leaving Angela standing awkwardly at Mr. Fisk's door. "I didn't mean to come unannounced and so late in the day—"

Mr. Fisk chuckled. "But when Violet learned you'd come to town to buy a violin . . ." He put a gentle hand on her back and urged her inside his cool dark-wood-paneled foyer. "Well, Miss Bellini, you're here now, and I've nothing pressing to attend to. Are you hungry? Where are you staying?"

More questions. People were certainly friendly and outspoken in Colorado, and her previous nervousness eased. She was so used to her father or brother criticizing her manner or her dress or some remark she'd make. Back home much propriety was expected of her. Here, in Greeley, she knew no one—well, aside from her brief acquaintance with Violet Edwards—and answered to no one but herself.

A giddy sense of freedom tickled her, and the weariness and worries of the former hours dissipated in the realization that she was now standing in the home of the famous instrument maker. She'd arrived.

She sighed and gave Mr. Fisk a grateful smile, remembering what Violet had said about his recent loss. While she was feeling a bit starved, food could wait, and she didn't want him to go to any trouble on her behalf. "Thank you, Mr. Fisk—"

"Please, my dear" he said, drawing out the word in his deep, melodious voice, "call me George. Everyone does. 'Mr. Fisk' sounds too formal."

Angela laughed. "All right . . . George. If you'll call me Angela instead of 'Miss Bellini.'"

"Angela it is. A beautiful name." He paused thoughtfully. "Beautiful angel," he added, translating the meaning of her name.

She liked this man. He was so different from the Italian men of Mulberry Bend. Here was a man of great talent, but he showed no haughtiness, as she'd expected.

He led her through the foyer and into a small bright kitchen, with sunlight streaming through yellow-and-white eyelet-trimmed curtains. Everything here, too, was neat and orderly, as if George, lonely and restless, had little else to do but straighten the modest furniture and wash his dishes. By the way his clothes hung on him, she wondered if he'd long ago lost his appetite and often forgot to eat.

As if hearing her stomach grumble, George opened an ice box and took out a wrapped block of cheese and a loaf of heavy crusted bread and set to work making a sandwich. He gestured her to sit in a chair at the kitchen table while he prepared the food. He then set before her a plate that held a ham-and-cheese sandwich, two fat dill pickles, and something she guessed was potato salad. He poured her a tall glass of sweet tea, then sat in a chair across from her.

"You're not joining me?" she asked, feeling uneasy at the thought of eating with him sitting there staring at her.

He shook his head and smoothed down his unruly hair as if suddenly aware that he hadn't had time to present a more neatened version of himself to his potential customer. "I've already eaten," he said. "Please." He waved a hand at her food. "I don't often have visitors dropping in from New York." He threw her a smile, and Angela sensed his loneliness fill the room.

She bit into the delicious sandwich and sated her hunger as George talked on, telling her how he'd lived in New York for a time, although he grew up in Vermont. He spoke of how this town began and why and how he'd come to live here—a close friend had introduced him to Mr. Meeker years back—and by the time Angela finished her meal and started on a second glass of tea, she'd learned much about him and found him wonderfully personable and sweet. He didn't mention his wife, though, while he talked, his recent grief was palpable in the timbre of his voice and the clouds of sadness that drifted into his eyes.

"So," he said, "now that you've eaten, tell me about yourself. You mentioned in your letters that your dream is to play in the New York Philharmonic. That's quite an aspiration, my dear."

Suddenly Angela was filled with doubt. George wasn't chiding or belittling her—not at all. But his words reminded her how desperately she wanted to play professionally. A horrific thought seeped into her mind. *What if those members of the audition committee were merely being polite when they told me I played well? What if they told me to come back with a better instrument only to get rid of me?* She'd never considered that they may have been merely placating her in a condescending way, and she, in her naiveté, assumed they were encouraging her.

Angela's stuffed stomach soured at the doubts gnawing at her. She pushed back in her chair and stood. The blood seemed to drain from her face. *Why did I come all this way? This was impetuous and foolish of me.*

George came to her side and took her arm. "My dear, are you ill?" He glanced at his ice box as if wondering if he'd unknowingly served her tainted meat.

"No, no, I'm fine," she said, assuring him. Had her face looked as stricken as she felt? "Perhaps . . . I'm just worn out from the long trip."

George studied her a moment, and Angela stiffened under his gaze.

"Where are you staying?" he asked quietly, looking into her eyes as if searching for something he'd lost in there.

"I've a room at the Greeley Hotel for the night. I'd planned to visit you tomorrow morning, and then catch the afternoon train to Denver—"

George took a step back and scrunched his face. "Catch the train to Denver . . ." His eyes suddenly showed understanding. "You mean, after you bought your violin." His words were flat and even, which gave Angela pause.

"Why, yes. I must get home as soon as possible . . ." Her throat tightened at the thought of her mamá and the way her papá had dragged her from the station platform. She swallowed back tears.

George looked at her as if able to read her mind. Flustered, she forced the words through her throat. "I live with my parents, but they're not very supportive of my interest in music. I'm . . . My father was not pleased when I left to come here."

George let out a sigh, nodding. "Those who don't know music can never understand." His eyes smiled at her, but his face stayed impassive. "We—you and I—know a world they can never fathom. We speak a language they can't learn." He paused. "Have you ever read Hans Christian Andersen's fairy tales?"

Angela nodded, surprised at this change in topic. Surely everyone had read them. She especially loved "The Princess and the

Pea" and, of course, "The Little Mermaid"—the story of a mermaid who so loved a man that she sold her beautiful voice to a wicked creature in order to be given legs and a chance to win his heart.

"Well," George said, "he once wrote 'Where words fail, music speaks.' This prolific author, who died not two years ago, knew that at the moments when words failed him, music would not. Come." He took Angela's hand in his warm large one and led her into his living room that was full of bookcases packed tight with books. He turned and looked deeply into Angela's eyes. "Music never fails," he said. "People will fail us. They will . . . let us down, and may even leave us, and at times we will be alone. But with music, we are never truly alone."

He grew quiet, and the room filled with the thick sound of silence, like the rush of quiet that followed the fading of the last bowed note of a violin solo.

"Here," he finally said, reaching for a small bound book from a shelf. The gray cloth cover was faded and threadbare, and Angela could tell this book had been read many times over many years. He handed the book to her, and she read the title: *Only a Fiddler*, by Hans Christian Andersen. She'd never heard of this book.

He took it back and flipped through the pages, then stopped and leaned close, narrowing his eyes to read the small text. "'Thou must also learn to play the fiddle, that may make thy fortune: thou canst win money by playing, and drive away thy sorrows when thou hast any. Here, thou shalt have my old fiddle, for the best I cannot give thee yet. In this manner place thy fingers,' and saying these words, he laid the violin on the little fellow's arm and guided himself the bow in Christian's hand. The tones rejoiced the little fellow; he had made them himself! His ear caught up each one, and his little fingers passed easily over the strings. Nearly a whole hour did the first lesson last. The godfather then took the instrument himself and played. That was fiddling! He trifled with the tones as a juggler who plays with his golden apples and sharp knives."

George smiled wistfully as if awash suddenly with sweet memories. He closed the book. "This is a story about a poor child named Christian who discovers his musical talent, but it's not supported. He thus goes through life striving but empty, for without the encouragement needed, he fails to find that fulfillment he yearns for." He frowned. "It's a sad tale, truly. But there is a rich lesson within these pages." He handed the book back to Angela. "Perhaps the story will resonate within your soul."

He seemed about to say more but fell silent again. Angela's heart felt heavy and pained, and she thought about what Violet had said about George's wife—her long illness and confinement. She imagined his music provided comfort for him now, but wondered if it truly was enough.

Was he right? Was music enough? If she devoted her life to it— if she turned her back on love and marriage and children—would it fail her? Or would it fulfill her? Was it possible to have both, as, no doubt, George once had?

"I think," George said, his voice rough with tiredness, "we should plan to meet in the morning, as you had suggested, and go to my shop, which is in the backyard. There, I'll show you some of the violins I'm presently working on, and we'll see if we can find one suitable for you."

He walked Angela to the front door, but before he opened it, he turned and gave her a hard look.

"Choosing an appropriate violin isn't something that can be rushed, my dear. While I know you feel the need to hurry home, it's . . . unlikely you'll have your violin tomorrow."

Angela's breath hitched, and her stomach knotted. "But . . . I must insist. You don't understand . . ." She could say no more. Her throat closed so that no other words could escape.

He rested a hand on her shoulder and opened the door with the other. A hot breeze assaulted her face as she stepped outside and tears stung her eyes.

"We'll discuss this in the morning, my dear. Whatever troubles await you back in New York will be there whether you return this week or the next."

"But I can't afford to stay longer," she blurted out, unthinking, immediately regretting her words. She hadn't wanted to reveal the dire financial situation she faced. Yet, if she had to stay longer—a week!—she would little afford a violin of quality. Unless she could find someplace else to stay. Maybe a room in a boarding house—if they even had such a thing in Greeley.

Her hope sank as she stood on the porch, unable to get her feet to move. *I should just leave in the morning.* She was on her own for the first time in her life, and she felt wholly incapable of taking care of herself. She'd never had to, and suddenly she felt scared and homesick and alone, here in this strange town halfway across the continent.

"I see," George said, standing in the doorway. "I suppose it's my fault. I didn't make it clear that you'd need to stay awhile. Just as it takes time to craft a fine instrument, that perfect match between musician and violin must emerge naturally. It can't be forced. But please, Angela, my dear—don't fret. I've a little cozy room in the back of my shop with a bed and all the comforts of a home away from home. Many a visitor has stayed there while searching for just the right violin to call his own. Just bring your things in the morning, and we'll get you settled in. All right?"

A room—for free? Then she remembered his letter, and how he said he'd take care of her lodging. Angela's stiff shoulders relaxed, and she let out a deep breath of relief. "Mr. Fisk, that's more than generous of you—"

"George—just George. So, will that suffice?"

Angela smiled and nodded. He was right, she told herself. Whatever awaited her in New York would still be there when she returned. And this was why she'd come—why she chose to purchase a violin from the famous instrument maker. He would ensure she got the perfect violin, one she could pour her heart into and that would, in return, respond with such sweetness, her soul would soar to the heavens. One that would speak, when words—and all else—failed.

"Yes, thank you, Mr. Fi—I mean, George." She gave him a wide smile and gripped the little book tightly in her hand. Tonight, she would read the story of Christian, but she would not share the boy's failure.

Nothing—and no one—she vowed, would ever get in the way of her dream.

Chapter 4

BRETT STRAINED TO OPEN HIS dirt-crusted eyelids. He rubbed a shaky hand over them and craned his neck up from the saddle to get a look-see of the land in the harsh glare of a noonday sun. His head pounded like someone was beating it with a hammer. A steady wind from the west blew grit into his eyes, and as he moved, just about every muscle he had yelped in pain and stiffness. He'd lost track of the days he'd been wandering lost, though he doubted he'd covered more than a few miles since he left Dakota behind for the buzzards and coyotes.

The thought of his poor horse sent a new stab of guilt and despondency through his empty gut. He'd failed to find any source of water, reckoning maybe his little Pinto might have died a more grueling death than the one he'd suffered. The way Brett felt, he prob'ly wouldn't last the day. His throat had swelled up as if a dry wad of clay lodged there, and as hard as he tried, he couldn't work up the spit to even swallow. His head wobbled on his neck, and his leg was a smoldering stick of agony.

As he tried to stand, searing pain shot through his back from the hours he'd foolishly hauled his saddle across this sorry wasteland of a prairie. His clothes were pretty well torn off, and his boots' soles flapped from the ripped seams.

Once he got some purchase with his feet, he looked far off to the west—to the mountains that beckoned heartlessly with their cool peaks of rarified air. The snow looked like cracked plaster.

He closed his eyes and saw his ma smiling at him, standing on some porch with brilliant light casting a halo around her whiskey-colored hair. She was younger than he remembered, and oh so beautiful, with soft skin and rosy cheeks, and a smile that gave no hint of the abuse or suffering she'd endured at the hands of his pa. She seemed so at peace. And happy.

"Come'on over, my sweet Brett." She reached out her arms to him, and Brett's heart surged toward her. But his feet wouldn't comply.

Then she seemed to slip back from him, getting smaller and smaller as the bright light sucked her inside and blocked her from his view, casting a long shadow over his heart.

"Ma!" he yelled, but his voice was swallowed up by the wind. He stumbled after her, grasping for the hem of her dress, which fluttered before him—all that was left of her.

"No, please, Ma! Don't go. Don't leave me . . . not again . . ." Brett's throat ached as the words crumbled to dust. His longing for her hurt more than all the pains in his body, and his heart wrenched as if someone was squeezing the daylights out of it.

"I'm sorry, so sorry," he sobbed, collapsing on the dirt, knowing he could never forgive himself for what he'd done, for her death.

After the tears dried on his feverish face, he lifted his head, then squinched his eyes. Not far off to the west, the ground shimmered wet. He told himself it was a mirage, another of the myriad delusions he'd suffered these past days. But he couldn't take his eyes off the rippling surface that promised soothing water. If only it was real.

What if it was? A tiny spark of hope lit under his doubt.

He crawled a few feet on hands and knees and stretched his neck. A wide, dark swath of water sparkled under the blinding September sun. His mouth salivated as he fixed his eyes on the river coursing across the endless desert. It seemed so close, yet as he crawled in agonizing slowness, the water inched away from him, teasing and tormenting.

Another few feet only confirmed his great fear. Through the wavering heat drifting up from the hot dirt, Brett made out a rutted road—dry and cracked like an old earthen crock. The despair rolled over and covered him—a blanket of surrender. He would go no further; he knew he had precious few minutes left. Here he would die—and he wasn't doing a gallant job of dying, at that.

He hardly had the strength to care. His life didn't amount to much anyway. Under all that cocky posturing, he was a coward at heart—truth be told. He'd run that day instead of standing up to his pa like a man. Instead of doing the right thing. Now he'd have to face his Maker. He doubted there'd be any forgiveness forthcoming for this son of perdition.

As he fell to the ground and laid his hot cheek against the hotter dirt, his mind emptying of thoughts and his heart hardening like a rock, he watched a plume of dust spin up from the road to the south. Like a tornado, it came for him, a steady approach. Brett lay there, resigned to his fate, a bit surprised at the manner in which the Devil was coming to collect him.

In a wagon drawn by two mules? A chuckle cracked in his mouth at the hilarity of his demise. Well, what did ya expect—some golden chariot to come down from the heavenly heights with the angel Gabriel blowing that trumpet and whisk ya away? The chuckle grew to an uncontrollable paroxysm of laughter as the ground vibrated with horse hooves and the jangle of breeching met his ears.

His final ride pulled to a stop before him, and as Brett's eyes closed and darkness enveloped him, he heard the Devil's footman jump down from the bench. Then his spirit cut loose from his body and commenced to seep away.

"Oh, Lord have mercy," Joseph Tuttle declared as he hurried over to the unfortunate young man lying half dead on the ground. *How in the world did this cowboy get here?* He doubted he was riding line for a ranch. There was nary a cow in sight, though Joseph knew this to be open rangeland, and the ranch of his friend Logan Foster wasn't all that many miles from here.

He threw his hand over his eyes and scanned the prairie around him, then spotted something in the distance that looked like a saddle. *A saddle?* He saw no horse wandering about.

He knelt by the fella who looked to be about his age, his medical bag at his side. It didn't take six years of medical school for him to assess what was ailing this poor sod. He was suffering from severe dehydration and hunger. The burns on his face and neck were bad, but Joseph's greater concern was the leg. A cursory inspection through the shreds of cloth that once were a pair of trousers showed what looked to be a gunshot wound, but while it didn't appear infected—thank the Lord for that mercy—the whole leg was swollen and red. He moved quickly, the heat of the day causing sweat to dribble down his neck.

The mules hitched to his wagon pawed the ground restlessly. They knew they were close to town and were tired from the trip to Loveland. Flakes of hay, a trough of cool water, and a rubdown awaited them at the livery.

"You'll just have to wait a little longer," he called out to them, then turned back to the cowboy lying beside him.

He gently tapped the man's grime-streaked cheek. "Hey, mister, wake up. You need to wake." Eyelids fluttered—enough for Joseph to think he might get some water down his throat.

"Here, drink." He held up his water skin to the cracked and bleeding lips, then lightly pried them open. They were stuck together with a glue of gritty dust. Joseph dribbled water into the fella's mouth, and most of it dribbled right back out. But he persisted until the head moved in response, then the tongue loosened and tasted the water.

After a minute or two, the man swallowed. Joseph let out a long-held breath. "Okay, we need to get you to town. I can't fix you up out here, in this heat." He rolled up his stiff starched blue shirtsleeves and rubbed his bearded chin. Moving the fella was going to be no easy task. Somehow he had to haul him up into the buckboard, and he had nothing he could use to aid him in this endeavor.

He hoped the fella suffered no broken bones or internal injuries. But there was nothing for it—he had to be moved, and it would be an awkward and jarring affair at best. But maybe the fella was so disoriented, he'd be oblivious to the pain.

It took Joseph the better part of a half hour and a slew of prayers, but he'd managed it. He made the young man as comfortable as possible and gave him more water to drink—most of which managed to get down the fella's throat, much to Joseph's relief. When he made to step down from the flat bed of his wagon, the cowboy moaned incoherent words.

"What's that?" Joseph asked, drawing close to the fella's mouth to hear him better.

The cowboy lifted a weak arm and gestured toward the east. "Saddle . . ." His face grimaced as he tried to say more, attempting to lift his head.

Joseph laid a hand on the fella's chest. "Easy now. I'll go fetch your saddle."

At those words, the cowboy's face loosened, and he let his head fall back on the folded-up blanket Joseph had bunched up under his head.

Joseph jumped down from the wagon, fetched the saddle—and a saddlebag and rifle lying nearby—then hefted the items into the back beside the cowboy, who seemed to have either fallen asleep or slipped into unconsciousness.

He studied the fella's face and sent up a prayer, thanking the Lord for sending him along this road this day. He'd seen only one other traveler that morning, and the farmer'd been heading south, down past Evans. Joseph believed the charge had fallen upon him alone to nurse this cowboy back to health. He hoped the fella would recover and Joseph could soon send him on his way—back to wherever he'd come from. Though, the wound in his leg suggested maybe this fella had reason not to return. For all Joseph knew, he could be an outlaw rather than the victim of some unfortunate encounter. But no matter. He was a doctor, just the person this fella needed at this moment, and Joseph's task was to see him back on his feet. He'd put the cowboy in his spare bedroom and tend to him till he was well enough to leave.

With his plans resolved in his mind, he climbed up onto the bench, picked up the reins, and got the mules moving north along the dusty road, much to their delight.

Chapter 5

THE MOMENT BRETT HENDRICKS JERKED his head up, he regretted it. It didn't take a genius to tell him he was bad hurt. Truth be told, he could hardly tell what didn't hurt.

A groan slipped out between clenched teeth as he edged himself upright, only now noticing the softness of a feather tick mattress underneath his bruised hips and the plump cool pillow behind his head.

A streak of morning sunshine spilled onto a dust-filmed wood-planked floor alongside the narrow bed Brett found himself lying in, the soft light revealing a bedroom with little adornment.

"Where in tarnation . . . ?" he mumbled, easing up a little taller and ignoring the painful stiffness in his joints. His belly felt cavernous and empty, and his hands shook like an old man's. He slid a hand down under the thin quilted blanket and gingerly felt for his wound. He grunted when his fingers touched on a wrapping of gauze that encircled his thigh. Through that, the skin was tender but no longer inflamed.

His clogged and woozy head cleared some — enough to stab him with the heavy memory of Dakota paddling the air in pain with his hooves and the sound of his gun going off when he aimed the Colt at the horse's head.

Brett squinched his eyes closed and let out a shuddering breath. Upon realizing he was wearing some man's long nightshirt, he knew he wasn't dead. He reckoned the afterworld wouldn't provide him the kind of considerations he was presently being shown.

Before the barrage of questions could crowd his mind, the door to the bedroom creaked open a few inches, followed by the spanking-clean face of a man about thirty. Thick dark-brown hair famed a pale narrow face that sported a trim beard, and a set of bushy brows hung over big green eyes that studied Brett thoughtfully.

Upon seeing Brett awake, the man straightened, and a grin revealed as fine a set of teeth as Brett'd ever seen. The man's eyebrows raised politely in question. "Mind if I come in?"

Brett gestured him in, wincing at the soreness in his shooting arm. "How long have I been here?" Wherever *here* was.

The man took three steps and came to his side, and Brett noticed his attire. Not a cowpuncher, this one, with his starched white shirt and pearly buttons. Brett's eyes took in the pressed brown wool trousers and spit-polished shoes. The neatly combed hair tucked behind the man's ears. He wasn't very tall.

"I'm Joseph Tuttle," the man said in a congenial manner, extending a very clean and manicured hand. Brett grunted. Was he back in Denver? He listened for sounds of a city, but the only thing he could hear drifting in through the half-opened window were songbirds warbling in a tree. The place seemed saturated in quiet as the man regarded Brett through curious eyes.

Brett shook the man's hand. "Brett Hendricks." He swallowed and noticed the dryness in his throat had eased, though he was fiercely thirsty. The hot windy prairie rushed into his mind, and

Brett recalled the mirage he'd seen while lying next to a road. The wagon pulled by a team of mules . . .

"Ohh," Brett said. "You're the fella who found me." His eyes drifted to what looked like a black medical bag sitting on the nearby dresser. Another cursory look around the room gave Brett the impression this fella lived alone—a keen lack of a woman's touch evident.

Tuttle nodded. "You were near dead about four miles south of town. Here," he said, reaching for a clay jug on the nightstand and pouring water into a tall glass.

Brett's mouth twitched as Tuttle handed him the glass. He took care not to spill it over his nightshirt as he drank. "I'm appreciatin' of your kindness." Cool water soothed his throat, and Brett couldn't recall a time when the simple act of drinking was so satisfying.

"I'm just thankful the good Lord led me to you." The man smiled, and Brett hoped he wouldn't get all religious on him. "Good thing you collapsed at the edge of the road and not out on the desert."

"What town is this?" Brett asked, his throat no longer scratchy. When he emptied the glass, Tuttle refilled it, then sat on a straight-back chair next to the bed.

"Greeley." Tuttle waited a moment, then said, "Where're you from?"

Greeley? Brett has heard something of this town. Some settlement by a bunch of folks from the East Coast. City of Saints or some such. Yep, religious folk. Prob'ly aimed to set up a bastion of purity and holiness in the middle of the lawless West. *Good luck with that.*

"Mostly down Texas way," Brett replied, not wanting to tell this stranger any more.

Seemed like these towns were cropping up all over the open range. Grangers—taking up rangeland, making it harder for ranchers to graze their cattle. First, the buffalo—nearly wiped out. Next—the cattle. In was only a matter of time, with all families heading west, now that the railroads crisscrossed the county. Soon he and all the other cowpunchers would be out of a job. He could see it looming on the horizon, and it weren't no mirage this time.

He drew a map in his head. Something like sixty miles or so north of Denver. He figured Orlander and his scalawags wouldn't chase him here. They'd probably turned tail back to Denver not long after he'd gotten shot.

He looked at Tuttle. "Did'ja fetch my saddle?" His roll of money was in his saddlebag—or so he hoped. Though, he didn't suspect a man like Tuttle would be the thieving type.

He suddenly felt trapped in the small bed. He'd hardly been inside a house more than a few times in the last two years, and the confining walls made his legs itch to get out.

Brett swung around, freeing himself from the unfamiliar tangle of covers and sheets, then tried to stand. His knees buckled, and a spear of pain shot up his thigh. His heart set off racing. He had to get shed of this room and fast.

"Whoa," Tuttle said, grabbing Brett's arm and steadying him. "You're in no condition to walk as of yet, Mr. Hendricks." He eased Brett back onto the edge of the bed. Brett's head spun riotously.

Brett conceded the man was right. *Just cool yer spurs, Cowboy. You ain't goin' anywhere right soon.*

Tuttle continued. "But you're welcome to stay in my house for as long as needed. I live here alone, and no one will bother you." He added, "And I have your saddle and saddlebags in the pantry in the back. Can I fix you some breakfast?"

At the mention of food, Brett's mouth watered. He nodded. "You a doc?"

Tuttle nodded in return. "I went to medical school in Ohio, then came out here about eight months ago."

"Seeking a new life in the West," Brett said, having heard it all many times afore.

Tuttle smiled and sat in the chair. "D'you mind if I check that gunshot wound?"

"Have at it, Doc," Brett said, pulling up the nightshirt to reveal the bandage. It looked clean—no blood staining the wrapping.

"Cauterizing that wound may have saved your leg," Tuttle said, carefully unwrapping the gauze. When he came to the end of the strip, Brett winced. Tuttle gently tugged the cloth free from the sticky skin and looked at the wound. The dark circle pinked around the edges, but the leg was only a mite swollen. "You took that bullet out yourself?"

Brett nodded, hoping the doctor wouldn't pepper him with too many questions. But the fella merely whistled and pulled out a roll of white gauze and scissors from his bag and rewrapped the leg.

When done, he stood. "I'll go fetch you some breakfast. Just stay here." He looked at Brett, his head cocked. The eyes studied him, but Brett sensed his kindness.

"I imagine you're keen to get going—to wherever it is you were headed. But healing takes time. You'll just have to let nature take her course. But I'm confident you'll make a full recovery, Mr. Hendricks, and you should be up and on your feet soon enough. I'll get you a walking stick. There's a privy out back, but I've provided you with a chamber pot." He pointed to the other side of the bed. "Would you like something to read?"

Brett snorted. He hadn't looked at the pages of a book since he was a young'un, when his ma used to set him on her lap and read to him from those picture books before tucking him into bed with a song. The image of his ma, all purty and smiling, beckoning him to come to her, set off an ache in his chest. He swallowed hard.

"Well," Tuttle said, "if you would like a book or the newspaper, just let me know."

"What day is it?" Brett suddenly asked. Just how many days had he been wandering lost?

"Friday. September fourteenth."

Brett whistled through his teeth. The competition in Denver was last Sunday. He'd never lost days like this before. "I c'n pay you—"

Tuttle waved him off. "No need, Mr. Hendricks. It's my pleasure and my Christian duty to help a stranger in need." He picked up his bag and walked out of the room.

A wave of weariness washed over Brett, and he felt weak all over. He hated feeling this poorly, wishing he could leap from the bed and get back to the open range. He was as helpless as a calf trapped in a branding pen.

Brett heard the kind doctor rattling pans in a kitchen, and he lay back against the soft, clean-smelling pillows in a room free of dirt, dust, and droning insects. Like a mud hog wearing Sunday best clothes, Brett felt wholly out of place. Closest he ever came to such luxury was a canvas cot in a crowded bunkhouse full of smelly, unwashed cowboys. Brett could tell the doctor had cleaned him up—even washed his hair. He pulled a crop of his red-brown hair to his nose and gave a whiff and winced. It smelled of flowers.

Brett shook his head. The sooner he got well and shucked this town, the better. He'd inquire of the local ranches. Surely he could find a spot in an outfit, even if he had to ride the drags. Wouldn't be long before the fall roundup. All the ranches hired on extra hands in the fall to cut the herds and send the cattle to market. So long as he stayed clear of Denver and Orlander's outfit, he'd be all right.

He closed his eyes, relishing the smell of toast and bacon cooking, his thoughts wandering to the horses he'd broken and gentled, to the cheers of crowds as he worked saddles and headstalls onto wild mounts and eased the fearful animals to their feet under his command. In the last few years, he'd spent more time on the back of a horse than off—and he preferred it that way.

There was nothing so freeing as being astride a horse in the wide-open range, thousands of stars twinkling in the night sky and the hoot of owls and lowing of cows to serenade you. Some folks considered it a lonely life, but Brett wouldn't have it any other way. He liked being answerable to no one but the foreman of his outfit. And while other cowboys bellyached about wanting a woman and settling down, Brett thought that the worst type of corralling.

Sure, he longed for someone sweet and soft to throw his arms around, but there was a difference between roping a gal in from time to time and having a tumble and one hitching you to the post and hobbling your legs so you could hardly take a step. He'd nearly been caught unawares twice, bespelled by such beauty that he'd almost lost his head. Those gals'd thought he'd make a fine catch, but they had 'airy a clue what kind of fella he was—what darkness brooded in his heart. What he was capable of. His hands clenched into fists as he thought on his pa's temper and the fiery blood that ran through his own veins.

Yep, he was safer on a horse on the range. Far from temptation. The distraction and hard work of cow-punching—riding point or swing twelve to sixteen hours a day, roping, herding, branding— was what he needed. No other life would suit him.

As his thoughts lapped against his sleepy head, lulling him, a strain of music drifted into his ears, a melancholy wailing, like a lone coyote pining for a mate. Sounded like someone playing a fiddle with a heavy arm and a heavier heart. The sound caused a twinge of pain in his chest, making him restless and irritable. The notes dug into his ribs, like worms looking for a dark, cold place to hide from the heat of the summer sun.

He threw off the thin quilt, which suddenly felt hot and cumbersome, and swung his legs over the side of the bed. Sweat beaded on his forehead. His body stiffened, as if ready to run for his life.

Joseph Tuttle strode in, a steaming plate of food on a tray in his arms, and halted in the doorway. "Are you all right, Mr. Hendricks?" His face registered alarm.

Brett managed a nod. He willed his heart to stop racing, wondering what in tarnation had come over him. "I'm fine, Doc. Jus' hungry, I reckon."

Tuttle's face loosened in relief. As Brett sat back, the doctor situated the tray on Brett's lap, the enticing aroma of the vittles wafting up into Brett's nose.

He listened for a moment and heard more fiddle music. He hadn't imagined it. The sounds were coming from the next house over. As Tuttle turned to leave again, Brett said, "Would you mind closing the window yonder?"

Tuttle seemed surprised at Brett's request, but he complied. Quiet filled the room. Brett relaxed his clenched jaw. "Well, then," Tuttle said. "I'll leave you to eating. I'll be in my office in the back — call out if you need my help."

"Much obliged," Brett said, his words thin and shaky. Yep, the sooner he got his legs back under him, the sooner he could get back on the Front Range and in the saddle.

Chapter 6

GEORGE FISK SWUNG OPEN THE door to his shop and gestured Angela inside. The smell of varnish and wood permeated the air—the redolence reminding her of the back room of the instrument shop on Second Avenue. She drew in a long invigorating breath as her eyes widened, taking in the dozens of violins in various stages of construction hanging from hooks on the walls and dangling from the low ceiling.

Two thick, long wood tables took up most of the crowded space, every inch of their surfaces covered with woodworking tools and pots of varnishes and unfinished pieces of violins, all neatly laid out. Numerous strung bows were propped up on a shelf against the far wall. One recently sanded violin lay completed in a stand before her, awaiting its first layer of varnish.

Angela had on occasion watched the old shopkeeper sand and re-varnish old instruments of various types, but she'd never actually seen an instrument built. Her eyes snagged on large blocks of beautifully grained honey-colored wood stacked on the floor against the wall. And smaller, thinner slices of dark wood sat stacked on one table's edge. She reached out and touched a bowl of nearly black tuning pegs that glistened in the morning light streaming through the two large windows on her right.

Angela turned to George, whose smile gleamed with pride in his work. "Those are made of ebony. All my violins have ebony pegs and fittings and tailpieces. Though at times I'll use rosewood, for a warmer look." He looked up to the rafters and took down a finished violin, then cradled it in his arms for her to see. It was yet unstrung and lacked the gleam of the instruments she'd played on. But it was beautifully crafted and made her long to pick up a bow and play.

"See the rosewood detail here on the fingerboard? It provides such a lovely contrast to the maple back and scroll and the spruce top. I take my time picking just the right pieces so that the grains blend in harmony." He gave her a wink as she gazed in awe at the swirling lines embedded deep in the wood. They almost resembled a line of music, the way the threads of grain danced across the surface.

"Once an instrument is completed 'in the white'—glued and sanded and ready for varnishing—it has to sit for weeks to dry fully. In the winter, I keep a fire going in the stove there"—he pointed to a small iron potbelly stove in a corner that she'd not noticed—"but I have to be diligent and keep the heat at a constant low level or else the wood will crack." He gestured around the room. "Building instruments takes great care and fine attention to detail, my dear. Not many have the patience to master the craft."

Angela thought about Violet's words—how Mr. Fisk and his wife never had children. He looked lovingly upon these instruments he made as if they were his progeny. And, she supposed, they were, in a way. They were certainly precious to him.

Angela was speechless as George continued to explain. He picked up a lightly varnished violin and held it up to the light. "This one has had the first ground layer applied. See, I'll share a secret with you—one I learned from a master craftsman in Vermont." She came closer at his urging. "The secret is in the ground coat of varnish. It must be mixed with minerals, such as silica and alumina. And then the subsequent coats of walnut and linseed oil must be sun-thickened." He pointed to a row of glass jars filled with amber oils lining the windowsill. "Good varnish will be translucent yet friable. And when applied, it should vary in color based on how thick the layer. A thin layer will be golden, and a thicker layer will have red hues."

He tenderly replaced the violin back on its stand and turned to Angela. "Well, my dear, if you're interested, while you're staying here, I can teach you some of the fine art of violin-making."

"I'd love that," Angela said, though she doubted there'd be much time for such a pursuit. She hoped she could choose her violin today, but she didn't want to voice her thoughts. George had indicated this decision couldn't be rushed. But what exactly did he mean?

"But, of course, that's not why you've come all these miles to this remote town, far from home. So, let's take a look at some possibilities for you, shall we, my dear?"

Angela nodded, her pulse starting to race in anticipation. George picked up a bow from the table and adjusted the tension in the strands of horsehair. He then narrowed his eyes as he perused the line of finished violins sitting on stands on the next table. While the violins looked similar, upon closer examination, Angela could see slight variations of color and style of detailing. They were all gorgeous, and she didn't doubt every one of them would have a beautiful sound. She didn't want to admit to this master craftsman that she hadn't the ear to distinguish between one fine instrument and another. She was glad she'd left her paltry violin in the apartment; bringing it would have been an embarrassment. Why couldn't he just pick one out for her?

"Let's start with this one," he said, carefully lifting a violin from its stand and handing it to her along with the bow. "Check the tuning, but it should be close to pitch."

She felt suddenly nervous, not wanting to play in front of George. But he laid a hand on her arm with a knowing smile, as if reading her thoughts—as if she wasn't the first to have a flutter of nerves in front of him. "I'll go make us some tea and be right back."

He ambled out of the shop back toward the house, and Angela calmed her nerves. She supposed she was more excited than self-conscious. She had never played an exquisite instrument of such quality before and hardly felt worthy of holding this violin in her arms. Yet, the moment she plucked the strings to tune them, a smile spread across her face. And after tuning the strings to pitch with those lovely ebony pegs, she tucked the violin under her chin, held the bow over the bridge, and rested her fingers on the neck.

She closed her eyes, taking in the feel of the instrument in her hands, the rich aroma of the room, and the quiet of the day. Not a sound could she hear but the thumping of her heart as she stood in the room surrounded by dozens of silent observers—George's many violins all waiting for someone to draw the sweet sounds from their souls.

With a tremble in her hand, she pulled the bow across the lowest string. A rich G resounded and seemed to fill her from toe to head. Slowly she moved her left fingers along the neck, playing random flights of notes and letting the music run loose.

The melody rose into the air and spread out like thick honey as she closed her eyes and relished the tones coming from this magical box in her hands. She envisioned the notes of music as fireflies lighting up the summer night. Images swelled through her mind of water skipping over rocks as the bow bounced lively on the strings. Her heart soared, like a bird on its way to roost in its nest after a long absence. Nothing else made her feel so content, so fulfilled, as this. She'd needed this reminder—of what mattered most.

Now she understood the difference between a good violin and a magnificent one. There was no comparison. She'd been limited, hindered, from playing her best on a mediocre violin. But with this instrument . . . it was as if it responded to the ache in her heart and sang for her without words—in perfect, exquisite tones.

She startled at the sound of the door opening, quickly lowering the violin to her side. George stepped inside, a tray in his arms with a tea service. "Here we are—some hot tea and a couple of biscuits." He cleared a spot on the table and set down the tray.

Words failed her. Then she thought of the quote George had spouted yesterday: "Where words fail, music speaks." That saying was never more true for her than in that moment. But clearly, he read her wordless expression.

George poured them each a cup of tea and handed one to Angela. She set the violin on its stand and sipped as George continued. "Each violin has its special qualities. Each has a unique voice that emerges over time. There is a bonding that must take place. The instrument and the musician must become one, inseparable. And not every union is a good fit—just like with a marriage. Love cannot be forced; neither can respect be demanded. Over time the musician learns the limits and potential of the instrument, and by honoring those things, the violin, in return, rewards the musician with beautiful music."

He walked over to the end of the table and chose a violin with a light varnish finish. He then picked up a bow and began to play. A flurry of notes burst from the violin, and she recognized the etude as one of Heinrich Ernt's.

A shiver traveled down her spine, and her jaw dropped as he played. He drew such exquisite melodies from the violin in his hand, as if breaking open a treasure box and spilling jewels into the air. She watched him—it seemed as if for hours, but she knew only a scant few minutes passed by the time he pulled the bow with a long final note and let the sound melt into the air. She now understood fully what he meant about becoming one with the instrument. It was as if they had merged and blended into one voice. She longed for nothing more in that moment than to experience that with her violin.

He opened his eyes, lowered the violin, and smiled at her.

"That was . . . I don't know what to say." Flustered, she took another sip of tea, and the milky sweetness soothed her dry mouth.

George set the violin down and rubbed his chin. "I need to purchase some things at the mercantile. Why don't you get settled into the room in the back, and while I'm out, you can try out a few of these violins. Then later, I'd like to hear you play, so we can begin determining which instrument might be a good fit." He took some time looking over the various instruments in the room, then collected four and set them in their stands on the table before her.

"Let's start with these. And then maybe tomorrow another four. Spend time with each one. Play outside as well, so you can hear the timbre in an open space."

Angela nodded, pushing down her desire to hurry back to her life in New York, though now she doubted she'd get another chance with the philharmonic. Though . . . there were many other symphony orchestras in the East—other auditions she could attend. With a superior instrument in hand, her chances of being hired seemed more than possible.

She knew George was right. While any of these violins would no doubt suit her, she wanted the one that would best bring out her music. She imagined she would play her chosen violin the rest of her life, for when would she ever have an opportunity like this again?

Which made her remember her resolve to ask her aunt about living with her when she returned to New York. Tonight she would pen a letter to Zia Sofia, telling her where she'd be staying and voicing her request. She wondered how long it would take a letter to get to her—at least as many days as a train trip, she assumed. Angela wondered if she would already be on the train to New York before she received word back from her aunt. She would be sure to plead with her not to tell her papá where she was, although she imagined he had pried that information from her mamá by now. And, she recalled, she'd promised to send her mamá a telegram letting her know she arrived safely.

That familiar despair welled up, but she determined to pay it no mind. She would instead think of how to help George Fisk, to thank him for his kind hospitality. Surely he would enjoy some home cooking, and he could use a few extra pounds on his wasting frame. When he returned, she'd offer to make dinner for them, and perhaps bake some bread or some sweet panettone cake with dried fruits and raisins.

She smiled thinking how George might be grateful for a womanly presence in his home, at least for the time she was here. She may as well do something useful while waiting for her violin. Though, the promise of playing night and day on these sweet instruments was tempting.

With that thought, she picked up one of the violins and tucked it under her chin.

Chapter 7

THROUGHOUT THE DAY, BRETT HAD dozed and awakened in a half stupor, only to drop off to sleep again. He hated how weak he felt, and though the food and water Tuttle had given him took the edge off his feebleness, still he felt like some old man every time he moved or tried to get up to stand.

But he was determined to get back on his feet and out of this confining pen as soon as his strength returned. Tuttle had left for the day, to tend to his practice in town, but assured him he'd be back by nightfall. He'd left Brett plenty to eat in the kitchen and told him it'd be good for him to walk around some. But the most Brett could manage was a handful of steps before he'd collapse into a chair or back onto the edge of the bed, frustrated and impatient. He'd done plenty of stupid things in his twenty-four years, but this was the worst. Still, Orlander and his men could've killed him. And at least his leg would heal. He s'posed things were looking up.

But the upshot was, he sure hated being an invalid and dependent on the kindness of others. Soon as he was able, he'd ask around town where he might find some ranchers—see who was hiring.

He rifled through the neat stack of his clothes that Tuttle had washed and line-dried for him that morning. He hardly recognized his blue plaid shirt—so clean and sweet-smelling. Usually he did his own wash out on the range in a creek or pond, scrubbing with a rock and sand to get the grime and stains out. He felt almost silly putting on such clean duds, but he felt sillier walking around in that long cotton nightshirt of Tuttle's.

He pulled on his trousers, wincing as the fabric slid across the bullet wound, and noticed how loosely they hung on his hips. He'd sure lost some weight wandering through the desert prairie in his fool attempt at escaping those men. He didn't bother to put on his socks and boots.

Brett gritted his teeth as he hobbled across the room and headed to the kitchen. He rubbed his raw clean-shaven face. It felt good to have gotten shed of that scraggly beard. He wished he had some whiskey, but the good doctor kept 'airy a drop in the house. Seemed this town had a prohibition on spirits. How in tarnation did folks get by without banking the fire from time to time?

He paced the floor, restlessness lassoing a chokehold around his throat. His fists clenched as the room closed in on him. He threw open the back door and lurched outside, sucking in long breaths and trying to calm his pounding heart.

The coolness of night rippled over his face, drying his clammy forehead. The damp grass felt cool and soothing under his feet. A waxing moon tangled in a listless elm's branches nearby.

Presently, the knot in his gut loosened, and his breaths evened out. He glanced around at the small grassy yard dotted with wildflowers. Tuttle had what looked like an herb garden by the back of the house, and not fifty feet away sat houses on both sides, also painted white and simple in design. Typical small-town dwellings similar to all the other towns Brett had visited on occasion.

And then he heard that music again. All through the day, bits of fiddling had drifted to his ears, but now, outside, it filled the night. He guessed it was some kind of fiddle, though he'd never heard this kind of music played on one before. Instead of a lively song, the notes sounded almost sorrowful. Maybe even full of heartache. He wondered who it was playing in that small shed out back behind the house to his right.

As he listened, his heart started to race, and his feet got twitchy. There was something haunting, unsettling, about the song filling his ears. He felt like a horse being soothed with deceptive words and sensing something wrong, fearing it was about to be roped and thrown to the ground. Yet, as much as he fought to resist the lure of this music, the more he was drawn to it in some strange, powerful way. The notes stirred in him a longing for something he couldn't name, causing a twinge of fear to tighten his throat.

Just when he was about to throw his hands over his ears and retreat back inside Tuttle's house, the door to the little shed opened, and out walked a gal in a long dress with a high collar and ruffled hem, a fiddle dangling from one hand and a bow in the other.

Brett stopped and stared, stepping back into the shadows of the eaves where he could watch without being noticed. He couldn't take his eyes off her. Moonlight splashed over her, lighting up her long black hair that trailed over her shoulders and down her back. In the glow of the light, her face resembled an angel's—soft gentle features, purty dark eyes, and the fullest lips he'd ever seen. He reckoned her to be about twenty, with a shapely figure he imagined drew looks from fellas wherever she went. Who was she? Did she live next door? Tuttle had told him a widower lived in the house. Was this the fella's daughter?

He sniggered at how smitten he was by the gal, like he was laboring under some spell. He blamed it on his exhaustion and the trick of the moonlight. *Not your type, Cowboy.* Seeing the way she held herself, so proper-like, and her fancy dress and all told him she was used to comforts. The kind of gal that wanted a trunk-load of purty things and screamed if she saw a mouse. Still, no reason he shouldn't enjoy drinking her in. It'd been many a month since he'd laid his eyes on a comely gal.

He leaned back against the house and propped his sore leg up on the wood siding. Being outside was a balm to his soul. He looked up at the stars spattered across the sky, and a wave of loneliness crashed over his heart. His life felt suddenly so empty, so meaningless. He'd been moving from one place to the next, one ranch to the next, year after year. For what? A few dollars in his pocket? Just what did he want to do with his life? His dream of starting his own ranch poked at him, but how would he ever save enough money for such a dream?

He looked back at the gal, who was now looking up at the stars. From where he stood, he could tell she was charmed by the sight, as if she'd never been outside at night. Then she put the fiddle under her chin and pulled the bow across it.

Brett couldn't move; he was transfixed by the haunting melody swirling about his head. He closed his eyes and rocked on his bare feet, drinking in the keening music coming from the fiddle as it sang to his heart. To his surprise, tears welled in his eyes. Something the bow drew from the strings fed his soul. He felt awash with sorrow once more, as if the fiddle was a key that unlocked a secret place in his heart. He opened his eyes in bewilderment, swiping a hand across them, stunned that he was so shook up.

A shiver ran down his spine, and his jaw dropped as she played. He watched her for what seemed like hours, but he knew only a few minutes had passed. Even the air and all the stars seemed to be listening. Never in his life had he heard such sweet music.

Then suddenly the night fell quiet. The gal with the fiddle was staring at him, moonlight swimming in her eyes. Once more he felt like a trapped calf in a corner of a pen, and his mouth went dry. He couldn't look away, and his feet were stuck in place. What in tarnation was wrong with him?

How long has that man been standing there, staring at me? Angela's arms dropped to her sides, and her face flushed with heat. She'd been so lost in the music, she hadn't seen him—only yards away, leaning up against the neighbor's house. But she wasn't surprised she hadn't spotted him. She'd been transported by the intoxicating tone of the notes coming from this violin. Playing outside in the cool, thin air, under such spectacular stars, brought out the notes buried deep in her soul. It was as if the instrument had awakened them from slumber and set them free, like releasing a flock of birds that had been caged for years. She couldn't have held them back if she'd tried.

Wanting to be polite, she waved and called out a timid hello. She could barely make him out in the shadows and felt suddenly self-conscious. She pushed down a niggling fear, then reminded herself that George was nearby, in his house, should this man act unmannerly toward her. He'd assured her she was safe in this town of wholesome, God-fearing residents.

But when the man stepped out into the moonlight, Angela stiffened. He had a rough look about him, though his handsome face was shaved and his shoulder-length chestnut hair was neatly brushed back behind his ears. Angela could tell he was a man of labor, with strong shoulders and powerful legs that could hardly be hidden beneath the neat shirt and trousers he wore. She saw he was barefoot, and his hazel eyes seemed to dive deep into hers, as if searching for something he'd lost. It was his intense gaze that unsettled her most of all. She saw hunger—and something like pain—in those eyes, and it made her take a step back as he approached.

He stopped about ten feet from her, and now that she saw him more clearly, her breath caught in her throat. His skin was rough and sun-darkened, and a scar ran from his neck to his ear. He was nothing like the men of New York. Every inch of him seemed tough and strong—even the thick cords of his neck that bulged under a chiseled jaw.

"Pardon me, honey," he said in a voice that had its own lilting melody. "I didn't mean t' startle ya. That's some purty music you were playin'."

Angela's eyes dropped to his chest showing through the open top buttons of his shirt, then she averted her eyes. His nearness unsettled her.

She cleared her throat, suspicious of his attempt at pleasantry. "Thank you." Her words seemed to evaporate in the night air.

"You live here?" he asked.

"Oh no . . . well, yes. I mean . . ." she answered quickly. "I've come to buy a violin from Mr. Fisk." Why she felt so awkward around this man, she couldn't say. She had a hard time meeting his eyes, for when she did, her heart raced. And when he smiled at her, she could hardly swallow. Everything about him exuded manliness and strength, and she sensed a wild spirit raging underneath his calm exterior.

"What's yer name?" he said, then winced as he shifted his weight onto one leg.

"Are you hurt?" she asked, for he surely seemed to be in pain.

He sighed and ran a hand through his hair. "Had a bit of a scrape. But the doc here has been tendin' to me." Before Angela could reply, he came toward her and held out his hand. "Name's Brett. Brett Hendricks."

She wasn't sure what he wanted, so she shook his warm, weathered hand, then pulled her hand away. "I'm Angela Bellini."

"Where ya from? I c'n hear an accent." His eyes lit up with moonlight as a coy smile graced his face. Angela felt flustered by his questions.

"I live in New York."

"Never would'a guessed." He turned thoughtful. "Italian, I reckon, by your name."

She nodded. "And you, Mr. Hendricks—?"

He chuckled and shook his head. "Just call me Brett." He reached up and rubbed his neck, and Angela watched the muscles ripple in his arm under his threadbare shirt. For a second she wondered what it might feel like to have such strong arms embrace her. Then she shook away the thought, remembering propriety.

"Do you live here in Greeley?" she asked, feeling more awkward with each passing minute, standing out here in the yard in the dark of night with a strange man. She certainly didn't feel comfortable calling him by his Christian name.

He laughed again. "No, I punch cattle. I'm between jobs presently."

"I see." Though she wasn't exactly sure what it meant to "punch cattle," she guessed he must be a cowboy. It took little to imagine him on a horse, wearing a brimmed hat and swinging a rope at some cow.

"What happened to you?" she said, nodding at his leg—the one he wouldn't put weight on.

"Got shot."

"Shot?" Was he serious?

He shrugged, and an uncertain smile touched his mouth. "It happens."

Angela blanched and fell speechless. Happens when, where? Herding cows? She'd heard the West was wild, but she really didn't imagine men went around shooting one another.

His eyes regarded her steadily, scrutinizing her. Her face got hot as a lengthy silence fell.

"Well, it's been a pleasure meeting you. I wish you a fast and full recovery from your . . . wound."

Now she was sure he was laughing at her. Though his eyes danced with mirth, his face settled into hard lines.

"Well, thank you, honey." He nodded and touched his forehead as if reaching for a hat he'd forgotten to put on. "When . . . uh . . . will you be headin' back to New York?" His eyes drifted down her body, then returned to gaze at her with a mischievous glint.

She restrained her hand from slapping his face. "Don't you think you're getting a bit too personal, Mr. Hendricks?" she said, her ire rising as she took a step back. She wrapped her arms around her chest, now regretting she'd said hello. It was highly improper for her to be talking to him like this. And he seemed just the kind of man who would sweet-talk a woman into his arms. Here in Colorado, she didn't have a stern father keeping unsuitable men from making advances.

He pursed his lips, and his eyes laughed at her. "Listen, honey. If a fella meant to hurt ya, he would'a done so by now." He towered over her by nearly a foot, and he intimidated her more with each breath he took.

"I have to go," she said brusquely. She hoped he'd get the message. She wasn't interested in getting to know Brett Hendricks beyond the usual pleasantries.

"Good night, then," he said with a chuckle, then turned and hobbled back toward the house he was staying in.

Angela waited until he went inside, then hurried into the shop and latched the door behind her. Her heart thumped fast as if she'd escaped some danger as her body went limp with relief. She couldn't get Brett's smile and laughing eyes out of her mind as she prepared for sleep. No doubt he was a reckless man—he'd gotten shot! He might even be an outlaw for all she knew. And the way he looked at her—with the hungry gaze of a wolf. She'd best steer clear of the man for the few days she was here. No sense giving him any idea that she was intrigued by him.

But you are, Angela. Admit it. Yes, he was intriguing, and utterly handsome, but she had not come here for adventure or romance—and especially not danger. She came to purchase a violin and then head home. Last thing she needed was a cowboy—or any man—in her life. *I will not end up like Mamá, trapped in an awful marriage.*

Angela fixed that thought in her mind as she crawled under the light patchwork quilt in the narrow bed and blew out the lantern, but sleep eluded her for some time.

Brett tossed in the too-soft bed, unable to snatch any sleep. That gal cut a wide swath through his thoughts. He replayed his feeble attempt at conversation, wondering what had gotten him so flummoxed. Sure, she was mighty fetching, with curves in all the right places and those gorgeous brown eyes and thick lashes. But he was never one to succumb to a fit of nerves around the female of the species. Being close to her had stirred something deep inside, like a sudden gush of blood. It was more than just carnal need— something he and every cowboy fought with, alone for months on the open range. No, there was something else there, something he couldn't right put his finger on. She'd stood in the moonlight, playing that fiddle, like an angel sent from heaven.

Well, Cowboy, get her out of your mind. She's heading home inside of a week. Not much ya can do 'bout that. And a gal like that is too good and proper for ya.

His mind flashed on the way his rage had erupted when he'd happened upon that Orlander kid with his hand squashed over that gal's mouth as she squirmed trying to get shed of her attacker. The kid'd pinned her against the side of the barn, just inside the open doors, and by the time Brett had heard her muffled screams, the kid had his pants down to his knees and the gal's skirts pushed up over her face.

What made Brett even more furious was seeing the three cowpunchers lollygagging nearby, joking and finding it all amusing—what the rich rancher's son was perpetrating. It took all his restraint not to shoot the lot of 'em. And, for the hundredth time, he reminded himself, that kid deserve what for. *But it felt too good smashing 'is nose. Ya knew it when ya done it. You lusted for blood and wanted more. Like a fever, it took hold of ya.*

Brett recalled the way his hands had shaken so fiercely with rage. He'd barely mustered the resolve to tear them from the kid's throat. What stopped him from crushing the kid's windpipe was the memory of the crazed look in his pa's eyes the last time Brett'd seen him light into his ma.

The familiar sinking feeling of guilt and shame settled back in his gut—though it hardly ever left him. He winced recalling how he'd stood there and done nothing, his fear of his pa freezing him in place, until he finally worked up the nerve to run out the door. He'd headed over to Newcomb's ranch and joined his outfit that day— he'd been all of sixteen. It was months later when he'd gotten the news, after coming in from a harsh winter in a floating outfit, having been far from Austin branding late calves and rounding up strays that'd escaped the roundup.

By then, it was too late to do a thing about it. His pa was in jail and his ma buried in the little plot behind the house, next to his sisters that'd succumbed to the influenza. Though the house had been sold, Brett had ridden over and put flowers on her grave. A sorry offering that did nothing to excuse his cowardice that day.

His hands were strong and able. With them he could bring horses under his command, throw lassoes and haul wayward calves into the branding chutes. His hands could fire a pistol or rifle with keen accuracy. But he also knew they were capable of killing, and he feared they'd someday wrap around a gal's neck with the ease they wrapped around the grip of a gun.

Chapter 8

HORACE ORLANDER PACED OUTSIDE THE bedroom door, his heavy boots thumping on the wood planks that had been smoothed and worn down over the years, though they gleamed with polish — as did every inch of his fine domicile. He wasn't a man who liked to wait for anything, and this fool doctor was wasting his time in there. Just how may more doctors would it take before he found one with an ounce of smarts?

He refused to believe Wade wouldn't walk again. The thought of his only son confined to a wheelchair for the rest of his life fanned his rage into a conflagration. He couldn't think of enough ways he itched to give that cowboy his just deserts. However long it took him, however far, he'd find that Hendricks fella and make him pay.

The big house was quiet, his wife prob'ly still in bed, crying — like she did most every day. He could hear his hands outside, breaking the horses and getting the next string ready for range work. Most of his punchers were over by Cal's Fork, near the Santa Fe Trail with most of the herd. *That's where Wade would be right now*, he thought bitterly, his mouth souring at the way his son just sat there in bed, his eyes glazed, all the life drained out.

He clenched his teeth and fists as he gazed mindlessly out the window, his thousands of acres of rolling grassland dry and brown in the September heat. Scatter Creek was as pathetic as he'd ever seen it, feebly pushing its way from the spring box only to be drunk up by the thirsty plains a mere hundred yards yonder. What used to bring him such pride and joy—looking out over his spread—now only gave him a big empty hole in his gut. He had one of the biggest ranches in southern Colorado, with two hundred thousand head of cattle. He'd spent decades making the name Orlander famous throughout the West, the admiration of ranchers from Texas to Montana. But what did it matter now?

His wife had given him three sons. The two oldest had died before age five, causing him and the missus unbearable grief. He'd trained Wade since he was four to ride and rope and run cattle. Though his son had always been testy and headstrong, Horace knew he'd one day do a right good job taking over the ranching business.

But now? How in tarnation would he be able to run a ranch if he couldn't even walk—let alone dress himself?

His chest tightened, and his breaths grew labored as his fury simmered to a boil. He turned from the window at the sound of the door opening.

The fastidious doctor he'd paid to come all the way from Fort Worth slipped out of the bedroom and eased the door shut behind him.

"Well?" Horace asked, reining in his impatience and frustration. He could tell from the look on the old man's face that the news would be bleak.

The doctor scrunched his lips as he approached Horace. His bag in one hand, the heavily mustached man wiped his brow with the other, then rubbed his chin.

"I wish I could give you a better prognosis, Mr. Orlander. But those other doctors were right. Things don't look all that promising for your son there. I'll allow he'll have a hard time of it. Usually if a man is injured like that and can't feel his legs within the first day or two, it's unlikely that'll change. Though, I don't discount the power of prayer. The Lord is a healer and can work miracles for those who have faith—"

"Spare me your preachin'," Horace snapped. "Is there anythin' at all—practical—we can do to help him walk again? Give him some kind of exercise?"

The doctor shook his head. "I don't see how. The boy can move his arms and his torso, and that's a blessing. He can feed himself and learn to dress and undress and be mostly independent. Give a boy meaningful work that can take his mind off his circumstance—"

"He's a cowboy, for heaven's sake! How's he s'posed to do that when he's confined to a chair? Running a ranch ain't done by sitting around."

The doctor shrugged and lowered his fearful eyes. "I imagine there's other work he can do. Keeping the books, tracking sales and cattle shipped to market—"

"I have a foreman who does all that."

"I'm merely suggest—"

"Jus' get out," Orlander said, seething at the man's "practical" suggestions. He was fed up and tired of hearing how he should have Wade push papers for the rest of his life. *My boy has strength and skill. He's almost a man, and a man needs to work with his body, not just his hands.* Then he thought on how Wade would never be able to love a woman and what that would do to him. *And that means no one to continue the Orlander family name. No one for Wade to pass the ranch to when he's old.*

His jaw hurt from clenching it so tight. He had to do something with this anger. If he didn't, who knew what terrible things he might do.

Without a further word, the doctor gave a nod that oozed with pity and let himself out. Orlander's eyes followed him as he fetched his wagon from his cowboys over at the barn. He stepped outside and watched Phineas Frye and Isaiah Cummings get the doctor on his way.

It was time to stop dawdling, hoping the doctors would come up with a miracle. He had to face the truth, but he didn't cotton to it one bit. He might not be able to get Wade walking again, but he could do something to ease his rage some.

He walked the fifty yards over to the hay barn. Frye and Cummings, his two most dependable punchers, spotted him and came over.

They'd told him the whole account of how that Hendricks fella had picked a fight with Wade over some fool thing, then, rather than take his punches, he fled on his horse north. Why his son felt he had to even the score, Horace didn't know, but he didn't fault him none for it. When a man insults you, you stand up to him. Wade had a bit too much pride, Horace had to concede. And he liked to fight — there was no denying that his son had a mean streak. Horace knew he'd spoilt his boy. But how could he not? He was all he had.

And how could Wade have known that when he caught up to Hendricks that the lily-livered buster would pull a pistol on him unawares? The shots missed, but Wade's horse got nicked and reared up, throwing him onto a pile of sharp rocks. Frye and Cummings said they'd fired back, but a dust storm had blown in, and Hendricks had ridden off. They doubted they'd hit him, but they couldn't go after him — not with Wade in such a bad way. Plus, being hardly able to see farther than they could spit.

They knew they had to get Wade back to the arena and fetch a doctor. They'd gingerly lifted him onto Frye's horse, laying him over the saddle. But they'd had miles to cover, and at a slow walk — taking care they didn't injure Wade further — night had fallen by the time they shambled in. Horace had been looking high and low for Wade, as the outfit had been all packed and ready to leave since midday after the contest.

And by then, Hendricks had to have been miles away. Now, more than a week later, he could be anywhere. Finding Hendricks was going to be no easy task, but he knew his men would do his bidding, though he was sure they'd buck a bit at the assignment. They only had two weeks till the roundup, and Frye and Cummings wouldn't like having to pass on their work to others. But they'd do what he asked, and they wouldn't return until the job was done and Hendricks was dead.

No, I want that pleasure. I'll just have 'em find the scalawag and lead me to 'im.

A man like Bronco Hendricks — with his talent at breaking wild horses — wouldn't go unnoticed. No doubt he'd land with some outfit somewhere. It was only a matter of time. And Horace had all the time in the world to find the man that destroyed his son and all of Horace's dreams.

Chapter 9

ANGELA SAID GOOD-BYE TO VIOLET in front of the church and walked over to join George. He stood on the corner speaking to Violet's friendly mother, whom Angela had met when they'd arrived at the small whitewashed clapboard building just blocks from George's house. He'd given her a tour of the neighborhood before the service began, and Angela found the wide streets and simple one-story homes delightful and the neatly tended flower gardens quaint and pretty.

Most of all she cherished the quiet. She hadn't realized how much noise invaded her world night and day in New York until she came to Colorado. Sounds flitted in the air here, like butterflies, tickling her ears, only to then be soaked up in the thick quiet of summer. A lazy drone of insects played a soft melody against the occasional clops of horses' hooves that punctuated the air when someone rode by or drove a wagon or carriage. She could get used to this quiet—and this simple style of life. Most of all she relished the freedom she felt away from the demands of her family and the tyranny of her papá. Though, she did miss her sisters and hoped they fared well.

But as appealing as this life out west was, she couldn't suppress the dream in her heart to play in a symphony. Would she feel as fulfilled if she settled on playing in a small town band, or for a local opera house, such as Violet did? Angela doubted she could ever truly be content on a small stage, playing with mediocre musicians. Perhaps she was being arrogant and thought too highly of herself. But how could she settle for less after hearing Miss Pappenheim play? For Angela to play the kind of music that would send her listeners into a state of bliss, she would need the backing of an exceptional orchestra—and a concert hall with perfect acoustics. And she'd need an audience with refined musical tastes to appreciate such magnificent music.

Maybe she would never grasp that dream, but she could never live with herself if she didn't try. She didn't want to end up like Signore Bianchi, the old frustrated shopkeeper whose dreams of being a famous violin soloist had been tossed by the wayside. All through those hours of lessons she'd taken from him, she'd sensed his regrets. There seemed nothing worse in life than letting go of a dream and watching it float away until it vanished, out of reach forever.

"Are you ready, my dear?" George asked her.

"I'm glad Mr. Fisk has you for company," Mrs. Edwards said, trying to pull her twin boys to her side. They seemed eager to run off and find trouble, and Angela could tell Violet's mother had her hands full with these two. Her own sisters were precocious but didn't have the wild energy these two boys seemed to have. They'd fidgeted all through the pastor's sermon, but she couldn't blame them. Few boys that age could sit still on a hard bench for an hour.

"She's spoiling me," George said, patting his belly. "She's trying to stuff me as if I were a pillow that's lost its feathers."

"It wouldn't hurt you to gain back a few pounds," Mrs. Edwards said softly, her eyes showing compassion. "And it's good to see you smile again."

George made a noise of agreement in his throat, and Angela could see he was trying hard to be cordial. But pain had oozed from his eyes every time someone came up to him and offered their condolences for his loss. She hadn't known when they headed out in the brisk morning that this was the first time he'd gone back to church since Lucy died, and while she and Violet had chatted right after the service, the pastor had taken George aside and spoken privately with him.

"I have a wonderful Italian dinner prepared for you," Angela told George. She'd spent an hour last night preparing a special pasta dish. His smile spread across his face.

"Violet mentioned she wanted you to come over sometime this week. Perhaps you might honor us with a violin piece after dinner?" Mrs. Edwards asked.

"I'd love that," Angela said, "though I'm not sure how long I'll be staying. I have to get back to my family."

Mrs. Edwards nodded in understanding. "Well, I hope you won't be rushing off too quickly." One of her boys tugged at her blouse sleeve. "Yes, Henry, what is it?"

"Please, can we go home now? Bandit and I wanna go ridin'." The other boy looked up with pleading eyes at his mother and bounced up and down impatiently.

Mrs. Edwards sighed. "I don't know what's taking Ed," she said, looking at the closed door to the church. "All right," she told Henry. "But you two go straight home and fix yourselves a snack. And don't make a mess. I want you back for dinner in an hour. You hear me?"

"Yes ma'am," they chimed in unison. Then, before Angela could blink, they were racing off up the street. Mrs. Edwards shook her head, but a smile graced her lips.

"As soon as George picks a violin for me, I'll come over," Angela said, giving George an entreating look. He merely shrugged. Angela was beginning to think he enjoyed being stubborn. In just a few days, she'd become fond of him, and it made her happy to know her visit was cheering him up and getting him to step back into the world of the living. But she couldn't stay with him forever, nor did she want to.

They'd spent most of Saturday inside the shop, and they'd had a wonderful time playing duets. She'd tried all his violins, and he'd narrowed down his choices to three that he felt might be perfect for her. But she couldn't tell the difference between them, and all three were exceptional instruments—she'd be thrilled to have any of them. Every time she pressed him to decide, he reminded her how such a decision couldn't be rushed. His reluctance to choose was beginning to irritate her to no end, but then she suddenly wondered if he was stalling for a different reason. He was a lonely, grieving widower, and she offered both distraction and company.

She chided herself for her impatience and selfishness. Here she had an opportunity to bring a small bit of joy into this man's life. Where was her Christian charity? She would be heartless to begrudge him for stalling if that's what he was indeed doing. Besides, she'd only sent her letter to her aunt three days ago. And while she'd also sent a telegram to her mamá, she didn't expect an answer. She hadn't said much in the telegram—only that she was fine and would return soon. She didn't want her papá to know where she was. Though, she'd told her aunt—who would keep such information to herself, at Angela's request. She couldn't leave Colorado until she knew for a certainty that she could live with Zia

Sofia. And if she said no? Angela pushed down the fear that lurched in the corner of her mind like a big spider. How could her aunt refuse her?

Angela and George said their good-byes and walked the few blocks back to his house, chatting about the sermon the pastor had given on generosity. Now, even more, she felt convicted about staying a while longer with George and helping him recover his joy for living. She'd seen how his eyes lit up when they'd played the Bach partitas. If anything, music was healing, and the more she could get George to play, the sooner he'd feel alive again. She was sure of it.

When they arrived at George's house, Angela stopped abruptly and bristled. Sitting on the porch of the house to the left was Brett Hendricks. She startled when she saw that he had a rifle on his lap and a rag in one hand. He was wearing a light-colored shirt with the sleeves bunched up at the elbows, and his wavy chestnut hair fell down over his eyes and tickled his shoulders. His injured leg was propped up on a stool. She'd thought him handsome in the dim moonlight, but in the bright late-morning sunlight, his features took on a bronze glow, and his hazel eyes sparked with light. The muscles in his forearms were firm and toned.

She tore her eyes away when he looked up and saw them come up the walkway. She reminded herself of his impertinence the other night, and it was clear by the way he was dressed that he hadn't made plans to attend church on this Lord's day. Instead, he was sitting and playing with his gun. She hoped Brett would ignore her, but he waved and called out a hello.

She stiffened when George turned upon hearing his voice and said, "Oh, hello there, young man. I've not met you before. Are you a relation of Mr. Tuttle's?"

"No sir," Brett said, getting up and setting his rifle down on the porch planking. He walked down the steps with a slight limp and came over. Angela avoided meeting his gaze, but she could tell he was looking at her.

He put out a hand for George to shake. "Name's Brett Hendricks. Doc Tuttle's been nursin' me back to health." Angela dared glance at him from under her lashes and caught him grinning at her. She seethed and dropped her gaze to the ground, feeling heat wash over her face.

"I met Miss Bellini the other evening—she was out back playing the fiddle."

George grunted, sizing him up. Angela sensed a fatherly protectiveness in his manner and was glad for it. Maybe this cowboy would leave her alone once George made it clear he should keep his distance.

George's manner was reserved. "Pleasure meeting you, Mr. Hendricks. I'm George Fisk. The doctor is a good man, and you're in good hands. Is he about?"

"At church," Brett answered with a casual wave of his hand, as if attending church was of little importance.

"And is that someplace cowboys don't deign to attend?" Angela blurted out, instantly regretting the harsh tone of her words.

Brett's eyebrows narrowed as he studied her. Her cheeks burned. George looked at her quizzically.

"Deign to attend?" He chuckled, and the warmth of his mirth set her heart racing again. Why did he have to stand so close to her? And why wasn't George saying anything to discourage him?

Brett shook his head. "I don't rightly know what you just said, miss. But I don't have much of a hankerin' for church. The great outdoors is the chapel I worship in, under the starry heavens. I reckon a body can get close to God just as easily outside as in.

Maybe even easier—without them walls and a roof blockin' the way." He laughed as if amused by his own humor. But Angela didn't find him funny. He sounded impertinent to her.

To her dismay, George smiled and patted Brett on the shoulder. "Are you employed by one of local ranchers?"

"Not at present. Though I'm looking to join up. Once I'm up to snuff."

"Where are you from?" George asked, seemingly happy to stand outside and chat with this cowboy all day—much to Angela's dismay.

"Texas, for the most part."

"Well, what brought you to Greeley?" George asked.

"He got shot," Angela said flatly, wondering how George would react to that.

To her surprise, he merely frowned and said, "Oh my, I'm sorry to hear that. But you look to be on the mend."

Angela's mouth dropped open. Was it that common for people to get shot in Colorado? Both Brett and George seemed to make light of it. She closed her mouth when she saw Brett staring at it. And then her eyes snagged on his. They again looked hungry and full of need.

Her jaw clenched and she sputtered, "Well, it was nice talking with you, Mr. Hendricks. I need to get busy preparing supper." She started up the walkway.

"Would you like to join us?" George asked Brett.

Angela cringed. *Oh please, say no.* Last thing she wanted was for this cowboy to be glaring at her across the dinner table.

Out of the corner of her eye, she saw Brett contemplating the offer. Then he looked at her again, thoughtfully, as if trying to read her mind.

"Mighty kind of you, Mr. Fisk. But I reckon I'll pass. I don't think the young lady is all that fond of my company."

"Oh, poppycock," George said. "She just hasn't been around cowboys before. The prosperity of the West is dependent on the fine work you cowboys do. I know what a hard and dangerous life you men lead and how much work it takes to get those cows rounded up and to market. You put the meat on our tables."

"Kind of you to say, sir."

Angela thought he saw Brett blush from the praise George gave him as she walked up the porch steps.

"But just the same, I'll be glad to take you up on your invitation some other day. Doc Tuttle should be back soon."

"All right, young man," George said.

Angela heard no more after closing the door behind her. Flustered by yet another encounter with the brash Brett Hendricks, she busied herself preparing dinner. Though, no matter how hard she tried to push his cocky smile and penetrating eyes out of her mind, she found herself unable to get the handsome cowboy out of her thoughts.

Chapter 10

IT FELT GOOD TO WALK in the warm sunshine of the late afternoon. The town was too sleepy and too religious for Brett's tastes, and he sure hankered for a drink. Well, he had to admit the peace and quiet of the last week had done some good for his soul. He felt rested and ready to get back in the saddle. But he was itching to get to work, for all this lollygagging was only good to a point.

Most of these townsfolk were farmers, come from back east, working the hard prairie ground with sweat and breaking their backs to grow crops, but their diligence was paying off. Though, Brett knew the locusts came nearly every year and gobbled up everything in sight. But this September, acres of wheat gleamed and rippled golden before him, surrounded by crops of potatoes and other plants he didn't recognize. The road he followed went along the town's wide ditch, where they channeled water across miles of open range from the Platte. The doc had told him about the town's beginnings and how a handful of people settled in the dust and wind and were determined to make the desert bloom.

Somehow, with grit and spunk, they'd done it. And encircled the whole place with wood fencing, to keep out the range cattle. But while this afforded the folks a good life, too many towns like this were springing up, following the railroad, crowded out the rangeland. He s'posed he couldn't rightly begrudge folks for wanting to start a new life—he surely had. But he kept wondering how long the cowboy would last if this kind of "progress" kept up.

He'd asked at the general store and feed store about local ranches and got some names, but how in tarnation could he get out to these places without a horse? He s'posed he could buy one with the money he had. But he didn't cotton to the notion of buying just any old horse, even if to ride it for a brief spell. But maybe he'd have to. He couldn't see any other way about it.

He was ready though. First thing tomorrow he'd find himself a horse and ride out to those ranches. He'd heard of Foster's Cattle Company. That one was prob'ly as big as Orlander's. And then there was Morrison's ranch direct east at Beaver Creek. He hadn't heard of Gerry's at Crow Creek, but it sounded like a small outfit. He'd do better at the big spreads.

As he turned down one of the wide roads that led into the heart of the town, he stopped. "Well, looky there," he said with a whistle under his breath.

Miss Angela Bellini was strolling down the side of the street in a purty lacy dress and pert hat, a large sack in her arms, with corn silk sticking out the top. She must have been out shopping for that fiddle maker. He didn't understand why the gal was living in the back shed. She said she'd come from New York to buy a violin. But she didn't seem all that much in a hurry to rush on home. She was a curious thing. Stiff and proper on the outside, but when she played that fiddle . . .

Brett remembered the way he'd felt hearing those sweet notes speaking to his soul, and how her playing had bewitched him something fierce. He'd even teared up, and he couldn't recall any time in his grown life that he'd cried—other than when he'd had to shoot Dakota. Maybe the unfortunate events of late had made him weak and sappy and that's why he'd gone all mushy. He didn't like the feeling. It made him twitchy. What good could come from getting weak and sappy like that? None at all.

He stopped at the corner and watched her come toward him. She was paying so much attention to her footing that she almost bumped into him.

As she looked up, she startled at the sight of him, then lost her balance. A cry of surprise escaped her lips. He steadied her with his arms.

"Whoa, there," he said. "Kinda hard to walk on this rutted road with them fancy shoes of yours." They were some kind of heeled boot but must have had slick soles.

She pulled back and narrowed her eyes, which made her all the more comely. "You can let go now, Mr. Hendricks."

He wanted to laugh at her flustered manner, but he swallowed it back and nodded politely, dropping his arms to his side. "Sure, honey. Just didn't want to see you drop all your vegetables."

"Don't—" She sucked in a breath and set about composing her face. "Please, don't call me 'honey.'" Her cheeks looked daubed with pink powder, and her sumptuous lips pouted. He could hardly keep from staring at them. It'd been a long while since he'd kissed any lips worth remembering. Lips like hers would burn in his memory.

She had her long black hair pulled up under her pretty bonnet, and the skin of her throat was milky smooth. He noticed her pulse throbbing under her chin and longed to reach out and run his fingers along her neck.

He gulped and took a few steps back, feeling way too hot under the collar.

"Lemme carry that for you," he said, reaching for her sack.

96

She started to protest, but he ignored her and took it from her. She pouted again and said, "Thank you, but I can manage."

"I'm sure you can," Brett told her, smiling. "But it's the gentlemanly thing to do, don't you reckon?"

Reluctantly, she said, "I suppose."

Pleased with his ploy to get her to walk with him, he started down the street, thinking how to stretch out the five long blocks to the house. She walked silent by his side, but his every sense was keenly aware of her. He smelled the lavender soap in her hair and clothes, and every nerve tingled in longing for her. It took some mighty hard determination not to pull her close and feel her body pressed up against his. He ached with need, for being next to her reminded him of how much he wanted a woman to hold and love and how hard he'd fought this yearning every day of his life since he'd run from home.

But, truth be told, he felt more than a man's need when he was around her. She wasn't just purty on the outside. And while that was a plus, comely looks never did much more than tantalize him for a spell. It was that music she played. As if she had something inside her that came out, something he needed. It made him think of a wild horse that finally gives up under his hand and goes limp. Its crazed eyes turn calm, as if the fear just melted away. One moment the animal's agitated and the next he's trusting. Something snaps inside, and there was no right way to explain it. But that's what happened to him when she played that fiddle. Oh, he was working himself silly over this.

He blew out a hard breath, tired of trying to untangle the knot in his head.

She stopped him and searched his face with those big brown eyes, and his throat went dry. "What's wrong?" she asked.

He rolled his eyes. As if he could conjure the words to tell her. He didn't rightly know what was vexing him.

He began walking again. "How'd you learn to play that fiddle so well?"

She seemed surprised by his question. "Do you like music?"

"I do," he said. "Though, I don't often git to hear the likes of yer kind o' music." *More like never.*

She nodded. "Well, to answer your question, I've taken violin lessons for many years. I hope one day to be a member of the philharmonic."

The phil . . . what? He caught her staring at him. Was she thinking he was stupid? So what if he didn't know a lot of big, fancy words?

"Mr. Hendricks?"

Something in the way she said his name made Brett spin to face her. He cocked his head. "If you don't want to call me Brett, that's fine. But don't call me Mr. Hendricks." His gut knotted up. "That's what my pa's called, and I don't want that name."

He didn't know why he said that, but when the words rushed out, he realized the truth of them. For most of his life, his pa had been seen as a respectable man in Austin. He'd brokered cattle into the Fort Worth stockyards. To all appearances, his pa had been a successful businessman, but none of his associates knew what a mean son of a snake he was at home. Not until he killed his wife in such a brutal fashion that his crony, the sheriff, had no choice but to throw him in jail. Brett knew his pa had cheated on his wife aplenty, yet she'd cooked and cleaned for him and kept up a right nice home. She hadn't deserved what he gave her.

Brett realized he was standing with his fists clenched, clutching the cloth sack tight to his chest. Air was snorting out his nostrils; he was sounding like a lathered horse after a hard run.

He shook his head at her consternation. "I'm sorry, Miss Bellini. I . . . uh . . . get upset when I think about my pa."

She made a funny sound in her throat. Brett turned and questioned her with his eyes. She shot a pained look at him, and it gave him pause. "I feel the same about my father," she said, touching a hand to her neck.

She bit her lower lip, and Brett's mouth went dry again as he tried to pry his eyes away from her mouth. He stared at the ground and kicked at the dirt as they stood under a languishing maple that gave little shade. "He's a mean man — Papá is. He beats my mamá. I can't . . . I wish . . ." She swallowed and looked at him through a blur of tears, her lips quivering.

"Does he hit ya?" Brett asked quietly, thinking maybe going back to New York wasn't such a smart idea.

She nodded, near tears, looking like a bunch of words were stuck in her throat.

The thought of any man striking such a sweet and gentle gal set afire his anger. He knew men like that — like his pa — did more than hit women. They brutalized and ravaged them. Just like that Orlander kid was trying to do that day. His head grew hot and heavy as blood pounded in his ears. He swatted the rage back into its pen and set the latch.

He wanted nothing more in that moment than to gently wipe those tears off her cheeks. But instead he stood there and nodded, feeling suddenly weak and irritable. He wished he'd never mentioned his pa.

"Tell me more about your music," he said, trying to lighten the mood off them both. For the life of him, he didn't know why all that hurt and rage came gushing out. But being close to Angela Bellini did something to him, and he wasn't sure he wanted to keep feeling like this. But he couldn't seem to yank away. She was like a river, pulling him downstream into a roaring current, sucking him under the surface. He could scarcely breathe around her.

She took some steps down the street while wiping her eyes with her sleeve. Then she straightened, and he saw how she pushed back the pain—just the way he often did. Locking it away but knowing it was always there. It never left for good.

"I got my first violin when I was thirteen," she said, working a smile back up her face.

She went on to tell him about her aunt and going to hear some orchestra play, but he didn't pay mind to her words. He was listening more to the sweet sound of her voice, her soft Italian accent smoothing over the words the way water played over rocks in a creek. They'd gone a couple of blocks when she stopped talking and turned to him.

"I apologize for rambling, Mr.—I mean, Brett." A smile lit up her face, the first genuine one he'd gotten from her. "I get carried away when I talk about music. It's what I care most about in life."

He nodded. "I understand, I think. I feel that same way about horses."

"In what way?" she asked. She genuinely seemed to want to know. And her eyes were no longer throwing knives at him.

He waggled his head and shrugged. "I don't know how to put it. There's just ain't nothin' like facin' a savage pair of bloodshot eyes, lathered flanks heavin', tail switchin', mane tossin'." He chuckled. "Cruel hooves flyin' at yer face, hopin' to gouge yer eyes out." He glanced at her as she listened, her gaze locked on his face. Then he looked down the road, out across the fields of wheat, feeling the open prairie call to his blood. "I love the challenge of gentlin' horses—'specially an outlaw horse."

"What's an outlaw?" she asked as they stood there, flies buzzing about their heads.

"It's a spoilt horse. One that's been cruelly broken in the early stages, so completely that he's bad to the end of his days, either as a bucker, kicker, biter, or backfaller. Usually master of all these accomplishments every time he's saddled."

She shook her head in amazement. "And you enjoy this? Don't you get hurt?"

"Yeah, I do--sometimes." He huffed. "But, well . . . I reckon I got this gift." He grinned at her. "Maybe not a purty gift like yours, but I have a way with horses. They know I don't want to hurt 'em. I respect 'em, and they tend to be fearful—it's their nature. Just gettin' 'em more scared only makes it worse. Horses have a keen sense of intent, if you catch my drift. They c'n rightly tell when someone means 'em harm. And they c'n tell when someone truly loves and honors their spirit. I believe they sense this from me. It might take 'em some time to calm down enough to feel it, but when they do, the battle's won. And a trust is born."

Brett shut his mouth, leaving his words to hang in the sultry afternoon air. He couldn't recall the last time he'd said so much in a breath.

He turned and looked at her, searching her eyes for understanding. He saw it there, and it made him smile. She was a bit like a scared horse, but now he knew why. She'd been beaten and mistreated, but instead of turning outlaw, she'd found comfort in her music. It soothed her the way his words and soft sounds soothed the horses under his legs. And he realized what soothed *him* was this gift of his. Getting horses to trust him, to know he meant no harm.

But that never truly calmed the raging inside him. Or the guilt and shame that haunted him. Nothing would ever cure that. Or at least that's what he'd reckoned until the night he heard her play her fiddle. Nothing in his life had ever given him such relief, such peace, from his suffering.

He suddenly wanted to feel that again, to let her music spill into him. As much as he longed to touch and hold her, to taste her sweetness, he needed more than that. More than just a moment of pleasure, a sating of his carnal desires. Could he have both? It was too much to wish for, but he was willing to take a chance and ask. For this one thing, leastwise.

Her name sat on the tip of his tongue. He was afraid to say it. Not because he worried she'd get mad. More like it would get tainted by his lips. Her name sounded like a prayer in his head, a pure white candle that burned with blue fire. He didn't think he could say her name in a way that it deserved. But he couldn't call her Miss Bellini anymore.

"Would you mind so terribly if I called you by your given name?"

The question seemed to break off and teeter for a moment before she answered. He expected her face to tighten into those hard lines he'd seen before, but she surprised him.

"No, Brett, I wouldn't mind. Not at all," she said, looking like she was waiting for him to continue. Then an unexpected chuckle came out of her mouth. "So long as you don't call me 'honey."

"Deal," he said. "Well . . . uh, Angela, I wonder if you would . . . that is, if I could hear ya play that fiddle again. Maybe I could come over when you and Mr. Fisk —"

He was back to fumbling with his words, but she interrupted and spared him.

"I'd be happy to, Brett. Why don't you come over after supper, around six? We'll play some duets for you."

"All right," he said, feeling empty and full at the same time. He was still a mite weak, and his body sagged with weariness. Though he wondered if it was due less to his ordeal in the desert and more from talking to Angela. *It's sure hard to breathe around this gal.*

Angela. The name tasted sweet on his tongue. How he wanted to taste her mouth and the sweetness he imagined waited for him there. But that seemed as impossible as getting a pig to fly.

He walked with her, lost in his thoughts, the final blocks to Fisk's house. He was careening down that river, starting to drown, the water way too deep for his liking. He needed to get back on the range, working cattle, breaking horses. There was nothing he could offer a gal like Angela Bellini, though his heart ached to shelter and protect her, to work the fear out of her so she could learn to trust again.

But she wasn't a horse, and he had no way with womenfolk. But at least before she left for New York, he'd get to hear that music again. He hoped it would take him to that peaceful place once more.

Chapter 11

ANGELA PUMPED WATER INTO THE big ceramic bowl on the counter, her head stuffed with confusion over Brett Hendricks. As she picked up the scrub brush and attacked the potatoes, working off the clumps of red dirt, she berated herself for letting down her guard and speaking in so personal a manner to that cowboy.

How had he done that—pry open her hurt? She'd meant to keep her distance from him, but seeing him turn so tender toward her had shaken her to her core. Underneath all that posturing lay a sensitive man who'd been through a lot of suffering. She didn't know just how badly his father had treated him, but she knew what he was feeling. She saw it in his eyes. It was the same pain she saw in her own eyes when she stared at her face in a looking glass.

But how in the world had she allowed him to get close? She gave him permission to call her by her Christian name, for heaven's sake—a stranger she hardly knew. *And a man who carries guns and gets shot at.* She fumed, thinking of the way he'd talked about taming horses. No doubt he thought she was just another animal to tame, to get under his control with sweet, soft words.

You're being too hard on him. You saw how he was. He opened up to you—and how many Italian men do you know who would bare their soul like that?

Maybe it was the untamed West that brought out such sentiments. That made people question their lives. Maybe men like Brett Hendricks had too much time on their hands, spending months with only cows and horses on the lonely prairie, with nothing else to do but think. *But why did you tell him about Papá, and that he hurt you?* That was something she would never tell a living soul. But somehow Brett Hendricks had pulled it out of her. *Him and his gift!*

She pushed wayward strands of hair out of her face with her wet hand—as if that might push away thoughts of Brett—and started slicing the potatoes to make her aunt's wonderful *patate al forno* dish. She wondered where George was, as it was nearly suppertime. He was probably napping. Well, she was glad he wasn't around to see her so agitated. He would ask her questions. More prying—the last thing she wanted. She adored the older man, but right now what she needed most was to be alone, to think. Talking with Brett had more than flustered her. Anger and hurt and confusion all mixed together so that she could hardly think straight.

Worst of all, she couldn't get his handsome face out of her mind. Those sparkling hazel eyes that dove deep into her soul, as if he could read her thoughts and memories. That quirky smile that exposed those straight teeth set in a strong jaw. She loved the way his wavy hair fell wild to his broad shoulders. His whole body exuded strength, every muscle taut and sculpted by years of hard ranch work. She pictured him galloping on a horse, a lasso swinging a wide circle overhead as he chased down a cow. She'd seen illustrations of cowboys doing that, their hats flying in the wind, hunched forward over a horse as they rode hard across a wide-open prairie.

Dime novels and magazines romanticized the cowboy life, but Angela had always imagined such a life as mostly drudgery and dirt. And danger. Even with the Indians gone, there were still other dangers out there—storms and outlaws and wild animals. *And don't forget—snakes.* What decent man would love a life like that? How could a man—like Brett Hendricks—find a life like that desirable. And would he even care about having a respectable place in society? Could a cowboy like him ever settle down and marry, raise a family? She imagined he'd be unable to stay put, wanting to run off and be free, answer to no one. A man like that lived for himself and his own pleasure. And Brett Hendricks seemed just that kind of man— restless and noncommittal. He'd run from some dangerous situation and now he was looking for a new job. How many ranches had he worked on? Did he ever stay long in one place?

A man like that would break your heart. Why was she even thinking of him? She scoffed at her endless musings about Brett and laid the potato slices in a clay pie dish, thinking how Lucy Fisk must have used this dish to make many pies over the years. Then she thought of how heartbroken George was. She could tell it lingered in his heart, a heavy pain, like a rock with sharp edges. He had surely loved his wife. He'd spent years devoted to caring for her, faithfully staying by her side throughout her illness. Perhaps he was the one who had made the pies in this dish.

Love that unselfish and true was a rare thing, Angela realized. She could hardly think of a handful of married couples who expressed such devotion. It seemed foolish to hope that she'd ever find true love. While her heart cried out for it, what good would it do for her to feed that longing? None at all. And what if her "perfect" man ended up like her papá? There was no way to tell.

Behind all those sweet words and gentle manners could lie a monster. And once married, it would be too late.

No, the only thing she could depend on to bring her joy, that wouldn't fail her, was music. She had to remind herself of that, of why she'd come to Colorado, and how close she was to grasping her dream. Soon she would have her violin in hand, and then she'd—

"Hello!"

Angela turned at the muffled voice coming from the front porch. She wiped her hands and hurried to the door, hoping George wouldn't be woken from his nap. When she opened it, letting in a draft of hot air, she wondered who this man was. He looked like any one of George's neighbors, neatly dressed in a starched white shirt and pressed trousers. His bearded face held a serious expression as he touched the brim of his bowler hat and said, "Are you Miss Angela Bellini?"

She paused, wondering what this man wanted from her—and how he'd known she was staying here. "Yes, I'm she."

He held out a hand that grasped a pale-yellow envelope. "A telegram came for you this afternoon."

A telegram? It must be from Tia Sofia. But why would she send a telegram? To ensure it arrived before I left Greeley?

She stepped out onto the porch and took it from him, noting George's address scribbled in pencil in the corner of the blank Western Union Telegraph Company envelope. "Thank you," she said, a shiver of worry running up her back. She wasn't sure she wanted to hear news from her family. Guilt over leaving her mamá so hastily pushed tears into her eyes. "Do I . . . owe you any money for this?"

"No, miss," the man said, again touching his hat brim. "Well, good day to you."

He marched down the walkway, and not until he was out of sight many blocks later did Angela turn the envelope over and consider reading it. For some reason dread filled her heart, but she told herself she was being silly. Zia Sofia was probably writing to tell her how much she'd love to have her come live with her.

The thought of returning home loomed large, like a giant gaping maw. She missed her family and the excitement of the city—the smells and flavors of her neighborhood, and her friends she often walked and picnicked with. But the longer she stayed in Greeley—in this quiet little town with the air so dry and clean—the less she felt the pull to go home. Even the prospect of auditioning with her new violin for a symphony chair hovered on the horizon of her thoughts like a receding mirage.

Still, New York was where her dream awaited. Despite the troubles and conflicts she'd surely have to face upon her return, she could see no other course. She had no money with which to support herself, which meant relying on her aunt's generosity until she could find suitable employment—hopefully by playing her violin. She couldn't bear the thought of living in the same apartment as her papá, nor could she start anew in another city—not without some savings to sustain her.

With a resigned sigh, she tore open the envelope and unfolded the single sheet of yellow paper. At first the words were confusing. The long paragraph ran on in capital letters, punctuated with *STOP* every line or so. But upon rereading the message, the meaning grew clear, and with that clarity Angela felt all the blood drain from her face.

Her knees buckled, and she dropped to the porch and plunked onto the top step. Her hand holding the telegram shook so hard, she couldn't reread the words. But she didn't need to. Her aunt's message was brief and to the point.

All the guilt and worry and fear she'd been pushing into a tiny corner of her mind now burst out in an explosion of pain and shock. *"Don't blame yourself,"* her aunt had said. But how could she not? It was all her fault her mamá was in the hospital. And what if she never awoke? *"A concussion, when she fell down the stairs at the station."*

Her papá had struck her mamá after dragging her from the train. When she tried to pull away, she tripped and fell. Angela squeezed her eyes against the flood of tears, picturing her mamá tumbling down the two dozen steps to the street below. She imagined the piercing sound of her mamá's scream of fear and her papá's angry scowl.

Angela wiped her eyes and reread the last lines.

"Don't hurry back STOP Papá is angry STOP Not safe STOP I will write again soon STOP Love you STOP Zia Sofia STOP."

Stop. Angela wished she could stop—stop the pain, the crying, the ache in her heart. Stop her papá's violence and the images assaulting her of her poor mamá crashing down the stairs of the El Train. *What can I do? How can I sit here and do nothing?*

Angela buried her face in her hands and wept. Great sobs racked her chest, hurting her ribs, but she couldn't stop. Then she startled at a hand touching her shoulder.

She twisted around and looked up into George's compassionate face. He said nothing as she dropped her head and held the telegram up for him to take from her hand.

After many minutes, she was emptied of her tears, and her sobs turned to painful heaves as she gulped air, unable to fill her lungs.

"Come, my dear," George said softly, reaching for her hand. "Let's go inside, and I'll make you a cup of tea."

Angela nodded, aware of what a sight she must look like to anyone passing on the street. But what did that matter? Here she was, a thousand miles or more away from her mamá, who needed her. Yet, her aunt had told her not to come home. She could go back and sneak into the hospital. She longed to leave this very minute. But if her papá saw her or knew she was back, what further trouble would erupt? Would he take out his anger on her sisters? She couldn't take that chance. She would just have to wait until her aunt wrote again. *But I will send a telegram back, telling Zia Sofia she must let me know how Mamá fares. If she dies . . .*

The thought brought on a new paroxysm of grief and tears. George—no stranger to grief—helped her to her feet with great care, as if she were an invalid. Her legs barely held her up as she stumbled into the house with George's help.

Oh, why did I ever come out here? This was a selfish, foolish decision.

Phineas Frye took a long pull of his beer, then wiped the foam from his moustache as he scowled, looking out the window of the empty saloon that faced the flour mill sitting like a lump of clay in the hot sun. Heat simmered on the rough wide dirt lane called Main Street in this sorry excuse for a town. Loveland. What was to love about it? There were only two stores, no railroad, and a measly hotel that even fleas wouldn't dare spend a night in. He scratched his neck, which itched something fierce. Probably all those fleas were in the saloon, nursing their cares on unsuspecting visitors.

"I still don't git why Boss sent us ta go find that Hendricks fella. He could be halfway to Mexico by now. We don't even know he went north."

Isaiah Cummings combed his fingers through his thick red beard. "Don't I know it? I told 'im half as much. But's he's got a burr in his craw." He fingered his vest pocket and pulled out his rolling papers and pouch of tobacco. "Listen, we'll make the rounds, then report back—like he told us. Boss knows it's a snowball's chance in hell we'll git word of 'im."

"Roundup's inside o' two weeks. If that buster didn't hoof it back to Texas, he'd prob'ly joined some outfit here in Colorady." Phineas upended the glass and gulped down the dregs of his beer. The barkeep was nowhere in sight, so he plunked down a coin on the stained and peeling counter. He thought on Boss's face yesterday when he told them to pack up and go on the scout for Hendricks.

He could still hear the gruesome crack of the kid's back when his horse dumped him onto those rocks. It was some miracle Wade was still alive. *Yeah, but what kinda life c'n he have? Better off if he'd died.*

Orlander loved that kid—and spoilt him thoroughly—though, if truth be told, Phineas reckoned Wade'd had it coming. More times than he could count, Wade had forced his way on a gal— everywhere and anywhere he went. Saw what he liked and took it. Didn't matter none if'n it was a little girl hardly out of her pigtails or a hitched woman. If his wily charms didn't get 'em willingly into his arms, then he used muscle or the threat of his knife. It sickened Phineas to no end—listening to the frantic pleas and screams and whimpers, and then hearing that mean laugh o' his. He'd had a knife to that Mexican girl's throat, and the terror in her eyes had made Phineas want to spit. But he did what the kid ordered—stood guard to let his boss's kid ravish that poor gal.

He ground his teeth as he ran his finger over his moustache again and again, thinking. But there was nothin' for it. He'd had to lie to Boss to cover for Wade—again. When Orlander had questioned them that night, Phineas had toyed with blurting the truth, once and for all—for it distressed him something awful to hold all that inside—but he reckoned it was too late. What good would it do? Not like Orlander would punish his kid—not now nor ever. Living the rest of his life in a chair was God's punishment enough, weren't it?

"What's got you so deep in thought?" Cummings cast a sideways look at Phineas as he stood to his feet and struck a match along the top of the counter and lit his cigarette. A hand mindlessly wandered to his shoulder to rub it. He'd been Boss's wrangler for years, but a rough fall had messed up his back, and he'd been relegated to riding point for the outfit most times, instead. Phineas got along fine with the fella, but it irked him some to see the way Cummings smirked and got pleasure off of watching the kid do his dirty business, though Cummings never said a word about it. But Phineas could tell—by that feverish look in his eyes and the way he grinned as he stood guard.

Out in cattle country, it was unwritten law that womenfolk were to be respected. It was the duty of cow men and horse herders alike to protect 'em and their innocence. A rich kid like Wade could have his pick from the purtiest gals in the West—*could have had.* So there was no excusing his bad behavior. He thought on the Hendricks fella, and how the instant he caught sight of Orlander, he went on the attack, swinging hard out the gate. Downright admirable. The right thing to do, and hardly a few fellas would dare risk a fight—'specially not over some Mexican gal's honor.

Phineas pushed back his stool and stood, then grabbed his hat off the nearby stool and stuffed it on his head. "Where to now?" he asked. It hadn't taken them long to suss out that Hendricks hadn't come this way.

"Well . . . Fort Collins's to the north o' here. Plenty of outfits runnin' around the Powder River and north o' the Platte."

"Still, we'll be meetin' up with most of 'em in the roundup, more'n likely."

Cummings sucked in a long draw from his cigarette, then blew out the smoke. "I know it. But Boss wants—"

"Boss wants, Boss wants . . . He wants that Hendricks fella to pay."

Cummings nodded. "So let's git."

He followed Cummings out the saloon door over to their horses tied up in the shade around the side of the building. The air was hot and thick and damp from the Thompson River flowing down the hogbacks at the edge of the town. He smirked, thinking of Wade's face when that buster yanked him off that girl, his pants down to his knees and so startled he'd dropped his knife. Before Wade had a chance to take another breath, Hendricks had about flattened his nose and gave a swift kick to those parts what were all exposed for the kicking.

Phineas had sucked back a laugh that almost snuck out as he watched Orlander's kid grab his privates and fall onto his rear in the dust. But when Hendricks sent the girl running off and then caught Phineas's eye, that laugh petered out and Phineas had felt ashamed. That's what is what—plain and simple. And now, here he was chasing down the fella, so's that Boss could put a bullet through his head. It just weren't right, no sir.

Well, he thought as he untied the reins and swung up on his horse, *maybe we'll get lucky and find 'im.* For then, he might get the chance to warn the fella. Yep, that's what he'd do. His ma had taught him that it was never too late to do the right thing. She'd also taught him and his brother about sins of omission—that's what she called them—and he shoulda followed her advice long ago. Phineas had stood by way too many times doing the wrong thing, and his sins were piling up to where they haunted his sleep. A body could lose his life at any time, 'specially in cattle country, and he'd put off too long making things right with his Maker. Yep, that's what he'd do—warn the fella.

With that resolved, Phineas put spurs to flank and galloped down the main street of the sorry excuse for a town, headed north for Fort Collins.

Chapter 12

"SORRY I WAS OUT TILL all hours last night. I was assisting another doctor with an emergency surgery," Doc Tuttle said, taking a big bite of toast and swallowing it down with the bittersweet coffee Brett was now enjoying while sitting at the table.

"This coffee's the best I've had in a spell," Brett said, savoring the flavor after he'd put a few spoonfuls of sugar in. Usually the kind of mud he got out on the range could make a horseshoe float — as the saying went.

"I been thinking," Tuttle said between bites of egg. "You still looking to get hired on with a ranch?"

Brett nodded and stared out the window and across the way at Fisk's house. All morning his thoughts were atumble over Angela. When he'd gone over last evening, figuring the old man and her had supped, the fiddle maker met him at the door with a strained expression and kept his voice low when he said, "She's received some bad news in a telegram, I'm sorry to say. I'm afraid she's retired for the night."

Brett guessed the news had something to do with her ma, and his first thought was that her pa had hurt the woman — just as

Angela afeared. Though he hoped the news spoke of her pa's demise, he didn't expect that'd be the case. Fellas like that—like his pa—rarely got their comeuppance. It was a God's miracle that his own pa was now rotting in the Alamo jail.

He hated thinking of Angela wearing her heart out with tears, alone in that back shed. His feet itched to run over and comfort her.

He snorted. Like she'd have any of that. Him trying to comfort her would be like barking at a knot to get it to untie. He had to stop thinking about her. Especially now. What with that news, no doubt she'd be jumping on the next train rolling east, and he'd never see her again. But maybe that was for the best—before his feelings got all tangled up like a calf in a patch of barbed wire. He needed to get on a horse and out on the open range before he got all sappy again. But he sure would've liked to kiss those scrumptious lips at least one time before she disappeared from his life.

Sadness sat heavy on his shoulders, like a sack of feed. He needed to shake it off. He pushed his chair back from the table, then realized Tuttle had been talking to him.

The doc looked at him and cocked his head. "You haven't heard a word I said, have you?" he asked good-naturedly. "You feeling all right?"

"Yeah," Brett said, straightening and busying himself with taking his dishes to the wash sink. "Sorry. My mind was wanderin'."

Tuttle smiled. "I was mentioning my rancher friend, Logan Foster. He owns a big cattle company."

Brett's ears perked up at the word *friend.* "I heard of it," Brett said. He doubted few hadn't. "How'd you get to be friends with a rich rancher?" Brett asked as he set his dishes down and leaned his back against the kitchen wall. His leg still ached some, but it was hardly noticeable. He doubted it would cause any trouble when he got back to riding with an outfit.

Tuttle cleaned his plate with a swipe of crust mopping up the last bit of egg. The fella sure had a big appetite, but nothing stuck to his bones. "Funny story, that," Tuttle said, smirking. "I'd just gotten to Greeley and opened up my practice on Sixth Street. It was an icy, cold morning after a bit of snow, and Mrs. Foster—Adeline—she had her little girls in tow and wasn't looking. Her feet slipped out from under her in front of my office, and she broke her ankle. I hurried outside when I saw the commotion. I think she was more embarrassed than hurting, for her skirts had flown up into her face, exposing her undergarments. The little girls were bawling, and a crowd was gathering.

"I managed to quickly get her up and into my arms. Good thing I only had a dozen or so steps to take, for she's not . . . how can put it delicately? She weighs a bit, and I'm not as strong or used to carrying heavy things as you no doubt are."

Brett sniggered, picturing this lightweight hefting a heavy woman with a flounce of skirts in his face and her arms flailing about.

"Needless to say, she was grateful for my quick action, and by the time her husband found her in my office, I'd set the broken bone and wrapped it in plaster and given her something for the pain. The little girls had nearly destroyed my office, so I was relieved when Logan arrived, and I helped his wife and children into the wagon. Which wasn't easy, seeing as Mrs. Foster was woozy and giddy from the medicine I'd given her, and she kept trying to throw her arms around me in gratitude while singing some silly song. Logan apologized and thanked me, appreciating my discretion and efficient handling of her injury.

"Ever since then I've been a regular guest at their ranch—for dinner and holidays and such. I think Mrs. Foster wants to adopt me, seeing as I have no family left back in Ohio. Her unfortunate accident, however, has established me in the town, and her word of recommendation has brought considerable success to my humble practice. For which I'm grateful to the good Lord."

Brett nodded, chuckling.

"So," Tuttle said, getting to his feet. "What do you say we pay a visit to Mr. Foster of the Foster Cattle Company this afternoon? I'm sure that if I introduce you to him and tell him what a fine cowboy you are, he'll hire you on the spot." Tuttle's smile turned into a frown. "Not that I'm eager to see you go, Mr. Hendricks—"

"Brett." He shook his head. "It's just Brett."

"All right, Brett. But I've thoroughly enjoyed your company and your stories. If my life were half as entertaining and adventurous as yours, I don't know if my constitution could take it." He gathered up Brett's dishes along with his own and set them in the wash basin.

Brett grinned. What a stroke of good luck—that Tuttle was friends with Foster. Now he wouldn't have to go buy a horse. If he got hired, he'd have a whole herd of 'em to work with. *If* he got hired. But he'd never had trouble landing a job once he showed off his skills. Every rancher needed a good wrangler or three, though Brett could do just about any job when it came to horses or cattle.

"When do you want to head out?" Brett asked, thinking he'd like to find some way to say good-bye to Angela, but he wasn't sure it'd be proper to impose. He wished he knew what that telegram had said, but it was none of his business. Well, it wasn't meant to be, and he knew it. Didn't hurt to entertain fantasies though. He couldn't think of a sweeter, purtier gal to settle his thoughts on, and he reckoned he'd be spending many a lonely night out on the range picturing her in his arms.

"How about in two hours? I have to do some things in the office, and I'm expecting an important delivery. I'll meet you back here."

He walked over to the door and grabbed his hat off the peg. "Oh, and when we get there, please don't say anything about Mrs. Foster's accident to her husband. I think he'd rather not be reminded of the incident."

"Oh, I wouldn't," Brett said, smiling and picturing the rancher's wife blathering after a big swig of laudanum. "But, there's some things I'll need to buy afore we go out there—just in case Foster does hire me on." He had his saddle and a few items he'd put in his saddlebags, and he was grateful the doc had fetched those things for him. Somehow he'd lost Dakota's bridle. He thought he'd put it in the bag, but he'd been so addled, he'd likely forgotten. He could do without a bridle, but he'd need some other personal items and clothes and such to fill his war bag. And he'd lost his bedroll, so he needed to pick up a good wool blanket or two and a tarpaulin, oh, and a heavy coat in case they ranged in the high country.

His head had been feeling right naked without a hat. His was blowing across the prairie somewhere, full of dirt. While he hated the notion of breaking in a stiff new hat and looking like a tenderfoot, he'd just have to make do. All those purchases would just about eat up his get-away money.

"All right. We can swing by the mercantile and wherever else you need." Tuttle tipped his hat at Brett and left.

Brett stood in the quiet house, feeling a rush of loneliness come over him despite his eager anticipation over a possible job. Usually he only felt like this when he'd been too long out on a cattle drive, and most often in the winter by a lonely fire. But this was more than the usual empty feeling. It was more like a hunger that a hearty meal couldn't satisfy. Or the kind of thirst that a bucket of water just couldn't slake.

He turned and looked out the window to the shed in the yard yonder. No, he was sure it had nothing to do with ordinary living and everything to do with Miss Angela Bellini.

When Doc Tuttle swung the buck-boarded wagon into the road that led them under the Foster Cattle Company sign, Brett whistled. He'd expected a big, nice spread, but this place was something else. Rich bottomland spread for miles from a wide fork of the South Platte that cut a swath through the valley, chock-full of cottonwoods and willows along the water's edge. As far as Brett could see, green pastures encircled the many barns and pens, which were sturdily built with fine woodwork. Nothing here had been thrown together, and Brett could tell the minute a post broke or a window needed replacing, it was done pronto.

The two-storied ranch house was the finest he'd ever laid eyes on, with all that fancy trim work around the doors and windows and a slate-rock entry, like something he'd see in a magazine on a rack in a general store. The whole front of the house was laid in slate, so that when Tuttle slowed the mules, their hooves make a loud clackety sound on the rock. A wide set of slate stairs led up to a landing that featured a fountain. Lordy, this was some spread.

Brett narrowed his eyes as he stepped down from the bench and nudged his hat back. The giant fountain had white sculptures of two ladies draped in gowns and pouring water from huge pitchers into the round tiled pool at their feet. It was surely a sight to behold, and Brett didn't know what to make of it. He'd never seen the likes of it in all his life.

A young cowboy ran over from the yard and took hold of the bridle of one of the mules hitched to their wagon and clucked at the animals to get them moving. He led them clacking along the rock and down to a carriage house with two wide hanging doors that sat off to the left of Foster's home.

Brett was staring up at the roof, at an enormous brass weathervane of a horse, when his attention was drawn to three riders galloping over to the horse barn that sat about fifty yards behind the house. The horses were nearly played out, their muscles heaving and manes tossing. The late-afternoon sunlight made their lathered flanks glisten, and Brett watched the fellas slide from their mounts with haste, their faces knotted with concern. Dust and grime coated every inch of their clothes, and their faces were dirty and haggard. One appeared to be a Mexican, with his silver-girt sombrero, and the other two Missouri types, from the looks of their features and dress.

Tuttle came to stand beside him and watched. An older fella, who could be no other than Logan Foster, strode up to the three men and had a powwow as their horses pawed the ground and snorted dust from their nostrils. Foster had a commanding presence, wearing a tall wide-brimmed black hat and a sparkling silver belt with a huge buckle. He stood nearly a head above his punchers and listened thoughtfully as the fellas gave him some sort of distressing news. Foster nodded and blew out a hard breath, then shook his head. Even from where Brett stood, he could tell the rancher was boiling up. *Maybe this ain't a good time for introductions—or to ask fer a job.*

"Roberts!" Foster caught the attention of a cowboy about Brett's age that was loading some bales of alfalfa onto a palette just inside the barn. The redheaded fella ran over to Foster, who nodded and grabbed the reins of the three horses and led 'em into the barn, likely to unsaddle 'em and give 'em a rubdown, then water 'em. Foster then dismissed the three riders, who stomped off in the direction of a bunkhouse situated behind the big barn.

Foster hadn't seen his visitors yet, so Brett waited at the base of the steps with Tuttle and used the time to take in the feel of the ranch. A few hands were doing the usual chores, and dozens of horses grazed lazily in the pastures, swishing flies with their tales. There was 'airy a cow in sight, but he'd expected that. With the roundup only weeks away, most of Foster's cowpunchers would be out with the herds, spread out in who knew how many directions over creation.

Funny how the buffalo were almost gone and the cattle had taken over the Front Range. Brett recalled hearing that after the War of the Rebellion between the North and South, upwards of a half-million wild cattle were roaming free on Texas soil—cattle that reproduced so fast, every four years the herds doubled. Free for the taking after the war.

Brett saw Foster turn and spot them, and he waved him and Tuttle over. When Brett stopped before the rancher, he took in the man's chiseled face, weathered from years on the range in hot sun and harsh winter winds. Foster was well-nigh sixty—a sinewy man with a shock of iron-gray hair tickling his buckskin shirt collar and a thick moustache to match that fell over his lip. He carried himself with confidence and dignity befitting his success, but his eyes gleamed warm and friendly. He gave Tuttle an unreserved smile and patted the doctor heartily on the back with hands as large as dinner plates. Whatever had distressed the rancher was no longer evident on his face.

"Doc, it's good to see you, as always," Foster said. "What c'n I help you with?"

"This is Brett Hendricks," he said. "He's looking for work."

Foster held out his hand, and Brett shook it. "Logan Foster. Pleasure to meet you, son. Where ya from?"

"I'm up from Texas." Brett hesitated. He didn't know what reason to give him and hoped the rancher wouldn't ask. "I've ridden for some big ranches, including Patterson's down in Austin."

Foster nodded in recognition. "What c'n you do?"

"Just about everythin'," Brett said. "I've punched in outfits year-round. Ridden point, flank, and swing. Spent a winter in a floatin' outfit near Houston and once as an outrider. But mostly I've worked at bronco bustin'."

"I see," Foster said, chewing his lip. "Well"—he looked at Tuttle, then back at Brett—"I could use a good buster right now. We got a wild string in, and more on the way. We need to get 'em ready for the roundup. I got two cowboys who do a right good job, but I'm guessin' they won't be able to work through the bunch in time."

Brett sensed there was something troubling the rancher's mind—prob'ly the news those punchers had given him. Maybe some problems with his herd. There were always problems cropping up out on the range. If it wasn't one thing, it was seven others— accidents, fights, cattle drifts. With thousands of head, it was to be expected. But usually a rancher took it all in stride. No, this had the smell of something personal.

Tuttle smiled. "Mr. Hendricks has been staying with me this past week. I can attest to his character. I think he'd make a fine addition to your crew."

"That so?" Foster said with a touch of amusement. "You jes found this fella alongside the road and took him under your wing?"

Brett cringed inwardly but kept his face unexpressive. Last thing he wanted was for Foster to hear his shameful tale of how he'd almost died in the desert.

But Tuttle—thankfully—only chuckled as if this was a joke the two fellas shared. Maybe Brett wasn't the first sorry sod to be rescued by the good doctor.

Foster turned to Brett. "Did'ya bring your rig?" he asked.

Brett nodded. "All but a bridle, Mr. Foster."

Foster grunted thoughtfully, then turned and gazed at the horse barn. Then he looked back at Brett, a sneaky kind of delight lighting up his eyes. Brett knew just what Foster planned to do, and a smile lifted the corners of his mouth.

"I got a pinto named Rebel that the boys jes can't seem to get under 'em. You wanna give it a shot?"

Brett grinned. He'd have this job in his pocket afore the day's end.

"I reckon I would," he said.

Chapter 13

WHEN ANGELA AWOKE THIS MORNING, she'd decided to push the guilt and grief to the back of her heart. She'd cried buckets of tears last night, mostly while pacing in the yard. The tiny room in the back felt like a prison cell, and it was too easy for her to wallow in her misery. In there, her flood of tears threatened to pull her under and drown her. But outside, the expanse of sparkling stars soothed her pain and enabled her to surrender to God's will. Seeing the heavens in such glory reminded her of how small and insignificant and powerless she was to fix or change her circumstances. It was all in His hands.

And so resolved, she prayed with abandon and with her "amen" felt the burden lift. She would trust that, in time, at the right time, she could return home. And that the Lord would make a way for her here in the meantime.

Meantime. What a strange word, she thought, and so appropriate. Her papá's meanness was the root of her suffering. And she would never be able to change him or what he thought of her and her dreams. She was an adult, not a child any longer, and it wasn't until last night—as she stood in the warm, dry wind that blew her hair into tangles—that she realized she didn't have to allow her papá to prevent her from becoming the musician she longed to be. He treated her as if she would always be answerable to him. And she'd wanted so much to please him and be an obedient daughter. But now she knew she would never truly please him. Not unless she dutifully married Pietro and suffered in silent misery in subservience to her husband and her culture. It wasn't until she'd spent her first week in the West that she saw the appeal of a life free of such expectations and encumbrances.

But how could she support herself here in Greeley, until the Lord made it clear it was time to return to New York? This was what worried her as she smoothed out her bedcovers and went to wait for George in the shop. She'd forgone joining him for his usual breakfast of eggs and fried potatoes, her appetite eluding her.

Presently, he came through the door, a concerned look filling his face and etching shadows into the lines above his brows. He'd kindly refrained last evening from pressing her to talk. Perhaps she had sparked his own grief, for he looked haggard this morning— much the way she had seen him when she'd first arrived. She smiled warmly at him; she didn't want to add to his burden of grief.

Surely her cooking and laundering and helping in other ways around the house was a blessing to him. And she hoped her company had been uplifting in some small part. But she realized she couldn't keep staying here and taking advantage of his hospitality. He was providing her food and lodging, and while he assured her she was more than earning her keep, it wasn't proper for her to stay here indefinitely.

What would George's pious neighbors think of a young woman spending so much time in the company of a recently widowed man? She was often in the house with him at night, eating dinner, sitting in the drawing room discussing books and music. He was old enough to be her father, but that still wouldn't stop tongues from wagging or hurtful gossip from spreading. Not from what Violet had told her about many in the town. "What's to be expected in a town as small as this, in which everyone thinks your business is their business?" Violet had said. It wasn't so much her reputation she was concerned with; it was George's. Though, she was sure he would deny caring a whit about such things.

Still, it was time she found a suitable position of employment and another place to stay. The thought befuddled her.

"Well," George said, his usual mug of tea steaming in his hand. "I've made a decision."

His declaration hung in the air between them. Angela wasn't sure what he was referring to. But then he reached across the table and lifted one of the violins she'd been playing.

"Let me hear one of the etudes you've been working on," he said, settling onto his stool and folding his arms across his chest.

No longer nervous playing for him—after so many hours of trying out his instruments at his direction—she picked up the bow lying on the table and quickly adjusted the tuning on the instrument. George, as was his habit, closed his eyes, as if that helped open his ears.

She smiled and closed her eyes as well as she tucked the violin under her chin and drew the bow across the top string. She especially loved this etude, and while in Greeley, she'd perfected the fingering and trills. It was a lively, cheerful piece that sent a rush of joy into her heart. She hoped her enthusiastic playing would buoy George's heart as well. She felt bad that she'd troubled him with her family problems, and he'd been so gracious and kind to her.

She wished her papá was half as thoughtful and considerate as George. If only she had a father like George Fisk. What a different childhood she would have had. *And Mamá. She deserved such a loving husband—not a harsh, ungrateful one.*

The thought of her papá striking her mamá caused such anger to flow through her fingers, a string snapped as she bowed the violin. She gasped, realizing she was gripping the violin so hard that her knuckles were white. The last lingering notes resounded in the small room with an edge of fury and defiance. The raw emotions hung palpably in the air.

She lifted her gaze from the bobbing broken string as she placed the bow on the table and set the violin back on its stand. Embarrassment kept her from looking at George, but she heard him clear his throat.

"Yes," he said thoughtfully, "this is your instrument."

She looked at him, curious.

He studied her face, then a smile lifted his pale cheeks. "A violin must be strong enough and sensitive enough to express any emotion its master desires. Our instruments are merely extensions of our arms—and our hearts, my dear." He shrugged. "When words fail us, our instruments speak for us. The right instrument will adeptly convey every nuance of our feelings as expressed through our musicality. It mustn't resist or transpose a jot or a tittle. It has to be the most faithful of friends, year in and year out."

Angela pondered George's words, which he spoke with great earnestness and conviction. While she still couldn't tell the difference between the three he'd narrowed his choice to, she trusted him. And she doubted he'd let her choose another. It was clear his mind was made up.

He picked up the violin and held it up to the light streaming through the window beside her. Dust motes danced in the air around the lightly varnished instrument. It lacked the rich red hues and luster the other two violins displayed.

"Two, maybe three more coats," George announced.

"Oh," Angela said, now understanding. "But . . . how long will it take?" She couldn't recall what he'd said about how much time each coat needed to dry.

George furrowed his brows. "Three weeks. Maybe four—"

"Four weeks!" That was a month. Could she stay that long? She supposed she could—and even longer—if she could find gainful employment. Though, perhaps if she went home, he could send the instrument to her by rail.

The thought of leaving Greeley without her violin caused an ache in her stomach. No, she would wait for the Lord to tell her when it was time to go back to New York, and she would return with violin in hand.

George thought for a moment. "The opera board is meeting for lunch tomorrow, and I'm certain that if I introduce you to some of the fine ladies there, they might have some referrals for students for you."

Angela smirked at George's unsurprising mind-reading ability. He seemed just as adept at reading expressions on others' faces as he did the timbre of notes coming from his creations.

"You see, my dear, I spent many hours a week teaching violin . . . up until Lucy's death. It was a . . . helpful distraction for me at times. But I found my patience stretched thin, having to listen to such inexperienced heavy-handed playing. I'm afraid I'm not all that good with children. And while there are a number of qualified violinists in town, none desire to teach. And the few music teachers in Greeley are lacking in the knowledge of stringed instruments. Most, like Mrs. Green, play the piano."

He walked over to the door, then turned back to her. "Which means, my dear, if you are willing to take on some squirrely young students, I imagine you'd do well for yourself here and be in high demand."

Angela was thrilled at the idea. She knew how much her mother had paid Signore Bianchi for her lessons, but she had no idea if he was charging her what amounted to city prices or if she'd been given a discount. She also had no idea how much it might cost her to rent a room somewhere—if there was even such a thing to be found in Greeley. Her head spun and began to throb from the questions circling inside.

She sighed and said, "I'd love to teach the violin. It certainly would suit me better than working in a shop or hoeing potatoes for some farmer."

George laughed. "Wonderful, my dear. Tomorrow, meet me on the front porch at eleven. And we'll get lunch in town—my treat."

Angela nodded, her affection for George filling her heart. Imagine earning money teaching music! She sent a prayer of thanks up to heaven, her heart light and happy for the first time since she'd received that telegram.

She stepped outside the small shop and breathed in the thin fresh air. Specks of white fluff from the cottonwood trees floated on the breeze, landing like fat snowflakes on the ground. Her eyes wandered to the house next door. She hadn't seen Brett at all since he'd walked home carrying her sack of vegetables. She felt bad that she'd promised to play for him last night and assumed he'd come over while she was burying her face in her pillow and drenching it with tears.

Her heart pounded a little faster at the thought of his strong arms, recalling how he'd steadied her when she nearly tripped. Brett Hendricks was certainly like no man she'd ever met. And not just because of what he wore or how he spoke in that uneducated manner. He was deep and complex, yet under that cocky, teasing demeanor she sensed a gentle spirit. She would never forget how his face filled with pain when speaking about his father. She of all people knew how awful it was to have a violent parent. As much as she and Brett were different—so very different—in this they were well met.

All the young men she knew in Mulberry Bend were cut from the same cloth as her papá. She blamed her culture, for it encouraged men to be arrogant and domineering. Women were only good for taking care of the home and birthing children. Men bragged about their large families, as if that proved their virility. And the men that showed any sensitivity or deference to women were chided for being weak, spineless.

She'd thought perhaps all men were like that everywhere, for what did she truly know about them? She'd been so sheltered and had never traveled more than a few miles from her apartment except on rare occasions. Other men she'd observed from a distance, and while their dress and mannerisms differed from those in her Italian community, she could hardly tell a thing about what they were like beneath their public face. Perhaps they all beat their wives.

But George would never harm a fly. And though Brett's eyes had flared with excitement when he spoke about the wild horses he broke, she heard the affection and tenderness in his voice, and it had tugged at her heartstrings like fingers plucking notes on a violin.

A yearning filled her as she stood there staring at the quiet house. A yearning to see Brett step outside. To look upon his sculpted muscles and strong shoulders. To gaze into those bottomless hazel eyes that glinted with specks of gold. And that mouth . . .

She swallowed, thinking of how it might feel to join her lips to his and taste his mouth. Heat spread down her body at the thought of him kissing her, his hands lovingly caressing her skin, his warm, hard body pressed against hers.

She tried to stop the images exploding in her head, but she couldn't. She hadn't ever felt such a strong need take over her—a need for a man's touch. For a man's mouth on hers. Never before had the thought appealed to her. Certainly not when she thought of Pietro with his small brooding eyes and fidgety fingers. He repulsed her.

Yet, she couldn't help thinking of Brett without her body responding as if being coaxed open like a flower. She felt weak and vulnerable at this rush of need, at this yearning that played over her like a caprice of gentle notes. When her imagination began unbuttoning his shirt and had her hands sliding down his taut stomach, she slammed the door to her mind in fear and shock. What in heaven's name was wrong with her? Was it the thin rarified air that addled her mind? Or the result of emotional exhaustion? Her thoughts were running as wild as the horses Brett tamed.

She hurried back inside, glad that Brett Hendricks hadn't seen her standing there and come out. Had he watched her from one of the windows? The thought made her face heat with shame. She saw the way he'd looked at her—that longing in his eyes. At first she thought it was nothing more than male lust—she'd seen that same look on Pietro's eyes every time she'd been near him. And on the faces of many of the old men who stood on the corners and talked in the evenings in Mulberry Bend. They thought nothing of staring lecherously at young women, teasing and flirting with them—even smacking their bottoms or trying to pinch them through the layers of petticoats. It disgusted her, and she couldn't understand how many girls she knew merely laughed and were flattered by the attention. She didn't want her younger sisters to be like that, but what could she do? It was the way of her culture.

But no, that longing of Brett's that she'd seen—it wasn't lust. She didn't know why she was so certain, but it made her think of the subtle differences in timbre in the violins she'd played. You could bow the same note on the same string on a dozen violins, and somehow each had a tiny variance in tone. Underneath the note lay the undertone, and often hidden even deeper were hints of harmonics. Angela understood that when a string resonated in just the right way, it would produce beautiful higher harmonic tones, adding richness to the sound.

When she thought of Brett, it was as if she sensed those rich overtones that resonated somewhere deep inside her—tones only she heard and felt.

She smirked at the silliness of her thoughts. He was hardly a violin to be played. But oh, wouldn't it be sweet to hold him in her arms and let her fingers play over his skin?

A shiver ran up her spine in the heat of the late morning. She again chided herself for her fascination with the footloose cowboy. Mere girlish fantasies. She imagined plenty of women romanticized falling in love with some wandering cowboy. The allure of a wild, untamable man was fine for a daydream, but in the harsh light of reality, such a man offered nothing but fleeting thrills and lasting heartache.

She had no doubt Brett Hendricks was trouble. Trouble seemed to chase after him wherever he went. And she had no interest in bringing more trouble into her life. She had a dream to chase down.

Chapter 14

BRETT, STANDING OUTSIDE THE FENCE, studied the pinto that the two wranglers had directed into the corral. A crowd of about ten cowboys gathered around, clambering onto the fence or leaning their elbows on railings, glad for a break in their workday and grinning at the prospect of seeing who they reckoned was some fool trying to prove his mettle.

Not a few jeered and hollered at Brett as he stood there, but he paid them no mind. This wasn't the first time he'd been asked to break a horse with folks watching—and hoping he'd be kicked seven ways to Sunday. A lot of cowboys took an evil delight in seeing a newcomer to their outfit suffer humiliation. Well, Brett had every intention of disappointing 'em.

He reckoned the horse was four, maybe five—an unusually stocky build for an Injun pony, heavier than average by at least two hundred pounds, lacking the typical long barrel, ewe neck, and light quarters of his breed. A powerful beast for his inches.

Brett climbed over the fence and jumped down into the pen, facing the snorting horse, his lariat in hand. With a gentle swing, the rope landed on the animal's neck, and the captive began surging on the noose tightening around its throat. The pinto then snorted and reared, paddling his forelegs in an attempt to strike Brett. But Brett kept working the horse around the pen, talking softly, while the beast kept charging and retreating, mouth open and teeth bared.

Brett lost track of time, and the effort nearly wore him out, considering his recent ordeal and too many days' bedrest. But he was determined not to show any weakness, though his shot leg began to throb something fierce. Presently, he worked up the rope hand over hand until, while dodging the horse's strikes, he succeeded in slipping a half-hitch over his nose. There followed another long tussle before he could approach the horse, but when he again got within arm's reach, he rested his palm on the animal's nose and lightly rubbed it.

The horse stood, astonished and wary at the tender touch and absence of harsh yelling or brutal treatment so many of these outlaws experienced. Brett knew right away that Foster's wranglers had lit hard into this poor animal, thus compounding the fear and mistrust it felt toward humans.

Brett then worked the half-hitch in his rope so that it encircled both forefeet, and with a hard yank, he dropped the pinto to the ground in a huff of dust. The horse squirmed and kicked as Brett lit on him, and soon he had the thrashing hind hooves safely half-hitched and all four bound in a hog-tie.

He pushed the shouts and cheers and jeers of the cowboys out of his head, as if they were the sound of distant water babbling in a creek, then sat on the pinto's side. He gestured over at the saddle sitting on the fence railing, and the redheaded fella with eager eyes who Foster had called Roberts—the one who'd taken hold of the three riders' spent mounts—rushed over, scurried over the fence, and hefted the saddle with a bridle thrown over its seat. The fella cautiously set the saddle down behind Brett, keeping distance from the struggling legs trying to break free of the restraints. Brett tossed him a smile of thanks as the fella backed away but stayed within reach should Brett need further help.

In moments, Brett had the pinto saddled and bridled, then he stood astride the horse and tucked his boot into the left stirrup. Quickly he seized the reins in one hand while with the other released the bound feet. The horse rose under him with Brett firmly in the saddle and bogged his head between his forelegs, then he started coming apart.

The violent bucking that would have unseated most fellas was only a matter of course for Brett. Twenty minutes of frenzied horse pitching wore out both horse and rider, with the beast repeatedly trying to bite him on the legs and falling backward to get shed of his load.

But Brett hung on, and when the pinto's flanks started quivering, and the horse could hardly keep standing, Brett stroked his neck and started up with the breaking patter he always used to wear down the last of a horse's resistance. Then he clicked his tongue against his teeth, touched the horse's flanks with his spurs, and the pinto took a few hesitant steps.

The nervous ears drooped lazily, and the resentful muscles relaxed under Brett's legs.

The thrill rushed through him as he sat straight and with a calm expression walked the pinto around the corral, giving him his head after a time, which allowed the pinto to toss his mane and snort, voicing his many complaints the way an old biddy might to the other old ladies in her knitting circle.

"I know, I know," Brett said, chuckling and patting the horse's neck. "It's a hard life, but it'll only get easier for ya from here on out."

One of the cowboys leaning over the fence called out, "Well, I'll be. If that don't beat th' Comanches. I'd never believed there was 'airy a puncher 'tween Texas an' Canidy could bridle an' saddle Rebel thataway without fightin' him all over a five-acre lot."

Logan Foster, who'd watched the whole thing from atop a table under a willow not yards from the corral, came over and entered the corral through the gate. Brett walked the horse right up to Foster, who laid a hand on the horse's nose, shaking his head as he studied the animal's now pacified demeanor. The pinto that had liked to kill Brett moments ago now looked bored and thought of nothing more than dozing lazily in the warm afternoon sun.

A man years older than most in the crowd called over to the rancher, "Boss, do you allow it's loco or sense an' sand the kid's sufferin' from most?"

The rest of the cowboys laughed, and most, shaking their heads in disbelief, jumped down from the fence rails and went back to work, the afternoon's entertainment over. As Brett'd expected, not a few showed a twinge of disappointment. But the redheaded fella caught Brett's eyes, nodded, and smiled wide at him.

"I never seen anyone do that—sit astride like that with the horse hog-tied—and not use a blindfold," Foster told him, still stroking the horse's nose. Brett slipped off the saddle, then lifted the reins over the pinto's ears and handed them to the rancher.

"I think you'll find him agreeable from here on out." The horse raised sleepy eyes and hardly paid Foster any mind, tired out from his cranky behavior.

Foster smiled with a grin that showed all his teeth. "And you can have him on your string, when you head out to camp, during the roundup."

Brett grinned back. He had a good feeling about Logan Foster. He seemed to deal an honest hand, and, from what Brett could tell, his punchers and wranglers liked and respected him. "I'm appreciatin' of yer kindness."

"Go get your rig, then. Roberts'll show you to the bunkhouse and get you settled in." He cocked his head at the fella, who was opening the gate for 'em.

Brett counted in his head. It'd been ten days since he'd fled from Orlander's men after winning those bronc-buster events. He'd nearly died, but now he'd been given another chance at life. He wasn't much of a praying man, but he thanked the good Lord for the recent events that led him here. He was back in the saddle, doing what he loved, free and unencumbered.

As Brett followed Foster and the docile pinto out through the gate, he spotted Tuttle off to the side, smiling and shaking his head. Brett went over to him.

"I'm impressed, Brett. I don't know how you managed to stay on that devil's back. And I have to admit, I worried about your stamina. How is your leg feeling?"

"No worse for wear," Brett replied, glad the throbbing had eased. If he could get through half an hour of that kind of grueling affliction, he reckoned he could manage a full day's work. It would be some weeks before he'd have to sit in the saddle sixteen hours straight for days on end in the roundup. By then he'd have his strength full back.

Brett imagined the thought of sleeping in a bunkhouse with a bunch of smelly cowpunchers wasn't something that appealed to a man like Doc Tuttle, but Brett knew he'd feel more at home there than in that purty little room with those lace curtains. He was grateful for the doc's hospitality, and he'd make sure to thank him sincerely, for he owed the fella his life.

As he walked with Tuttle to go fetch his wagon, Brett's excitement waned, and an empty feeling grew in the pit of his gut.

His thoughts drifted to Angela and the way the tears had smeared those striking brown eyes when she talked about her pa.

A sudden longing to hold her seized him, and it startled him with its ferocity. Like a wild weed entangling his heart, it seemed to squeeze the breath out of him. But there was nothing for it, no lovely waist to pull her to him so he could kiss away those tears. She was in Greeley, and he was here on Foster's ranch, miles away. Angela Bellini would be on a train in a few days' time and out of his life forever. *You gotta stop thinkin' about her, Cowboy. It'll only make your heart hurt.*

He looked around at the thousands of acres of open range off in the distance, the pinks of dust sketched like chalk against the big bowl of sky. A coyote howled afar, and the smell of rice and beans and cooked pork wafted on the air. His mouth watered, and his stomach growled. He was peckish and thirsty, but those needs paled compared to the gnawing hunger he felt for Angela. How long would it take for him to forget her—for the painful ache to leave for good?

Well, it'd better not take too long. You got ridin' to do and a life to live—one that doesn't include a woman.

"Where'd ya learn how to do that?" Foster asked Brett as they stood near the fountain, waiting for the wagon to be brought around.

Brett shrugged. "I've always had a way with horses, Mr. Foster."

Foster's bushy eyebrows lifted. "Well, I'm impressed, young man. You'll be a fine asset to my outfit." He nodded at Tuttle. "Sarah Banks should see this kid work."

Tuttle chuckled. "If she does, she'll want to steal him from you."

Foster laughed. Brett wondered who this Sarah Banks was, but he kept quiet.

"My foreman, Mack Lambert, and most of the punchers should be back tomorrow. That'll give ya time to get situated in the bunkhouse. Tate Roberts—the redheaded cowboy yonder—will show you around and tell you how things are run on the ranch. I expect all my hands to work hard, and I don't brook fighting or bickering. I pay forty dollars a month. You'll get three squares, and drinkin's your own business after hours. But I'll toss any puncher on his ear if I catch him drinkin' on the job. Understand?"

"Yes sir," Brett said without hesitation. The rancher's rules were the same as any other's, but Brett knew there were always some hands that snuck a flask into their saddlebag and tucked into it from time to time. He didn't see no harm in it so long as they did their job proper.

The thought of a shot of smooth whiskey set his mouth watering. He'd been two weeks without a drink, and he wondered if this fella Roberts had any in the bunkhouse. A drink or two late at night helped him relax and get to sleep, and the way his thoughts kept circling back to Angela Bellini, he figured he was going to need something to get his mind off her.

A kid about fifteen rode the wagon over, then yanked the mules to a stop and hopped out. Brett walked around to the back of the flat bed and pulled out his saddle and bags and bedroll and set them on the slate rock. The blankets looked squeaky clean, and he figured they'd be a bit itchy until they were washed a few times. He stood, feeling restless and wanting to get to work. Foster must've noticed his twitchiness.

"If'n you want to, after lunch you c'n round up some of those *mestengo* broncs in the pasture yonder and work with 'em in the corral. Rusty should be around somewhere — he's one of my busters. I'll have him join you."

Brett nodded, feeling that tickle of eager anticipation at spending the day breaking broncs. He couldn't think of anything he liked doing better — other than enjoying the affections of a purty gal. Though, there was only one gal roping in his thoughts presently, making him forget every lovely face he'd ever laid eyes on. Every time he thought of Angela, he felt a sour ache in his chest, as if he'd been punched. Why'd he let himself get smitten with a gal he could never have? She must have bespelled him with that fiddle — that's all he could think of to explain why he couldn't shake her from his head. Well, work was the best cure for a lonely heart.

Brett turned at the sound of the front doors blowing open. Foster and Tuttle, engaging in quiet discourse between them, spun around. A lady who looked to be about busting out of her seams in a pale-green silky gown with a half-dozen rustling petticoats flounced down the steps and came over to them. Her hair was a mass of whiskey-colored curls pinned to her head, and she oozed elegance and money. Brett knew without an introduction that this was the rancher's much-younger wife. Her cheeks had a pink powder on them, and she'd painted up her eyelashes so they were long and thick. But in a tasteful way — not like some saloon gal.

"Oh, I'm so glad I caught you before you left," the woman said with a Southern drawl to Doc Tuttle. Foster seemed to want to roll his eyes, but he merely smiled and introduced his wife to Brett. Her name was Adeline, and she gave him a polite hello before turning back to Tuttle with a breathy sigh.

"Joseph, darling," she said, laying a gloved hand on his arm. Tuttle smiled at her, and Brett pictured Miz Foster slipping on the ice and her skirts flying into her face. He held back a chuckle. "You live next door to that violin teacher, is that so?"

Tuttle's lips pursed together. "I'm not sure Mr. Fisk teaches violin. He builds them; they're purported to be some of the finest instruments made in the country."

Adeline nodded, flipped open a fan, and waved it vigorously at her face. "Well, my girls were given violins from their aunt in Savannah for their birthdays."

At this, Logan Foster did roll his eyes. Brett could only imagine the screechy sounds two girls with fiddles might fill a house with.

"I'd very much like to have Mr. Fisk come to the ranch and teach Clementine and Madeline how to play. They didn't do well with Mrs. Green. She . . . lacked the patience."

Brett guessed from the look on the rancher's face that he wished his girls never got those fiddles. He reckoned it took a whole lot of years of diligent practicing to play the way Angela did. The sweet sounds of Angela's music drifted into his head.

Tuttle nodded respectfully, fully attentive to Miz Foster.

"Would you please ask him to pay a call, as soon as possible?"

"Yes, Mrs. Foster. I'll do that."

She clapped her hands in delight. "Ah, thank you so much, Joseph. Will you and . . ." She looked at Brett as if seeing him for the first time. Her eyes took in the length of him, and she smiled approvingly. Brett felt a little hot under the collar and kept his eyes cast down. He felt like a calf on the auction block.

"Brett Hendricks, ma'am," he said when he realized she'd already forgotten his name.

"Yes," she replied, her words bubbly as she flicked her fan faster and turned back to the doctor. "Will you and Mr. Hendricks join us for lunch?"

Brett smiled, but inside he cringed. Last thing he wanted was to sit down at some fancy table and try to figure out which fork he was s'posed to use for what food. Thankfully, Tuttle shook his head.

"That's kind of you, Mrs. Foster. But I have to get back to my practice." He gave a slight bow, then shook the rancher's hand. "I'm glad Brett will be working for you. I'll be sure to give Mr. Fisk your message."

Adeline nodded her thanks and flounced back up the steps. Brett heard a girl's shrill voice coming from the second story. Then he heard something crash to the floor.

Brett looked over at Foster, who hardly flinched at the sound. He shrugged and said, "Those girls fight like alley cats." His face glowed with adoration for his young'uns. "They got a lot of spunk. Like their mother." He said this to Tuttle, as if looking to the doctor to agree.

Foster added, "When're ya goin' to nab yourself a wife, Joseph?"

"Ah, don't you start in on me. Adeline is always trying to fix me up with one of her friends."

Foster gave a playful frown. "It ain't good for a man to be alone."

Tuttle waggled his head like a guilty dog that had stolen a hunk of meat off the counter. "In due time," he said. "When I find the right woman." He added, "They're not always easy to come by."

"Ain't that the truth," Foster said, grinning and slapping the doctor on the back. "I'm a lucky fella to have found Adeline."

All this talk about getting hitched was making Brett prickly.

"Well, I'll be on my way, then," Tuttle said as he hopped up onto the wagon and sat on the bench. He tipped his hat at the rancher and then at Brett, then clicked his teeth at the mules.

As the wagon rolled across the fancy slate, Brett caught sight of Tate Roberts, then took his leave from Logan Foster, who went back inside his ranch house. He hefted his saddle and bags and gave the puncher a wave as he headed off to find the bunkhouse.

Chapter 15

BRETT SWIPED HIS FOREHEAD WITH his shirtsleeve. Grit stung and clogged his eyes as he leaned back against the breaking pen fence in the cool of morning and watched Tate Roberts deftly take over with the last of the bunch of green geldings. He regarded the capable Missourian who Brett could tell was an all-around cowman. Brett figured Roberts had no more than two years on him and grew up in a saddle. He was the kind of fella that said a whole lot in mighty few words. Roberts broke with a light hand, something Brett was glad to see. For he detested the way some wranglers treated horses with harshness. It was usually a matter of arrogance or impatience or both, but Brett had no tolerance for such bullying.

They'd spent the afternoon yesterday, along with the buster named Rusty, on three of the most ornery mustangs Foster had. Today, they'd had an easier time of it.

Across the yard, beyond the hay barn, two punchers were sliding off their mounts. They'd brought in a dozen or so cattle — mostly young bulls but a few heifers among them. They'd led them into a pen, and Brett figured they'd culled them from the herd to brand them, since a branding chute was attached at the far end.

They were prob'ly ones that had been missed during the last roundup and range branding.

While it was common for punchers to brand in the open, as needed, if the herd wasn't too far from the ranch and the punchers were heading back there anyways, they'd lead 'em back. Usually a ranch this size had a brander on site.

"Let's see what's goin' on," Roberts called over, reins in hand, nodding at the barn. The horse he was presently working was bridled and huffing through his nostrils as he stood staring at Roberts expectantly. Roberts doffed his hat and slicked down his thin red hair, then replaced the hat. Brett noted he had a lean shaved face except for a pencil-thin mustache that tickled his upper lip.

Brett followed Roberts out of the corral and waited for him to let loose the animal into the nearby pasture. After the buster pulled off the bridle, the little pinto kicked up his hind legs, then galloped off across the fields of tall brown-tinged grass. Roberts turned to Brett.

"I'm s'prised we got the load of 'em cooperatin' so fast. A good day's work," he said with a genuine smile. "I'm glad ya joined up." He glanced over at the two punchers who were standing at the fence talking to a young kid who looked all knees and elbows.

Roberts narrowed his eyes, and Brett sensed the fella's immediate disapproval in the set of his jaw. Every muscle in Roberts's body appeared to tense as they walked over to the punchers.

One of the fellas was about thirty, thick in the gut and wide-shouldered, with a swarthy complexion that hinted at some Mexican blood. Thin brows lay over small eyes that looked like hard chunks of coal—eyes Brett instantly distrusted. The other fella was closer to Brett's age, but the lines and scars on his face attested to a harder life. He was tall, lean, and sinewy, and a shock of thick wheat-colored hair fell into his eyes, though the puncher did nothing about it. Their clothes showed they'd been out on the range some days, and their hats were coated in that film of red dirt that seemed to dust everything in Colorado.

Both fellas had cruel smiles as they chatted up the kid, who was clearly a newly arrived tenderfoot. His clothes looked like they'd just been purchased out of the Montgomery Ward catalog, and his too-large hat swam on his head. Brett figured the kid to be about sixteen. It would take him a few years to grow into that hat.

Brett could tell right off these fellas were giving the kid grief, and the poor fella didn't have the guts to stand it. He looked like a lost calf stuck in a thicket and about to wail.

"Well," Roberts said cheerily, slicing through the obvious tension in the air as he sidled up to the tenderfoot. "Who do we have here?" Roberts kept that narrowed gaze on the two punchers even though his voice sounded jovial.

The fellas, who'd been up close to the trembling kid, took a couple of steps back, and their tense stature relaxed.

The kid sucked in a big breath, and relief lit his eyes as if he'd just been rescued. Maybe he had, Brett thought, sizing up the two fellas before him.

"I'm Archie," the kid said in a rush. "Archie Halloran, from over Loveland way." A band of bright freckles streaked across his nose, and Brett could tell he'd recently had his hair cut—probably at a barber shop. The kid looked squeaky clean, and Brett wondered how he'd gotten hired on here. Maybe some kid of a friend of Miz Foster's needing a job.

"Nice to meet ya, Archie," Roberts said. "I'm Tate Roberts. This is Brett Hendricks." He nodded at Brett. "And I s'pose you've met Ned Handy and Rufus Shore."

The tenderfoot nodded, and Brett saw fear flare up in his eyes.

Brett exchanged hellos with the two punchers, who eyed him warily. Brett paid them no mind. He'd seen their type on every ranch he'd ridden for. Fellas full of themselves, and while it was true that cowboys often joshed each other and played jests and roughed the tenderfoots, it was all in good humor, for the most part. But when Brett had first started out as a tenderfoot, he'd been sorely mistreated by a few fellas like these two, and he'd been grateful that Ol' Tex had stood up for him and told the others to leave him be, which they did, though he'd still been the brunt of their jokes, and they regularly snickered at the fun they had at his expense.

"We were jes tellin' the kid how things work round here," said the swarthy fella name Rufus Shore.

Roberts nodded, and Brett read a lot behind the buster's cool green eyes. "Well, let's git those beeves inside so Collins can check 'em over."

It took a moment for Brett's eyes to adjust to the scant light inside the barn. Handy and Shore had goaded the animals, and they were now pressed into a small pen. Kicked-up dust choked the air from the cows that surged and lowed against the fence. Brett, standing outside the pen, noted a few golden duns among the piebald black and whites, some longhorns. All were cooperating agreeably except one big white heifer that kept charging back to the gate despite Handy's yelling and arm-swinging.

"Stand over yonder," Shore directed the kid, whose eyes looked about to bug out of his head. Brett reckoned he'd never even seen a cow up close. He knew what Rufus Shore was up to, and he didn't like it one bit. Brett headed toward him around the outside of the pen.

Archie stood transfixed near the gate as the heifer charged at him, his mouth open wide enough for a frog to jump into it. Brett knew he couldn't get to the kid in time, but he spotted a shovel propped up against the fence railing.

He grabbed it and tossed it over the railing at Archie. "Here, use this," Brett yelled, then scrambled over the fence in time to see Archie rush to scoop it up. Both Shore and Handy had cocky grins on their faces as they watched to see what would transpire. Brett wanted to kick them into next week. A mean heifer would as soon kill a man as snort at one.

The tenderfoot thrust the shovel in front of him, hoping to ward off the heifer's advances.

"Smack her between the horns!" Brett yelled, catching a glimpse of Roberts out of the corner of his eye. The buster was inside the pen, working his way around to the kid's left.

The heifer's tail lashed as she slid to a halt, then she whirled and charged at Roberts, who stopped abruptly about ten feet away. To Brett's surprise, the kid raced at the heifer like some wild dust devil, shovel swinging, yelling and hooting. Then, as he neared, his feet slipped from under him, and he landed flat on his back.

Brett sucked in a breath as the shovel went flying across the pen, and the heifer, bracing her forefeet, slid through mud right up to where her two hooves practically dug into the kid's ribs.

Then, to everyone's surprise, she backed away a couple of feet, nuzzled Archie's body and face in inquiry, and lightly prodded him with her horns—prob'ly to see if he was alive.

Smart kid, Brett thought, watching Archie lie there unmoving, his eyes closed, playing possum. Brett saw the fury raging in the animal's eyes soften to wonder and curiosity. He imagined her wondering how a body could go dead so quickly. Then she lightly leapt across the kid and ran over to join the other cows pressed against the fence, as easy as you please.

Inside of five seconds, Archie had scrambled to his feet and mounted the fence, panting hard and shaking his head. Brett imagined every inch of that kid was shaking like a leaf.

Roberts whistled. "Hooey, who'd a thought a kid like you was loco enough t' tackle a fightin' heifer afoot? That heifer was hell bent fer trouble. Kid," Roberts said, shaking his head, "ya got a lot of sand in ya—more'n what appears. That was right kind of ya, what ya did."

Archie looked too shook up to say a word. Maybe a frog *had* hopped into his wide-open mouth. He pulled his hat off his head and scrunched it between his hands.

Brett went over to him and said quietly, "Come'on, let's git ya some water to drink. Prob'ly time to wash up for supper too."

Archie looked up at Brett with eyes filled with gratitude. As he helped the shaky tenderfoot down from the fence, Brett caught the scowls on the two punchers' faces. They stood outside the pen next to the now docile cows. Roberts dusted himself off and came over to Brett and Archie.

"Stay away from them two," Roberts said under his breath, checking Archie over. Roberts glanced at Brett, and Brett realized those words had been meant for him as well.

"Just stick with me," Brett said to Archie in an amiable tone. "I'm new here too."

"Really?" Archie asked, all innocent and naïve. Brett had to laugh. Had he ever been this green? He didn't reckon he had, not even on the day he arrived naked out of his ma.

He tousled the kid's mud-caked hair and let Roberts, who was chuckling, lead the way back to the bunkhouse.

Chapter 16

"YOU 'BOUT READY, MIZ BANKS?"

LeRoy Banks stood, a hand on his hip, alongside the wagon hitched to their two mules, watching his fine young wife fuss with the basket under the wagon's bench seat.

"I reckon," Gennie said, a playful smile lifting her rosy cheeks and her emerald-green eyes sparkling with happiness. She grabbed hold of her skirts as LeRoy helped her down from the buckboard. The day was cooler than yesterday, and LeRoy was glad. It'd make for an easier ride over to Foster's ranch. He reckoned the trip would take about three hours, and Gennie had spent the evening with his ma, making bread and concocting a batch of stinky paste used for treating horse ailments, from swollen muscles to sore teats, to bring to Logan Foster as requested.

He'd been so thrilled to see the way she'd adjusted so quickly to what he called a normal life—Gennie's prior life being nothing that resembled normal. She'd had him so fooled—dressed like a man, masking her sweet voice to sound like a man. She'd even chopped off that purty hair of hers. When he thought on the kind of life she'd led for years, so alone up in the mountains, what kind of inner strength it took to get through the brutal winters and long stretches of loneliness—his heart overflowed with deep respect and abiding love. He didn't think he could ever love anyone as much as he loved Gennie.

As they headed over to the horse barn, where his ma was gathering up the lead ropes, bridles, and halters for the dozen or so horses they'd be taking over to Foster's, he took her hand in his and gave it a squeeze. She shot him a look that sent fire right to his loins. There was still plenty of wild left in his now "domesticated" wife. Though, there was hardly much domestication to speak of when you scratched an inch below the surface.

Gennie was every bit her own woman—just like his ma. And, to his great relief, when he'd brought the poor gal to the ranch the day after he'd coaxed her down the mountain last fall, she and his ma had gadded about the spread like two hens excited over a passel of worms. He chuckled recalling the relief he felt, knowing he'd have to leave her for a few weeks and finish up his work with Whitcomb to break in all those wild horses he and Eli'd driven into his corrals.

Those three weeks had been agony for him. All he did night and day was pine away for Gennie. And while he knew he was foolish to worry about her, he couldn't help hisself. He felt such a need to protect her and keep her safe—a feeling that had stunned the boots off his feet.

While he'd wanted to go back to the ranch those weekends, to check up on her—and, if truth be told, to hold her again in his arms and kiss the living daylights out of her—his ma forbade it. That was one of the few times he'd dared argue with her so adamantly. But she wouldn't back down—stubborn as always and had to be right. But she was. Gennie needed those weeks to settle into the little cabin Ma had cleaned and readied for her—*for them*, LeRoy corrected.

She'd known somehow—through her crazy Cheyenne medicine—that LeRoy would be bringing her back. Not just to civilization but to life proper.

He was so grateful Gennie and his ma got along. And he'd been determined to brook no argument from either of 'em when he'd finished up at Whitcomb's and galloped the whole way home, chewing up the miles from Fort Collins as fast as he could. But neither woman voiced objection when LeRoy swooped Gennie up in his arms and told her he wanted to marry her as soon as was humanly possible. He'd worried so that her affections might have cooled for him, but upon seeing her, he knew his fears had been ungrounded. She'd kissed him passionately and thoroughly until his ma had to loudly clear her throat and get 'em to wash up for supper.

Not three days passed before Miss Gennie Champlain was all his. A simple ceremony with just Eli and Clare and Lucas and Emma by their sides, to witness the vows. Ma had made a ceremonial cake, and they'd all sat at the kitchen table eating a hearty, simple stew as fat flakes of snow fell and the fire sparked and crackled in the hearth in the living room. LeRoy would never forget the way the firelight danced in Gennie's eyes—eyes so filled with joy. He'd gone up the mountain to hunt down a bear and returned with the gal of his heart. Like Eli and Clare—and like Lucas and Emma—theirs was a perfect match. He felt as if he'd waited his whole life for her and she for him. The passion that flared hot that night had hardly cooled in the nine months they'd been together.

"What's with the big grin?" Gennie asked, cocking her head and staring at his face.

"Oh, I'm jes thinkin' 'bout how much I love ya." He grabbed her tiny waist and squeezed. She squealed and slapped at him with the buckskin gloves she held in her hands.

"And that gives you the right to pinch my sides?" She lunged for him and wiggled her fingers under his armpits.

"No fair!" he cried. He was fiercely ticklish, and this woman of his took advantage at every turn to remind him of it.

"You two," his ma yelled from the barn, sticking her head out. "We're burning daylight. Fetch them horses and let's get a'goin'."

LeRoy and Gennie exchanged guilty looks, then broke out into laughter as they strode to the fence and swung open the gate. His ma had been getting grumpy of late. Complaining about her old bones and threatening to give up the ranching business. She claimed she was too old to chase horses all over creation and wanted to spend the rest of her days doing something less taxing. Like what? He could hardly picture her sitting in her stuffed chair knitting like the old ladies in Greeley liked to do.

It took 'em inside of ten minutes to get halters on the bunch, and when they'd led 'em out to the barn, his ma already had her favorite mustang bridled and saddled. But then his eyes caught on the mare with the strain of Arabian blood. She was tied to the post, digging the dirt with her hoof.

"What're ya doin' with her?" LeRoy asked, nodding his head at the horse while fetching his saddle off the fence rail.

"That's Ehase'o, isn't it?" Gennie asked his ma, who took the leads of two of the horses in her hand. "Isn't that the brood mare you'd decided to keep?"

Sarah Banks nodded but said nothing as he and Gennie watched her tie a long lead line to a gelding of fifteen hands that was the gentlest of the bunch but who always had to be in the lead. LeRoy noted his ma had necked Renegade to trail alongside.

LeRoy threw his saddle up over his pinto he'd named No'kest'a, short for the Cheyenne word for "handful," and cinched it up. He took a bridle from off the fence post where his ma had hung 'em and got his mount ready to go. He then turned to her, unable to keep the question from working its way out his mouth.

"I don't figure why you're takin' that mare. You ain't givin' it to Foster, are ya?"

"No, LeRoy."

LeRoy shook his head, wondering what his ma was up to. She was humming an odd tune—something he'd never heard before. Sounded like a kind of folk tune. His ma rarely ever hummed. Something was up, and he knew better than to press her with useless questions.

His ma looked over the remaining bunch of horses with a thoughtful eye, then reached out and took the reins for O'asé— named for the bright blaze on his face. His ma rode every horse she broke at least once a week, and on deliveries like this one, she always picked the most ornery, to iron the kinks out before the horse left her hands. Some of their horses liked to tie themselves in knots now and again just to remind themselves they once used to be wild. His ma would just huff at such antics. Few horses every gave his ma much lip, and if they did, they got an earful of Cheyenne words that even LeRoy could hardly figure out. But those animals shaped up quick enough.

LeRoy walked Gennie over to the wagon and helped her back up. She picked up the reins and leaned over to give her husband a kiss. He took every advantage of the moment to get his fill, waiting until he heard his ma clear her throat again. She did an awful lot of throat clearing these days on the ranch.

He wished Eli was coming along. They'd always delivered horses together—LeRoy couldn't count the trips over the last ten or so years. The place still felt way too empty with him gone. Off living in Fort Collins and running a freight company. Clare about ready to pop out that baby any day now—no doubt the first of a dozen, if'n you looked at the size of her Irish family. But Eli was happy, and life was treating him well. Besides, up till recent, when Clare got too big to make the fifteen-mile trip, they'd come over for Sunday supper every week. LeRoy hoped once the baby came and Clare was back to snuff that they'd make their regular rounds again.

He had to admit he was looking forward to being an uncle. He loved Ben—Grace and Monty's little fella—and he did secretly wish he and Gennie would be blessed with young'uns. But she'd been bad hurt when young—harshly abused—so they reckoned she might not ever be able to bear a babe. And if that was so, they'd accept that as their lot. They had plenty of love 'tween 'em to keep 'em happy.

With the horses all bunched together and ready to go, his ma trotted ahead and out the gate, setting the pace. LeRoy hung back on the right flank a few yards in front of the wagon. He threw Gennie a kiss and thought she looked right perky sitting on the bench holding the reins.

The wagon's wheels clacked along the dusty road in a soothing rhythm, and the horses trotted along, alert, with ears twitching and some tossing of heads. LeRoy didn't expect much fuss among the group, seeing as Renegade wasn't able to wander off to graze and get into trouble. He smiled at the orderly conduct of animals that had not all that long ago never seen a human nor had any reason to trust one. The transformation from wild to tame never ceased to astound LeRoy. It was as if, deep inside, a horse yearned for human companionship and when it was offered, gladly embraced it.

He glanced over at Gennie in her purty calico dress—the gal who'd worn men's clothes for years and had lived as wild and isolated a life as he'd ever seen. It had only taken a few days to get her to trust him, and that in itself was some miracle. One he'd forever cherish.

After Angela and George had dined in the lovely café next to the Greeley Hotel, they strolled along the storefronts on Eighth Avenue on their way to meet the members of the opera board, discussing her favorite subject—repertoire.

"When we get back, I'd like to show you some lullabies I transcribed from Schubert's piano music," George said. "I wrote some little duets I thought you'd enjoy playing."

"I love Schubert. That would be wonderful!" Angela couldn't wait to pick up one of George's violins and play again. All she wanted to do was play, night and day. She'd never felt so at one with the violin before, and truly understood what George had said about bonding with her instrument. She longed to hold it in her hands and pull the beautiful music from its heart. When she wasn't playing, she felt anxious, her mind distracted with melodies, her fingers aching to move across the strings and wield the bow.

But even as this passion rippled over her unceasingly, another passion simmered under the surface. She didn't want to heed its call, but how could she not? Every pore in her skin, every nerve in her body, vibrated and hummed as if in resonance with another. And the more she sought to deny the yearnings she felt, the more they fought for her attention.

It was all Brett Hendricks's fault. He had done this to her—somehow. As if he had plucked a string inside her—a deep, rich, beautiful tone that sent her heart racing.

From the moment she'd awoken this morning, she couldn't push thoughts of him from her mind. Thoughts of them in embrace, their bodies hot with desire and their hands and mouths exploring the other. Her imaginings made her blush in shame, and she chastised herself for her ungodly and improper thoughts, but they ran roughshod over her. No matter what she did to push them away, like a stubborn dog, they kept coming back again and again.

She'd hoped playing the violin and losing herself in the music would prove to be the antidote for this madness that gripped her — her own strain of "Western fever" — but playing music made it worse. In some crazy way, her yearning for Brett ignited her passionate playing, which only stoked the fires of her longing for him. She played as if possessed, carried off by the exquisite and frightening feelings emerging from the recesses of her heart. Feelings she never knew lay hidden there — so intense they were almost palpably painful.

Would this madness never cease? She feared losing the passion, but how could she cut away the fervent desire she felt for the rough-and-tumble cowboy without destroying this precious gift of music that seemed to bleed from her heart? They seemed enmeshed, like two threads twined in a tapestry. Surely in time her inexplicable attraction to him would wane. It was childish — a fantasy. Merely her natural urges manifesting because of her encounters with Brett.

Yet, the thought of losing these feelings — *losing him* — detonated a burst of panic inside her chest. She'd never felt so alive in her life and couldn't bear the thought of losing this feeling. This glorious, tortuous feeling . . .

"Well, if it isn't my neighbor, the good doctor," George said, stopping and laying a hand on Angela's arm.

She looked up, unaware of the blocks they'd walked. They were now in front of the mercantile, and a youthful fastidious man with short dark hair, thick eyebrows, and a smart neat beard hurried their way, an eager smile on his face. *This must be Dr. Tuttle — the man Brett is staying with.* She imagined he was very busy with his medical practice, for though she'd been residing in the instrument shop for nearly a week now, she'd not caught sight of him once. Her first thought was to inquire about Brett, then she chided herself once more.

"Ah, Mr. Fisk. Just the man I wanted to see," George said. The doctor stood a hair taller than Angela, wearing a starched white shirt tucked into loose gray trousers that only stayed up over his narrow hips by the grace of a pair of striped suspenders. She imagined he'd normally wear a proper coat and vest, though the day's heat precluded even the thought of such attire.

"May I introduce you to Angela Bellini? She's recently come to Greeley to purchase one of my violins. This is Joseph Tuttle, one of Greeley's newest physicians."

Dr. Tuttle gave Angela a polite little bow. "I'm pleased to make your acquaintance, Miss Bellini." His eyes lit up in understanding. "Oh, so you are the one I've been hearing play out in the shop in the back."

Angela nodded. "I'm pleased to meet you as well. I hope my playing hasn't bothered you."

"Oh, not in the least." He waved a hand dismissively. "I've greatly enjoyed it, as it drifts into my house late at night. A very soothing sound—to my ears, at least." He grinned as if something tickled him.

"Well, Joseph, how might I be of service?" George said, his face curious as he stroked his side whiskers.

"Oh, I've just returned from visiting the Fosters. You remember the rancher and his wife?"

"Oh yes, they are strong supporters of the opera, and his wife serves on their board." He turned to Angela. "No doubt, my dear, you'll meet her. She's very . . . exuberant."

The two men shared a knowing chuckle. "Well, George," the doctor said, "Mrs. Foster wondered if you might consider coming out to the ranch and giving her girls violin lessons—"

George threw his hands up into the air. "Oh heavens, no."

Dr. Tuttle frowned, but Angela could tell he wasn't at all surprised by George's response.

"I promised her I'd ask," he said with a shrug. "I've faithfully discharged my duty." He added with a warning tone, "But Adeline will be very disappointed. And surely, we need to find a way to keep the rancher's wife happy."

Or what? Angela wondered. She sensed this Adeline Foster had great influence in this town. Or perhaps it was her husband they meant to please. But the solution was obvious, wasn't it?

"I'll teach her girls to play," she announced.

Both the doctor and George stared at her as if they'd forgotten the English language.

"Ah yes, you of course would be perfectly suited for the task, but . . ." George hesitated and searched for words. ". . . let's pay a visit before you make such an offer. Those girls are a handful. And Adeline Foster is a very exacting woman. But then, you two might just get along fine." His brows knitted in thought.

Angela frowned. "But, how would I get to this ranch? Is it far?"

"About a half-hour's ride from here," the doctor said, pointing south.

"I'd be happy to take you, but I don't own a horse or a wagon presently," George said. "Though, we can hire one from the livery," he added, looking with eagerness at her, as if she'd offered to bail him out of hot water.

"I appreciate your offer," she told him. "But surely I can't depend on you to take me there for every lesson. Or to pay for the wagon."

"Why, it would only be once or twice a week, my dear. And we could include the extraneous expenses of time and travel in your fee. I have no doubt she'll pay whatever price you ask."

How hard could it be to teach two girls to play violin? Angela smiled—maybe these girls would be her first students. How long would it take—and how many students—before she saved enough money to rent a room somewhere? And could she truly trust that when her violin was finally ready, she could safely return home? Just the thought of facing her papá and seeing her injured mamá twisted her stomach into a knot.

"I'd offer you the use of my wagon," the doctor told George, "but you never know when an emergency might call me out of town."

"Of course, of course, dear Joseph. You mustn't think of it," George said.

"I have an appointment in"—the doctor pulled a watch dangling from a chain attached to his trouser pocket—"ten minutes. So I'll bid you two a good day."

"Of course," George said, then as an afterthought asked, "How's that cowboy of yours? Has his leg healed? We met him the other day."

Angela's breath hitched as she waited for his response.

"Oh," the doctor said, turning to hurry off, "he's left. Got a job breaking horses. He's quite amazing to watch. Good day, George, Miss Bellini."

"Good day," George said, watching the doctor go in through a door halfway down the block.

Left? Angela felt as if she'd been kicked in the ribs. *Just like that?* No wondered why she hadn't seen any sign of him these last couple of days. Her throat constricted as she pictured Brett riding a horse across the open range, the glistening mountain peaks in the distance, the lonely sounds of night owls hooting. She knew he'd return to the life he loved and the freedom that called him, but she hadn't expected it so soon. Surely it took longer than a week to recover from a bullet wound, didn't it?

Well, no matter, she told herself. He was bound to leave, whether sooner or later. And, why should you care? He was probably just toying with you all along.

His departure would only expedite her recovery from this strangling malaise she was feeling because of him. Maybe now that he was gone from her life, she could forget him—once and for all—and focus on her music. Even if thoughts of him had somehow inspired her playing, she would find a way to perform just as passionately without him as her muse. For she knew that even when men and love and dreams failed her, her music never would.

However, this assurance did nothing to smother the persistent ache in her heart.

Chapter 17

BY THE TIME LEROY AND his ma drove the bunch of horses onto Foster's ranch, a half-dozen hands had come out to the front of the big fancy house to watch their arrival. The neighs of Foster's horses back in the pastures were answered with enthusiasm by the dusty and tired bunch he and his ma directed toward the corral.

Behind them, Gennie rode in the wagon, and the mules huffed and snuffled as she pulled them to a stop on the gray slate driveway fronting the ranch house. He knew she'd be right cared for — offered some elaborate lunch and a pitcher of sweet tea by Foster's talkative wife.

LeRoy chuckled as he slid down from No'kest'a's saddle alongside his ma and slipped the reins over the animal's head. He wondered what Gennie would make of the rancher's wife and hoped she didn't retreat like a turtle inside its shell. The woman had a tendency to talk a body's ear off, given half a chance. And LeRoy reckoned Gennie would give her that chance, polite and shy as she was around strangers. He didn't know whether she'd ever lose that fear. Hard to think she'd stayed that shy what with being around his ma so much every day.

LeRoy took a look-see around him. The ten geldings they'd brought were handily encouraged into the corral alongside the hay barn, where they were presently being rubbed down and watered. LeRoy smiled thinking about the new adventure awaiting the horses. They'd have a whole new bunch of brothers to meet, and LeRoy knew Foster would ensure their fair and kindly treatment.

How they'd do out on the range driving cattle would be anyone's guess. You never knew which horse would take to the task and which wouldn't. But he and his ma had broken and trained this bunch so they'd be fine cutting horses. He glanced over at Renegade, who tried to take a nip out of his ma's backside when she loosened the lead rope. He sniggered. *That one might be another story.*

She gave the horse her meanest eye and said, "You want to be meat for some wolf? Jus' keep that up." Renegade promptly dropped his head and studied the ground as if he'd all of a sudden found a hill of ants highly entertaining.

LeRoy chuckled again, noticing his ma had tied Ehase'o—the brood mare—to a nearby fence post. He understood why she'd not wanted the mare in the pen with all the other geldings. But he still had no clue why she'd brought the horse in the first place. She'd raved about that mare for weeks, saying what a calm and steady spirit she had. Just what was his ma up to?

After she unsaddled O'asé, she eased him into the corral to join the other horses. Then she turned and cast her eyes around the ranch, clearly looking for something.

LeRoy went over to her, brushing dirt off his trousers. A few hands were working in the hay barn, loading up a wagon. Then LeRoy saw Logan Foster come around the back of the house toward them, a big grin on his face. The rancher came over and nodded hello, sticking his thumbs under that big shiny silver buckle of his.

"Sarah, that's a fine-lookin' bunch y'all brought over. I never have to worry none about any of the horses I buy from y'all. I won't buy from any other."

LeRoy's ma smiled and pulled her hat off her head. Her silver-streaked black braids fell over her shoulders and shone in the afternoon sunlight.

"I'm pleased to sell these'ns to you," she told him. "Jus' one a bit ornery, but nothin' your cowboys can't handle. He'll be handy for roundin' up the drags. Good for him to eat a little dust now and then."

Foster laughed along with her. Then his gaze caught on the little brood mare tied to the fence. His smiled turned curious. "What do we have here?" He walked over to Ehase'o and looked her up and down. "That's some fine pinto mare ya got there—mighty fine conformation. What's her name?"

"Ho'ehase'o'o," she said. "Cheyenne for Fire Starter."

LeRoy noticed how his ma wasn't paying the fella any mind. Her gaze kept sweeping the ranch with narrowed eyes and bunched-up brows.

"Well, I'll be pleased to have her. I've got one particular stallion I've a mind to breed her to—"

LeRoy's ma turned suddenly and stared at Foster. The man cocked his head and smoothed out his thick silvery mustache as he stared back.

"What?" he asked.

"That mare's not for you," she said, plain as day.

LeRoy scratched his chin and pushed his hair back over his ears. *Then why'd she bring the mare along? For exercise?* It made no sense. But, much of what his ma did and said made little sense at first. Later was another story.

Although Foster flinched at Ma's rebuke, the rancher knew LeRoy's ma well enough to know when it was time to stop asking questions and just wait. Folks did an awful lot of waiting around her.

"That one," she said, finally, pointing to a cowboy closing a gate to one of the far pastures. A horse nickered at him as he set the latch, and the fella stroked the animal's head. He seemed ordinary enough, LeRoy thought, not recognizing him and guessing he was new to Foster's outfit.

"The cowboy yonder?" Foster asked, his face scrunched in puzzlement. "He jes joined up yesterday." LeRoy watched as the cowboy strode over to the corral and climbed up on the railing to look at the horses they'd brought that were lazing in the warm sun.

His ma nodded. "I want him to have Ehase'o."

Foster's eyes widened, and he opened his mouth to speak, then promptly shut it. Without another word, LeRoy's ma made a beeline for the cowboy.

"Why she wanna give that buster a horse—and such a fine one at that? She know the fella?"

"I don't reckon she does," LeRoy said, surely as befuddled as the rancher. "But there's no explainin' her ways."

Foster nodded. "Your ma's highly regarded around here. Hands down, y'all have the best horse ranch in all of Colorado and further parts." He turned thoughtful and lowered his voice. "When Dunnigan and Woodson and them were killed, I know a lot of ranchers got in a huff, and there was a lot of talk—some pretty nasty." He shook his head. "Still a lot of hatred t'ward the Red Man. But I knew y'all must've had your reasons. Then when the sheriff explained how they'd ambushed ya at your ranch and set your horse barn afire . . ." His words dropped off, and he stared at the cowboy on the fence. "I'm jes glad y'all weren't hurt—your horses neither. I didn't know Dunnigan well, but I'd heard things. You can't help hearin', what with punchers moving from ranch to ranch. It was despicable the way they was tryin' to force y'all off your ranch. Your ma's a strong woman, and you should be proud o' her."

"I am," LeRoy said, reflecting back on that night and how Lucas had ridden all that way in the middle of a blizzard to warn them and help stop those scalawags. LeRoy had never killed a man afore that night, and it'd sure rattled him—Eli too. But there was nothing for it—'twas either kill or be killed.

He shook off the jittery feeling the memories gave him and turned to watch his ma. She stood beside the corral fence and tapped the cowboy on his shoulder. Logan Foster just shook his head again—LeRoy could tell he was more than a mite displeased that the mare wasn't going to be his—and walked over to the barn.

Brett spun around at the touch on his shoulder and found himself face-to-face with an old Injun woman. Cheyenne, from what he could tell by her features. She gave him a toothy smile and introduced herself as Sarah Banks.

So this is the woman Foster was talkin' 'bout—the one Doc Tuttle said would wanna hire me. Bet these are horses from her ranch.

"Name's Brett Hendricks," he told her when she asked. He'd been around plenty of Cheyenne over the years. She had the look of a medicine woman, with that pouch noticeable around her neck, and he wondered why she'd stayed on the Front Range when all her people had been moved to Oklahoma. Injuns like her were now few and far between, and they still faced a lot of hatred and mistrust. But Brett commiserated, knowing what it was like to lose your home and family. At least to some measure.

"C'n I help you with somethin'?" he asked when she didn't say anything. She looked long and hard at him, and he politely waited for her to speak. The Cheyenne he'd known had taken their time to fashion their thoughts into words, something Brett respected. Too many a fool let their mouth run off without their head and got into a world of hurt and trouble for it.

She suddenly smiled at him and nodded. "I want to give you somethin', Brett."

Brett frowned as she turned and walked over to a pinto mare that was maybe four or five leaning half asleep against the fence.

"This is Ho'ehase'o'o. Her name means Fire Starter." She grunted. "But now I see I need to change her name."

Brett frowned deeper. "I . . . don't understand. Uh, what does this mare's name have to do with me?"

Brett startled when the woman put her hands on his shoulders and stared hard into his eyes. She searched in there, like looking for something lost. He caught a strong whiff of sage brush and creosote and something spicy like cinnamon. A shiver passed over his neck, and a pain started up in his chest, as if his heart was being squeezed by a strong fist.

"Wha-what are ya doin'?" he asked, a strange sinking feeling growing in his gut.

She broke off her gaze and looked to the north. Then she turned and patted the mare's neck. "He'kotóo'moehá." She nodded, and the mare tossed her mane and snorted. Sarah laughed. Brett coulda sworn that horse knew what the word meant.

"You can call her Kotoo." She gave him another mysterious smile. Why was she saying all this? "Calm water. Calm in the midst of fire." She nodded, making a kind of grunting sound of approval. "She will teach you how to go through the fire. And come through without gettin' burned."

"I don't under —"

"I want ya to have her, Brett Hendricks."

Brett whistled and shook his head. "I . . . I couldn't, ma'am. She's a fine mare — that's clear to see. But I —"

"You lost your horse." She said the words so matter-of-factly, they stabbed like a knife in his gut.

He drew in a shaky breath. "Yes'm," he said, barely getting the word out. The world around him grew fuzzy, and the sounds of the ranch activities were muffled, the way a ground fog snuffed out the cows' scuffling and lowing on the open range. He pictured Dakota lying in the dust, squealing and kicking. He squinched his eyes shut, trying to push away the pain and guilt and shame of it. Tears pushed at the lids of his eyes, and he swallowed them down.

"Sometimes we have to pay a high price when we do the right thing."

He forced his eyes open, as if she'd commanded him to look at her. He saw no condemnation in her gaze though — only compassion. Oddly, it sent a rush of relief through his limbs. *What right thing?* He guessed she was talking 'bout the way he'd tried to defend that Mexican girl, but how would she know that?

"Not too many stand up. No, not many at all." Her eyes flashed with sadness. Brett rubbed his forehead, feeling a headache coming on behind his eyes.

"So," she said abruptly, untying the mare's rope from the fence rail. She handed him the end of the lead. "I want you to have this horse."

There was no arguing about it, Brett knew. He could barely speak — his throat was raw with emotion. All the anguish and guilt he'd felt in that moment, when he'd watched Dakota thrash on the ground, gushed like an open wound. And then, to his shock, it vanished in one blink of his eyes.

He looked at the mare's face and saw the wildness deep inside her. Yet, he also saw something he knew all too well—trust. He hadn't personally broken her—clearly this Cheyenne woman had— but the pinto looked to him the way a hundred or more horses had done. And when he laid his hand on the horse's forehead, the animal closed her eyes with the contended look that only a horse could convey. A look that made Brett's heart swell with affection. He had a sudden urge to gallop her across the range.

Sarah Banks nodded. "When the fire rages, look for the calm water. You will hear the song." She added in a solemn tone, "Follow the song. It will lead you out."

Brett looked at her, confused, her face as undisturbed as a lake covered by morning fog.

"When a fire races across the prairie, it burns the grass to stubble. It is not a bad thing. From the ashes, new grass sprouts. New life begins. It must be."

Brett suddenly saw in his mind his pa slapping his ma and knocking her across the kitchen. He heard the thwack of her head hitting the wall and winced. But at that juncture, instead of his ma's face, he saw Angela's. She glared at him in shock and horror. The sight of blood trickling down her forehead sent a fierce wave of panic through his heart. His body shook, from head to toe.

"The song is the path through the fire, the way to peace." Sarah's words sounded far away, underwater, muted and faint. He then heard a ripple of music, a thin strand—as thin as a hair on his head—and an ache swelled inside his chest. It was a high keening note of a fiddle bowing a string. Or was it the voice of a woman singing? It made the panic erupt inside him—just like that day he lay in Tuttle's little room and heard that music coming in through the window.

Angela . . . Her face filled his mind, and he thought his head would explode from the pressure.

Then he felt Sarah's hand light on his wrist. The anguish and pressure and emotion blew away like a leaf in a mighty wind.

"Why don't you take Kotoo for a ride?" Sarah said softly, smiling as if she hadn't a care in the world.

Brett couldn't think of a thing to say. His tongue was stuck to the roof of his mouth. He nodded, thinking how he had about a half hour before the dinner bell rang. But a horse! His own horse. He couldn't fathom it. He'd have plenty of horses to ride here on Foster's ranch, but he never thought he'd own another horse—not for a long spell. Not after what happened to Dakota. He didn't understand why this Injun woman wanted to give him the mare, but clearly she wouldn't take no for an answer.

He managed to get a thank-you out of his mouth, her words swirling in his head. "When the fire rages, look for the calm water. You will hear the song. The song is the path through the fire, the way to peace."

He didn't have a clue what Sarah Banks meant by all that talk of fire and song and calm water. But somehow he knew they were important to stick in his mind. He didn't dare dismiss the words of a Cheyenne medicine woman.

He felt her eyes smiling at him as he led Kotoo to the barn to saddle her up. He had no doubt that Dakota's saddle would fit the mare just fine.

Chapter 18

ANGELA LOOKED AROUND AT THE beautifully appointed foyer of the Fosters' ranch home. Her reflection gleamed back up at her from the polished marble floor that stretched out into a spacious living room filled with elegant furnishings — upholstered sofas and chairs of exquisite imported damask fabrics, cut-glass oil lamps, thick Oriental rugs, and vases overflowing with flowers of every color, including gigantic purple and yellow peonies alongside blood-red and white roses. Not a speck of dust lined the floors or surfaces of furniture, and Angela imagined Mrs. Adeline Foster kept a staff of servants polishing the silver and dusting with lemon beeswax for many hours each day. With all the dust flying around the ranch from the many animals and cowboys working outside, it seemed an impossible task.

Her aunt's apartment displayed the luxury and wealth Angela noted here, but on a much smaller scale. Angela imagined the Fosters' home had at least six bedrooms and boasted indoor piping and heated water. How wonderful to live in such comfort, but the sheer size and opulence adorning every corner intimidated her. Every piece of artwork and table runner and sofa coverlet seemed painstakingly designed to coordinate in pattern and color. She felt as if she were looking at a photograph in *Harper's Bazaar* or *Vanity Fair.*

George stood admiring a painting of snow-dusted mountains that hung on a foyer wall, his hands clasped behind his back as he rocked on his feet, the soft light of dusk creating a halo around him. He'd dressed in a fine suit—perhaps the first he'd worn since his wife had died—and he nervously raked his hand through his thick dark hair. The Mexican maid that had shown them in could be heard upstairs speaking in quiet tones that were answered by a woman's boisterous and confident voice. The heat of the day—which had made Angela feel grimy and disheveled during their hour-long ride in the wagon—waned to a comfortable warmth interspersed with hints of a cool breeze. Angela loved the way the hot days gave way to chilly nights in this high altitude, making it so easy to sleep. Her hot and stuffy New York apartment was an oven all summer long, without reprieve until late fall.

Presently, someone came traipsing down the wide polished mahogany staircase, layers of stiff petticoats rustling and ringlets of golden hair bouncing along the sides of a cheery face of a plump woman of about thirty years. She waved her arms excitedly, her eyes lit with excitement, as she hurried down to meet her guests. No doubt this was Adeline Foster. George had succinctly described her, having engaged her in conversation at numerous past opera events.

Angela had worried that they'd be interrupting the Fosters' dinner upon their late arrival, as the aroma of freshly baked bread and stewed meat and vegetables wafted through the house from some unseen kitchen. But it appeared to Angela that the rancher's wife had just dressed for the evening meal, as the dark-blue satin gown she wore—not to mention the elbow-length white gloves—could hardly be attire she'd spent the day in. The style of dress would befit a woman of high society in New York, though Angela wondered why a rancher's wife in the wilds of Colorado would bother to dress in such fashion. Did Adeline Foster wish for a citified life rather than this dust-choked one? How would such a woman find joy living so far away from town, with no neighbors for dozens of miles?

"Ah, Mr. Fisk!" Adeline announced in a lilting Southern accent, her smile genuine and welcoming. "So wonderful to see you again. And such a prompt response to the request I sent by way of our good doctor Tuttle."

She held out her hand to him, and he pressed his lips to it with a bow of his head. "How could I delay with such a summons, my dear?"

Adeline's face flushed even pinker—if that were possible. Angela felt an immediate affinity for this gregarious woman who reminded her in some small way of her zia Sofia with her piquancy and enthusiasm. Joy exuded from this woman—something so lacking in Angela's home life. Rarely had she seen her mamá ever smile with such abandon, such lack of care.

The thought of her mamá lying in a hospital bed sank Angela's spirits as quickly as a heavy stone sinking to the bottom of a dark well.

"And whom do we have here?" Adeline said, taking Angela's hands in her own. The rancher's wife gave a few little squeezes, much the way Angela would her younger sisters' hands. Angela's face heated like an iron as Adeline studied her from head to toe.

George gestured with his hand to the rancher's wife. "May I introduce Angela Bellini, who has recently come to Colorado by way of New York? Angela, this is Mrs. Adeline Foster."

Adeline gave her head a slow shake with widened eyes. "My, what a beauty you are—exquisite European stock. And that skin—

ah! How I envy your olive complexion. I can hardly stand outside in the sunlight for more than a minute before my skin begins to burn and my freckles pop out across my nose!" She looked down at the hands she was still squeezing.

"And unmarried! How is that possible? My . . . I do declare, you must be twenty years at least. Why has no man yet snagged your heart, Angela?"

Taken aback by such forwardness, Angela tripped over her words in an effort to reply. But before she could untangle the words, Adeline said, "Well, I imagine you have high standards, and, of course, one *must* if one is to go far in life. No doubt you've had many suitors, but none has yet won your heart. Is that right?"

Angela, feeling a bit overwhelmed by Adeline's probing of her romantic life, could only nod, keenly aware of George's nervous but silent fidgeting at her side.

The rancher's wife tipped back her head and laughed merrily. "Well, Angela Bellini, one must never compromise." She leaned in close as if about to share a secret, and her lilac perfume wafted over Angela's face. "Somewhere out there"—she turned her head and looked upward as if searching the heavens with a wistful look of longing—"is your true love, waiting with open arms. And when you find each other . . ."

Angela waited while Adeline kept gazing aloft, perhaps imagining Angela's perfect beau floating on a passing cloud. She abruptly turned and questioned Angela with her eyes. "You do want to marry, don't you?"

"I . . . I suppose . . ." Her thoughts filled suddenly with Brett's teasing smile and broad, strong shoulders rippling under his shirt. Heat collared her neck and seeped up into her cheeks.

"Oh . . ." Adeline said with a knowing grin. "There *is* someone tugging at your heartstrings."

Angela looked at the floor, awash with embarrassment.

Adeline laid a hand on Angela's arm. "Well, Mr. Fisk," she said, turning to the instrument maker, "is this darling girl one of your students?"

"On the contrary," George replied, giving Angela what looked like an apologetic smile, no doubt due the personal inquiries of the rancher's wife. She had to repress a smile. No wonder George and his doctor friend felt a bit unhinged around a woman like Adeline Foster. Both were presently unmarried, and Angela held little doubt that Adeline Foster was the consummate matchmaker.

George continued. "Angela is a superb violinist, and she traveled halfway across the continent—from New York City—to purchase one of my violins."

Adeline threw her hands up in surprise. "My word—you traveled all this way from New York, alone, just to acquire one of Mr. Fisk's violins? How . . . daring of you!" Her corpulent body shivered with feigned fear. "You must truly love to play."

"I do," Angela said in all sincerity, suddenly longing to bow the delightful violin George had lent her in the interim.

"Then, you must play—for us all, after dinner. Of course, you will join us at the table, will you not? My girls will be thrilled." She cocked her head at George with pursed lips. "Have you brought Miss Bellini here to teach my girls to play?" Her head swiveled back to Angela. "How long do you plan to stay in Colorado, darling Angela?"

Angela looked to George, the woman's questions befuddling her.

George cleared his throat. "I'm finishing a violin for her. It will take some weeks. In the meantime, Angela is hoping to teach violin lessons—"

Adeline clapped her hands in delight. "You'll be perfect for my girls," she said, giving Angela a wink. The tinkle of a high-pitched brass bell sounded from down the hallway. "Ah, it's almost time for dinner. Let me show you where you can freshen up. You will dine with us, of course. And after dinner, Logan and the girls and I would be honored to have you both perform some pieces for us. Oh—you did bring your instruments with you?" When George nodded, she added in a quiet conspiratorial voice, "I can't tell you how excited I am to hear more about your passion for playing music, Angela. I do hope you'll consider staying in Greeley and sharing your talents with our fine community. We so very much need musicians of high caliber to not only perform works of the masters but to teach our young ones professional technique and repertoire."

"We'd be honored to join you and your family for dinner, Mrs. Foster," George said. "And we have some duets we'd be happy to play for you."

Adeline rolled her eyes. "Please, Mr. Fisk. Just call me Adeline. There is no need for such formalities between us." She linked her arm with Angela's. "Ah, I'm so thrilled you've come. You'll love Madeline and Clementine. They don't like to practice their violins, but I'm sure once they hear you play . . ."

While Adeline chattered on about her girls, leading her guests up the wide staircase in the exquisite ranch house, strains of Schubert's lullabies tickled Angela's mind. The violin sitting in the case in the foyer called to her, and the longing to play it made her fingers move over imagined strings. While Adeline's effervescent personality overwhelmed her, she felt oddly comfortable here in this ranch house—a place as different as could be from the life she'd left behind in New York.

Adeline's urging her to stay in Greeley sparked doubts in Angela's mind. In the brief time she'd been in Colorado, the stark beauty of the high desert and open plains—with the stunning array of stars that blanketed the night sky—called to her heart and inspired her playing. From the sparkling snow-packed peaks of the majestic Rockies to the miles and miles of golden wheat fields they'd passed on their drive over to the ranch, Angela found the expansive and unmarred landscape soothing to her troubled soul. As much as she longed to return to New York—she so missed her mamá and aunt and siblings—she hated the thought of leaving behind such a wild, untamed place that stirred her passion for playing violin more than any other. She feared that, upon her return, her inspiration to play would shrivel—or dry up like a shallow pond under a hot summer sun. She also feared that the guilt and worry and fear of her papá's wrath would suck away every last vestige of musicality she coveted so tenaciously here in the West.

Yet, how could she stay in a place like Greeley? A tiny town with few residents, and a small opera house and community orchestra? How could her aspirations to perform magnificent music on a stage before hundreds of appreciative listeners ever be satisfied? *But you don't know if any symphony will hire you. Maybe your dreams are too big, too unreasonable.* She swallowed back the rising fear and frustration. *But I have to try. If I give up now, I'll regret it.*

For the first time since she'd heard Miss Pappenheim play all those years ago, Angela was riddled with doubt. Maybe it wasn't the big stage in a crowded city that was calling to her. Maybe it was the big open sky of the unspoiled, uncrowded West that tugged at her heart. What mattered most? Playing on stage for accolades or playing under the heavens with a heart full of gratitude for the gift of music? What if the reason she had so longed to play for the philharmonic came from her need for approval—for the praise and love and adoration she'd never gotten from the one person she needed it from—her papá?

The thought shook her to her core. She knew in that moment, as Adeline stopped in front of a door at the top of the second-story landing, that, up until now, her aching need for approval was what had driven her to play. Only when she played for George, on his beautiful instruments—away from the pressures and problems of home—had music flowed unfettered from her heart. If she wanted to be the caliber of musician she longed to be, she couldn't allow guilt or hurt or fear to contaminate the wellspring of her inspiration. But how could she ever purge those feelings from her soul? Was it even possible? If so, how?

"Here we are, darling. You'll find everything you need to freshen up," Adeline said, gesturing Angela into a boudoir that featured a claw-foot tub with copper pipes coming from the wall and a dressing table displaying brushes and combs and pins for her hair. Thick white towels sat folded on a side table in the prettily wallpapered room. "All the hot water you desire—just with a turn of a knob." Adeline gave Angela a big smile. "Listen for the dinner bell in a half hour, then come downstairs when you're ready."

Before Angela had a chance to thank Adeline, the rancher's wife had already taken George by the arm and was leading him down the hall, speaking quietly to him in a patter of words that sounded like a susurrant melody to her ears. Maybe soaking in a hot bath would dissolve the thoughts troubling her heart.

Hoot owls called one to the other as Brett walked Kotoo through a patch of squishy marsh weeds not far from the bank of the river. A full moon sat on the edge of the world, fat and blotchy, lifting into the night like a heavy balloon. The searing September heat of the day slipped into the cool sheath of evening, and a light wind tickled at his ears. Ever since that Cheyenne woman gave him the mare yesterday afternoon, he'd felt wobbly—like his saddle was loose. But it was more than that. He couldn't get shed of that picture of Angela, with her head trickling blood, out of his thoughts.

You didn't hit her, he kept telling himself. But maybe the vision he'd seen meant that he would. That the rage and temper he tried to keep in check would detonate—just as he feared.

He told himself for the millionth time that this was why he had to forge ahead in life alone, not let his heart get pulled into loving a gal—any gal. But the force of that current, that need, was surely strong and abiding. He'd have to fight that current, like a salmon thrashing upstream, against the powerful forces of nature—to make it. The prospect of a loveless life was sorely unbearable, but he'd just have to buck up. He could no sooner get the wild out of his soul than he could get the wild out of this mare he was riding. It was a fact of nature.

He sighed and patted the mare's shoulder and ruffled her mane. She tossed her head and picked up her pace, seeming wholly content with the world and her lot in life. If only he could feel such contentment. The soft throb of his shot leg reminded him of the constant ache in his chest—an ache that never let up, never gave him a minute's peace. Shame was like a piece of lead lodged in his rib. He couldn't pry it out without killing himself—and in dark moments he'd considered that as the only way to lift the burden that often sought to crush him. The only thing that helped was burying himself in his work. Riding and busting twelve hours a day, thinking on the tasks at hand and locking the door to his memories. But at the end of the day, as he lay on his bed in the bunkhouse or slept on the range under the stars, that door creaked open, and those memories and bad feelings came gushing out willy-nilly.

Yet, when he rode Kotoo—gave her her head with a loose rein to run at will—he felt a strange calm come over him. Like a warm, soothing poultice spread over a wound. Is that what the Cheyenne woman meant when she gave the horse a new name? *Calm water in the midst of fire.* That's just what Kotoo felt like underneath him, as they raced across the prairie.

He'd had many horses in his life, and Dakota had been the best. But none had ever given Brett such a sense of calm. The constant nudge of restlessness and anger seemed to get chewed up over the miles they rode, and the feeling was so much a relief, he'd taken her out again last night, long after the other cowboys had dropped off to sleep. And then again before dawn, an hour before the breakfast bell sounded. Too bad he couldn't take her out on the range, during the roundup—only geldings were ridden then. He'd already gotten so attached to her, he knew he was gonna miss her during those weeks. He grunted, wondering why that Injun had given him this horse. No one had ever given him a gift like this, and it perplexed him.

As they turned onto hard-packed ground, Brett caught sight of the ranch house, all lit up with warm yellow lights from the oil lamps lit in the rooms. He caught glimpses of movement in the upper windows and shimmers of cloth as the curtains riffled in the breeze like ripples in a stream. It was a cheery sight that reminded him painfully of how much he wished he'd had a real family and a home.

He didn't care about wealth such as what Logan Foster enjoyed. But he saw the way the rancher adored his missus and girls. He'd watched those two young'uns throw their arms around their pa and hug the daylights out of him before jumping up into the wagon to head to town with their ma. There was no missing the true affection between Foster and his missus when he pecked her cheek and sent her on her way, waving until the wagon turned down the drive and out of sight. Brett had stood transfixed, envy coursing through his veins, wondering for all the world why he'd been stuck with such a viper for a pa. If only his ma had met someone else along the way. Someone kinder, gentler. Instead of a rogue and a scalawag like Jed Hendricks. She'd deserved better. *If only I'd done the right thing. I shoulda killed him. I had plenty of chances.* But he'd been a coward, and he'd walked away. *And sealed her fate.*

He reined Kotoo to a stop a dozen or so yards in back of the house and listened to the night, trying to cool his spurs. A few cows lowing in the pens. A horse nickering in the pasture. A tickle of laughter and conversation drifted past his ears, so quiet it sounded like the murmur of water over rocks. The guilt that had welled up unbidden seeped out into the night, the way thirsty ground soaked up rain.

He lingered in the peacefulness cast by the moon, again keenly aware of the quiet inside him—a quiet so foreign to him, he didn't know what to make of it. Did the horse put some kind of spell on him? He knew when he let her loose in the pasture, those old uneasy feelings would wash back in and engulf him again. He couldn't rightly stay on her back all the time. But somehow he had to find a way to get that feeling of calm to stick around. Nothing else worked—not drinking, not women, not even wrangling till he dropped from exhaustion.

His ears perked up at a new sound puncturing the quiet. Someone in the big house was playing a fiddle. His breath hitched as he strained to listen, remembering the silky, smooth notes he'd heard that night when he stood against Tuttle's house and watched Angela play, the moonlike gleaming in her hair and lighting up her face that looked like an angel's.

He breathed deeply, drawing in the music that set his bones trembling. Who was playing so beautifully? Was it Miz Foster? It couldn't be. No one could play like that—except maybe that violin maker. Maybe Fisk was visiting. Seemed everyone in that tiny town knew everyone else. Had he been called out to Foster's ranch to play for the family? Brett had known ranchers that hired musicians to come play at shindigs and for special events.

He closed his eyes, sitting still on Kotoo, and let his mind run wild. He thought on Angela's beautiful brown eyes and her full lips and the way she smiled. A fierce longing seized him again—just at the thought of kissing those lips. Every inch of his body erupted in need, and he wanted nothing more in that moment than to pull her into his arms and smother her with kisses. Somehow he knew if he held her like that, he'd never feel the same again. Could it be possible that a gal like that could snuff out that anger raging inside him? Why couldn't she be the one to quench that fire Sarah Banks had talked about? *"Follow the song—it will lead you out."*

He shook the thoughts from his head, like flinging water. What song? It made no sense. A song couldn't lead anyone out of a fire. And surely not away from the kind of hellfire raging inside his soul.

Besides, you fool, the gal's off to New York. Get over her.

He listened awhile longer, mesmerized by the lively tune being fiddled. He clicked his teeth at Kotoo, and the horse walked ahead. Brett stopped only yards from the house, under the branches of a wide-spreading willow, staying in the shadows in case someone had a mind to look out the window. From there he could make out the rancher and his wife sitting in big padded chairs. And the two girls sat at their feet. They were all looking in the same direction, listening to whoever was playing that fiddle.

Then he heard two fiddles. Their notes bounced off the other's like bullets ricocheting off rocks. He'd never heard the like. Sure, he'd listened to some fast fiddling, but this was different. Instead of a ragged, rough kind of fiddling, this was like honey—every note sweet and smooth. Then, the fiddling stopped, and when it started up again, Brett sucked in a breath.

The silhouette of a woman moved into view, pulling the bow across the strings.

Angela! There was no mistaking her shape or her music. The strains of the fiddle soared into the night sky like tiny birds glinting with moonlight. He stiffened as the notes pricked him almost painfully. He fixed his eyes on her, both astonished and confused. What was she doing here, at Foster's ranch? And just when he began to doubt it was her, she turned toward the window, and he could see her eyes were closed as she lost herself in her playing.

He could barely make out her features, but it was enough to set his heart pounding. The thought of her so close yet so out of reach made the ache in his chest feel like a rock lodged in a crevice. He had to talk to her—one last time before she left. He didn't know why—it wouldn't do any good. But here she was, like he'd been given another chance.

Fool! What do you plan to do? Knock on the front door and invite yourself in? Wait until she's getting into the wagon to go back to town and scare the living daylights out of her?

He couldn't figure why he was so smitten by her. And then he realized—her music made him feel just the way riding Kotoo made him feel. But was it her music *or was it her?*

Don't matter. She's up there, and you're down here. She's a refined gal from the city, and you're just a restless, homeless cowboy. More than ever, his dream of owning his own horse ranch seemed impossible—a foolish dream to cling to.

He sat his horse, listening until the music stopped and the last notes floated away, leaving him empty and feeling more alone than ever. He heard talking and laughter as if he gazed across a chasm that he could never cross. He considered taking Kotoo out for another ride, but the mare was nearly asleep on her feet.

With a heavy heart, he led the horse out from under the tree and headed over to the barn to unsaddle Kotoo and brush her down. The thought of slipping into the smelly bunkhouse with a dozen snoring cowboys at his elbows soured his mood even further.

He glanced back at the window, but the lamps had been snuffed out, and the room was dark. He felt his momentary joy at seeing Angela snuff out as well. She was so close, but she might as well have been on the moon for all he could do about it.

Chapter 19

"ANGELA, DARLING. ARE YOU STILL in there?"

Angela sniffled and wiped her eyes with the sleeve of her blouse as she sat on the ladder-back chair in front of the dressing table. Adeline Foster pushed open the door to the boudoir and peeked inside. The rancher's wife gasped as she studied Angela's face.

No doubt her eyes were red and puffy from the crying she'd done. She hadn't meant to fall apart, but somehow playing those pieces with George after dinner and seeing the Fosters listening so intently, their darling girls cuddled at their feet, made her homesick. More than homesick—the pain that crumpled her was from seeing the warmth and affection between the rancher and his wife as they sat on the divan, holding hands, Adeline leaning against her husband with such tenderness. And the way he mindlessly stroked her hair while listening to the music made Angela's anger toward her father boil—to the point that she had to stop playing and excuse herself.

Yes, she was feeling sorry for herself, and it was unbecoming. But life was so unfair. She couldn't recall a time—or even imagine one—when her papá had shown even a smidgeon of such affection for her mamá. Living in their tiny apartment in a climate of loathing and cruelty made it worse than a battlefield. Her heart ached for her Rosalia and little Maria, who had years still ahead of bearing up under their papá's hard hand. While a mother's love could make even the most horrible situation tolerable, since Angela had arrived in Greeley, it seemed everywhere she turned, she saw more and more how much she suffered from the lack of a father's love.

What would it have been like for her had she grown up with a father like George, who not only loved music but understood and respected her need to play? George was exactly the kind of father she wished she had—a gentle man with a humble heart. And here was Logan Foster, a busy man running one of the most successful cattle ranches in Colorado—yet he had time to attend to his wife and children, and showered them with affection, even indulging them to the point of excess.

Angela felt more tears coming on. Oh, why was she so emotional? She'd never had a problem barricading her feelings before coming to Greeley. Maybe it was because of her mamá's accident. She hated being so far away and not being there to sit by her bedside. She felt so useless, so helpless.

A great sob burst from her throat, and Angela buried her face in her hands. Adeline hurried to gather her up in her arms.

"There, there, darling," Adeline said, shushing her softly, much the way Mamá used to do when Angela was little and fell and scraped a knee or elbow. It had been so long since anyone had held her this way, and Adeline's strong, warm arms made Angela's tears fall anew. She hadn't realized how starved she was for human touch, for some comfort. She'd been holding so much inside, so much pain . . .

After she'd cried, soaking the shoulder of Adeline's beautiful blue satin dress, Angela sniffled and gladly accepted the handkerchief Adeline pulled from a hidden pocket. The rancher's wife smiled sweetly at her as she said, "Always carry one on me. You never know when a tear or two might fall when you have rambunctious girls living on a cattle ranch."

Angela mustered a smile, grateful for Adeline's kindness and surprising lack of prying. She'd expected the woman to drench her with a flood of questions, but she waited quietly, seemingly content to let the room grow silent. After a moment, Angela started to get up from the chair, but Adeline motioned her to stay.

"George is downstairs with Logan, enjoying cigars and brandy." She winked and added, "We should let them have their time together. I imagine George hasn't been out in company much since Lucy passed."

Angela looked at the rancher's wife with new eyes. Her face was full of compassion for a man Angela assumed Adeline hardly knew.

"Did you know Lucy Fisk?" Angela asked, the soreness in her throat easing.

Adeline reached for the silver-handled hairbrush and, to Angela's surprise, pulled the pins from Angela's head and let her long hair tumble down her shoulders. As she ran the brush through Angela's hair with long, gentle strokes, she said, "Oh yes. Lucy was on the opera board too. Such a brave woman. And how she suffered those many years with seizures and a weak constitution. But not a word of complaint." Adeline shook her head and clucked with her teeth. "Poor George. He looks completely lost without her. You can see it—in his eyes. So sad, so sad."

Adeline's eyes filled with tears, and then she abruptly laughed and said, "Soon we'll both be weeping, and then what will we say when the men come and find us in such a sorry state?"

She straightened up and set to work re-pinning Angela's hair. "Oh my, you have such beautiful hair. Do you ever curl it with a hot iron? It would look . . . ravishing."

Angela couldn't help but giggle, feeling the heaviness finally lifting from her chest. "I'm not sure I want to look ravishing."

Adeline grunted and waved her hand full of pins in the air. "Of course you do! Though, you hardly need to do a thing with your hair or your face. Your natural beauty glows, but more than that," she said, tucking and pinning more hair, "it's the beauty of the soul that shines the strongest. That's something a woman can't hide or fake, truth be told."

When she finished with Angela's hair, she went over to the wash basin and wet a laced-edged hand towel. "Here, let's wipe those tears away and go downstairs. We've peach cobbler for dessert. I do hope the girls left us some."

"Thank you," Angela said, feeling drained and exhausted.

Adeline studied her. "Where are you staying? With Mr. Fisk?"

Angela nodded. "In his small shop. Where he builds his violins."

Adeline threw her hands up again. "Oh heavens, that won't do. All those varnish fumes and dust. I don't imagine you would have a toilet inside?"

When Angela shook her head, Adeline make a whimper of protest. "Darling girl, we have rooms upon rooms that no one ever uses. While you're waiting for your violin, you must stay here, with us—"

"Oh, I couldn't," Angela began to say.

Adeline frowned, and her perfectly plucked brows knitted in disapproval. "I insist. And I know Logan will as well. Now, don't worry—you'll still be paid for teaching the girls to play the violin. But this way, they can have daily lessons. And you'll find that living on a ranch can do wonders for your constitution. George can bring round your things as soon as it's convenient. Or perhaps the next time one of the hands makes a trip to town, he can drop by George's house and fetch your belongings. In the meantime, I'm sure I can provide you with all you'll need in the way of clothing and womanly necessities."

Adeline wrapped an arm around Angela's shoulder and helped her to stand. Angela smiled at the change in the rancher's wife — back to her boisterous, talkative self. But she had to find a way to gracefully refuse. She didn't want to take advantage of this family's hospitality — or impose on them.

"I'm grateful for your offer, Mrs. Foster —"

"Oh puleeze, you must call me Adeline."

"Adeline, it's very kind of you, but —"

She put her hands on her wide, full hips. "I won't take no for an answer, Angela. I know you hardly know me, but when I put my foot down, there's no lifting it. Whatever your troubles, the last thing you need is to be alone with a sad widower. Yes, George could use the company. And I'm sure you've helped lift his spirits. But it's hardly proper for you to stay at his house for an extended time, don't you know. Small towns have big ears."

Adeline confirmed what Angela feared. She didn't want gossip that might hurt George. And she had no other place to go. Her money had been meant to feed and house her for a day or two — not a month or more. But she could hardly accept Adeline's offer of being paid when she would be living in their home and eating their food.

"Well, I'd have to do more than teach the girls violin lessons —"

"What about Italian?" Adeline asked, walking toward the door.

Angela stopped. "Italian what?"

"Why, the language. And cooking. You could teach the girls. I can tell that they already adore you. Would you be willing to do that during your stay?"

Angela smiled, thinking of how her little sisters helped her roll out dough and layer pasta in the big iron casserole pan. "I'd be pleased to teach them."

Adeline clapped her hands. "Well, that's settled, then. Oh, I'm so thrilled. If anyone can get those two to produce beautiful sounds from those violins, you can. The sooner the screeching starts sounding like music, the happier we all will be." She gave Angela a little wink.

Angela joined Adeline in a hearty laugh, excitement bubbling up at the thought of staying here with this wonderful family. She never imagined she'd live on a cattle ranch, surrounded by horses and cowboys, and though it would only be for a few weeks, it seemed a thrilling adventure—something to take her mind off her worries while she waited for George to finish her violin. *And I'll have plenty of time to play, with no one to complain.*

"Now, let's join the men and let them know of our plans. And then indulge in a dish of peach cobbler. After that, I'll show you to your room and get you settled in. Oh, the girls will be so happy to hear you're staying with us."

Adeline strode with renewed purpose out the door, and Angela followed, wondering just what a peach cobbler might be.

Chapter 20

"**S**EE, HOLD YER HAND STEADY—out here, like this."
Brett told hold of the kid's arm, standing at his shoulder, and straightened it so that the pistol lay in a line of direct sight from Archie's eye to the tin can on the fence. "Ya can't have your gun hand loose like a noodle, floppin' hither and yonder."

Archie heaved a sigh while narrowing his eyes and setting a bead on the target. "I know, Brett. Listen, ya know the safest thing around me is the thing I'm aimin' to shoot at."

Brett chuckled and released his hold on the kid. It was those bruises spattered on the kid's forehead from his Colt .45 six-shooter recoiling in his face that led Brett to take him aside for some mighty needed shooting practice.

"Well, like they say: 'practice makes . . . uh . . . better.' Suck in a breath and hold it. There ya go."

The powder exploded, and the ball whistled across the yard. Archie scowled and dropped his firing arm. "Dang it all. I missed by a mile. Agin."

Brett clapped him heartily on his back. "But ya didn't smack your face—that there's a fine improvement, don't ya think?"

Archie fumbled with swinging open the chamber and stuffing more bullets in from his pouch. "I reckon." He sounded downright despondent.

"Well, keep at it. Oh, and if ya see any horses come wanderin' through the pasture, hold off shootin' till they pass. I don't reckon the boss will take kindly to you killin' his animals."

Brett was joking, but Archie nodded solemnly. His face was clouded with trouble.

"Hey," Brett said. Archie stopped messing with the pistol and turned to Brett. "Those punchers botherin' you?" Ever since those two—Handy and Shore—played that dangerous prank on the kid with that heifer, Brett'd been keeping one eye on him. But what with all the busting Brett'd been busy with—he and that good fella Tate Roberts—he hadn't had time to pay Archie much mind. The kid was gonna have to learn fast to keep watch and stand up.

Archie shook his head, but there was no mistaking the worry in his eyes.

"Listen," Brett told him. "You gotta have the guts to stand the life of a cowboy. Like the boss said: 'Make good or make tracks.' You're young—and ripe pickin's for the likes of Handy and Shore. Just keep close to my flank—or Tate's. In a few days we'll be dumpin' our blankets and tricks at the chuck wagon, and you c'n make down with me and him. The punchers are gonna rough you up some, but most of it will be good humored. So don't get over-sensitive about it. A tenderfoot's always gonna be the brunt of jokes, so try to laugh good-naturedly about it. But keep an eye out for them two. I c'n tell they're nothin' but trouble. Every outfit's got one or two bad apples."

"Alright," Archie said, listening hard and nodding.

Brett took a look-see around him. A flock of songbirds dove into the giant willow beside them and erupted into song. Flies buzzed around their heads, and a jackrabbit rustled through the sage brush down by the riverbank. Brett relished the cool quiet of the morning—a welcome feeling after his restless, sleepless night. He wasn't a man immune to the beauties of nature, as some were. He liked nothing better than taking in the world around him, setting his gaze on the mountains that rose like a wall of jagged teeth in the west. The air was so clear this morning, he could almost see into next week.

The wide lazy creek shimmered in the morning light, and a few prairie dogs sat and barked on their haunches, looking like spinsters in church with their paws folded on their stomachs. Brett chuckled at the sight, then turned back to Archie.

"Kid, you gonna keep practicin'?"

"I reckon." He smirked. "I don't guess I'll have to run back and forth much to that fence yonder to set up more cans." He looked at the half dozen lying next to his feet. "I'll be lucky if'n I hit that can even once."

"You will," Brett assured him. "Listen, I gotta drop my twine on that brute called Renegade over in the pen yonder. That Cheyenne horse breeder told me he's got some kinks to iron out. You gonna be okay out here?"

Archie nodded, getting ready to aim at the tin can on the fence. Brett figured that can would probably still be sitting there if he came back in an hour, and Archie'd still be in a snit.

"Alright, then. I'll see ya back at the bunkhouse round lunchtime." He gave Archie a slap on the shoulder. "Keep that arm straight and stiff, now."

"Thanks, Brett," Archie said. "I really 'preciate the help."

Brett left the kid to his devices and headed over to the pasture below the hay barn. Roberts and the others were out on the range, rounding up some strays that'd been spotted to the north, so he was on his own today. He scooped up the rope he'd left hanging on the fence post and presently looped it around the dun horse's neck. The look in Renegade's wide eye told Brett he'd have a time of it, but he was glad for it.

Since the moment he'd seen Angela playing in that upstairs room in the ranch house, she'd been cutting a wide swath through his thoughts, and he needed the distraction. What were the odds she'd pay a visit to the ranch he was riding for? Would she come back? What if she'd changed her mind about New York and decided to stay in Colorado?

Whoa, there ya go again—gettin' up your hopes. You're headin' down a slippery trail.

She was like a pesky mosquito nipping at his ear in the dark of night, and the more he slapped her image away, the more she pestered him. Seemed the only thing that eased the throb of desire for her was getting in the pen with an ornery horse.

The antsy gelding pulled at the lead and pranced about as Brett led him to the fence, where he'd set out the bridle and saddle after breakfast on the top rail. He studied the dun—a powerful sixteen-hand beast with stocking legs—then let him loose. "Alright, mister—let's see what ya got."

Renegade broke apart and thrashed his forelegs in the air, but drifting through the noise of the horse's prancing, Brett heard something else. He craned his neck to see over the fence to the ranch house up the hill. He must've been imagining things. He coulda swore he heard the sweet sounds of that fiddle—the way Angela played it.

He chided himself with a huff and turned back to Renegade, who was doing fine working his kinks out all on his own, running around the pen and kicking up the dust enough to scare the Devil.

Two bright-faced girls poked their heads into the study, where Angela was working on polishing one of the Schubert lullabies. She lowered her instrument and noted the way they bounced up and down in excitement. They were garbed in matching green calico dresses and had on ankle-high button-up boots that had seen a lot of the outdoors.

"Mama says to ask if you'll take us berry picking," Clementine said in a voice that brooked no argument. She had her mother's blond curls and bright blue eyes—every bit her mother's daughter. Last evening, Clementine made it clear she was the "older sister," and it was evident that she took her role seriously. Madeline, not even a year younger, stood shyly behind her sibling, her brown eyes and hair showing more resemblance to her father. At eight and seven, they were a tad older than Rosalia but so much taller.

"Please say yes," Clementine pleaded. "If we bring enough home, Cook will make us berry tarts!"

"Yum," Angela said, putting the violin back in its case. "That sounds like a wonderful plan. Where do we need to go to find the berries?"

"Not far," Clementine assured her, taking her hand and yanking her toward the door.

"Wait, I need my bonnet." Angela went over to the dresser and fixed the hat on her head. She supposed she was dressed in a manner befitting blackberry picking. Adeline had lent her a soft cotton blue blouse to wear, and though it was a bit loose on her, she'd tucked it into her skirt's waistband. But her shoes wouldn't do. They were fine Italian leather slippers with embroidery and button closures, given to her by her aunt.

Madeline noticed her studying her shoes. "Those are pretty," she said. "I like the pearly buttons."

Angela smiled at the girl's sweet innocent face. She missed her sisters so much and wished they could be here to see this beautiful wide-open land. When would they ever have the chance to pick berries? Everything her family ate was purchased at the local grocers or butcher shop.

Sadness welled up once more at the thought of her sisters hiding in their beds at night with their hands over their ears, trying to drown out Papá's shouts. Now, more than ever, Angela dreaded the thought of returning home. If only she could steal away her sisters and bring them here. She frowned in frustration as she tucked a stray strand of hair under her bonnet.

Madeline tugged on Angela's skirt. "Mama has lots of mud boots. I bet something will fit your feet. Pretty shoes belong inside, not outside—Mama always says."

Angela took her hand and headed out the door. "Well, she's right. Same goes for pretty dresses."

Clementine huffed and tossed her curls, just like Adeline. "We know that. Why'd you think we wore these old things?"

Angela couldn't help but laugh at Clementine's expression. She was a perfect replica of her mother, only smaller and with a higher-pitched voice.

As they made their way down the staircase to the foyer, Angela said, "Don't forget—before dinner we're going to have a violin lesson."

As if on cue, both girls groaned. She wondered what kind of teacher Mrs. Green had been to make these girls so loathe playing their instruments. Perhaps they'd been forced to practice scales without having a bit of fun. But Angela knew how to remedy that.

True to Madeline's word, the room off the porch had plenty of worn, sturdy boots to choose from, and Angela found a pair that fit fine with thick stockings. A cool breeze greeted them as they headed out of the house and down the back porch, baskets in hand.

Gratitude welled up in Angela's heart for the Fosters—for inviting her stay in their home. And for George, for having treated her so kindly and graciously, in the midst of his own lingering grief. She thought about Violet and how nice it would be to get to know another woman near her age, realizing everyone she'd met thus far in Colorado had been genuinely friendly and helpful. Perhaps all that noise and crowding in the city set people on edge. In New York, everyone seemed to be in such a rush most of the time, finding few moments—and few quiet open spaces—in which to covet peace and solitude.

She didn't miss the noise, nor the way the women in Mulberry Bend were treated as if they had little worth. Most of the women she knew in her neighborhood worked their fingers to the bone to cook and clean for their husbands, who gave them little regard and even less respect. Italian wives were practically servants, answering to every whim of their husbands. She was so glad to have escaped marriage to Pietro. But how would she ever return? How could she be with Mamá but not face Papá? She would have to find some way.

Guilt weighted her steps as the girls led the way along a narrow pack-dirt path bordered by tall brown grass. She couldn't help but remind herself yet again that it was all her fault her mamá was in the hospital. If she hadn't left on the train . . .

Movement caught in the corner of her eye. She turned and looked over at the corral, and the girls halted in front of her.

"Hey," Clementine said, "that's the new buster. I heard Mama talking 'bout him yesterday."

"Buster?" Angela said.

Clementine made a face at her. "You don't know what a buster is?" She seemed altogether shocked at the thought.

Angela smiled and shook her head. "I'm from New York City, remember? We don't have 'busters' there." She added, "You have heard of New York, haven't you?"

Clementine rolled her eyes and flipped her curls with her hand. "Of course."

Madeline said in her soft voice, "Busters train the wild horses so they can be used out on the range. Every cowboy gets a string of them to ride." She spoke authoritatively and matter-of-factly, which made Angela grin. "Herding cattle is hard on horses, Papa says. That's why they have to change mounts all day long."

"Come on," Clementine said, "let's watch awhile, then pick our berries." She gave Angela a sly smile, and her eyes sparked with mischief. "I like to watch the busters get thrown off. It makes me laugh."

Madeline giggled too, but Angela imagined getting thrown wasn't all that much fun for the cowboy. Taming wild horses had to be hard, challenging work. She recalled the way Brett had described it—the way his eyes had shone with exhilaration when talking about breaking an outlaw horse. How could something that dangerous be thrilling? She wondered at this strange thing called "The Cowboy." The men she knew would never risk life and limb like that. Reckless and childish, she thought, to find danger enticing.

"Well, look at that!" Clementine pointed at the man inside the corral.

Angela froze, and her breath caught in her throat. *Brett?* She walked a few steps closer to the fence, looking between the poles. It was Brett! *What in heaven's name is he doing here?* Doctor Tuttle had said he'd gotten a job on a ranch. *But he hadn't said where, and you didn't ask.*

Angela felt flustered all over and told her heart to slow down as she watched Brett in the corral. He had his back partially turned to her and seemed unaware of the three gawkers at the fence. And he was sitting on a horse that was lying on its side, with its head pinned to the ground by Brett's hand.

Angela didn't dare breathe. The girls gaped at the sight, mouths dropped open. With those strong muscular arms, Brett held the horse down, but he didn't seem to be scared at all—though she couldn't imagine how he could be so calm and cheerful, perched on top of a snorting powerful beast like that.

Tufts of chestnut-brown hair strayed out from under his hat, and Angela's eyes riveted on the way his body moved with grace and confidence as he slipped off the horse and brought the animal to its feet. A chuckle came from his throat as he took the horse's rope and walked it around the pen. The big horse danced and pulled at the rope, but Brett lightly tugged on it and muttered words in its ears. Angela smiled at the way the horse's ears twitched as it listened, and she wondered just how much it understood what Brett was telling it.

Angela stepped back, hoping he wouldn't see her. What would he think? What would he do? She didn't want to startle him and make him lose his concentration and get injured.

The sight transfixed her. The rapport between man and animal was astonishing to see. Even from where she stood, the bond between them was evident—which reminded her of George's words. About how she had to bond with her instrument. She well knew now what he meant—how it felt to surrender to the music, to let herself go, let go of all restraint and judgment and allow the songs to emerge from the sound board as her fingers danced over the strings.

She saw this same thrill, this same abandonment, in Brett. There was no mistaking the deep joy in his eyes as he got to his feet and prodded the horse into a smooth run, paying out the rope attached to the bridle, his eyes locked on to the animal as he turned in slow circles, bringing the horse in closer and closer until it stopped mere inches from him. Face to face they stood. And as Brett looked deep into the horse's eyes, Angela's heart pounded hard in her chest. The morning stillness wrapped around her like a shawl, and she shivered as if something tickled her neck.

She couldn't take her eyes off him. He seemed utterly handsome standing there in his dust-coated canvas pants and cotton shirt that couldn't hide the lines of his taut muscles. And when he pushed the rimmed brown hat from his head and raked his fingers through his thick tousled hair, the muscles in his strong jaw twitched. His was a body hardened from hours of roping and riding. There was nothing soft about him; he was so unlike the men she'd known, who sat behind desks or store counters. Who hardly lifted more than a fork to their mouths. Angela couldn't help but imagine again those arms encircling her, gently brushing her hair from off her face, his fingers trailing down her neck and his lips . . .

Heat rushed to her cheeks just as Brett turned and saw her. His face reflected the same surprise, but his shocked expression quickly turned to pleasure as a grin lit up his face.

He squashed the hat back down on his head, brushed off his trousers, and headed straight to the corral fence, a compliant horse in tow.

Panic made blood pound her ears at his approach. His smile nearly melted her heart. If she was flustered before, she was practically apoplectic now. Why did this cowboy unhinge her so? What could be so attractive about an uncouth, uneducated, and unrefined man like Brett Hendricks?

"Angela? I can't believe . . . What're ya doin' here, at Foster's ranch?" He stopped merely inches from her and stepped up onto the bottom rail to get a clear look at her.

Angela searched for words to say, but they eluded her. She was aware of two small sets of curious eyes staring at her.

"She's here to teach us the violin, mister," Clementine declared, as if challenging him to refute her.

He gave the girl a big grin, but his piercing eyes remained fixed on Angela. A shiver ran all the way up her spine at his hungry expression. What frightened her more was knowing she felt a hunger herself, a fierce longing to pull him to her, to feel his body pressed against hers. Were her unbidden feelings giving her away? She tried to wrench her gaze from his but couldn't. Her face turned as a hot as a flame—even her ears burned.

"That so?" he said to Clementine.

"Mister, why were you sitting on that horse?" Madeline asked.

Brett pulled his gaze from Angela's face and looked at the girls. "You must be . . . uh, let's see—Clemaline and Madetine. Did I get that right?" He frowned as if he were puzzling a problem.

The girls erupted in laughter as they clambered up to the top of the fence and sat on the rail in front of him. "No!" they said in unison.

"I'm *Clementine*, and this is *Madeline*."

Brett frowned deeper, but his eyes glinted in merriment. Angela loved the affection she saw in his eyes directed toward the girls. She wondered if Brett had any younger siblings. "Ain't that what I said? Clemaline and Madetine."

"No!" the girls shouted, snorting with laughter as if he were deaf.

Brett shook his head. "Well, how 'bout I just call ya Clem and Maddie?"

Madeline gave him a big smile, her eyes wide in surprise. "That's what Papa calls us."

"All right, then." He blew out a breath and wiped his forehead with the back of his hand. His eyes drifted over to Angela's once more, which set her heart galloping away again. She lowered her gaze, feeling suddenly awkward and self-conscious. "I sat on the horse," he told the girls, "to get him to respect me."

"Huh," Clementine said with a frown. "Doesn't seem like respect to pin someone to the ground."

Brett laughed and threw back his head. "I reckon that makes a lot of sense, Clem. And don't let that give ya any ideas." He blew out a long, tired breath. "But horses, ya see, have to learn respect a different way. Through trust."

"You mean, if you sit on 'em, they can tell you're not gonna hurt them," Madeline said. "And then they trust you."

Brett nodded with eyes wide. "That's exactly right. My, you girls are plenty smart . . . for being so little and rascally."

That made the girls giggle and blush. Angela was more than stunned at his easy way with these girls. He knew just what to say to make them respect and trust him—just like he did with that horse. He truly did have a gift, and it was no less special than hers, she realized. Sometimes it was a lot harder to understand people than it was to figure out the bowing of an etude.

"So," he said to her, hesitating. "You're stayin' here? For how long? Aren't ya s'posed to be gettin' on that train back to New York?"

"Her violin's not done yet," Clementine offered. "It needs three more coats of varnish. George says you can't rush things when it comes to making a violin."

"I see. Well, George'd know," Brett replied thoughtfully, scratching his chin. "So . . . Miss Bellini here is stayin' with y'all till her violin's done cookin'."

The girls laughed again. Madeline shook her head vigorously. "No! You don't cook a violin."

"Ya don't? Ain't that how it gets all brown—from cookin' on a grill?"

"Noooooo!" the girls shouted again, followed by another eruption of giggles. Madeline said, "It has to sit and dry between coats. That's how it gets pretty."

"Ohhhhhh, I git it now." He stepped down from the fence and led the horse over to the gate, then opened the gate and came out of the corral. The girls ran right up to him and the horse, but Angela hung back, intimidated by the big animal—who looked much more menacing up close.

Brett looked at her and pursed his lips as the girls reached up and patted the horse's neck and nose without a care in the world. Angela worried the wild horse might bite them, but it only made a huffing sound and pawed at the dirt. Surely Brett wouldn't have let them approach if the animal was any real threat. *And those girls have been around horses all their life—they're probably just as comfortable around them as you'd be around a kitten.*

Still, she couldn't get her feet to take even one step forward.

"You ever been on a horse, Miss Bellini?"

Angela noted Brett's propriety in his address of her—no doubt for the sake of the young girls. "Uh . . . no, I haven't."

"Well," he said, looking at the girls sandwiching him, "we'll just have to remedy that, won't we, girls?"

"Yessir," they said.

"But not now," Clementine added. "We're s'posed to be picking berries for tarts."

"Ohhhhh." He rubbed his head, pretending to think hard. "So if I come with y'all, does that mean I can get a tart?"

"Only if you help pick," Clementine answered in all seriousness. "It's a lot of work, doncha know."

"Don't *you* *know*," Madeline corrected, scowling at Clementine's butchering of the English language—for perhaps the fourth time that day.

Brett chuckled. "I'm not opposed to hard work. I reckon I'm up to it—that is, if Miss Bellini don't mind."

The girls spun around, bouncing on their toes and giving her eager looks. Clearly they wanted this cowboy to come along. Angela did too, but she would never say it. She didn't dare give him any reason to think she had feelings for him. *Unreasonable, silly feelings!* Her stomach did flips thinking of him close by her side. She still couldn't believe he was here, working for Logan Foster.

She cleared her throat. "Well, Mr. Hendricks is welcome to come along."

Brett looked at her sideways, those hazel eyes sparkling with mirth. "It's always good to have the womenfolk in the protection of a big, strong cowboy—in case a bear or a wolf tries to attack—"

The straw basket fell from Angela's hand to the ground. "Bears? Here?"

Brett lowered his head and shook it, smiling. But Angela sensed he was laughing at her ignorance and fear. Her face heated again.

"You should see your face," Brett said, chuckling again.

"Of course there's bears. And wolves," Clementine said with enormous eyes. "This is the wild West, doncha know? Papa shot a bear once—just the other side of Johnson's Creek."

"Don't *you* know," Madeline muttered with a frown.

"And we had bear steaks for a week—yum!" Clementine added.

Angela couldn't open her mouth. She looked from the girls to Brett, utterly horrified. It was one thing living in a town like Greeley, where perhaps the only dangers were blizzards or sickness. It was another thing altogether to be living where animals might wander across your yard and . . . eat you.

"Don't worry, Miss Bellini," Brett said, stuffing down his laughter. "I'll bring my Winchester." He winked at the girls. "Wouldn't want some pesky bear snatchin' those berries we picked, would we?"

"No sir," they chimed, beaming and rocking up and down on their toes.

"All right, then. I'll be back presently, and we'll git on the scout for them berry bushes."

He gave Angela a wink, and she thought her heart would turn to mush. The hunger had returned to his eyes—and she was sure it had nothing to do with blackberries.

Chapter 21

BRETT WALKED ALONGSIDE HER, HIS rifle slung over one shoulder by a strap, near enough to make her unsteady and self-conscious. He made a pretense of looking for ripe blackberries, and from time to time plopped a handful into her basket, but she was aware of his eyes on her when he wasn't scanning the creek bank or looking over at the girls, who were hard at work in a nearby patch, bickering over something—Clementine's voice dominating her younger sister's.

"Tell me something about your family, where you grew up," she asked, realizing she knew almost nothing about him. He flinched — just a little—but it made her think of his remark about his father the other afternoon. She quickly asked, "How did you get to be a cowboy? Did you grow up on a ranch?"

Brett chuckled and popped a berry into his mouth. "Well. You're suddenly full o' questions." She clamped her mouth closed, but that only made him laugh harder.

"Let's see—I grew up near El Paso—that's down Texas way— most o' my life. I avoided the big war between the states by joining up with a cattle outfit in Mexico, where I rode for a time. Till the war was over, leastwise." He stopped and held out a giant berry between his thumb and forefinger. "This here's a whopper. I bet it's juicy sweet." He came closer and held it up to her mouth.

A flutter of nerves tangled her stomach. Once again she was drawn into his gorgeous hazel eyes that seemed aflame with mischief and desire. Was she mistaken? Perhaps he was just teasing her, being friendly. But no, there was no mistaking his desire. Though she'd never had a man look at her in such a way, every pore in her skin responded. He was like a sublime melody that seeped deep into her soul.

He waited until she opened her mouth for him, then dropped the berry in. Angela abruptly closed her mouth and chewed.

"Good, huh?"

She nodded, wishing her stomach would stop doing flips.

"Sweet for the sweet." He winked at her and took a step back.

She finally remembered to breathe. As he told her about living in Texas and working on cattle ranches, she found her thoughts drifting. His words strung together in that lilting way of his, reminding her of a caprice she'd played last week, with her bow skipping delicately across the strings. She realized she was listening more to the tone and timbre of his voice — his husky warm voice that coated her like treacle — than she was hearing his actual words.

Her eyes kept returning to his deft hands working through the sharp thorns of the bushes to pluck the ripe fruit. Those hands were his livelihood, and they were rough and cut up and scarred. But they were the hands of a man who calmed the wildness out of wild animals with a gentle but firm touch. Hands she imagined touching her in such a way.

"I didn't have no proper schoolin' such as ya must've had. Most of what I learned came while on the back of a horse. Contrary-wise to what some folks think, cowboys ain't uneducated. They're just educated differently, about different things." He pushed his gray hat back on his head to get a better look at her. "Just about any cowboy can tell ya all ya need to know about anyplace in the West. If'n you're in Texas and ya want to know about the Gallatin River in Montana territory, just 'bout any puncher can give ya all the details—every peak and valley, every creek, best place to fish, where the trails lead. Better'n any map. Cowboys spend a whole lot of time observin'. They can spot anything out o' the ord'nary from afar. Tell whether an approachin' rider is a line rider or an Injun, and what kind, by his dress. Many a cowboy's observed new species of animals, studied the way they move and eat and live, learned about the migration of birds. This here open country is like a book, filled with hundreds of pages of knowledge the likes of which any ol' stuffy Easterner wouldn't have a clue about. There's no replacin' real experience for book learnin'—wouldn't ya say?"

"I'm inclined to agree with you, though there is a big world out there. Wouldn't you want to learn all about it?"

"What for? How'll that help me any out here in cattle country? Why should I learn about some city or mountain in a foreign land? Or study paintings or ancient pottery or the like? I don't see the point."

"It's culture, heritage."

"Not mine. I c'n see ya wantin' to learn about Italy and yer people from there. Maybe ya got a hankerin' to go visit back there someday. But . . . the way I see it is this: where yer people come from or how they lived might be nice to know, but it don't define who ya are. You aren't where you're from. You aren't an Italian or an Irishman or an Injun. Yer behavior, the way ya treat others— that's who ya are. Too many folks use their fine and educated pedigree to excuse their mean treatment of others. I seen a plenty of it in cattle country. Englishmen and Easterners who can list back all their ancestors to some earl or king or t'other. But they don't have a lick o' sense or decency, and would jus' as soon steal the clothes off your back as say 'how-de-do.'"

Angela studied his face, surprised at his words and the passion behind them. And his words rang with truth. She realized she had spent her life defining herself in just that way—as an Italian woman bound by her culture and required to play the part defined by the men surrounding her. Proud men who often felt they did no wrong, who rarely apologized for any mistreatment of others. Who bragged and flaunted their money or station in the community. She'd tried hard to fit in, to accept her lot, but she saw now that she could never fit. How could she, when it wasn't proper for a young woman to seek a career, to want to become a professional musician and play on the stage? Was there anyplace she could fit in and still realize her dreams? She doubted it, feeling that familiar heavy sadness seeking to pull her under.

"So, ya have any siblings?" Brett asked.

"An older brother. And two younger sisters." She tried not to look at him, knowing she'd get lost in those eyes again, and her cheeks would give her feelings away. As she pulled the fat black berries from the vines and dropped them into her basket, she noticed the juice was staining her skin purple.

"Ya miss 'em?"

Angela nodded, wondering if he planned to ply her with questions now.

"They all live with that pa of yours?" His tone had grown quiet and serious.

At the mention of her papá, her mouth tightened. Why had she mentioned him to Brett that day? How could she have told a complete stranger that her papá beat her? *Come stupido.* She looked at him, and he just stood there, waiting for her answer. Her nervousness shifted into irritation.

"Let's just enjoy this beautiful day," she said, turning abruptly and walking over to the girls. She hoped that would put a stop to the subject.

Her eyes dropped to her feet at a tiny rustling sound, and she half-expected a snake to slither out from under the prickly berry bushes and bite her. Her imagination had run loose upon his mention of bears and wolves. It took all her resolve to hide her fear, and she felt altogether foolish to be so frightened.

She noticed the girls were without a care in the world. Ten feet from her, they concentrated on the task, filling their baskets with berries—though a good portion ended up in their mouths instead, staining their lips purple. What a happy, carefree life they lived.

The thought soured in her mouth as if she'd eaten an unripe blackberry. These two girls not only had their own violins, they had parents that encouraged them to play music. Who loved and adored them.

The fuller her basket, the emptier her heart felt. What was she doing here watching over someone else's girls instead of protecting her own sisters? How could she be so self-indulgent, chasing her dreams instead of facing reality? Her mamá was lying in some hospital bed, alone, no doubt worrying herself sick over her eldest daughter, who'd run off to some Western town to buy a violin. What was she thinking when she got on that train?

The heavy weight of her guilt and fear over her mamá came crashing down on her shoulders. She stifled the sobs as best she could, keeping her face turned from Brett so he couldn't see her tears. The last thing she wanted was for this uncouth cowboy to try to comfort her. *But you want to be comforted. You'd like nothing more than those strong arms to hold you and for Brett to tell you everything will be all right. Tell you that Mamá will recover and Papá will have learned his lesson and will never hurt her again.* She choked back a new flood of tears. *But those are lies, and you know it. Papá will never stop, never change.*

She realized she stood frozen in place, staring out at the horizon stretching for endless miles, which only emphasized the distance that lay between her and New York. The sea of tall brown grass was a vast ocean separating her from Mamá.

A hand touched her arm, and she flinched. She turned her head and locked eyes with Brett. Before she could turn away, he stopped her with his hand on her shoulder. She shuddered, her throat raw and her face wet.

"Angela, I'm sorry." He gave a quick glance over at the girls, who had run over to another patch of berries nearby.

"Sorry?" Her thoughts clustered thick in her head. What was he apologizing for?

"I shouldn't'a mentioned yer pa." His mouth tightened into a hard line of self-recrimination.

She stared at the ground, her feelings aching to gush out. It was all she could do to keep them bottled up in her chest. "It's . . . not you—or anything you said. I . . . I just shouldn't be here—"

"At the ranch? Or ya mean Colorado?" When she didn't reply, he said in a hushed tone, "Or ya mean here, with me?"

The way he said the words caused her to tremble. His voice was so thick with longing and tenderness, she could hardly breathe. The air seemed suddenly stifling, choking her. All she could do was shake her head and let the tears fall. She couldn't have been more embarrassed by her emotional display.

And Brett was just standing there watching her—maybe studying her the way he did those volatile horses. Was she just another thing to calm with his soft words? She didn't want to be calmed or reassured or comforted. She didn't deserve it. But the ache inside would explode if she didn't say something to ease it.

"My mamá's in the hospital. I don't know how badly she was hurt . . . I should be there, helping her . . . But my aunt told me to stay away, that Papá was furious I'd left . . ." She could say no more. Her eyes brimmed with more tears, and her throat pained her such that she couldn't swallow.

After a long stretch of quiet—the air so still now, the silence seemed to pulse—Brett said softly, "It's not your fault—"

She spun around to face him. "It is! What do you know about it? Nothing!" A string of Italian curses flew out of her mouth—to her shock. Words her papá often flung at her mamá.

"Whoa, whoa, there," he said, shushing her. But she didn't want to be "shushed."

She wanted to run. To be free, like a wild horse. To race over the open prairie and leave her pain drifting behind. But there was nowhere to run. She was trapped inside this burning fire with no escape.

"It's *not your fault*," Brett repeated, this time with firm insistence, hands on his hips. "You didn't make your pa the way he is. And you cain't change him and make 'im different. The only person you c'n change is yourself. It don't do any good beatin' yourself over the head with a stick."

Angela saw pain in his eyes, and she suddenly understood. *That's what you do.* She drew in a long breath and swiped the back of her hand across her eyes. *And that's why you run.* She huffed, seeing him as clear as the air around her. *Because you can.*

How many men sought a new life in the West because they were running from something? She narrowed her eyes at him. He was just a coward—the same as she.

"Running doesn't solve anything either," she said, her words biting and sharp.

He looked stunned, as if she'd slapped him. She regretted her thoughtless retort.

"I'm sorry," she said, feeling his hurt ooze out like an untended wound.

He grunted, and his features took on a hard edge. "No. You're right. I run from trouble." He shook his head slowly, and a sour smirk rose on his face. He stuffed his hands deep into his pants pockets. "Always have. Prob'ly always will." He came up close to her face and looked down into her eyes with a scowl. His words hung in the inches between them. He smelled like horse and grass and sweat, but it was an intoxicating, heady scent that made her falter.

She tried to take a step back, but a hedge of tangling blackberry bushes prevented her.

"Hey, are you two having a spat?"

Angela turned her head and saw Clementine marching over to them, her basket full to the brim with plump blackberries. Madeline trailed a few steps behind her.

Angela forced a smile onto her face, feeling as if she'd just escaped some danger. "Of course not. Let's see those berries."

Clementine held up her basket, then frowned. "Your basket's only half full. You've been dallying, I'd say."

Brett raised an eyebrow at the girl, and Angela almost laughed. Clementine's tone was so chastising and parental, it was comical. Apparently the cowboy thought so too, for the dark cloud that had momentarily engulfed him had shredded and blown away, and that sweet, arresting smile had returned.

Madeline came over to Angela and took her basket. "Clem and I'll finish picking for you. We're experts."

"Apparently so," Angela said, throwing a quick look at Brett. He stood with his arms crossed over his chest, thoughtfully watching as the girls scampered off, back to the patch they'd been picking at. Clem stopped and yelled to them.

"And the sooner, we're done, the sooner we'll have tarts!" She ran over to her sister and got busy again.

Brett gave Angela an apologetic look. "Maybe we should help 'em."

"Oh no," she said, "we're not *experts*. We'll only get in the way." She gave him a smile, sorry for snapping at him. What in heaven's name had gotten into her? She'd never uttered such awful words before. Good thing Brett didn't understand Italian.

Her own dark cloud seemed to have blown away too. Though crying hadn't solved any of her problems, it had at least emptied her of her pain and sorrow for the moment.

"So . . ." he said, running his tongue across his lower lip. Angela felt a new surge of desire wash over her. A smile snuck up on his face, which only heated the flames more. "Under that sweet demeanor of yours there's a bit of a temper, I'd reckon."

She shrugged in resignation. "That's the Italian part of me."

He stepped closer, then stopped and cocked his head. She swallowed and met his gaze. "What's the other part?"

His question flustered her. Or maybe it was his nearness and the way his eyes searched her face, as if looking for the answer there.

"There . . . there is . . . I mean, there is no other part," she said, feeling like she had cotton in her mouth.

"Oh yeah there is," he was quick to say. "A whole lot of *other*."

"I don't understand—"

He took up the distance between them such that she could feel heat from his body. There remained a hair's breadth between them. Angela froze, though her arms started to shake.

Brett fastened his eyes on hers, his face impassive.

"What I mean to say, Miss Bellini, is . . . you've got this sweetness about you." His warm breath now tickled her cheeks. She held her own breath, unable to pull away from his mesmerizing stare. "Sweet like honey and as soft and gentle as a spring lamb."

Angela burst out in laughter, startling him.

"What'd I say that was so funny?" He looked entirely flustered, and it was utterly endearing.

She waggled her head at him. "No one's ever compared me to a sheep—"

"Not a sheep. A *lamb*. A *spring lamb*." He frowned, taken aback.

When she laughed again, he threw his hands in the air and made a noise of frustration.

"Well, what's the difference?" she asked, trying to get her chuckling under control. But the look of confusion in his eyes only made her erupt in giggles once more.

"See here, miss. I'll not brook such impolite teasin'—"

"Oh? What do you plan to do to stop me?" The brash words spilled from her mouth before she could stop them.

With raised brows, he pulled her swiftly into his arms—those strong muscular arms that she'd dreamed of feeling again. Her breath whooshed from her body.

"Oh I know jus' the trick," he sighed into her ear, making her knees so weak she thought she'd fall. But he held her firm against his chest, and she could feel his heart hammering to match her own beat.

What was she doing? How could she let this man hold her so? And she was supposed to be watching Adeline's girls. *And they're probably watching us right now.*

Angela tried to pull back in protest, but before she could manage, Brett's lips found hers, and his tongue ran across her upper lip. Angela gasped, and Brett pulled her even closer, almost crushing her against him. But it felt good, oh so good. Her head spun with dizziness as his moist tongue worked its way past her lips, forcing her mouth open.

She was like a fish out of water, sucking for air, yearning for more but not able to get enough, not enough of him, as his lips teased and kissed hers. Every inch of her body was set afire, craving him, needing him. She trembled in his arms as she fought to pull back, fearful and shocked by the passion that he'd sparked inside her.

But Brett didn't put up a fight. To her surprise, he dropped his arms to his sides and pulled back, tenderly tucking a strand of hair back under her bonnet. He bit his bottom lip as if tasting her still on his skin. Her heart hurt from its fierce thumping.

She'd never been kissed before — not like this. And though she'd imagined what it might be like, a million times over, Brett's kiss was nothing like she'd pictured. It had shaken her to her toes, and now she felt as fragile and weak as butterfly emerging from a cocoon.

He cleared his throat and gave her a crooked smile, those hazel eyes making the embers flare again and filling her with such a rush of passion, she could hardly look at him.

"That's . . . the *other* part I was talkin' 'bout. I knew it was in there, somewhere."

She gaped at him, flustered, tongue-tied, torn between wanting to be furious at him and longing for him to kiss her again. His smug smile made her think he'd been playing her like a violin — seeing if he could get this naïve, emotional woman to succumb to his wiles.

A cowboy! She'd let a cowboy kiss her. And not just a little tiny peck on the lips either.

She put her fingers on her mouth and spun around. Dizzy, she strode to the girls, who'd filled her basket almost to the top.

"I think we have plenty for tarts," she managed to get out of her mouth. Her heart still raced, and her tongue tasted Brett's lips on her own lips. She wanted to run into her room and hide under the coverlet. "Let's head back to the house."

The girls chattered with excitement about the delicious hot tarts Cook would make them, leading the way along the creek trail. Angela followed, and Brett fell in step behind her, his boots making a soft thud in rhythm with her beating heart, her head filled with a new and frightening kind of music that made her hurry all the more to the sanctity of the ranch house.

Chapter 22

A NGELA'S FACE PALED UNDER THE overcast sky. "Are you sure this is safe? He's awfully big."

Brett stood in front of Miz Foster's appy gelding, holding the reins loose in his hand while trying not to gawk at Angela, who looked purty as a picture in that split riding skirt and high boots the rancher's wife had given her to wear. Her thick black hair was pinned up under her straw hat, exposing her milky neck. Brett swallowed back a sigh.

Miz Foster smiled, gave that high-pitched titter of hers, and put her hands on her wide hips. "He's a cotton puff," she said to Angela, with a thick drawl. "He won't do a thing unless you make him. The girls learned to ride on him."

Angela looked about to swoon as she studied the horse from hoof to head. Ol' Nicker couldn't have been more bored. *Prob'ly knows it's Sunday. Folks and horses were meant to have a day o' rest.* But a pleasant little ride round the ranch wouldn't take long. *Then you c'n git back to nappin',* he told the horse silently with a pat on the neck.

He had approached the missus when the family — and Angela — had returned late morning from church, after Angela had gone inside the big house and the rancher's wife was giving some instruction to the cook out in the garden. Miz Foster about turned pink when Brett had inquired whether he might take Angela out for a ride, explaining that she'd never sat on a horse afore.

Brett's affection for Angela must've been written all over his face, though he tried his darndest to hide it. But women like her could smell a man courting a mile away, and her eyes lit up in a kind of conspiratorial way. He knew Angela would need some riding clothes and a lady-broke horse and reckoned he'd have to ask Miz Foster's help in that regard. Plus, if Angela was staying in the big house, he'd best get in the missus's good graces.

She'd been more than happy to comply. Truth be told, the idea had sent her in a tizzy, with her hands flapping and mouth working, looking like a busy bee off to fill the hive with honey. Brett had rushed to clean up and put on his nicest clothes — a pair of brown denim pants and a pale-yellow shirt he'd bought at the Greeley mercantile he'd not yet worn — wanting to make the right impression on Miz Foster. And, he had to admit, on Angela.

Archie and Tate had given him looks when he changed out of his busting clothes after supper. But Brett reckoned if he smelled like a sweaty horse, he might not get another chance to kiss those delicious lips.

Standing there, watching Miz Foster help Angela up onto the side saddle and instructing her how to sit and use the reins, Brett could hardly contain his fidgeting. He knew he had to do the proper thing and be all gentlemanly — 'specially riding around the ranch for all eyes to see. The cowboys doing their chores or just lazing around on their day off would catch sight of 'em, and he also knew the kind of talk that would follow. But Brett didn't care a whit about the joshing he'd get. All he cared about was spending as much time with Angela Bellini as he could before she left to go home.

It was a kind of torture—he readily admitted it—hankering for something he could never have. But after spending the night reliving that kiss over and over, so utterly bewitched by her charms, he knew there was no use fighting it. He could no more keep away from her than the sun could keep from rising in the morning sky.

A tiny spark of hope had lit in the night, as he lay in his bunk. What if he could convince her to stay? He mulled over all the things he could say to her, but his thoughts kept circling back to the same spot. What would a gal like her want with a cowboy like him? He had nothing to offer her. She deserved better. And then he'd reminded himself about the bad blood that flowed in his veins. About his wild temper that might take hold of him without warning. He'd kept seeing that image of him hitting Angela, and the blood dripping down her face. He knew it was the Cheyenne woman's way of warning him.

But she'd also told you of a way out—a way through the fire. "Follow the song. It will lead you out." He wished he understood the meaning of her words.

If he truly cared about Angela, he wouldn't let her heart get tangled with his.

But he already had. It was evident in that kiss, plain as day. She had the same longing for him as he did for her. A tiny voice screamed a warning in his head, telling him he'd only end up hurting her and to stay away. But the other part of him squashed that warning—like a stampeding herd of buffalo riding roughshod across his heart. How could he ignore the fervent desire he felt for this gal? Even standing here, a few feet away, he thought his heart might burst out of his chest. It took every ounce of restraint not to rush over to her and swoop her into his arms.

He was sure Miz Foster sensed his every thought, for once she situated Angela up on the saddle, she gave him a chastising look that told him to be on his best behavior. He appreciated the trust she showed him, for she didn't know him at all, and plenty of cowboys couldn't be trusted as far as you could spit. Angela was a guest at her ranch and came under her care and responsibility, and Brett intended to prove worthy. He could thank Doc Tuttle for that kind testimony of character.

"Take her along that trail that starts back behind the bunkhouse," she told him. "It follows the Platte for a half mile east along a stand of cottonwoods, then opens up to the prairie."

She turned and patted Angela's leg. The gal sat nervously on the horse, gripping the reins hard in fisted hands. "He'll go nice and slow. Nicker's about the gentlest horse you'll ever meet. Nothing flusters him."

She added with a reassuring smile, "Relax and enjoy the ride. There's nothing more peaceful than seeing the wide-open country from the back of a horse. Isn't that right, Mr. Hendricks?"

Brett nodded and touched the brim of his hat to thank her. Then he walked over to Kotoo, who was standing alongside the corral fence, and swung up on her. He'd packed some water and tied his rifle to his saddle, just in case of trouble.

"You alright, Miss Bellini?" He brought his mount alongside Nicker. Kotoo stepped about, eager to run. But there'd be no letting loose today. Both horse and rider would have to exercise some mighty restraint.

Angela blew out a shaky breath, looking like she couldn't wait to get this over with.

Brett chuckled. "This ain't like a visit to the dentist. And ya don't have to hold on so tight."

He noticed her hands loosen a bit on the reins, but she sat stock-still, her face as tight as a drum. The sight made his heart swell with affection. She looked like a little girl up there on the saddle, afraid she might fall off. Her right leg was hooked around the large horn, and her skirts spread out like a fan over her leg. She was so fetching, she about took his breath away.

Miz Foster shook her head at Angela, amused. Brett imagined she'd never seen the likes of a lady who'd never ridden a horse. "Y'all have a good time." Brett coulda sworn the rancher's wife winked at him. Maybe she'd merely had a speck of dust in her eye.

Brett clicked his teeth and got the horses walking. Angela made a little sound, like a gasp, and Brett saw her fists tighten again. But he could tell she was trying to look brave, though her gaze was fixed on Nicker's head as if worried it might fall off.

He hid his smirk and pushed down his excitement. He'd pictured this moment many a time—him and Angela riding out on the range, just the two of 'em. Stopping along the bank of a babbling creek and laying out a picnic. Then, pulling her into his arms as they watched the clouds drift by, and dropping a line of kisses along her throat and down the swell of her chest.

His hands twitched as he thought on all the ways he would tenderly love her, drawing moans of pleasure from her as he ran his fingers and tongue over every inch of her body, and especially the secret parts he longed to discover. She was an enticing wilderness waiting to be explored, and he wanted more than anything to be the one and only explorer to venture into that untamed country.

He realized he was breathing hard, and now it was his hands that were balled into fists, the yearning tying him in knots.

As he moved out in front of her horse, Brett caught a glance back at Miz Foster. She was standing with arms crossed watching them. He sure hoped she couldn't read thoughts—the way Sarah

Banks had seemed to do. He kept Kotoo moving at a slow and easy amble down past the bunkhouse, feeling those curious eyes burning into the back of his head.

He figured he'd give Angela a bit of time to get used to having a horse under her. So he kept quiet and led them toward the river, leaving the sounds of the ranch behind them. Soon, the warm damp air by the riverbank hummed with insects, and shiny blue-winged dragonflies darted in and about the water reeds.

Brett pulled Kotoo to a stop, and Angela and the appy came alongside.

"Well, how d'ya like riding Ol' Nicker?" He studied her face, and she seemed much more relaxed than when they'd started out.

She wiggled a bit in the saddle and gave him a smile. His heart 'bout melted at the sight of her warm brown eyes looking at him with such affection. His words snagged in his throat.

"I'm right glad ya took me up on my offer to take you out ridin'. It ain't so hard, ya reckon?"

She laughed, and he wished he could pull her down from the horse and cover her with kisses. But he had a mind to show her he could be just as gentlemanly as those stuffy Easterners he'd met from time to time. Though, if the opportunity presented itself sometime along the trail, why, he wouldn't turn down another chance to kiss those plump lips of hers.

Just the thought set his limbs afire once more. He wanted more than just a kiss. He had to admit it. The need to have her in his arms, to entwine his body with her soft, luscious one made him ache all over. How long could he bear such torture? *Long as ya have to, Cowboy. Rein it in. She's a lady, and you'd best remember that.*

She patted the horse's neck. "It's a bit awkward sitting like this. I don't know how women stay on if they have to ride fast."

He nodded, taking a look-see at the river valley spreading out for miles around them. Fat cottony clouds drifted overhead, promising thundershowers and maybe lightning up in the mountains. While plenty common in the late summer and fall, those storms posed a mighty danger to a cowman and his herd. When cattle bunched together in a storm, especially when there was no lowland or ditches to run 'em in, dozens sometimes died from lightning strikes. Brett recalled plenty of nights when he'd had to ride through a storm on a trembling horse, rain pouring and thunder crashing. Lightning flashing downright close about him, attracted to the heat rising from the heaving herd. He'd even seen those uncanny round balls of fire hovering on the tips of his horse's ears as cattle fell beneath the lightning strokes. Such was the life of a cowboy on the open range. You took the weather as it came.

But there'd be no rain on the prairie today. Just those fat clouds casting dark shadows that moved like ghosts over the ground.

"It's so beautiful and peaceful here," Angela said, her eyes gazing off across the river. The wide swath of water moved sluggishly this time of year, looking like thick molasses. Easy for a man or beast to get stuck knee-high in the mud if he weren't careful.

He thought on all the dangers the open range presented, so many he half ignored. But with Angela riding beside him, his eyes were alert to any danger, and a strong hankering to protect her welled up in his chest.

Brett studied her with adoring eyes. It was like he couldn't get enough of her, his eyes as hungry as the rest of his body. He recalled that fierce thirst he'd suffered in the desert, but this was just as painful a thirst. And his mouth now felt full of dust, unable to open and say the things he yearned to say. He just knew if he started talking, he'd make a fool of himself. So he urged the pinto to walk on, and Angela followed behind on the narrow trail, wads of tall cattails banking the sides.

Soon the way opened up to the prairie dotted with the usual sage brush and occasional prickly pear—some towering over ten feet high. The horses' hooves pattered along on the hard-packed ground as a breeze lifted thin blankets of dirt up into the air and swirled them around. Then he reined Kotoo to a stop and let the mare nip at the tufts of prairie grass, seeing as both mounts had hackamore bridles on. It didn't take more than a second for Nicker to take the hint.

Angela chuckled at Nicker's long-reaching tongue wrapping around the bunches of grass, and she held on to the saddle horn as the horse took little jerking steps this way and that as he grazed. Even out on the range, under a cloudy sky, in ordinary clothes, Angela looked like an angel sent from heaven. He wouldn't have been a mite surprised if the sky opened up and a chorus of heavenly beings broke out in song above her.

He couldn't bear it a second longer. After clearing his throat, he turned to her and said, "About yesterday . . ." He just had to know what she was feeling. After that kiss, she'd practically run the whole way back to the house. Was it from embarrassment? Or did she regret kissing him? He'd taken advantage of her—he knew he'd overstepped. But she'd kissed him back. Oh, how she kissed him. *Ya don't kiss like that if ya don't really wanna be kissed.*

A flush of red leapt to her cheeks as she dropped her gaze to the ground. She looked about to say something, and Brett waited. But when no words were forthcoming, he said quietly, "I shouldn't've been so forward. I apologize." Though, he wasn't a bit sorry. When she still didn't answer him, fear gripped him. "I mean, I hope you're not mad. I didn't mean—"

"Please," Angela said, pleading with her eyes, "it was as much my fault as yours . . ." She looked away, her face still flushed with embarrassment.

Fault? So she did blame him. She did think he'd done wrong by her.

Looks like you're not gettin' any more kisses today, Cowboy. He could kick himself into tomorrow. He just knew he was asking for it when he kissed her. Proper ladies didn't go around kissing fellas they hardly knew. *But ya couldn't help it.*

He grunted and slid down from the horse, his feet yearning to run. He dropped Kotoo's reins, walked a few steps, and looked out over the hot, dry desert. Desert that had almost been the death of him.

He'd been given another chance at life. Didn't that mean another chance at love too? If anything, that brush with death shoulda taught ya to think first afore actin'. Rushin' off into the desert without water was a fool thing to do. And so was rushin' to kiss that gal. He always acted without thinking—that was his problem. He fired off on a whim, letting his emotions get the best of him. He'd stormed out that fateful day, aggrieved at his pa, fed up and thinking only of himself and his own wants and needs. He'd had 'airy a thought for his poor ma.

"I'm sorry," Angela said, interrupting his rant at himself.

He turned and looked at her. She was attempting to get down from her horse, but the stirrup was tangled up in her skirt.

"I didn't mean to upset you," she said, tugging at the cloth and leaning precariously off the saddle.

"Whoa, wait there," he said, coming around Nicker's neck and putting his hand on her leg. "Lemme get you free."

"I . . . I mean, I'm not angry. It's not . . . I didn't . . ."

He felt her leg quiver at his touch. He stared at her skirt-covered leg, and he couldn't help but think about the creamy smooth skin of her flesh underneath. A heatwave of passion flushed his neck.

He looked up into her flustered face, feeling sore at himself and frustration at his predicament. Here was a beautiful gal—one who'd stolen his heart from the first moment he'd laid eyes on her—and he couldn't have her. She was being all polite and trying not to hurt his feelings, but he read her face, and the message was as plain as day.

His words came out rougher than he'd intended. "No need to apologize. I understand." He added, "It won't happen again." He yanked at the fabric caught in the crease of the stirrup, and it ripped, freeing her leg. He felt his own heart tear in two, as if someone had grabbed it like that and pulled.

Brett eased her down off the horse, his hands tight against Angela's soft waist. The moment her feet touched ground, he let go and stuffed his hands in his pants pockets, keeping them out of trouble. He couldn't trust his hands or his heart. Not around her.

Knowing she'd start asking questions, he strode off toward a jumble of rocks. He wouldn't go far, but he needed to simmer down. He felt about to explode with all the conflicting feelings warring inside him. He plopped down on a boulder and huffed out air as he stared off at the mountains.

Angela smoothed out her skirt and stared at Brett sitting on the rock a dozen yards away. Why was he so angry at her? She should be mad at *him*. He'd apologized for kissing her, acting as if he'd never really meant to. All but admitting the kiss had been impulsive. She knew the moment she'd run into the house after picking berries that he'd been toying with her. Taking advantage of her naiveté and inexperience. And how could he have kissed her in front of those little girls? Did they tell Adeline what they'd seen? The thought horrified her. What kind of woman would the Fosters think they had staying under their roof? Would she be asked to leave?

Angela fumed as she held on to Nicker's rein as he ate the grass at her feet. What was she thinking, letting this cowboy take her on a ride, far out of sight from the ranch? She doubted he'd do anything to hurt her—not if he wanted to keep his job. But how would it look to others?

You know why you agreed to ride with him—because you can't stay away from him. And you want another kiss. Admit it!

She didn't want to admit it. Of course she longed for Brett to press her against his strong, broad chest and kiss her with the passion he'd shown yesterday. But it would only lead to trouble—big trouble. It would give Brett the wrong idea and open a door to more intimacy. She couldn't trust that a cowboy like him would have any honor. What code did he really live by? He said he worshipped God under the stars, forsaking church and the fellowship of other good Christians. He lived a carefree, "do as he pleased" life, not answerable to family, friends, or church. So how could she trust him?

She was playing with fire—and if she didn't stop this now, she would get burned. Badly burned. Already her heart was smoldering, threatening to explode into flames of passion she would never be able to douse. Had she forgotten why she'd come to Greeley? Had she forgotten her dream?

She had to put Brett Hendricks out of her mind and heart. He'd weaseled in there somehow when she wasn't looking, when she was vulnerable and lonely. *Well, he can just weasel back out. Just march over there and tell him to take you back to the house. Before you change your mind.*

228

She dropped the rein she'd been holding and headed over toward Brett, taking a deep breath and trying to prepare what she planned to say to him. But then every word flew out of her head as her eyes caught on something moving over the dirt.

Fear bolted her feet to the ground. Not inches from her boots, a giant brown snake with diamond-patterned skin stretched out, its tail flicking and making a rattling sound. Her hand flew to her mouth but did little to stifle the scream escaping her throat.

Brett leapt up from the rock. "Don't move!" he ordered.

Angela gulped as bile rose to the back of her throat. To her horror, another giant snake slithered out from a nearby rock, coming her way.

"Oh, Lord, save me!" she cried, her knees threatening to give out. She sucked in air that failed to reach her lungs. The ground erupted in undulating movement. Snakes were coming at her from every direction, hissing and rattling in a symphony of death. Her heart raced so hard, she thought she would faint.

"Please, help me!" Why was Brett just standing there? *Oh, Lord, please, please . . .*

She whimpered, shaking so hard her teeth hurt. She couldn't bear to look down and squeezed her eyes shut. Her body stiffened, awaiting the first bite to her ankle.

"Just don't move!" Brett repeated. She could tell he was running. Running away? Surely he wouldn't leave her—

A gunshot blasted loud and close, and Angela jerked in surprise. She couldn't help but jump back, her eyes wide. Her foot landed on a snake, and she screamed in horror at the top of her lungs. The snake's head darted at her, and its gleaming forked tongue stabbed at her boot, causing her to scream even louder. She nearly stumbled backward onto a tangle of slithering snakes as another gunshot rang out by her foot. The snake's head exploded in a pulpy mass of blood. Angela grabbed her head as her ears rang painfully, spinning this way and that, trying to find purchase on the ground with her feet.

She spun again and saw Brett striding toward her with a rifle in his outstretched arm and an angry scowl on his face. Another three snakes made toward her, and she froze, her stomach about to vomit its contents onto her boots. She wrapped her arms around her waist, moaning and trembling as more loud shots echoed through the air.

Snake after snake exploded around her. Screams flew from her mouth, one after the other, as she pranced like a terrified horse, trying to find a way out of the writhing mass surrounding her.

There! A narrow path opened up as Brett fired again and again. Dirt flew up around her in clumps as bullets hit the ground, the snakes still alive moving quicker in anger and agitation. She ran as hard as she could toward the horses with her hands over her ears, but Brett marched toward the snakes with narrowed eyes and a meanness in his gaze that shocked her.

She stopped and panted next to the horses, stunned at their calm demeanor. Their curious eyes watched Brett, but they didn't flinch at all when he fired the rifle. But what was he doing?

Her mouth dropped in shock, her body still shaking uncontrollably, as she watched him stand in the midst of a dozen or more crazed snakes. As they lunged at him, he shot their heads off, and when the rifle clicked, Angela panicked.

He was out of bullets! Why was he standing there? Why didn't he run away?

Then she stared at his face. He was like a man obsessed. He threw his rifle to the ground and pulled a knife from somewhere. The blade glinted in the sunlight streaming through rents in the clouds. She stood, unblinking, and watched as Brett became unhinged.

With fury he slashed at the giant creatures who thrust their heads at him, tongues flickering and tails rattling. Brett roared and lunged, grabbing one snake after another by its neck and slashing off its head, blood splurting all over his clothes.

Angela watched—mesmerized and horrified, both—as he attacked with vicious intent. Even after the last snake had died under his hand, Brett stabbed the thing over and over, screaming in rage, consumed with some terrifying bloodlust. When at last he paused and caught his breath, he turned his head and glared at her. His eyes were dark and stormy, the pupils like black, cold marbles.

The sight made Angela suck in a breath and tremble in fear. Blood soaked Brett's shirt and had splattered his strangely calm face. His hair dripped with blood under his hat as he stood ankle deep in dead snakes. The screams and the cacophony of rattles dwindled to soft echoes bouncing off the rocks, leaving a silence that seeped into the prairie that lay heavy and oppressive.

Brett shook off his stupor and looked around as if surprised at finding himself in a pile of dead snakes. When his eyes met hers, he seemed to look through her, as if she wasn't there.

Angela's heart finally slowed to a normal beat, but she knew the horror of what she'd experienced would be forever branded in her memory. She sidled up to Nicker, glancing nervously around. Her every thought was on fleeing. The sooner she rode back the ranch house, the sooner she could breathe again.

She waited for Brett to come to her and help her up into the saddle, but he stood frozen, as still as a statue, his face impassive.

"Brett?" She waited, then called to him again. "Brett, please. Let's go back." Flashes of Brett shooting and slashing the snakes played over and over in her mind. And while those snakes had terrified her to her core, what frightened her even more was the venomous look on Brett's face as he brutally attacked the creatures. She was utterly grateful to him for saving her, but instead of feeling relief, she felt another fear slithering into her heart—the same sensation of fear she felt around her papá.

Despite Brett's calm and friendly manner, there was an angry, violent man deep down inside. Who knew what other things might spark that anger? A wrong word? A late dinner? She saw in her mind her papá screaming at her mamá, then striking her hard with the back of his hand—his eyes brimming with the same fury as Brett's eyes had held.

Perhaps the snake attack was a blessing in disguise. It had revealed to her the truth about Brett Hendricks. Now, more than ever, she knew it was time to return to New York—violin or no violin.

Chapter 23

ACHEERY FIRE BLAZED AT the tail end of the chuck wagon, but Brett felt anything but cheered on this dead-calm evening. He reined in the gelding he was riding, while Archie Halloran and Tate Roberts rode the string over to the rope corral the wrangler had set up a ways past. About the fire sat a dozen or so punchers, who eyed him as they ate from plates loaded with beans and beef and powder biscuits and drank from tin cups. A coffeepot bubbled over the fire, the strong aroma drifting into Brett's nose, and the small Mexican cook busied himself with his pans of food.

Brett dismounted, and a kid in a hat too big ran over and took his horse, then led it over to the makeshift corral where all the strings were put up for the night. The punchers ranged in age — young like Archie, some of 'em, and others maybe sixty. As he approached the fire, he noted all were grimy and dusting and reeking from the lack of a bath. Included in the bunch were Ned Handy and Rufus Shore, whose narrowed eyes followed Brett as he introduced himself and got back nods and hellos.

Roberts and Archie joined him over at the wagon, where the cook handed them tin plates loaded with steaming food. Archie blabbered on excitedly, and Brett politely nodded. His stomach grumbled. He'd hardly eaten a thing since they set out to join the roundup. Truth be told, he'd hardly eaten much all week, his appetite soured. Foster had Brett stringing the last of the broncs late yesterday, and so he and Roberts and the tenderfoot had set out at dawn. They'd led the bunch without incident north and east across the desert, passing herds of Foster's cattle and giving a wave to the riders moving the animals to the roundup location.

Usually Brett looked forward to a roundup. It was a time for sharing stories and meeting punchers from other ranches. But Brett had no hankering for comradery here. Ever since last Sunday with the snakes, his spirit had snuffed out, like a candle in a strong wind. He felt nothing but emptiness. Emptiness and shame. He couldn't get Angela's horrified expression out of his mind. And he knew it wasn't just the snakes that had scared her.

He found a secluded spot on a log away from the campfire and ate his food without tasting it. He noted Roberts had taken Archie under his wing and was introducing him to the punchers around the fire. He was glad for it, for last thing he wanted was to swap pleasantries.

Angela had said 'airy a word to him when they rode back to the ranch. He knew he'd lost his temper. He'd lost her. Yet he hardly recalled what he'd done. One moment he was grabbing his rifle and running to save her, and the next moment he was covered hat to boot in snake blood. His eyes had dropped to his hand, which held his big Bowie knife. He had no memory of pulling the knife from its sheath on his calf. Or of cutting all them snakes into pieces. Something had come over him, something awful.

He groaned as despair sucked him under. He'd known his pa's blood ran through his veins. But up until that moment he'd hoped that he'd mercifully been spared the curse. All it took was a pile of rattlers to show him the truth. That, and the look in Angela's eyes, condemning him.

The whole rest of the week, he saw no sign of her. Nor had he heard her sweet fiddle playing. He knew she was still at the ranch — Foster's little girls had told him so — but Angela had stayed out of sight. *Out of yer sight.* He couldn't blame her. He just wished he'd had the chance to apologize before the roundup. Who knew if he'd ever see her again. Foster had told 'em this roundup would be a small one — maybe only four ranches and take about two weeks. Even so, he reckoned Angela would be long gone by the time he got back to the ranch.

Well, it was for the best. Better that she saw his true self. Better that *he* saw. For it drove home the truth of the evil residing in his heart. Never, *never*, could he allow that rage to bust out of its cage around a woman. He was destined to spend his life alone and lonely. So be it. A wildfire burned hot across the barren wilderness of his soul, and no calm water or sweet song would lead him out, despite that Cheyenne woman's proclamation.

He finished off his food and wiped his mouth with the back of his hand. He sat there, wallowing in his misery and knowing he had to get over it. *Get over her.* A big empty hole sat in his heart, as if someone had shot him. He'd never loved any woman before. Never really knew what *love* meant — all that mushy talk he'd heard cowboys blather about, their eyes moony and their spirits low, missing some gal back home. Cowboys often spent the long hours under the stars talking about some gal or other they had their heart set on or broken by. But Brett thought it mostly wishful thinking or some sort of delusion or fever.

Lovesickness. It surely was a sickness, truth be told. He could hardly deny it now. For that pain in his chest never let up, and the longing for her drove him mad with need and desire, worse than any sickness he'd suffered. He sorely rued the day he'd laid eyes on Angela Bellini.

It would take time, but he'd purge that sickness from his bones if he had to dig it out with a knife. That, or end his life and the suffering. *You're stronger than that, Cowboy. You don't have to end up like your pa.* But what was his life worth—without Angela? Nothing. Why run cattle twelve hours a day, year in, year out. What was the point? *There ain't none. But ya don't have a choice, do ya? This is yer work, yer life.*

He was good at running. Angela said it plain as day. Well, then, he'd just keep running from trouble, even it if dogged him like some hound of hell. If he ran fast and long and hard enough, he might be able to keep one step ahead of his simmering rage. He didn't see any other choice. And maybe if he chewed up enough miles, he'd forget the haunting face of that the gal he loved.

They finished breakfast just as the sun glared over the rim of the horizon. Punchers were rolling up blankets, stuffing war sacks, rounding up their string. The cook was rattling camp kettles, packing up the chuck wagon for the move. The camp was astir with activity and chatter, horses and punchers alike eager to get a move on. Brett's back ached from the lumpy mattress of buffalo grass he'd slept on. Didn't help that he'd tossed like a land-bound fish all night.

Word had it the five ranches had converged at the appointed site—a place called Willow Creek—inside of ten miles from where Brett stood putting a saddle on Rebel. The deplorable mood Brett was in, the pinto had better not even blink his eye in a thought of defiance. Rebel must've sensed Brett's threat, for he hung his head like a sorry dog.

Brett tightened the cinch with a sharp pull, waited a minute until Rebel puffed out a breath, then yanked once more and ran the end of the strap through the cinch ring. Brett had five other horses in his string—ones Foster had kindly let him choose. He'd met the wrangler before dawn—a grumpy squat fella named Templeton that looked to need two pots of black coffee each morning before he could utter a word. And last evening, as Brett was rolling out his bed, Mack Lambert, the foreman and wagon boss, had introduced himself.

Brett heard his name called and turned. Lambert was heading his way. And Roberts was a step behind him, his expression grim.

Brett pushed his hat back and studied the foreman. He looked as distressed as Roberts, but it was a telltale riffle under his calm. Though a foreman dressed like any other cowboy, he had an air of smarts about him. He needed to know the layout of the land, the general count of the herd, the punchers and others that made up his outfit. Lambert had a head full of wild black hair that could hardly stay stuffed under his hat. With thick side whiskers and moustache and beard, and monstrous shoulders, he resembled more bear than human. Contrasting that, his eyes were the palest, clearest blue Brett'd ever seen, set in a face that had seen plenty of years in the hot sun, though Brett took him to be around forty.

Mack only needed to cock his head at the stand of cottonwoods to let Brett know he had something to tell him. Brett threw Rebel's lead to the kid helping the wrangler and followed afoot. When they were out of earshot from the outfit, Mack drew them close and spoke in a hushed voice.

"I need t' ask you boys a favor," he said with his heavy Texan twang. He waited till he was sure they were paying attention. "Logan's been losin' cattle to rustlers. It's been ongoin', and he has some notion who it might be."

Roberts chewed his lip. Judging by his expression, Brett guessed he'd known about this trouble.

He reckoned this was what those riders had talked to Foster about the day Brett had shown up on the ranch, when Foster looked perturbed at their report.

Rustlers showed up all over the Front Range at times—as it was a sore temptation, all those animals freely ranging over hundreds of miles—and Brett had seen a few caught and brought to justice. But they were slippery, and over thousands of acres of rangeland, it was easy enough to cut some of the cows off from the main herd without being seen. 'Specially where there was heavy brush and places to hide. Sometimes they'd snatch young animals that hadn't yet been branded or ones that had missed the spring roundup. Other times rustlers would just steal a rancher's marked cattle and rework the brand out on the range and let the animals go. At the roundup, the rustlers would cull out all their stolen cows, proving ownership with the false brand. It was the worst kind of thievery, and the punishment was hanging.

"We'll be headin' east first up Crow Creek and Pawnee butte country, then along to Fremont's Orchard. If'n ya two don't mind, I'd like to have ya ride the drags—just for a few days. Seems these rustlers dally around the edges of the herd, then work some of the beeves back and into the brush. They're range brandin' 'em."

Roberts didn't look eager to eat dust, but he readily agreed. Lambert continued. "I'll be riding point, and I've got Daniels on swing. If'n you see somethin', git to him. Y'all will be paid fightin' wages."

Brett's eyebrows raised at the hint of danger. Though, confronting a rustler was danger aplenty. "Why ya want me on this?"

Lambert studied him. "New set o' eyes. You're new to the outfit. Ya may notice somethin' no one else will. Plus, word has it you're the best buster and rider in the outfit. Ya may need to chase these fellers down. I know Roberts c'n keep up with ya."

Brett nodded. Normally a compliment like that would make him feel right proud. But seeing as he presently felt as big as a worm, the words just slid by him matter-of-fact.

"Alright," Brett said, "but I don't need no extra pay. I'm glad t' help."

"Same here," Roberts said, a determined look etched into his features.

"Well," Lambert said. "Sorry to stick ya back there, but Foster'll greatly reward the one that can nab them scoundrels. Go on, then. Mount up and head on out."

When out an hour from the camp, they caught up with the herd, which was strung out a mile or more along the south bank of the Platte. From where Brett sat his horse, the many-tinted ribbon of cattle moved ever forward across the sea of rolling buffalo grass upon the hillocks, and two punchers riding drag were shouting and pounding the lazy, lame, and footsore animals to keep up with the rest.

Roberts rode over to the punchers and had a powwow with them. Presently, the two riders loped off along the flank leaving Brett and Roberts to take over their task. This part of the range had little cover, so Brett doubted he see signs of trouble, but he kept vigilant, rounding up strays and prodding the cows that fell behind or tended to wander off.

Brett kept as busy as he could, letting the heat of the day pound his shoulders and back and draw the pain and heartache from his body like a poultice. Only when the sun was westering above him did he take a break, coming up beside Roberts, who was drinking water from his canteen and sitting his horse on a hill thick with sage brush. Green trees to the north edged into hilly shrub land.

"Over yonder." Roberts pulled off his sweat-soaked hat and smoothed down his red hair. "By that slow piece o' water."

Brett craned through the evening haze choked with dust and made out the mass of bodies congregating along the river in the midst of an abandoned apple orchard. He spotted the chuck wagon backed up against a rocky hillock and made out other riders swinging round from the north, pushing the strays back into the main herd. An old corral teeming with lowing cattle, with posts lashed together with strips of cowhide, stretched out beyond the orchard with wings running out at least a hundred yards. Brett could tell by the hard trampled ground that it had been used plenty over the years for rounding up cattle.

"So, what're ya thinkin'?" Brett asked Roberts.

The Missourian shrugged. "I got a notion." He scrunched up his face as he looked off at the camp. "You reckon ya wanna give my hunch a spin?"

"Let's hear it," Brett said.

Roberts didn't name names, but he outlined his plan to Brett. It made a lot of sense. Clearly he'd been on the scout for some time sussing out the rustlers.

"So, I figure we got a half a moon—'nough light to see by." Roberts kept staring, his mind working the angles.

"Ya really think they'll take a chance so close to camp."

"I do." He left it at that. Brett sensed Roberts knew a whole lot more than he was telling. And maybe more than he'd told Lambert or Foster.

"Where ya want'a meet after supper?"

Brett listened as Roberts laid out the last details. He knew there could be a heap of trouble if they ran up on those rustlers in the dark. But Brett trusted Roberts—not just with his good aim and keen eye. He trusted the cowboy's character. And that was more important than a fast trigger finger—by a long chalk.

"Let's bring these drags in," Roberts said suddenly, then kicked his mount and loped off across the prairie. Brett itched to get into some action after spending the day at the tail end of the herd. It was a thankless job, but it felt like a kind of penance for Brett. Though, he doubted even the flames of hell could burn out the evil in his soul. He wished with all his might there was something he could do, some way to purge the blood of his pa from his veins. If it meant bleeding to death in a confrontation with rustlers, so be it. Maybe dying a noble death would give him reprieve for the perdition awaiting him.

In the meantime, he'd planned to stay as far away from the fairer sex as was humanly possible.

Well, that wasn't going to be hard to do so long as he rode with an outfit. Maybe after the roundup ended, Foster would keep him on. So long as cattle needed punching on the open range, Brett would always be able to rustle up work. And keep running from his life.

Chapter 24

"DARLING, I WISH YOU WOULD change your mind. The girls will miss you something awful." Adeline stood in the bedroom doorway, arms crossed, giving Angela her most pathetic look. But Angela was decided. And George had graciously agreed to allow her to move back into the small room behind his shop until her violin was ready.

After Brett had escorted her back to the ranch that awful day—saying not a word, even when he'd helped her dismount and watched her storm into the sanctity of the Fosters' home—she'd calmed down and told herself not to be hasty. Getting her violin and pursuing her dream was more important than anything—or anyone—else, and that included Brett Hendricks. She could wait a couple of weeks.

But not here. Not if there was any chance she'd see the cowboy again.

"I'm sorry, Adeline. You've been so generous and kind to me. But I can't stay."

"If it's because of those rattlers, you can stay close to the house—"

Angela stopped packing her small carpetbag and looked at Adeline. The rancher's wife had a knowing frown on her face.

"It's not about the snakes, is it?" she asked delicately in her Southern drawl. "It's the cowboy."

Angela's cheeks grew hot, and she returned to packing.

As she put her hat on her head and picked up the bag, Adeline added, "From what I hear, Brett Hendricks is a good man, and"— her frown turned into a mischievous smile—"anyone can tell by looking at him that he has it bad."

"Has what bad?" All Angela could see in her mind was the crazed rage in Brett's eyes as he slashed at the snakes with that knife, followed by the black emptiness she saw in his soul when he'd killed every last one of them. Was Adeline talking about his bad temper? But no—her entreating look said otherwise.

Adeline shook her head and gave Angela the kind of smile a mother would give a naïve child. "Darling, I saw the way Brett looked at you. The man's mad in love—can't you tell?"

Angela huffed. *In love? If so, he sure has a strange way of showing it.* She started to walk toward the door, but Adeline blocked her egress with her large form, which filled the doorway. Clearly Angela was not going to be permitted to leave until Adeline said her piece.

Angela sighed and set down her bag, then rubbed her weary eyes. She'd hardly slept a night since she'd been attacked by those snakes. The creatures invaded her dreams and chased after her in the dark hours, making her jerk awake in sweat and fear. Not even playing the violin helped pacify her tremors.

She had wished for Brett to hold her in his arms and comfort her once the snakes were dead. But he'd turned into some kind of monster—standing there glaring at her, covered in blood. She couldn't wash away the image of him like that—as if the snake blood had indelibly stained him. She couldn't bear to see him like that ever again.

"Don't you want a man to love you?" Adeline asked pointedly.

Angela's mouth dropped open at Adeline's forwardness, but no words came out.

Adeline pressed her further. "It wasn't his fault that the snakes attacked. They're everywhere on the Front Range—"

"Just another reason to leave," Angela sputtered with haste, wrapping her arms across her waist. "I just . . . I can't take this life. This isn't what I'm used to. I just want to go home." Without warning, tears pushed out of her eyes.

"Oh, I understand, darling," Adeline replied, her own eyes glistening as she put her arm around Angela and led her to sit at the edge of the four-poster bed. She plopped down next to her, and the feather mattress sank low. "I felt that way when I first came out to Colorado Territory. Here I was, not even twenty, and I'd hardly been ten miles outside of Savannah. I'd met Logan at a party given by his great-aunt—a woman of means and prominence among the great families in that part of Georgia." Her eyes turned dreamy at the remembrance as Angela sniffed and wiped her face.

"He was so handsome, and he asked me to dance. I had no idea he ran a cattle ranch in the West. I wanted nothing more than to stay in Savannah. But he'd swept me off my feet, and we were soon married. When we arrived by coach to Evans, I was horrified. What had I gotten myself into? I thought. The place was desert as far as the eye could see, and Evans was hardly what one would call a town, with one street and a handful of clapboard storefronts. How could I live in such a place?"

She smiled wistfully at Angela. "But Logan aimed to make me feel at home and, bless his heart, did everything to please me. He built me this beautiful house and keeps me in comfort and security.

And he's such a good, doting father to the girls." She took Angela's hands in hers and squeezed them, as if that would drive home the truth of her words. "Darling, when a man loves a woman the way Logan loves me, there is no greater joy. You need a man in your life, sweet girl, and there's no better catch than a cowboy with a true and loyal heart."

Angela bit her lip, thinking of how good, how right, Brett's arms had felt around her. And that kiss . . . Heat washed over her thinking of how his lips had tenderly met hers, and how his hot tongue had played with her mouth. Oh, how she longed for the kind of heated passion his kiss had promised. And the comfort and security Adeline spoke of.

But Brett was much too like her papá. There was no escaping that fact. No matter how much Brett might love her, or claim to love her, she knew, in the end, a marriage to a man like him would end up just like her parents' marriage. Marriage to a man like Brett — like her papá — would be a prison sentence and not the bed of roses Adeline gushed on about.

Adeline hadn't seen what Angela had in Brett Hendricks. And she probably wouldn't understand. She has no firsthand knowledge of what a violent-tempered man is like. And besides — what kind of life could Brett offer me? He wasn't wealthy, like Logan Foster, or from a fine, established family. And while Angela wasn't looking for riches, she didn't want to live in poverty either.

"Promise me, this, then, darling," Adeline said, still squeezing Angela's hands. "That you won't leave Greeley until after Logan's birthday party." When Angela began to protest, Adeline held up a hand and gave her a chastising look. "I've spent nearly a year planning his fiftieth bash. It's going to be a magnificent party, and ranchers and those of high-society from all parts will be attending. George Fisk has promised me a string quartet, and I want you to play." She added, "It's the very least you could do, and Logan will be so thrilled to hear you play again. As will the girls."

Angela buckled under Adeline's urging. It *was* the least she could do to show her gratitude for the Fosters' hospitality.

"When is the party?" she asked with a sinking heart, feeling trapped in a corner.

"Right after the roundup. On October thirteenth. By then, surely your violin will be ready. What better way to finish up your stay in Colorado than to play your new violin at Logan's birthday party."

"Will . . . all the cowboys be there too?"

Adeline frowned at Angela, but her eyes took on that glint that Angela saw often enough. "Of course. His cowboys are the lifeblood of this ranch, and they rarely get to dress up and partake of such fine food and drink."

"I see," Angela muttered, wishing there were some way out of committing. But if Brett showed up, she would be polite and brush him off. She would be there to perform—nothing more. And then George would take her back to town, where she could pack and leave Greeley on the next train south to Denver. Surely she could manage that. She straightened in determination.

"So, you'll play at the party?"

"Yes," Angela said with a sincere smile. "I'd be honored." It would be an honor to play for Adeline and her guests. No doubt George had already picked out the music. And the thought of playing in a string quartet sent a surge of excitement through her. She'd never played with more than one other musician before.

She stood and picked up her bag. The jangle of breaching outside the window told her the wagon was ready for her departure. Cook was heading into town for groceries and would drop her off at George's house.

"Will you at least come by a few times in the next two weeks to give the girls their lessons? All the cowboys will be at the roundup. The ranch will be like a ghost town."

Meaning, Brett won't be around when I come.

Angela nodded. "I'll see if I can arrange it."

"Cook can pick you up and bring you here on Mondays and Thursdays, after doing the shopping. And there is always someone at the ranch that can take you back to town. Thank you, darling. The girls love you so."

"And I love them," Angela said, for she did. They were adorable despite their precociousness. The kind of children Angela would love to have someday—full of spirit and free to express themselves. She recalled the way Brett had playfully teased them, eliciting their trust and laughter. He seemed to have a big heart full of love and would make a wonderful father.

How deceiving appearances are, she reminded herself emphatically.

As she headed down the grand staircase to the entry, she couldn't help thinking with bitterness how she'd had such dreams about Brett Hendricks. No other man had ever stirred her with such longing and desire. He alone understood her. He knew the pain and hurt a child felt at the hands of a mean father. Would she ever meet another man that spoke so truly and deeply to her heart as he had?

But he's just like his father. The apple never falls far from the tree. There was truth in that saying. And she'd do well to remember that.

Chapter 25

T HE MAKESHIFT CORRALS WERE FILLED with wild range cattle that glowed in the evening light—golden duns, pales yellows, soft reds, piebald black-and-whites. Brett hung back and watched as Foster's punchers yelled and waved their hats, funneling the last of the cows in. Above the din of the snorting and stomping and lowing, Brett heard the supper gong ring.

From his reckoning, it was a Tuesday. The four-mule team pulling the supply wagon could be seen cresting the ridge, heading back to the ranch, a plume of dust like a feathery tail trailing behind it. He'd been with the outfit rounding up cattle for more'n a week, the orchard jam-packed full of punchers from the five ranches. And while he and Roberts had scoured the range for signs of rustling, they'd seen 'airy a clue. Still, Roberts was both keen and certain about the scoundrels being among them, and whatever suspicions he had, he kept to himself. Roberts wasn't a man of many words— and few words that jumped to hasty conclusions. Brett liked the Missourian more every day that passed.

When the last of the bunch were shooed into the pens, Brett tapped Rebel's flanks and rode him over to the wrangler, where he slid off and uncinched the horse. The aromas drifting over from the chuck wagon made his mouth water. He was sore tired after thirteen hours in the saddle, though glad his leg had mostly healed and wasn't throbbing the way it had those first few days. Tuttle had done a right good job on him, and Brett was grateful.

A huge campfire crackled and sent sparks up into the night sky by the time Brett had washed up. Twenty or more cowboys sat on logs or stood around the warm blaze that cut the chill out of the air, eating with gusto and bandying jokes about. Brett smelled the season shifting—almost like he could tell the earth was tilting a little further away from the sun. This time of year the light thinned out, casting soft, long shadows across the ground. He caught a whiff of winter coming his way, the scent mingling with burning creosote and fir and strong coffee bubbling in a pot set on a rock next to the fire.

Laughter rose into the air, along with the murmuring of quiet talk among cowboys that had done this very thing more times than they could count. Brett thought on the many campfires he'd huddled in front of on cold Texas winter nights, and on the many times he'd laughed at some cowboy's funny tale or antics. But he'd lost all his mirth since that day Angela walked out of his life. *More like stormed.*

He sighed. He still hadn't been able to squash thoughts of her. She kept seeping into his mind, like black ink spilled onto a white page. Thoughts of her blotted everything else out. *In time. You'll forget her.*

He sighed and made to go join Roberts and Archie, figuring he may as well be social and could use some distraction. The nights were the hardest—when he lay in his bedroll and stared up at the stars. He'd never been lonely on the open range, but every night since coming to the roundup, the ache he'd pushed down all day floated to the top of his heart and hurt something fierce. All the while his hope for any kind of happy life sank like a boulder. Some nights he fantasized the way he would love Angela, imagining her warm skin as he held her in his arms under the blankets and under the stars. Other nights he swore he heard her fiddling—soft and low and sweet, a balm to soothe his ache, his need.

Just as he stepped into the circle of light, firelight flickered on the faces of the punchers. Brett froze and studied the man sitting beside Roberts. He'd seen that short, crusty fella with the thick red beard somewhere. His every nerve went on alert. The man wore a dark hat with a wide brim, and he nodded at something Roberts was saying. Archie's face lit up and he started in gabbing, while another fella—this one with sandy hair tickling his shoulders and trim side whiskers—glared at Archie, who seemed to be telling some funny story. Roberts was chuckling, but those two punchers acted like they weren't listening.

Brett dropped back into the shadows and eased his way over to where Roberts was sitting. Close enough to listen, Brett ducked his head down and turned his back. He only needed to hear the cowboys' voices to know who they were. *Them two are Orlander's men. I seen 'em standin' by the barn when I gave that kid what for. They're the ones that chased me.*

While Brett didn't imagine they'd still be on the scout for him, he wasn't going to take any chances. Riding the drags each day kept him well away from the other outfits, but evenings, all the punchers wandered about, chatting up fellas from the other ranches—just like they were doing now by the fire. Not much chance Brett could keep from being found if Orlander's men were still searching.

He caught snippets of their talk, though Archie's voice rang loud above the rest. Brett couldn't hear what Orlander's men said, but he stiffened when Archie said, "Hendricks? We got a Brett Hendricks in our outfit."

Brett turned enough to glimpse Archie swiveling his head this way and that—looking for him, no doubt. Brett dropped back a few steps behind two fellas smoking cigarettes and talking between themselves. He could still hear Archie, who was now telling these fellas what a great buster Brett Hendricks was, and how he could work the wild out of any horse in a few seconds flat.

Brett blew out a breath. Every nerve in his body tingled, telling him these fellas were fishing. *Orlander prob'ly sent 'em to the roundup to find me. And to finish what they started.*

He slipped away from the crowd and went to fetch his bedroll. Tonight he'd sleep somewhere else—and not tell Archie or Roberts. And he'd keep his Colt by his side.

He'd thought he gotten away scot-free. Colorado was big, but word passed between ranches and punchers like wildfire. And he imagined plenty of fellas had spread the word about the new buster who had a way with wild horses. He'd been a fool to think Orlander wouldn't catch up with him somewhere. So long as he stayed a cowboy, he wasn't safe.

But why in tarnation would Orlander be dead-set on findin' me? The answer shot into his mind, fast as a bullet. *I must've shot his kid.* Brett strained to recall what went down in that sudden dust storm. He'd taken that bullet in the leg, and the pain had all but erased the minutes that followed. But he did recall firing off some shots over his shoulder as he spurred Dakota into a run. *And right after that, the cowboys stopped pursuin'.* He'd reckoned it was due to the dust and poor visibility. But now he wondered.

Maybe I killed him. And Orlander wants revenge. The thought made Brett's gut ache.

Well, the roundup would be over inside of a week. He could probably stay out of sight until they broke camp. *And then what? Ya can't run forever.*

Well, why not? That's all he'd been doing since the day he slammed the door on his ma. While he really liked Foster and this outfit, clearly he hadn't put enough distance between Orlander and himself. Maybe if he went into Montana Territory. Or Oregon —

"Hey, Brett."

Brett spun at the whisper reaching his ears. He stopped, and Roberts came up to him. They stood close to camp, near the rope corral where their strings were kept for the night. Horses snuffled and nickered, but no other cowboys were close by.

Roberts cast a glance around, doffed his hat, and smoothed his hair. "Seems some cowboys are lookin' for ya, from the Flying Y Ranch," he told Brett, then got quiet for a moment. "They appeared all friendly, but I could tell somethin' was up. Smells a whole lot like trouble."

"I saw 'em — sittin' with you and Archie."

Roberts nodded and chewed his lip. "You know 'em?"

"They chased after me in the desert a few weeks back." He touched his thigh. "One of 'em put a bullet in my leg."

Roberts gave Brett a knowing look. Brett figured he'd noticed the bit of limp Brett'd had when he first joined Foster's outfit.

True to Brett's expectations, Roberts merely nodded and didn't ask any more questions. Brett was glad — he didn't want to tell the story or explain how he ended up being chased by those men. Still, he didn't want Roberts to think he was an outlaw.

"Their boss's kid was mistreating a gal. I interfered. Busted the kid's nose, I reckon." He let the words sit between them. Enough said.

After a time, Roberts shifted on his feet and looked out over the dark plains. A sliver of a moon sat high in the bowl of stars, and the Milky Way stretched in a thick cinch overhead. Night owls cooed in their holes. "Not likely them fellas are lookin' for ya over a busted nose."

Brett snorted. "Nope, not likely." Brett sorely hoped he hadn't killed that rich rancher's kid—though such a fate might be considered justice. Problem was—if he did kill that kid, there might be a price on his head. The thought soured his gut further.

"Well," Roberts said, "ya wanna go ride over yonder and check out what's behind them hills?"

Brett nodded. He wasn't sleepy even though he was plum tuckered out. Prob'ly wouldn't get any shut-eye tonight, what with his longings for Angela warring with his unease over Orlander's men close by.

"Alright, let's see if we c'n catch us some rustlers." Roberts smirked and patted Brett on the shoulder—the gesture telling Brett he had his back.

A feeling of gratitude filled him. Tate Roberts was a good fella, and good fellas were often rare in cattle country. Roberts reminded him a lot of Ol' Tex—the foreman at Lazy R who'd watched out for him, though Roberts was Brett's age.

After a quiet and lonely ride of a few miles through hilly country pockmarked with dry gulches, the wind kicked up cold. Brett tucked his chin as they loped past tall pines and broad balsams and slender birches, keeping his eye on Roberts's coat as it flapped against his cantle in the scant light.

"Looky there," Roberts said as he drew his horse to a halt and Brett stopped beside him.

Roberts pointed at a clear trail through some brush—easy enough to see by moonlight.

They tracked in and found the remains of a campfire with the embers still smoldering enough to give off an ashy smell.

They dismounted and looked around. Roberts scrounged through some nearby brush and presently brought up a stick of metal. A running iron.

Brett went over to him.

Roberts nodded, thinking. "I seen some of the cattle marked with a lazy eight." He ran a finger along the brand, which looked like a wave. "They're usin' this to alter Foster's brand."

"Ya think these rustlers're pullin' cattle out at night? Range-brandin' them?"

"Disfigurin'," Roberts said. "Yep. Look at the brush, how it's been trampled. I figure two fellas—one to hold the rope and the other t' work the brand."

"Workin' for someone else?" Brett asked. It seemed likely.

Roberts nodded. "Someone, sometime, will be gatherin' up them beeves. Boss might know who's got that brand." He took one of the irons in hand.

His look told Brett what he already knew—that just knowing who owned a brand didn't prove a thing. Only that cows with your brand were yours. If the branding was done well, there was no telling it was an alteration.

"Now what?" Brett asked, feeling twitchy about the whole thing.

"We catch 'em," Roberts said. "I got a feelin' they'll be back tonight. Maybe went back to get a couple more cows."

Roberts pointed at a stand of small pines that bunched thick passed the gulch they'd last crossed. "Let's head over yonder and sit awhile."

They mounted and made their way over to the trees, but as soon as they entered under the canopy of branches, the low, heavy rumble of horse hooves drifted to Brett's ears.

Presently, two riders came into view, bringing their galloping horses to a stop not more than ten feet from the fire pit.

Voices carried on the chill air, but Brett couldn't make out either words or whose voices they were. But he recognized the horses. So did Roberts.

"Just as I thought," Roberts hissed to Brett. "Handy and Shore."

Brett thought the two punchers were arguing about something. Rufus Shore was wildly waving his arm and shaking his head. Ned Handy slid down from his chestnut gelding, his lean, sinewy body easy now to make out in the moonlight. He walked over to the fire pit, kicked something, then marched back to his horse.

Brett and Roberts sat their night horses, watching until the two punchers rode away.

"Don't prove nothin'," Brett said.

"Nope, it don't. But it'll be enough for Mack to set them afoot. Chances of catchin' 'em brandin' are little t' nothin'."

Brett whistled. Having recently experienced the mercilessness of the desert, he knew that could be a death sentence. Punchers dreaded more than anything being discharged in such fashion. And these two would have at least ten miles of wandering across sage brush in the heat—stripped of weapons and packing no water—with only a coyote chorus for company.

"Ya really think Lambert will do that to 'em? They won't take it lightly."

Roberts shifted in his saddle to look at Brett full-on. "I reckon there'll be gun play. I doubt the two'll confess who they been rustlin' for. But Boss'll worry 'bout that."

The night fell thick with quiet as they waited a few more minutes before heading back to camp. Roberts said, "Let's go back thataway—jes in case those two stopped somewheres."

Brett nodded and fell into a lope behind Roberts's horse as he led them over the desert to the north and east. Rebel whinnied, and Brett felt the horse yearn to run. The powerful muscles worked under his legs, and Brett wished he could give Rebel his head so together they could outrun the wind.

He didn't look forward to the confrontation awaiting the outfit when Lambert dealt with the two scoundrels. It could only get ugly. As the cold wind bit his cheeks, he turned his thoughts to a warm fire—and the warm body of Angela Bellini lying next to him, her big dark eyes filled with love and desire, and those full tender lips parted and waiting for his kiss.

He flinched with need as he kicked Rebel with his spurs. Sure, he could run—run hard and fast, away from this life, this world of cattle, this country. But no matter how fast he ran, he would never be able to outrun his fervent need for Angela—that was the God's honest truth.

Chapter 26

"I SEE YOU SEEM TO be enjoying the book."

Angela looked up from where she sat on the porch chair. George held out a tall glass of iced sweet tea, a smile wide on his face.

"Thank you," she said, taking the drink from him, grateful for his consideration. Never once had her papá ever served her a drink. "Come sit." She patted the chair next to her, and the violin maker eased onto the cushion. He seemed pale and weak today.

"Are you unwell?" she asked, setting down the little book about the fiddler and dabbing her brow with a handkerchief she'd kept in her lap. The day was horribly hot and so dry that her lips hurt from the tiny cracks that had developed. She'd meant to go to the druggist's to get some cream, but had been so engrossed in the lives of the characters Christian and Naomi that the thought had slipped her mind.

"No, no, my dear. Just weary with age." He gave her another sweet smile. "Something you won't have to worry about for some years."

The noonday sun made the air so bright, Angela could hardly look at the glaring white paint on the steps to the house. She sipped the tea, and the cold liquid soothed her dry throat. Colorado was so dry all the time—even when thunderstorms drenched the earth in passing squalls. "You mentioned you had spoken to Violet. She's going to play with us at the party on the thirteenth?"

"Yes, and I've written out some parts for her, since the pieces for string quartet, of course, don't include flute. But I think these Beethoven compositions will provide the perfect music to entertain Mrs. Foster's guests."

"So do I," Angela said, her fingers itching to get playing once more. She'd hardly touched the violin at Adeline's house. Just knowing Brett might have been outside listening to her made her leave the instrument on its stand. She'd been silly, not wanting him to know she was still staying there—as if he couldn't find that out. In fact, the day before she left to return to George's house, Madeline had snuck up to her as the family gathered for the evening meal and whispered in her ear that "the handsome cowboy's been asking about you."

She'd wanted at that moment to rush out the door and search for Brett. She'd imagined him dusty and sweaty, his hair matted under his hat, as she ran and threw her arms around him. Why did she find such an image of him so intoxicating?

Even now, she ached for his kiss and tender embrace. Nights were torment, for instead of sleep they ushered in visions of Brett's hazel eyes sparkling with mirth and tinted with pain. She knew in that kiss that he hadn't been toying with her. She'd felt his need— and not just his physical craving for her. It was as if his soul played a song that made her soul cry out in kinship. The way two instruments or voices perfectly harmonized in timbre and melody.

Two people could hardly be more different, she admitted. But did those differences really matter when it came to the heart? She'd been trying to convince herself they did. But with every day she was apart from Brett, her conviction weakened a tad more. So much so that now, merely ten days after she'd run from his arms, she couldn't imagine anyone else holding her and kissing her. She longed for him to love her—to touch every inch of her body, to explore her with his fingers. Just as she longed to run her hands over his tightly muscled limbs and taut stomach. He was like a rock—solid, strong, unbreakable. She'd felt so right in his arms . . . and then . . .

Then she'd seen what was beneath his tenderness and affection. A man driven by rage, out of control. Violent, heartless, killing with cold passion. She winced recalling how he'd slashed at those snakes again and again. He'd become possessed with rage. Just like her father. And just as with those snakes, there was no telling when such rage might strike—without warning, without a care. How could a woman truly feel safe in arms that might go from embracing to strangling or striking?

"Perhaps I can arrange a rehearsal for tomorrow with all the musicians," George said, interrupting her dark thoughts.

She turned to him and pushed away the images of Brett with a knife in his hand dripping with blood. "Yes, I would love that."

He stood and said, "Wonderful, my dear. Violet has been nagging me to send you over to her house. Perhaps you'd like to take a walk with me after supper to pay a visit. We can bring her the flute parts I've written out."

"Perfect." Angela's mood lifted at the thought of seeing Violet again. She needed a girlfriend now more than ever. Though, she wasn't sure if she could tell Violet about her conflicted feelings for Brett. But why should she? In two weeks' time, she would be on a train, and Brett would become a memory—a cherished memory of her first real kiss. Someday she'd look back on this time and think how silly she'd been to romanticize love with a rough-edged cowboy.

No, now was the time to immerse herself in music. That would cure her melancholy and bring peace into her heart. Music was the great healer. *If only my music could heal Mamá.*

Angela suddenly noticed George studying her face. "Are you still troubled over your mother?" he asked.

His words made her realize she had hardly given thought to Mamá in the last few days. How could she have so easily forgotten the suffering she herself had caused? The reminder stabbed her with guilt. She'd been so absorbed with her own trite feelings.

George laid a hand on Angela's shoulder. "You mustn't be so hard on yourself, dear girl. Each must take responsibility for his own actions. Sometimes the powerlessness we feel over changing another is one of the most difficult things in life to accept." He picked up the book about the fiddler and thumbed through it. Then he stopped and read: "'Would that all the past could crumble into nothing. Yet, I will not be my own tormentor. I will enjoy the fragrance of this life.' Wise words, my dear. Life is too short for regrets. Live with passion and embrace all that God offers us in this world. Don't let guilt or fear hold you back from reaching your dreams."

Angela sighed, grateful for the reminder. And for George's wisdom and kindness. She was glad she'd come back to spend time with him. And she would do all she could to encourage him as well — and add a few pounds to his languishing frame.

She jumped up from the chair. "I'll make us a special meal tonight. And after that, we can visit Violet and her family."

George slipped his hands under his suspenders and rocked on his feet, his delight evident. "In the morning, I'll pay a call on Daisy and Rebecca—they play viola and cello, respectively, with the Greely Orchestra. We can rehearse in the Opera House building."

"I'm excited," Angela said. "Do you have time now to spend with me, reading through the movements? I have to admit—I'm a bit nervous about playing in an ensemble. It was hard enough to play for you when I arrived."

"But now you're not nervous, are you?"

"Not at all. When I'm playing one of your magnificent instruments, I seem to disappear. Only the music exists."

"As it should." George took her hand. "Come, my dear. Beethoven awaits your sensitive ear and touch."

She followed him inside the house to the living room, where the violins sat in cool repose, waiting for them. Her violin needed one more coat of varnish, George had told her this morning while showing her the rich red tones that highlighted the exquisite grain of the wood.

One more week. Then she'd have her very own Fisk violin—made by the man the newspapers called "The Stradivarius of the West." How many twenty-year-olds could boast of such a thing?

As she picked up the violin George had lent her and tuned the strings, a smile spread across her face. Before even running the bow over the strings, music washed her soul and lapped against the wall of her heart. The melodies of the many pieces she'd played with George since arriving in Greeley ran through her head. She felt about to burst with anticipation as George scooted over the music stands and opened up the folded sheets of paper dotted with notes that danced and leaped across staves, filled with promises of joy.

Rich, deep notes sounded as she played the music before her, filling her with a calm, serene feeling. But that feeling grew heavy with overtones and harmonics of loneliness and desire as, unbidden,

Brett Hendricks's face appeared in her mind—the way he'd looked at her when she played the violin.

She suddenly knew what she'd seen in those eyes—why the sight had riveted her. Her music had brought a measure of healing to his hurting heart. Just as it healed her own heart.

She let this thought settle into her bones as she played on, the strains of the violin erasing her with every note, until only the music remained.

Brett stood off to the side as the punchers and others in the employ of the Foster Cattle Company gathered in camp in the ruddy dawn light around the campfire. The dusty-booted punchers with spurs clanking shifted restlessly as wind canted smoke into their faces. The cold air danced across Brett's neck, but it was more than the air that chilled him to the bones. He knew this was going to turn ugly fast, and Lambert had told him and Roberts to be ready for lead to fly.

When he and Roberts had reported what they'd seen last night and showed the foreman the branding iron, Lambert hardly flinched. Brett knew then that Lambert'd had his suspicions confirmed by the news. Though Roberts had reminded the boss that "those two kin draw 'n' kill ya 'fore you could git your gun out," Lambert replied, "I gotta take the chance. Maybe they won't call the play. But if'n they do, there's nothin' for it."

A glance over to Roberts showed him moseying up behind Ned Handy and Rufus Shore. Both scalawags showed bored expressions, but even from where Brett stood ten feet away facing them, their shifty eyes flickered with worry.

As Brett's fingers twitched near the Colt in the holster at his side, he eyed Archie, who rubbed sleep from his face as he stood yawning among the bleary-eyed punchers shuffling restlessly, no doubt wondering why breakfast was delayed. The smell of hot coffee wafted like a temptress around Brett's head, along with the aroma of eggs and beans and bacon.

But breakfast would have to wait.

"I know y'all are eager to eat," Lambert announced to the silent, surly outfit, "but there's a matter that has to be dealt with afore we git to work." Lambert tugged on his big thick beard and pursed his lips in thought. Then he lifted his face toward Shore and Handy and took a step toward them, looking every bit the bear.

Brett let his hand slip down to his pistol, his eyes locked on the two men, who stiffened with eyes wide and hands hovering over their guns. Roberts moved in close behind them, watching Lambert like an eagle fixed on a mouse.

"You two." He pointed a steady finger at the pair of scoundrels. "Ya got ten minutes to quit the camp and hit the trail back to the ranch." His words hung like molasses in the thin air. "An' don't fetch yer things. Just git a move-on."

At first the punchers' expressions were of blank astonishment. And then, as realization came over them that they'd been found out and were about to suffer the indignity of being set afoot, their lips tightened and their eyes glowered murderous hate. Like most cowboys, Brett reckoned these two had hardly walked a total of ten miles in ten years, and without food or water or mounts, they'd have a tough time of it.

More than that, their days as punchers were over. *At least they weren't caught with cattle in hand. Then they'da been hung.* They were getting off easy, the way Brett saw it.

Handy screwed up his face. "Fire us to hoof it to the ranch? Fer what?"

"For engagin' in unlawful activity."

Handy snorted. "Why, you . . . It's a dog trot to hell for you, 'n' you starts right now!"

His hand flashed to his pistol, but before his fingers could tighten on the butt, Brett landed a violent kick on the flat of his shinbone. At the same time, Roberts threw an arm around Shore's neck as the scoundrel reached for his gun.

Lambert stood and watched as Handy doubled up, howling with pain—which gave Brett a chance to snatch the fella's pistol from its holster and smack him upside the jaw. Brett felt the bone crunch through the tips of his fingers.

Brett then whirled out his own gun and set a bead on Handy's head. Gasps erupted from the crowd as cowboys jumped back out of the fray.

Shore wriggled free enough from Roberts's grip to pull out his pistol and aim it at Lambert, but the foreman was ready. He punched Shore's face with a terrible crack, breaking his nose and laying him out stiff. Presently, both of Shore's eyes swelled until they were in poor shape for any accurate shooting, and blood trickled down his cheeks. Dust motes danced in the crisp morning light streaking across the camp and settled to the ground as the outfit fell quiet.

Brett caught a glimpse of Archie, who stood trembling with his heavy long-muzzled pistol in the air, his hand shaking so hard, he'd have probably end up shooting himself in the face if he pulled the trigger. Brett pushed down a grin.

"Whoa there, kid," he said, coming over and taking the gun from Archie's hand and returning it to its holster. The tenderfoot blew out a hot breath of relief, and his body slumped like a sack of rocks. Brett threw him an appreciative smile, admiring the kid's bravery and gumption.

With Handy moaning on the ground—Lambert's gun trained on him—and Shore unable to see straight, the fight was over. Roberts came alongside Lambert and dropped the guns he'd taken from the two at his foreman's feet. The rest of the outfit stared in stunned silence.

"Alright then, entertainment's over," Lambert finally said to the outfit under his charge. "Let's git to eatin' and to roundin' up Foster's cattle."

Punchers moved away from the fire, saying little, gathering up their things and fetching plates. The mood was thick and solemn. Cowed and defeated, without another word, the two scoundrels stumbled to their feet at the boss's urging, eyes downcast.

Lambert patted Handy and Shore from hat to boot and pulled out a couple of knives. Shore had a Derringer tucked into his belt at the back, which the foreman threw into the pile.

"The ranch is thataway." Lambert pointed south and west. "I reckon if you don't run into trouble, you'll make it there by nightfall. I'll send word so's Foster'll be waitin' for ya."

Brett knew there'd be little chance those two would make it that far—seeing the shape they were in. While they might be inclined to find refuge to nurse their wounds, Brett hadn't seen hide nor hair of a dwelling anywhere between Foster's ranch and Fremont's Orchard. The punchers might wander north and catch up to the river, but it would be a fool cowboy that'd wander afar without a gun or food or bedroll to stave off the cold of night.

He thought back to his ordeal in the desert not a month back, and he'd been lucky the heat had been so fierce as to keep the warmth locked in the rocks and dirt through the night. Otherwise he would have died for certain. Plenty of cowboys had met their death from a cold night on the open range. The way the frost had been icing the ground in thin sheets, without a bedroll those two'd be froze-stuck to the ground at first light. Lambert had given them good as a death sentence.

As Brett stood off to the side, waiting till the other punchers got their vittles, he kept an eye on Shore and Handy. They faced Lambert, scowls set hard on their faces, then, saying 'airy a word, they stumbled off in a westerly direction, which took them presently past Brett.

Pulling his coat tight around his neck in the cold breeze skittering across the prairie, Ned Handy slowed, his hand cradling his cracked and swollen jaw, a hard limp evident in his gait due to Brett's kick to his shin. Rufus Shore, his eyes swelled like black plums, hung on to the hem of Handy's coat like a blind man. Brett had hardly seen a sorrier-looking pair.

Brett stiffened when Handy stopped in front of his face. But he didn't expect more trouble. Handy'd be a fool to try to incite him into a fight in his condition. Brett caught sight of Tate Roberts in the corner of his eye, watching and ever ready to jump into action, if the situation warranted.

Brett clenched his jaw and glowered back at Handy, saying nothing, keeping his face as still as a pond at sunrise.

"I know 'twas you," Handy sputtered through clamped teeth. Pain swam in the puncher's eyes. Pain and hatred. "You 'n' Roberts." He spat on the ground in disgust. "You set us up. We don't got nothin' to do with no rustlers."

Brett grunted. "Who said anythin' 'bout rustlers?" A smile inched up Brett's face as Handy realized how he'd good as admitted his crime.

Shore merely hung his head and moaned. "Come'on, Ned. Let's just git goin'. We got a long ways back." He tugged on Handy's coat and was met with a slap to the head.

"Shuddap," Handy said. He turned and looked hard into Brett's face. "You're gonna pay for this. You 'n' Roberts. You'll see."

"Handy!"

Lambert's voice bellowed. The two scoundrels looked behind them. Lambert was marching over to them. "Git a move-on, or I'll kick you seven ways to Sunday."

"Alright, we're leavin'!" Handy muttered.

Handy and Shore trudged off with the glare of the sunrise at their backs. Lambert and Roberts came alongside Brett and watched to make sure the two left camp. Hands in pockets, the three stood, unspeaking, as the sounds of cowboys packing up bedrolls and clanging dishes filled the morning air.

Phineas Frye swung his lariat at the pesky calf, finally coaxing it out of the stand of creosote bush. His horse was already played out after a hard morning's work, but they'd pretty much gotten all of the Flying Y's cattle over along the northwestern ridge beyond the Platte. Instead of a month, they'd be done and heading back to Denver inside a week. He'd thought there'd be more ranches taking part in this year's roundup, but only five came. Then he'd learned that the three others had run their cattle up into the northeast corner of the territory—by the Overland Trail coming down from Nebraska.

"Hey!"

Phineas pushed back his hat and squinted under the hot sun as he watched Cummings gallop over to him and rein to a hard stop.

"There ya are. I wondered where ya'd run off to." He looked at the calf that was trotting over the hill bellowing, having gotten free of the brambles. "That one o' ours?"

Phineas shook his head. "Second time I seen that lazy eight brand. Whose is it?"

"Don't know," Cummings said, wiping his forehead with his shirtsleeve.

"I gotta switch out my horse."

Cummings nodded, then stiffened in his saddle. He threw a hand over his eyes and looked afar. "What's that?"

Phineas trained his eyes on the wavering horizon, where Cummings was pointing. "Huh. Someone's afoot." His nerves tingled alert, slacking off his tiredness.

"Who'd be out here, if'n it's not someone with one of the outfits?" Cummings cocked his head, a wary look on his face. A fella without a horse was a rare sight on the range, and it often spelled trouble. Back in the day it usually was Injuns, but Phineas hadn't seen hide nor hair of one in more than a year. "Let's check it out."

Cummings kicked his horse into a slow lope, and Phineas followed. Before long he made out two shapes—male, dressed like cowboys. Maybe they'd run into wolves, or they got thrown from their horses. *Not likely. One might. But two? And why would they be out thisaway?*

When they got within hailing distance, Cummings called out. The fella in front—limping hard—stopped and turned. The other one—shorter and fatter—slumped like a drunk behind him. They didn't carry a pack or water jug—nothing. Just had coats slung over their arms, which Phineas thought odd in this heat. And as far as he could tell, neither fella carried a weapon. Leastwise nothing in plain sight.

"Got . . . got any water?" the taller fella asked, his voice rough and dry.

"Sure," Phineas said, sliding down from his horse and offering his canteen. "What're ya two doin' out here?"

Cummings sat his horse, eyeing the two with suspicion. But Phineas could tell these fellas were in no shape to start throwing lead. They looked to be on their last legs. They had the appearance of longtime punchers.

The tall fella glugged down the water, then handed the canteen to his pal. The two looked beat up—with swollen faces turning black and green in bruised patches.

After they'd drunk their fill, the tall fella wiped his mouth and said, "We were with Foster's outfit. But we had a . . . scrape with the foreman. We was wrongly accused of somethin'."

Phineas could barely make out the cowboy's words, but the fierce expression on his bashed-up face told all.

The shorter one with a mess of brown hair matted to his forehead said, "C'n ya help us?"

"Mebbe," Cummings said. "We heard there's a fella recently joined up with y'all. Name of Hendricks. C'n bust horses like nobody's bizness."

The two footsore cowboys shared a look. Then the squat one said, his eyes nearly swollen shut and gummed with dirt, "Yeah, he's there."

The bitter scowl on both faces told Phineas these two had little love for Hendricks. The taller one narrowed his eyes. "What ya want with 'im?"

Cummings said, "He hurt the boss's son. Mr. Orlander wants that buster to get his comeuppance. But, uh, we cain't jes march into yer camp and take 'im."

"No, that ain't gonna happen. Plus, that kid see ya comin', he'll shoot. And he's got an aim and an ornery temper to boot."

"So, ya see our little dilemma. We gotta find us a way to nab the fella and haul him back to Orlander."

The short cowboy snorted. "Ya wouldn't git three yards afore you'd be stopped. Hendricks is Foster's pet."

Phineas took it all in as he got back up on his horse, and he could see Cummings's mind working.

"But I know jes the way fer you to catch 'im," the tall one said. "Foster's having a big party in a week. Saturday next. Big bash at the ranch house, for the boss's birthday."

"So?" Cummings said.

"So all o' the cowboys'll be there. Hendricks too."

Cummings's brows lifted. "Any ranchers comin' to this party?"

The short puncher said, "Yup. Your boss wanna come—if'n he's not already invited, no reason he wouldn't be welcome. Don't all them rich ranchers know each other?"

Cummings said, "I reckon."

"Easier for him to show up unannounced than the likes of you," the tall one said, having trouble staying on his feet. He came over to Cummings and rested a hand on the horse's neck, breathing hard. "Listen, you help us, and we'll help you. Saturday, right at dark, you meet us at Logan's ranch, behind the bunkhouse. There's a well and spring box set back by a gulley. Hendricks ain't the type to be caught off guard, and we c'n set a trap for 'im, so's your boss can . . . *see justice done.*" He gave Cummings a big smile full of crooked teeth.

Cummings looked over at Phineas. All Phineas could do was nod. He didn't like this one bit, but maybe he'd still get a chance to warn the buster. Orlander would be out for blood, but this Hendricks fella would have his outfit and his boss there to cover his back should things get ugly. Even so, Phineas doubted Orlander would call him out. He'd just as soon lure the fella out into the night and shoot him in the back. And that would be a low and dirty way to get revenge.

Not if I c'n help it. It weren't right that an honest and decent fella would get killed for some foul-headed spoilt kid's misdeeds. But ya cain't say a word—not if'n ya mean for Boss to ask you to come with. Ya gotta play along—and hope ya git the chance to warn Hendricks.

"So, c'n ya get us two horses? Jes anything so's we can make it back to town." The tall fella stepped back away from Cummings and implored him with his sorry expression.

The shorter cowboy looked confused. "We ain't goin' to the ranch? Lambert tol' us to head—"

"What for? Foster'll just give us a grillin', and then boot us out anyways," the other said, snarling. He turned back to Cummings. "Ya help us, and we'll make sure your boss gits Hendricks."

"Saturday next?"

"Yup, that's it. At sunset, behind the bunkhouse. Rufus an' I'll be waitin' for ya."

The short fella named Rufus nodded, and his gunked eyes tried to blink.

"And what's yer name?" Cummings asked the tall one.

"Ned Handy. I been with Foster's outfit six years. And this is the thanks I git," he ground out with bitterness. "Ya think yer boss would give some kind o' reward? For helpin' him nab Hendricks?"

"I reckon." Cummings pursed his lips and looked back behind him. Phineas heard the cattle lowing over the hills to the east.

"Alright, you two wait over yonder." Cummings pointed at a stand of scrub pines. "Here." He threw them his canteen and then dug into his saddlebag for some hard tack and threw that too. "We gotta get back, but I'll fetch ya two horses."

"How ya plan to do that?" Phineas blurted.

Cummings shot him a look. "Leave it to me. They won't be missed." He glared at the two punchers. "Ya better not double-cross us or you'll be sorry."

Handy forced out a gravelly laugh. "We wanta see Hendricks get his comeuppance jes as much as yer boss. We'll be there."

And so will I, Phineas thought, not looking forward to next Saturday — no, not one bit.

Chapter 27

ANGELA CAREFULLY TUCKED THE VIOLIN into the hard case, the strains of Beethoven wending through her mind, the lingering notes soft and sweet, feeding her soul. What more did she need? Music filled and overflowed in her, and she was so grateful for this gift. How could she ignore or squander it? If only she could find a way to support herself playing music.

As she watched Violet talking to stodgy Mrs. Green by the stage in the small and unadorned auditorium that seem buried in a film of dust and grime, her dream to play with the New York Philharmonic seemed nebulous and out of reach. While it had taken a measure of courage—and desperation—to board the train to come west to Greeley, she didn't think she had what it took to carve out a life in the city—or any city—living alone in some tiny apartment and practicing her violin and going to rehearsals and performances. If she indeed did get lucky enough to land a position in a symphony orchestra, she doubted she could earn enough to pay the high cost of her living expenses. And that would mean taking on some other job. Perhaps she could trade for a room, by cooking and cleaning for some wealthy matron. Or she could find a position as a nanny for a rich woman's children. If there were such positions.

Her dream seemed entangled with so many complications and "what ifs." Every possible path to her dream landed her back on her aunt's doorstep, depending on Tia Sofia's charity. And while she was certain her aunt would welcome her gladly, living in New York in the sticky heat of summer and the piercing cold of winter, trudging through city streets amid noise and the stench of horse-drawn carriages, grew more distasteful with each day she was in the West.

True to her expectations, the undeveloped open space of the Front Range and the simple, unpretentious town of Greeley provided the peaceful and inspiring tableau she needed to let loose the music that had been trapped in her heart. She couldn't help but fear that if she returned to the big crowded, noisy city she might lose her way to the heart of her music. For the first time since she'd come west, the niggling question had grown into a full-fledged possibility. *What if I stayed here and chose not to return to New York?*

As impractical and defeatist as it sounded to her mind, her heart argued otherwise. For what was truly awaiting her in Mulberry Bend? Only anguish and heartache and opposition. Yet, the thought of being so far from her mamá and sisters and aunt stabbed her with guilt. *But they are only a five-day train trip away. You could visit anytime.*

"Angela, dear. I want to introduce you to these lovely women who serve on the opera board."

Angela turned at the sound of George's voice and swallowed back the tears that lodged in her throat. Three old women in pretty dresses and summer bonnets came up to her, their petticoats swishing and gloved hands outstretched to clasp hers. Angela felt genuine warmth in their smiles.

"Oh, Angela," crooned a matronly woman with a head of tight white curls and cheeks as big and round as apples. "Your violin playing is divine. I've never heard such celestial music come from any instrument."

Angela's cheeks heated at the praise. George, standing alongside her, sported the smile of a proud father. *Not a smile I would ever see on Papá's face*, she thought with a sharp pinch of hurt. She glanced at the women hemming her in. She hadn't known they'd had an audience during the quintet rehearsal, but she'd been so lost in the music, she hadn't looked out into the dark auditorium.

"I'm Lavenia McConnoly—one of the founding members of Union Colony and chairwoman of the opera board." The elderly woman fingered a strand of pearls around her neck. "And this is Arta Pilsbury and Berta Gilmore." She gestured to the two other silver-haired ladies whose faces shone with excitement. Soon hands were patting and squeezing her arms.

Mrs. Pilsbury rolled her eyes while shaking her head. "Utterly divine—just as Lavenia said. My dear girl, you have such a gift. And we are so honored to have you here in our quaint little town. George told us you'd come all the way from New York to buy one of his violins. Such a brave undertaking for a young woman all alone."

"Indeed," Mrs. Gilmore added. A tiny woman, her voice fluttered like a warbling wren. "Please tell us you'll be making Greeley your new home. We have such a need for a violinist of your caliber. The fall season at the opera is already in progress. Did George tell you we are beginning rehearsals for Verdi's *Ernani*?"

"And as coordinator of the Greeley Orchestra," Mrs. Pilsbury said, taking Angela's hands in hers, "I can assure you a position of first violinist. Ever since Mr. Fisk vacated the chair, we've been in dire need of finding a replacement." She gave him a sympathetic smile.

"And Angela would more than fill my shoes," George said, lifting a foot and wiggling it—which made the ladies titter in amusement.

Angela, cornered on all sides, saw the spark of conspiracy in George's eyes. No doubt he'd put these women up to this onslaught of persuasion. But how could she be upset? Their accolades were sincere—and they gave Angela such a warm feeling of acceptance and appreciation.

Wasn't that why she played? So that she could move others with the music that so touched her own heart? Did it matter where those listeners lived or what kind of room they sat in to hear her play? She thought of the many families that braved a move west, into unknown reaches of the country, facing life-threatening hardships and difficult living conditions. Didn't they deserve to hear beautiful music? Wouldn't they be all the more grateful an audience?

Angela had never consider this—considered what a blessing she could be to those who needed to be comforted and uplifted by her gift. Did she really want to perform for wealthy city patrons only—those who could afford the high-priced ticket of an opera or symphony in a fancy performance hall? She suddenly realized she had been equating success and fame with self-worth, thinking that if she played with the New York Philharmonic, that would somehow prove to the world—*to Papá*—that she was worthy, that her life had value apart from her expected role of wife or mother.

Now she saw how wrong she was. All her dreams had been built on a lie. A lie she told herself. Her music wasn't about *her*. Her gift wasn't given to her to make her feel special. It was a gift given to be shared to others. And Angela wanted more than anything to inspire and move those who most needed the healing power of music. Regardless of their station in life.

"Angela, dear?" George's voice startled her. She realized the women were still chattering at her, but she hadn't heard a word.

"Oh," she said, "my apologies. My mind wandered off."

"These ladies would love to take you and Violet to lunch."

Just as he said the words, Violet came hurrying over, an bemused look of exasperation on her face. Angela guessed her discourse with Mrs. Annie Green was the reason for her expression.

"We're taking Angela to lunch," Mrs. McConnoly declared to Violet. "And we'd love to have you join us. Are you free to come?"

Violet's eyes sparkled. "Oh yes, I'd love that." She turned to Angela. "These ladies are the most wonderful supporters of the arts in our town. And the funniest." She cocked her head at Mrs. Gilmore. "You'll have to tell her the story of how you and your husband showed up in Union Colony in the middle of a blizzard."

Mrs. Gilmore's eyes went wide. "Why, Violet, dear, do you mean to scare Angela away? We're hoping to convince her to stay."

Violet laughed, and the other ladies cackled in merriment. "A good blizzard story will be welcomed in this heat." She patted her forehead with a handkerchief. "I could use two or three feet of snow right about now."

She linked her arm around Angela's and added, "Besides, the stories of how this colony was founded are tales of courage and vision and hope. They're inspiring. We may still have plenty of hardship and setbacks, but life is so much easier than it was five years ago. Why, who would've thought back in seventy-two that we'd have an opera house? At this rate, by 1880, we'll be known as one of the country's top centers of culture."

Angela smiled, astonished at Violet's words. "You have big dreams, Violet."

Mrs. Pilsbury nodded with the others. "We all do. That's why we came here. To make our Colorado dreams come true."

Angela's mind spun with their words, which tangled her heart with warring desires. But beneath it all, the truth of their comments plucked a loud string in her heart.

Admiration for these pioneers swelled. They'd given up secure, comfortable lives and risked all for a dream. A dream that was no less daunting and as seemingly impossible as hers.

In that sense, she and the founders of Union Colony were well met. She'd thought she would find the residents of Greeley, Colorado, to be entirely different from her—in background, in personality, in attitude. But they were much like her—chasing a dream. The difference being that they had grasped that dream and made it a reality. She could learn much from these people, she realized, greatly humbled. From George, from Violet, from these kind ladies standing beside her.

"I'm starving," Violet announced.

"Then let's be off," Mrs. Gilmore answered with a brisk wave of her hand.

Angela smiled, feeling a strange sense of freedom come over her as Violet, her arm still linked in Angela's, led her out of the building and into the hot fall day. A steady wind chafed Angela's cheeks and tugged at her bonnet as they marched down the wide boardwalk behind the three older women, leaving George to close up the auditorium.

Violet stopped suddenly. "Oh, tomorrow we're picnicking at Island Grove Park. My mother asked if you'd join us. Some of the ladies in her reading circle will be there with their families. They all love to bake, so there will be lots of yummy pies."

"Sounds wonderful," Angela said, trying to adjust to this surprising sense of belonging coming over her. She could think of nothing she'd like better than to spend a day at the local park eating pies and conversing with her new friend and hearing tales of the early days of this small and simple town in the West.

Well, there is one thing you'd rather be doing—even though you don't want to admit it.

Brett's face reappeared unbidden in her mind—as it often did throughout the day and in the late lonely hours of night. An ache of longing spread through her body as she once more imagined those muscular arms pulling her close to his chest, his lips finding hers. And once more tried, unsuccessfully, to force him out of her thoughts.

Brett's first thought when he'd slid down from Rebel's saddle was of Ned Handy and Rufus Shore, wondering if they'd made it back to the ranch that day last week when they'd been set afoot. Word at the roundup was that no one had seen 'em and that they'd probably ended up as lunch for the wolves. If that had been their fate, it was likely no one would ever know for sure. Brett wasn't going to lose any sleep over it, at any rate. Even if those two had somehow survived, he didn't think Handy would make good his threat to get even with him and Roberts. They'd be fools to show up at Foster's ranch at this juncture.

Wind from the west blew hard, churning up grit and causing Brett to squint as he looked around the ranch. The place was like a ghost town in the late afternoon, with all the punchers wrapping up the roundup and driving the cattle to the rail station for transport to Denver and the stockyards. As the other outfits and their chuck wagons were pulling out around noon, Lambert had told Brett and Roberts to go off herd and head back to the ranch, saying the boss had something in mind for them. No doubt Foster'd heard the whole account about Handy and Shore. Maybe he wanted to hear Brett's accounting of the events.

Tate Roberts trotted up to a halt beside him, his bandana covering his nose and mouth, the rest of his face coated with a layer of dirt. The fierce wind whipped bits of his red hair about his face as he pulled off the cloth and blew his nose. Their horses, weary from fighting the headwind and being pelted with hard grit, dug at the ground with restless hooves, heads hanging.

"Let's get these animals into the barn and rubbed down," Roberts said, then spun around at the sound of neighing and whinnies.

As Roberts dismounted, Brett stared into the hazy dust-choked air and made out shapes coming from the north toward the ranch. A tight herd of horses materialized—mostly Injun ponies and a few mixed breeds that were bigger and stockier. Out of the corner of Brett's eye, he saw Logan Foster come out from behind the big ranch house fifty yards yonder. He watched the herd of about two dozen move at a slow lope toward the far calf pen with the wide wings feeding into a narrow chute.

Now Brett made out two riders flanking the herd, and the young kid Brett had seen his first day raced over to open the pen gate. Just in time too. For not a moment later the first of the ponies stormed into the chute.

Brett watched in quiet astonishment. The wild horses ran into the corral with 'airy a complaint—as if they were happy to oblige. He'd never seen the like. Not a look of panic or fear on their faces. Yet, it was clear they were of wild stock. It wasn't until the two riders sat their horses after the kid latched the gate that Brett realized who they were.

Roberts whistled. "Ya see that?"

Brett nodded. "Some good-lookin' bunch there."

"Yep. Wonder how far away they fetched 'em." There were still plenty of wild horse herds on the Front Range, for the taking. But the numbers had been dwindling, along with the buffalo. Brett remembered many a time seeing hundreds of horses roaming across the Texas prairie, along with thousands of cattle, belonging to no one.

The wind died down like a flapping hen settling on her nest. The air cleared, exposing bright-blue sky. Sarah Banks—the Cheyenne horse breeder—sat astride her pinto in deerskin chaps and a cowboy's clothes. Her son sat his horse next to her. LeRoy—that was the fella's name. He had her dark Injun looks, but now, seeing him clearer than he had the other time, Brett could tell he was a half-breed.

An uneasy feeling seeped into Brett's gut as he thought on the words she'd said to him that day—that stuff about the calm water in the midst of fire and some song leading him out. And the pictures that had seared his mind—of his pa striking his ma, and Angela's face with blood trickling down her neck.

He knew not to take a medicine woman's words lightly, and they worried him. Was that vision just a warning, or was it something that one day would come true? *Well, if'n ya never see Angela again, you won't ever hurt her.* But what if he did see her? What if he tried with all his might to contain his anger? Could he do it? *Ya might as well try catchin' the wind and stuffin' it inside yer hat.*

He thought about Sarah Banks giving him Kotoo—a mighty generous gift. Something a person would hardly do for someone he knew and cared for, yet he was a stranger to her. He still couldn't reckon why she'd done it. Most folks would want something in return, but she'd given him the horse because he'd stood up, because of that Mexican girl he'd rescued from the clutches of Orlander's kid. *But how in the dickens did she know about that?*

He looked afar over the miles of pasture. Where was Kotoo? Probably out with the other ranch horses, clustered with them under a tree out of the wind. Just as he thought to find her, he heard her.

Brett swiveled around to see Kotoo running to the fence, then sliding to a stop in the brown pasture grass. The mare nickered and tossed her head, but she wasn't looking at Brett. She was calling over to Sarah Banks.

The Injun woman slid off the pinto and walked the fifty yards over to say hello to the mare. Brett reckoned he ought to join her, though his insides flipped at the thought of hearing more of her mysterious pronouncements.

"Go on," Roberts said, "I'll take care o' Rebel and Star." He took up both horses' reins and led them away. Brett slapped at his dusty pants and wiped his face with his sleeve. A dip in the river and some clean clothes would have to wait a spell. As he headed over to the pasture, he saw Foster talking to LeRoy Banks by the corral filled with the range horses.

Sarah Banks wore an old beaver-skin hat with a woven band, the kind cowboys used to wear back before the war between the states. She gave him a toothy grin when he came beside her. Kotoo nickered at him, then and pushed her nose toward him so he could rub her head. A big smile rose on his face at the sweet nature of this horse — *his* horse — and the way the mare made him feel every time he was near her. It was like all his cares just blew away on the wind. He couldn't explain it. But who would believe him if he tried?

"Your horse missed ya," Sarah said, patting Kotoo's neck.

"I missed her too."

Sarah nodded and kept patting, a thoughtful look on her face. Brett felt like he should say something, to thank her again, but the words wouldn't come out.

"Some wind, eh?"

Just as she spoke, the hot, dry wind kicked up again, twirling dead leaves around their feet. Kotoo threw back her head, tossing her whiskey-colored mane.

"Thunderclouds're movin' in," Sarah added, nodding at the foothills stretching out in front of the Rockies, the clouds casting dark shadows that drifted like ghosts over the land. "Hot dry wind and lightning—dangerous combination."

Brett nodded, wondering why she was going on about the weather.

"Tomorrow, you be sure to ride Kotoo." She turned to look him directly in the eye. "Remember what I told you? When the fire rages, look for the calm water."

She fell quiet, but Brett heard more words loud in his head. *"You will hear the song. Follow it. It will lead you out."*

The wind whistled through the stand of pines and cottonwoods to the north, near the river. The lonely moaning sound made Brett shift on his feet, the uneasiness growing in his gut.

"There *is* a way out," Sarah told him, still studying his face. "You don't have to burn in the flames."

Her matter-of-fact words startled Brett, but then he thought maybe she wasn't talking about a real fire. Maybe she meant the fire of rage burning in his heart. Still, it was a plenty odd thing to say.

He looked at her and she nodded. Then a smile lifted her wrinkled brown cheeks, and she patted Brett on the shoulder.

"I will see you on the other side, Brett Hendricks." She chuckled as if she'd said something funny, then strode off to where Foster was talking to her son.

"What the . . . ?" Brett blew out a hard breath. All that funny talk made him edgy. Best he go fetch his towel and head for the river to wash up and cool off. As he made for the bunkhouse, though, Logan Foster waylaid him on the path, Roberts right behind him.

"Hey, Hendricks," the tall man said, his iron-gray hair splaying out from under the wide-brimmed black hat he always wore. The boss's smile told Brett he was glad to see him, and Foster wasted little time telling him and Roberts what he'd learned about the rustlers. Seemed that altered Lazy 8 brand had led to a couple of disgruntled cow punchers that had a beef with Foster from long days past. "Slackers is what they were, and I'd let 'em go. They'd put up a big fuss, and I thought that'd be the last I'd hear of 'em. I reckon it were more greed than spite that drove 'em to do what they did." Foster snorted in disgust. "They got what was comin' to 'em."

Neither Brett nor Roberts asked for more details. But Roberts then said, "What 'bout Handy and Shore?"

Foster shook his head as his lips pinched tight. "Don't rightly know. And frankly, I don' care, long as they stay away from my ranch and my cattle. Not likely they'll be gettin' involved in more rustlin', seeing as their pals got caught."

Brett didn't imagine they'd dare try to join any outfit in Colorado—if they were still alive. Someone, sometime, was bound to recognize them and send word back to Foster. *If I was Ned Handy, I'd hoof it to Mexico and stay there.*

"So listen, I got a job fer you two. Bill Johnson over Greeley way is lookin' to put on a cowboy contest this weekend—just for some of the small local ranches, for the punchers to blow off some steam after the roundup. While I reckon you boys'd like to compete, Saturday's my big birthday party"—he gave a twisted smile that showed he wasn't all too keen about the idea—"and I'm 'specting all you cowboys to attend. It's just as much a party for y'all as it is for me. There'll be music and food and dancin'. Once the rest of the outfit gits back, y'all will hear more 'bout it."

"Alright," Roberts said, shifting his weight and looking every bit as eager as Brett to jump in the water and wash off two weeks of grime. "How c'n we help?"

"That lot of wild horses yonder?" Foster pointed at the corral behind them, where Sarah Banks and her son had driven in the herd. "They need to be taken over to Island Grove Park, to the fairgrounds, where they'll be holdin' the contest. I reckon if'n y'all head out at dawn, you'll make it back in time fer supper. Usually I'd send out a half-dozen or so cowboys for this many head, but Sarah Banks said you two'll do. She said to keep that little mare of yours in front, and the rest would follow." He shrugged as if to say, "Who am I to argue with a Cheyenne medicine woman?"

Brett and Roberts exchanged looks. Since when did a wild herd ever follow a young mare? "Ain't there a stallion in that bunch?" Brett asked.

"A couple of young bachelors, but no," Foster said. "I reckon Sarah and LeRoy cut that group from a bigger herd. Though, how they'd managed that . . ." His voice trailed off as he looked over at the corral. Sarah and her son were back on their horses and walking up toward the road. Foster gave a wave, and with a nod of heads, the two Injuns urged their mounts into an easy canter, heading north. Brett wondered why Sarah and her son hadn't run the herd over to the park themselves, but then, he figured maybe Foster's ranch was closer to where they'd rounded 'em up. Made sense to pen 'em up, feed and water 'em, give 'em a night's rest. Putting in a few broke horses overnight did wonders to calm down a nervous bunch.

Brett looked back at Kotoo, who still stood at the fence, looking at him as if reading his thoughts. You volunteerin'? Since that

Cheyenne woman wants you in the lead, you prob'ly oughta spend the night with that bunch, settin' the rules straight.

Kotoo threw her head, and Brett shook his, just this side of astonishment. *I'll pretend I didn't see that.*

"So, y'all good with the plan?" Foster asked. Brett and Roberts nodded. "Alright, then. I got some nice whiskey back at the house, and I think you both rightly deserve a glass. I'd like to hear y'all's version of what all happened that mornin' when Lambert told those two scoundrels to pack it in. But after you two clean up. The missus wouldn't cotton to havin' you step inside her clean house smellin' like y'all slept in a pile of cow pies."

Brett smiled along with Roberts. He could already taste the fancy rich whiskey soothing his dry throat.

"Yessir," the two said.

Brett glanced up at the big house, and his eyes snagged on the second-story window where he'd seen Angela playing her fiddle. The window looked like a lidless eye, staring him down, and the room beyond was dark and empty—just like his heart.

Chapter 28

FAT GUN-METAL-GRAY CLOUDS skittered overhead as the October wind buffeted Brett's face. The smell of rain clogged the dusty air, and wide dark streaks fell like curtains from the thunderclouds, the water drying up before making it halfway to the ground. The thirsty land begged for rain, but Brett doubted he'd see any water hit the red clay this day.

The years he'd spent living out of doors on the open range gave him and every cowboy a keen sense of weather. And of all the things the heavens threw at a puncher while driving cattle, one in particular sparked fear. Brett felt it now — in his fingertips as he held Kotoo's reins loosely in his gloved hand and all over his skin. Electricity tickled even the parts of him covered by clothing, and the hairs on his neck bristled.

He glanced back at Roberts trotting at the rear of the dozen horses in their orderly procession. He kept one eye on their charges and another one on the sky. No doubt he sensed it too. But not much they could do about it. They were on open rangeland between Evans and Greeley, nearing the fairgrounds set beside the South Platte on the outskirts of the town. It felt odd to be off herd for the day.

Brett made out the dull silver of the wide, slow-moving river to the north and a hint of the wood fence erected around the farmland. He'd heard that shortly after the shareholders of Union Colony had arrived at this dry godforsaken part of the desert, they'd build ditches to carry water twenty miles *uphill* to found their town. Brett couldn't believe the gumption of folks so determined to irrigate the desert, but they'd done it. And to keep out the range cattle, they'd built a fence—around the whole town.

What had driven them to such a hard task? And it wasn't just the Greeley folks. Towns like Loveland and Fort Collins and Longmont had been started by rich folks back east in places like Chicago and New York and Boston willing to give up a soft and easy life for a dream. A crazy dream—beset by blizzards and locusts and drought and Injuns.

And what about your dream? He hadn't much thought about his secret hankering to start a horse ranch. He'd always chided himself, thinking such a dream was foolish, that wishing for something that grandiose would only cause disappointment. Be glad for your lot in life, he told himself over and over. Could be worse. *Yeah, you could be dead, like a lot of other fool cowboys.*

He thought about the bullet he'd pulled out of his leg. About his nearly dying in the desert. About the times he'd been shot at and thrown from a horse and trampled and bit and kicked. Foster had told him and Roberts this morning as they saddled up how Sarah Banks's husband had died when a horse threw him and he hit his head against a post. It could happen to the best buster. To anyone, on any given day. He'd been lucky, so far.

So, you c'n try to play it safe, but there're still no guarantees. Why not go after your dream?

But how? Those folks that came west and founded towns—they were rich. *You got nothin'.* Well, lots of folks started with nothing.

Nothing but a dream. A dream plenty of gainsayers probably told them to quit wasting time on.

Fact was, the whole country was built on dreams. Dreams of freedom, of a better life. If you didn't go after your dreams, what was the point of living?

He thought about Angela—for the hundredth time that day. Seemed she was never far from his thoughts. She had a dream, a big one. The kind of dream not many gals chased after. Most gals he'd met wanted to settle down and have a passel of kids. And he reckoned there was nothing wrong with that. But Angela wasn't most gals. She had a gift with that fiddle. He could tell that when she played it, the music that came out fed her soul—just as it did his. It was some kind of magic. And he wanted nothing more than to be wrapped up in her spell every day for the rest of his life.

All morning, a tune had been playing in his head. He'd even started to hum it. For the life of him, he couldn't recall where he'd heard it or why it was stuck between his ears, playing over and over. But the notes were ones Angela had played—he was sure of it. The tune filled him with a heavy sadness. Yet, at the same time, he felt something else. Something he couldn't put a finger on. A kind of peace or calm. Soothing, the way a babbling creek sounded. Or evening crickets chirping at the end of a quiet fall day.

He'd been so deep in his thoughts, he hadn't seen Roberts trot up beside him. They'd covered the miles at a steady canter a good part of the morning, but now that they had Greeley in their sights, Brett had slowed the herd to mostly a walk—to let them cool down gradually and keep them from foundering when they hit the river to drink.

"Hey," Roberts said. "You seem a million miles away. Thinkin' 'bout a girl?"

Brett raised his brows in surprise. He hadn't known Roberts to talk about women—not like most cowboys did. Which made him wonder why the Missourian hadn't quit punching to settle down. He suspected Roberts was good-looking enough—had a set of straight teeth and an unscarred face and the kind of features most womenfolk took a fancy to.

"I might be," Brett replied.

Roberts laughed—a hearty laugh—as he looked over at the horses following Kotoo with 'airy a fuss.

"What's with that Injun pony o' yours?" Roberts asked, tipping his head at Kotoo. "Ya reckon that Cheyenne woman put a magic spell or somethin' on the mare? I never seen wild horses follow a mare hardly five years old like that. Like a schoolmarm keepin' the li'l rascals in line with jus' a look."

Brett shrugged as they neared the fence line. He thought about telling Roberts how it felt to ride Kotoo, but he knew he'd sound foolish. But there was no denying the odd sense of peace Brett felt the moment he lit onto her back. Soothing, just like that tune going through his head. It didn't squelch the loneliness that needled him, though. He knew only one cure for that, and she was out of his reach.

"What 'bout you?" Brett asked. "You ever think about gittin' hitched?" Brett hadn't known many punchers that quit the range to get married. Most that did had gotten hurt and couldn't ride in an outfit like they'd been doing. Cowboy work was hard on the bones, but it appealed to a certain type of fella. Mostly the kind that liked the company of a gal, but not every day and not under the same roof.

"Sure," Roberts said. "All the time."

Brett looked at him sideways. "Ya do?"

Roberts nodded, keeping one eye on the horses. They were getting twitchy with the wind blowing hither and yon and pelting them with dirt. Brett hunkered down and squashed his hat over his ears.

"I been punchin' for ten years straight," Roberts said with a sigh. "I've saved up a bit o' money. Figure mebbe next year I git me a homestead out Fort Collins way, along the Powder River. Good fishin' there."

"An' ya got a gal you're sweet on over yonder?"

"Nope. But I reckon I'll find me one. Plenty o' nice spunky gals in Colorady—same as anywheres."

"An' you'll jus' quit ridin'? What'll ya do instead?"

"My pa's a woodworker and taught me the trade. I reckon I can set up a shop, or work for someone already in the business."

Brett shook his head. "Ya mean you build tables and chairs and such."

"Yep. But also houses and window sashes and custom moldin'. Things all them rich folks want done to their fancy houses—like Miz Foster's place."

Brett thought of that fountain spewing water with the slate rock all around. "I s'pose there'll always be rich folks needing moldin'." Whatever that was.

The fields to the east, on the other side of the fence, lay fallow, the brown-red earth churned up in rows of clods, all the wheat and corn and potatoes harvested for the year. The first snows weren't long in coming. Though, on a hot, dry, and windy day like this, it was hard to believe.

"There's the park," Roberts said, pointing. "Every July Fourth the local folks have a big picnic and shindig there and horse contests. Them Banks boys—they win jus' 'bout every ribbon. 'Cept for a few Lucas Rawlings snags each year."

"Who's he?" Brett asked.

"Local vet. Comes out to Foster's ranch on occasion. Right nice fella. He—"

A loud rumble broke out across the sky above them, followed by spears of lightning striking the ground off to the west, near the hogbacks. Wind rose to a gale, and Brett grabbed his hat that danced madly behind his head, pulling on the strings under his chin.

The horses behind them startled and pranced, and without a word, Roberts fell back quickly behind them, pushing them against the fence and keeping them moving forward. Brett clicked his teeth at Kotoo, who alone looked not a bit fazed at the storm. Still, not a drop of rain fell, and the air thickened with dust. The hair on Brett's forearms stood on end as another three spats of lightning struck near the river. Thunder rolled in loud waves overhead, and Brett yelled over the hot wind.

"Let's git 'em movin'. I don't know what this bunch'll do if lightnin' gits closer."

Roberts nodded, and the two broke into a run, sending hooves flying. Roberts brandished his quirt and yelled "Haw! Haw!" at the ponies.

As Brett led the tight bunch in a gallop along the fence line past the fallow fields, the cluster of fairground buildings in his sights, his every nerve tingled. A twinge of fear raced across his neck before he could figure why. Then he smelled it.

Smoke.

Strong, acrid, and close.

The prairie was on fire.

Angela took a sip of her sweet tea as she and Violet sat underneath the branches of a small willow tree. The remnants of their picnic lunch lay scattered on the white china plates Mrs. Edwards had brought—crusts of blackberry pie and smears of mustard tinging leaves of lettuce from the sandwiches they'd enjoyed. They'd had a wonderful time at the park, talking about music and cooking, with the Edwardses sharing some of the funny tales about the colorful people who founded the colony.

Violet was so gregarious and naturally friendly, and Angela warmed to her as a friend unlike any other. Sharing a love of music gave them a special bond and made Angela feel her dream to play music wasn't all that silly or unattainable.

And then the weather had shifted without warning.

Hot wind wreaked havoc with Angela's hair, pulling strands loose and whipping them into her eyes. She was losing the battle to stuff it all back under her bonnet. Violet fared little better with her thick tresses. Angela had never seen a storm move in so quickly.

"Did you see that?" Violet said, suddenly getting to her feet. Crumbs fell from the lap of her brown-and-yellow calico dress. Flashes of lightning speared from the thick clouds overhead, just the other side of the park. Deafening thunder followed on its heels. The air felt heavy with dust and moisture.

Angela wasn't alarmed by the heavenly turmoil. In New York, the summers were punctuated daily with thunderstorms. But Violet's expression of fear gave her pause.

"Are we in danger?" Angela asked her.

Violet frowned. "We're not on the highest ground, but there's always a chance of getting hit by lightning out on the prairie. I'm more concerned about the animals."

Angela stood and looked to where Violet's gaze landed. Her father, Ed Edwards, was fussing with the breeching attached to the two mules, who pranced nervously as the thunder undulated overhead.

"They're not usually bothered by anything," Violet said, her frown deepening. "I don't know what's upsetting them so."

Mrs. Edwards, who had been playing a game of catch with Violet's young brothers, said something to the two boys, gesturing to the buckboard wagon. She then hurried over to Violet and Angela, agitation plain on her features as the brothers ran to help their father.

Around them, other families gathered up their baskets of food and folded up blankets. Women chattered excitedly as men loaded wagons and helped their wives and children onto benches and into saddles. Soon, Angela and Violet's family were the only ones left in the spacious riverside park. From the looks of the clouds, a deluge was about to be unleashed.

"Hurry up, girls," Mr. Edwards yelled over the moaning wind. Within seconds, the wind had gone from a slow and steady breeze to a violent gale that threatened to knock Angela off her feet.

"Oh!" she cried as her bonnet took flight from her head. Before she had a chance to chase after it, it had tumbled across the grass on its way into the river. Her skirts wrapped around her legs, entangling her.

Violet bent down, one hand anchoring her hat, and hurriedly threw the plates and glasses and silverware into the straw basket. Mrs. Edwards helped her and Angela fold up the checkered blanket as the ominous clouds roiled overhead.

"Girls, hurry and get in the wagon—"

Another bright splat of lightning struck the ground, this time only yards from the mules. Mrs. Edwards screamed and threw a hand over her mouth as one of the mules reared up and nearly struck Mr. Edwards in the head.

He jumped back, and the boys ran behind him, cowering. As lightning speared the ground again, a mule brayed in terror and broke free from the leather straps attaching it to the wagon. With a jerk and heave, the wagon lifted up sideways, then crashed back to the ground as the mule raced off down the road. One of the wheels broke upon impact.

Mr. Edwards's mouth fell open, but if he said anything, his words were sucked up into the wind that whipped and whirled like a dervish. Angela fought down the fear rising in her throat as Violet took her hand and stood huddled next to her, shaking.

Then, to her further shock, the other mule screeched as if something had bit it, then bolted. Still attached to the wagon by its side straps, it pulled the heavy contraption behind it for a few halting yards. But in its frightful effort to flee, it upturned the wagon altogether. The wooden sides crunched into the dirt in pieces as the mule kept pulling and pulling.

Mr. Edwards managed to grab the mule's headstall and bring the frantic animal to a stop. But behind it, the wagon lay crushed and mangled.

Mrs. Edwards froze halfway to her husband, and the picnic basket fell from her hands. Henry and Thomas threw their arms in the air, voicing their astonishment.

"What should we do?" Angela managed to say. "How will we get back to town?" The park was on the far south edge of town, perhaps only a mile or two from any houses or structures that could provide shelter.

"We'll just have to walk," Violet said with determination in her voice. "It's not all that far. Though, I wish I'd worn different shoes." She gave a smile that was clearly intended to reassure Angela. No doubt her own face revealed the fear she was trying so hard to keep at bay.

Angela stood beside Violet and watched as Mr. Edwards fumbled with the tangled breeching and extricated the panicky mule. Mrs. Edwards watched on as well, her feet stuck to the ground and her hands covering her mouth. When Violet's father finally got the animal free, he calmed it by walking it in circles. Angela could tell he spoke soothing words into the mule's ear, to keep it from bolting after its companion, who was far down the road, heading toward town.

"Leave everything," Mr. Edwards yelled when his wife lifted the basket from the dry brown grass. Violet set down the folded blanket. "Hurry!"

He looked up at the sky just as lightning struck an elm tree at the other side of the park, near the corrals and wooden stands that Violet had told her was the arena for the summer horse events. Flames erupted in the branches and ignited the few desiccated brown leaves clinging to the tree. Sparks flew into the air and blew their way, landing on the grass.

Angela stood transfixed, staring at the glowing orange tendrils that gobbled up the fingers of grass as if a voracious beast. Violet yanked on her arm, pulling her toward the road. Suddenly the air was filled with smoke.

Angela looked around her. Smoke billowed in the distance, the Rockies poking their peaks out the top of a blanket of gray that seemed to coat the entire prairie. Her gasp caught in her throat.

She swiveled around, looking in the direction of the wide river. The far bank was lined with a ribbon of flickering flame. She ran alongside Violet toward the others huddling on the road. The mule reared and brayed, and now Angela understood why the two animals had panicked. They'd smelled the smoke before the humans had. Mr. Edwards could barely keep hold of the mule.

"Just let him go," Mrs. Edwards said, her voice a hysterical pitch. "He'll hurt someone."

Mr. Edwards, clearly frustrated and at wit's end, stepped back as he threw the ends of the reins in the air. The mule wasted no time and ran off to join its partner.

"All right," he said, gesturing everyone to come close as he looked in all directions. "The wind is pushing the fire our way. But if we stay on the road and run as fast as we can, we should make it."

He looked at Henry and Thomas. "Stay with the girls. I don't want you running ahead." He took his wife's arm, and they exchanged a glance of courage. And then they all took off running.

Angela's heart pounded as the wind thickened with smoke. She pulled the top of her cotton blouse up over her nose once she loosed it from the waistband constraining it. Violet did likewise. Together they ran over the uneven ground, Angela squinting hard as smoke stung and forced tears out the corners of her eyes. Then, she tripped.

A cry of pain shot from her mouth as she tumbled to the ground, wrenching her hand from Violet's grasp. She grabbed her ankle and groaned in pain. A quick feel assured her she hadn't broken anything, but when she struggled to stand, the moment she put weight on her foot, she collapsed in a wash of new agony.

Violet knelt beside her. "Is it broken?" Her eyes were wide as she darted glances down the road, her parents and brothers widening the distance between them, as they were unaware Angela had fallen.

"No, but I can't put any weight on it." Angela berated herself for her clumsiness. She turned her head, and to her horror, the entire park seemed engulfed in flames. Now the wind was so hot, it seared her cheeks. Gray ash lighted like snow on her face and caught in her eyelashes.

Presently, Violet's father looked back, spotted her and Violet crouched on the road, and halted.

Angela's mind went numb as she straightened to stand with Violet's help. Fire swept across the prairie around them, closing in on them. Violet whimpered and clung tightly to Angela's arm. Tears fell hot onto Angela's cheeks as if drops of lava.

"Go!" Angela told her friend.

Violet shook her head hard, her face tight with refusal.

Hope of escape evaporated in the conflagration raging around them. Stabbing pain ringed her ankle as she dropped back to the ground and waited and watched in horror as fire consumed the world around her.

Chapter 29

AS BRETT KICKED KOTOO INTO a run, the prairie laid out before him burst into flame. He pulled leather and brought the mare to a sliding stop. The dozen horses behind him bumped into one another, whinnying in protest and fear. Roberts trotted up beside him, and together they gaped at the sight.

"That fire's headin' to Greeley," Roberts muttered.

Brett lifted his chin, feeling the searing heat of the wind and sensing its erratic shifting. Sparks flew like fireflies around him, lighting on his hat and shoulders and on Kotoo's mane. Even now, his horse stood unruffled, eyes and ears alert, making 'airy a sound. *How had that Cheyenne woman knowed this was gonna happen?* A tendril of fear slithered up the back of his neck.

"We gotta head back," he said. "Leastways, Foster c'n keep this herd awhile, till the wildfire burns out." He'd seen plenty of fires sweep across the desert, but always from a safe distance. Something about this one made the hairs prickle on his arms.

"Seems like we should jus' let 'em loose. Folks in town might need help with a fire brigade," Roberts said, chewing his lip and staring at the prairie. His gelding tossed his head, itching to bolt.

"Foster charged us with deliverin' this bunch to the fairgrounds. Seems we oughta—"

Brett froze. He heard something tucked into the wind. It sounded like a woman's scream—coming from the park area. He swiveled in his saddle and looked at Roberts.

"Ya hear that?"

Roberts nodded, narrowing his eyes and craning to see through the thick wad of black smoke ahead.

Crimany! There's someone smack dab in that fire.

He hesitated only a second before deciding. The wild horses would run to safety; they maybe could find them later. Or not. But now, delivering horses was no longer his first concern.

Brett spun Kotoo around and waved his arms at the herd. "Git! Go on!" Roberts joined in the effort to scatter the bunch, but they huddled ever closer, snorting and prancing, paralyzed by the smell of smoke and fire. They were used to a stallion leading the way, and though Kotoo had led them this far, she wasn't budging an inch at his urging.

"Oh for the love o' God . . ."

Brett reined Kotoo back around and kicked with his spurs toward the fairgrounds. "Haw!" he yelled.

Roberts rode hard beside him, and together they headed toward the brushfire that slithered across the open range like spilled oil, the herd blindly following them. Brett's face burned, and his eyelashes and eyebrows felt as if they were melting on his face. To his amazement, Kotoo remained calm under him—not a flinch of fear could he detect as she ran headlong into danger.

Calm in the midst of fire. Brett snorted as he hunkered down over the saddle, passing flaming fields as he found the wide dirt road leading to the park and turned onto it. *Didn't think that Cheyenne woman meant a real fire.*

"Looky there!" Roberts pointed as he ran his horse up alongside Brett's.

Brett's heart pounded as he strained to see through the heavy soup of smoke choking the road. He made out two shapes on the ground. Arms around each other. Dresses fluttering in the wind. *Two gals! What in tarnation are they doing sittin' in the road in the middle of a fire?*

He kicked harder, then some of the smoke cleared, and he spotted some other folks. They were running back to the gals. Looked like two grown-ups and two young boys. Six in all.

Brett's heart sank like a rock into his gut. Fire crackled and hissed all around them, flanking the road. No way could he and Roberts get all those folks out—not on their two horses. Maybe that fella and his boys could hoof it fast to town and outrun the fire. He and Roberts could each take a gal and ride hard, try to get help, more horses . . .

Ya have horses. A dozen of 'em. He shook his head as he pushed Kotoo harder. Yeah, wild horses. Ones that ain't never been ridden.

No way could he put any of those folks on these animals. *Besides, they aren't jus' wild. They're scared outta their minds.* And he had 'airy a halter or bridle for them.

But if he didn't try, he knew what fate awaited the pa and his boys. Afoot, they'd never outrun the fire. And that other grown-up's a woman, he now realized. You could put two of 'em on Kotoo and one on Star and git yerself on one o' the wild ones . . .

As his thoughts warred inside his head, he glanced back. The bunch stuck close to Kotoo's tail, trusting her lead, though their eyes stayed wide with terror. Trees on both sides of the park exploded in bursts of bright-orange flame as one after another fell victim to the wildfire. Above, the iron-gray clouds hung heavy, but not a drop of rain touched the scorched earth. Brett knew the fire would just have to run its course until it died out on its own. And with the wind this vicious and as feisty as a cornered wildcat, there was no saying when that'd be.

After what felt like ages, he reined to a stop in the road a few yards from the gals on the ground. One, without a hat, gripped her ankle, her head down, black hair falling around her shoulders. The other turned and looked up at him with scared, pleading eyes. Roberts jumped off his horse and hurried to their side. Star stood stock-still by Kotoo's side, while the other horses jostled and snorted.

Brett clenched his jaw, noting the fire had them surrounded. Only that thin strip of road held a tiny bit of hope of a way out. He heard Sarah Banks's words in his head. *"There is a way out. You don't have to burn in the flames."* Then he remembered her also saying: *"When the fire rages, look for the calm water."* Yeah, and *she also said somethin' about hearin' a song and followin' that. Fat lot of good that'd do presently.*

The man and woman—who Brett took to be the fella's wife— ran over, breathless and panting, the two boys close behind.

"Please!" the large woman cried, wringing her hands, "can you help us?"

The big fella with a bushy beard said, "Take the women. Get them to safety." He pulled his boys into his arms, as if trying to shield them from the scorching heat of the flames.

Roberts took the wife's arm, but she pulled away. "No! Take the girls! Please!"

Brett looked down from where he sat Kotoo. The gal looking at him from the ground had tears running down her plump cheeks. She was the spitting image of her ma.

"You have to help her," she said. "She's hurt her ankle."

The raven-haired gal, still clutching her foot, looked up. And when her eyes met Brett's, he sucked in a shocked breath, then swallowed hard.

Brett's heart lurched at the sight of her hopeless expression. He almost fell out of his saddle. "Angela . . ."

"Brett . . . ?"

Angela's pulse raced at the sight of Brett looking down at her from his horse. Confusion clogged her head, and she couldn't gather her thoughts. Where had he come from?

Every inch of her body broiled from the heat of the fire. She tried to stand once more, and while she couldn't put weight on her foot, at least the pain was now a bearable throb.

He slid off his horse and rushed to her side, helping to steady her. His touch sent another kind of wildfire racing through her limbs. His eyes were filled with concern and worry as he pulled her into his embrace and gently pushed hair out of her eyes. She longed to linger in the comfort of his arms—arms she'd dreamed of, night after night, holding her tightly against his broad chest. But this was hardly the time for such thoughts.

Violet stepped back, and Angela caught the stunned look on her face, questions about this cowboy swimming in her eyes. Then Angela turned. Behind the two cowboys, a half-dozen or so horses danced in fear. Brett and his partner must have been taking them somewhere nearby.

"Oh, Angela," Brett whispered hot into her ear. "I thought I'd never see ya again."

She felt his arms tremble, longing pouring out of him as he stood there holding her. She believed she'd convinced herself to forget him, but all the warnings about his violent temper burned to ash as his face pressed against her cheek and he held her tenderly, as if she might break.

The other cowboy—a tall, lanky man with red hair—took Violet's arm. "Miss, lemme help you up on Star."

Violet pulled away from him and scowled. "No! I won't leave my family."

"Violet . . ." her father began, his voice firm.

"Father, no. I won't." Violet planted her feet.

Angela pulled away from Brett and turned to her friend. "Violet, get on the horse." She looked at Mrs. Edwards and imagined how her husband and children would feel if they lost her in the fire. "Please, Mrs. Edwards. You and Violet should go with these cowboys."

Violet's mother shook her head in stubborn refusal.

Brett's face scrunched in frustration. "Listen, we ain't got time to argue. Roberts, git those gals up on the horses." He turned to the boys. "You fellas know how to ride?"

Henry piped up. "Yessir. We sure can."

"Okay," Brett said, looking at Mr. Edwards. "Start ripping up your shirt. I need long strips o' cloth." Mr. Edwards did as Brett said, pulling his shirt over his head and tearing it apart.

Brett looked hard into Angela's face. In a quiet, calm voice, he said, "Will ya trust me?"

Angela marveled at Brett's calm demeanor—so different from the day he attacked the snakes. But there was no time to ponder her choice. She had to trust him. She would.

She nodded, then turned to Violet. "Just do as he says."

Violet let out a frustrated sigh and ran her hand across her brow. The heat was unbearable, and Angela's throat and chest burned with every breath. The fire was inching ever closer, and more sparks and embers struck the ground around them. Wind etched her face with unbearable heat.

The cowboy named Roberts helped Violet up onto his horse. Hitching up her skirt, she threw a leg over the saddle and sat like a man with her legs on both sides. Then he managed to get Mrs. Edwards up onto the horse, situating her behind the saddle with her legs off to one side. She wrapped her arms around Violet, who took up the reins in her hand, still scowling, and waited.

Angela let out a little yelp when Brett hefted her into his arms and eased her onto his horse. The pain in her ankle erupted anew. She gritted her teeth.

"Get your leg over here," Brett said, helping her swing her leg out from under her skirt. He was having her sit astride, the way Violet was. While awkward, she felt a whole lot more secure than when she'd ridden sidesaddle that day at the ranch. "You won't likely fall when we git runnin'," he said.

"But what about you? And—"

"Jus' trust me, honey." He gave her a smile that sent her heart racing. His hazel eyes shone with affection and reassurance.

Roberts, standing beside his horse, laid a hand on Violet's and patted it. "Jus' sit tight a minute." He hurried over to Brett. "They're ready."

"We cain't jus' send 'em off runnin' to town. That herd'll follow."

Before Roberts could reply, Brett rushed over to Mr. Edwards. The grass stretching from the road to the river smoldered anew as the wind shifted east. Angela shook in terror, losing her last vestige of hope that maybe they might get out alive. A new eruption of fire now engulfed the wooden corrals and benches, and the wind gyrated once more with embers and ash.

Violet yelped. Angela saw her smack at her dress, putting out sparks that had drifted onto her. Mrs. Edwards clenched Violet's waist as the horse they sat on began sidestepping and neighing. Roberts wrapped one arm around the horse's neck, but that did little to calm it.

"We gotta git these horses outta here fast," Roberts told Brett. "What're ya doin'?"

Brett ran over to the horse Angela was sitting on—a strangely calm horse—and pulled a loop of rope from out of the bag behind the saddle. Then, to her consternation, he yanked the bridle off her horse, then pulled the reins over the horse's head.

"What are you doing?" Her voice pitched with hysteria, but she couldn't help it. Her horse, though, stood curiously calm.

Brett worked quickly, muttering to the group of horses as he approached one and slowly slipped the bridle over its head. The horse protested a moment, throwing back its head and flattening its ears, but then it calmed.

"You boys," Brett called out, gesturing them over. "Ya ever ridden a horse that wasn't broke?"

The brothers gave each other a nervous look. "No sir," Henry said, but he put on a brave face. "But we'll stay on. Don't you worry." Thomas nodded but looked utterly frightened when Brett handed him the reins.

"Alright. But first, we gotta get this bunch into the water." He gave the boys a smile. "Y'all stay here."

Angela's mouth dropped open. The river lay a hundred yards away—with a wall of fire between it and the road where they congregated.

"Can't we just take the road?" Mr. Edwards yelled over to Brett.

His answer was a tip of his head. They all looked to the north, where he'd indicated. Flames spun and twisted, dancing across the road as if daring them to approach.

"Roberts," Brett said to the other cowboy, "blindfold the rest."

He took the strips of cloth from Mr. Edwards's hands and handed them to Roberts. The cowboy quickly went from horse to horse and tied the strips of cloth over each one's eyes. Angela wondered why he was doing this but said nothing. She watched, astonished, as the agitated horses immediately settled down, despite the fires burning all around them.

Brett barked out instructions, his voice clear and loud over the roar of the fire and wind. Angela watched, mesmerized, as Brett had Thomas and Henry and Mr. Edwards each grab on to a wild horse's mane as they stood alongside it.

"Jus' walk fast 'n' steady. Follow Angela 'n' the others."

Roberts did the same with two horses in the rear, a hand on each blindfolded animal. Then Brett, guiding the last unclaimed horse, ran up alongside Angela. After a quick glance at his terrified and waiting group, he turned and looked at her. His face wrenched in concern for her.

"Lean down and tuck your head into her neck," he told her. When she'd complied, he yelled to the others.

"Hang on and don't let go. And for God's sake—don't try to stop, whatever ya do."

Before any of them could question or protest, Brett slapped her horse on the neck with a loud "Yehaw!"

Her horse took off running—toward the wall of fire leaping up from the park's sprawling fields. A scream caught in her throat. Was he mad? They would burn to death before getting anywhere near the river.

But he asked you to trust him. What other choice do you have?

She leaned forward and pressed her head against the horse's muscular neck as it rocked up and down, the strong scent of burnt hair and earth and horse filling her nostrils. She clamped her eyes shut, feeling the rush of scorching heat drench her as the horse plowed through the flames, moving so quickly that she felt as if they were riding the wind.

An eerie calm soothed her heart—so much so that she found her hands unclenching the horse's mane, though she dared not open her eyes. She wondered at the puzzling sensation, for her fear melted away as if the fire had reduced it to steam. Brett's voice played in her head like a soothing sonata. *"Trust me . . ."*

Chapter 30

BRETT HELD THE FIDGETY HORSE tight in his arms, feeling the animal's frantic need to race after Kotoo. But before he could head to the river, he had to make sure every last one of the horses — and the scared humans — made it through.

He couldn't get Angela's face out of his thoughts. Sitting there on Kotoo, her cheeks flushed red from the heat and her hair blowing wild around her shoulders. Her beauty and courage had struck him hard. He would do all he could to save her, even if it cost him his life.

Brett watched Star, glued to Kotoo's tail, run toward the water, the two gals hanging on tight and burying their heads. The pa and his boys were having a time trying to keep the blindfolded bunch moving forward, running alongside and avoiding the hard-pounding hooves. But they kept them heading in the direction of the river.

Brett hadn't harbored a hope that they'd cooperate, figuring the second they felt those nipping flames, they'd rear and bolt. But they didn't, and Brett had never seen the like. He shook his head, thoroughly astonished, as the fella and his two boys ran headlong right into the wall of fire. He needed those wild horses to stick with them, for his plan to work.

He'd wished some other way would've opened up, but nothing had. Every which way looked as deadly as the next. But Sarah Banks's words pounded like an Injun drum in his head. *"When the fire rages, look for the calm water."* He'd had no other choice but to take the medicine woman's words as literal. And the only calm water was the Platte.

Roberts had his hands full with those two last mustangs, but, seasoned horseman that he was, he clucked and yelled at them, yanking on their manes, keeping them moving forward.

Kotoo's whinnies were a rallying cry to the herd, but they sounded far from panicky. He wondered what she was saying to the horses following her. *"Thisaway, fellas!"* or the like. Brett knew a whole lot of talk could take place in a few neighs or snorts. He thanked the heavens he'd been given that mare, once more reeling in astonishment over such a priceless gift.

To his great relief, as each of the horses and humans ran through the flames, they seemed unsinged. By some luck or divine hand, wind blew the fire in all directions, as if confounding it, while they rushed through it.

The moment Roberts disappeared from Brett's view into the smoke and conflagration, Brett swung up onto his blindfolded horse and found his balance as the wild animal fought the startling weight on its back. Brett had picked the pony he knew would give him the most trouble, and, as expected, the horse began to break apart and rear up, turning circles at this new terror.

Without a bridle or saddle, it took work to get the animal properly under him and complying, but within a minute Brett leaned hard into its neck, kicked flanks with his spurs, and got the horse into a run. He trusted the animal's urgent need to join up with its pals. With his legs and arms, Brett guided the blind horse through the searing fire, hitting its rump with his quirt and allowing no hesitation.

Smoke slapped his eyes, but when he reopened them, he found himself galloping on smoldering blackened earth, the fire behind him and the river ahead. And at the water's edge, Roberts held the group, all eyes on Brett as he ran up to them, his heart battering his ribs.

For the moment, they were safe. But there was no time to waste.

Brett slid off the horse and yanked the blindfold off his mount. Roberts pulled the cloth from the eyes of the two horses he'd been leading. Then he ran over to the others and removed theirs.

With one eye on the brushfire gobbling up the edges of the park, Brett strode over to the two boys, who huddled beside the horse Brett had slipped the bridle onto.

He smiled and patted one on the shoulder. "Up ya go." With one hand tight on the side of the bridle, he put his other hand under the kid's foot and pushed him up onto the back of the horse. The animal took a few steps backward, looking as if it would start rearing, but Brett wrapped his arms around the horse's neck and spoke into its ear. Presently, the horse relaxed, and Brett let his arms slip off. He patted the horse's neck and said to the other boy, "Now you."

He lifted the wide-eyed kid and set him on the horse's bare back behind his brother. "Hold tight."

"Yes sir," the boys chimed, looking more excited than fearful. The one in front clutched the reins, and his brother wrapped arms around the other's waist.

Their father stood in his undershirt beside Roberts. His face seemed as white as a washed sheet. "I . . . I'm not much of a rider."

"Don't need to be," Brett said. "Now," he told him, "I'm gonna help you up onto this horse." He led the pa over to one of the smaller horses. "Ya don't have to do anything but hang on to the mane, alright?"

The fella nodded, but Brett could tell he was stricken with fear. Somehow Brett managed to heft him up and onto the horse, and the fella hunched over the animal's neck and grasped handfuls of mane. He gave a hesitant nod. The horse shifted with the new weight on its back but didn't fuss, much to Brett's surprise and relief.

Angela watched Brett help Violet's father. She couldn't believe this was normal behavior for a horse in the midst of a firestorm. She could only assume that Brett must have used that gift of his to calm these horses. What other explanation could there be?

Somehow, through all this, the fire sizzled and danced behind them and on the opposite side of the river, yet it no longer encircled them. What was Brett planning? She hadn't a clue.

Without bridle or reins, Brett trotted his horse over to her side. Her horse nickered at him, and Brett reached over and rubbed its forehead, his face troubled.

He scanned the river downstream, toward town, then he turned around and looked at the others. Violet and her mother sat on Roberts's horse behind them, and Roberts, who'd gotten up on one of the wild horses, waited at their side. The boys sat on their horse behind Violet, with Mr. Edwards in the rear. The last two horses pranced and paced but didn't run off.

"Jus' hold on," Brett yelled back to them all. He turned and looked at Angela, and his hazel eyes searched deep into hers. The nearness of him took her breath away. She wanted nothing more in this moment than for him to kiss her—the way he'd kissed her that day they picked berries. It seemed so long ago, and her desire for him was so potent, it made her ache all over. She'd all but forgotten her twisted ankle.

"Don't be afraid," he whispered, leaning close to her. "If ya feel scared, just hum one of them tunes ya play."

And then he wrapped his hand over hers as she clutched Kotoo's mane. The warmth of his rough hand made her desire for him flare. "I gotta make sure the boys' pa stays on his horse. Kotoo will lead ya home."

She nodded, but the thought of Brett leaving her side unnerved her. Yet, she was glad for the concern he was showing for Violet's family. In the midst of this danger, he displayed surprising calm and clearheadedness. This was a Brett she never thought she'd see.

"Alright, Kotoo. Lead the way," he ordered.

To Angela's shock, Brett slapped her horse's rump with a loud "Haw!"

Before she could utter a cry of surprise, the horse broke into a run into the river, and water splashed all over her skirts as the powerful animal's hooves galloped toward Greeley. She hung on for dear life.

Brett dropped back as the horses ran. He smiled at the sight. His ragtag outfit followed Kotoo, every one of them still on their horses. A steady lope would keep them from falling, rather than a bumpy trot. His biggest concern was the wife sitting on Star's rump. But she seemed to be holding tight to her daughter's waist—and that young gal knew her way around a saddle. The pa was clinging to his pony's mane. Brett didn't expect the fella would get dusted anytime soon. Still, Brett needed to be by his side when they entered the river. No telling what his horse might do—especially if they happened into some deep holes.

Brett's head was still reeling over finding Angela here, in the middle of the prairie fire. Her presence both distracted and spurred him into action. Some crazy twist of fate had brought them together again. He'd thought she'd long gone from Colorado with her newfangled fiddle. He'd never expected to see her again.

A grain of hope lodged in his heart. Maybe the good Lord was giving him a second chance. Just as he had when he'd sent Tuttle to find him in the desert. He knew he didn't deserve one, but he was grateful for it. Still, it puzzled him. The vision he'd seen—him hitting Angela, blood dripping down her face—told him he had to stay away from her. It was a warning, of what would happen if he got too close. If he let Angela trust him.

He loved her—he knew that now. There was no denying what he felt when he saw her on the ground, clutching her ankle. Every bit of him wanted to protect and save her. Same way he felt right now. The thought of losing her made him sick all over.

Ya don't have time for these thoughts, Cowboy. Git these folks to safety. Ya can moon over Angela later.

Fire now blocked the road that led into town and gorged at the western bank, taunting them. But they were safe in the middle of the wide river.

He used his legs and body to keep his pony from bolting ahead, then once the last of the horses splashed into the water, Brett raced it across the smoky stretch of burnt grass and plunged into the Platte, where the eight horses ahead kept up a steady gallop, stumbling and splashing.

Brett had heard the Platte was a shallow, wide mud pit this time of year, inching its way across the Front Range. If they could keep to the middle of the river, stay in the water, they'd be safe, even if the fire burned both shores. What they'd find once they got to town . . . well, they'd deal with that once they got there.

As he urged his pony on, prompting with his legs to bring it alongside the boys' horse, Sarah's words kept swirling in his head along with the ashes and smoke in the air. *Calm water in the midst of the fire.* That was the meaning of Kotoo's name. And he was sure it was Kotoo's calm spirit that made all the wild horses settle down. It wasn't anything he'd done. Fire terrified horses, as it did all creatures. He hadn't thought his crazy idea to lead these folks out on wild horses would've worked. Without Kotoo, he was sure the bunch would've scattered long afore they got to the park.

He grunted. Now he understood why the medicine woman said she needed to change the horse's name. Somehow, when she met him, she'd seen this moment. She knew Kotoo would lead 'em out. Maybe that's why she'd given him the mare that day—to save him and the others. The rest of her words came to him.

"When the fire rages, look for the calm water. You will hear the song." She'd added, "Follow the song. It will lead you out."

What song? He guessed the calm water was the Platte, but he didn't hear any song. Kotoo was leading them out, not some music.

He blew out a tired and frustrated breath. He and Roberts had ridden all morning, from Evans to Greeley, with hardly a break and hadn't stopped for lunch. And then this. Hunger gnawed at his gut, and the raging heat from the fire had given him a mighty thirst.

Oddly, he wasn't all that perturbed anymore about the fire. It still ate up the prairie all around them, but it had already raced across most of the park, leaving it scorched and smoking. The wind had eased some, and the churning black clouds were drifting east. Some blotches of blue peeked through, and the air wasn't as hot as it had been ten minutes prior.

But the road north was still ablaze. He hoped it didn't reach the town, but if it did, he and Roberts would help however they could.

All that mattered right now was getting Angela and these folks to a safe place. And by some uncanny miracle, his plan seemed to be working. Seeing the boys were handling themselves just fine, he rode up alongside their pa, who was trotting behind 'em, water up to their horses' knees.

"You alright on that horse?" Brett asked.

"So far." The fella turned his head for just a second, then went back to staring at the horse's neck. "Thank you for helping us. I'm much obliged." Brett heard the thick emotion in his voice.

"No need to thank me," Brett said. "I'm jus' glad we found y'all."

"We would have died back there." He clenched his eyes shut when his horse tripped up a bit. "I can't believe I'm on the back of a wild horse. Without a saddle or a bridle."

"You're doin' jus' fine. We'll be back to town in no time."

"How're my boys doing?"

Brett glanced ahead at the two youngsters. Just like boys, they were having the time of their life, ignoring the dangers around them, blabbering happily about something. They reminded him a bit of what he was like at that age. Fearless on the back of a horse. They rode well, with confidence.

"Nothin' to worry 'bout," Brett assured him. "Someone taught 'em well." Though, he wondered who that might have been.

Brett looked ahead and saw that Kotoo had slowed to a walk. Water came to her shoulders, and Brett was glad to see her wading through the water without sinking into the mud. She'd no doubt found a sandy bar underfoot.

"I'm Ed Edwards, by the way," the fella said, gripping tighter as their horses entered deeper water and slowed down. Cool air rose from the marsh weeds and water, and Brett longed to dunk his head in the river. The horses' hooves sank an inch into the soft mud, and Brett noted the hot summer had mostly dried up the red mud along the bank and hardened it to clay.

"Pleased to make yer acquaintance," Brett said, touching the brim of his hat. "You and yer family live in Greeley?"

"Yes. I'm a house builder and an architect. Been here since the colony began."

"How're ya acquainted with Miss Bellini?" Brett longed to ride back over to her, but he wanted to make sure Mr. Edwards got through the water without mishap. He reckoned distracting him with small talk might ease his fears. Much like the way it did a nervous horse.

"Angela's friends with my daughter, Violet. They've been playing music together. Angela is quite a talented violinist."

"I've heard her play," Brett said, his weary mind hearing the notes she played that night as he stood under the stars behind Tuttle's house. Even now, even here, her music filled him with a strange and unsettling longing. He heard one particular melody, sad and simple, and it made him feel empty and full at the same time. He shook away the glittering notes that burned like sparks in his soul.

He raised his head and looked at Angela's back. She sat tall and straight in the saddle as Kotoo plowed steadily through the water. The other horses followed Kotoo's lead without hesitation, as Brett reckoned they would. He smirked, thinking of the story he'd tell Foster when they got back to the ranch. *Those ponies'll prob'ly wonder why we took 'em on such a long ride. And that fella Bill Johnson won't be puttin' on a cowboy contest here at the fairgrounds anytime soon, that's for certain.*

Maybe Foster would keep this herd. They sure wouldn't need much busting after today.

"When we get back to town," Edwards said, bringing Brett's thoughts back around, "no doubt the missus will cook up a big supper. I hope you and your friend will stay and join us. It's the least we can do. That is, if the fire doesn't burn down the town."

He frowned and looked back at the smoldering park.

Brett saw the flames nibbling at the edge of town. But the wind presently turned into a gentle southerly breeze. From where they waded through the water, clanging bells warning of fire could be heard, blending with alarmed voices.

Just then, the clouds overhead let loose a downpour, and water sluiced down his hat and neck and soaked his shirt, front and back.

Brett turned his grateful face upward to heaven. Cheers of joy erupted around him.

"Well, would you look at that?" Edwards said, smiling wide and letting rain splash on his face. "God is surely smiling on us today."

Brett wasn't much of a praying man, but he gave thanks for this unexpected gift. Maybe all those religious people in Greeley held some sway over the Almighty. No doubt their prayers were a whole lot weightier than his.

Whether divine providence or just plain luck, though, it looked like the town wouldn't suffer the same fate as the park and fairgrounds. The rain fell in sheets, and the sound of sizzling steam and downpour was more music to Brett's ears.

The thought of a home-cooked meal sounded better than just about anything right now. He reckoned the town had a livery or some corral they could herd these horses into. And while he wished he could bathe off all this grime and smoke in the river, he'd settle for a towel and a bar of hard soap if it meant he could be in the same room as Angela for the evening.

Why, he imagined Tuttle would welcome him and Roberts and give them a bed for the night. *Prob'ly wash and iron our clothes, too, while we sleep.*

Brett laughed. The heavy sadness he'd been plagued with since he last saw Angela was gone. The fire had sparked more than a conflagration across the Front Range. It had sparked hope in him. If he could beat a wildfire that hemmed him in on all sides, why couldn't he beat the fiery rage lodged in his bones? Sarah Banks had told him that fire wasn't a bad thing. From the ashes, new life sprouted. New life begins. *"It must be so."*

While he didn't much understand what Sarah had told him, he felt the truth of her words. He felt the hope. It was well worth clinging to.

Chapter 31

"SO, WHILE WE WERE ENGAGIN' in all that cowboy frolic, some fat black clouds come rollin' in. The temperature dropped forty degrees in one fell swoop, forcin' us inside the hotel."

Angela watched Brett across the dinner table as his friend Tate Roberts told his tale, his face glowing in the candlelight. Brett chuckled as he scooped the last bit of apple pie off his plate and into his mouth, and Angela couldn't take her eyes off him. Scrubbed clean and in a fresh shirt Mr. Edwards had given him, his rugged features and crooked smile set her heart racing. But she watched from under lowered lashes, hoping no one—especially Violet— noticed how flushed she felt having him sitting only a mere two feet across from her.

Exhausted from the day's terrifying ordeal, she could hardly keep her eyes open. She sipped at the sweet tea that Mrs. Edwards had poured for her, and the cold liquid soothed her raw throat. Miraculously, they'd all escaped the fire without a single scratch or burn.

Angela would never forget the look on the faces of the townspeople they'd passed as their group trekked wearily through the streets of Greeley, their clothes drenched and punched with holes the embers had burned in the cloth. When they'd arrived at the outskirts of the town, rain dumping in buckets on their heads, they'd all dismounted—even Brett and Tate. Brett had wanted to put her back on his horse because of her ankle, but it no longer hurt. The horses hung their heads and plodded behind them, with no inclination to run off—no doubt as drained and weak as their human companions were. They must have all looked as if they'd been to hell and back, for the faces she saw expressed utter astonishment, and many ran over to them and asked if they needed help.

While Brett and Tate settled the horses in at the local livery, Angela went with the Edwardses back to their home, where she and Violet each took a brief turn bathing in a large claw-foot tub. Violet had insisted Angela come directly to her home and not first stop at George's. After the luxurious warm, soapy bath, Violet lent her a simple green cotton skirt and a chambray blouse, and since Angela's shoes were soaked and caked with mud, she gladly accepted a pair of satin slippers from Mrs. Edwards, who seemed to have an entire wardrobe of spare clothes in the armoire in the hallway.

Angela and Violet had been helping prepare supper when the two cowboys tromped up the front porch and were welcomed inside by Mr. Edwards. He wasted no time offering them something to eat to tide them over until the meal was ready. He then showed them to the bathing room and found them some clothes to wear, though, from all appearances, the shirts and trousers Brett and Tate wore hung loosely on their lean and muscular frames. Mr. Edwards was a big, wide man, so the two cowboys had to wear suspenders and roll up the sleeves of the shirts. But even dressed in poor-fitting clothes, Brett looked dashing and more handsome than ever.

". . . we were little more'n sheltered behind closed doors before the rain blew in, great gusts like a hurricane," Tate relayed, taking a respite to down the dregs of his coffee. Mr. Edwards poured him another cup and urged him to continue his tale.

A glance at Violet showed Angela she was all ears, engrossed in Tate's story. Or maybe she was more riveted on Tate himself. Angela noted the tall cowboy had a strong, kind face, and his green eyes lit up with merriment. He seemed in his late twenties, from what Angela could tell—perhaps the same age as Brett. Violet's smile stretched from ear to ear as she leaned forward and listened.

"It picked up a chair and dashed it to splinters against the wall. An' while our ears were still stunned by the roar, suddenly there came floodwaters pourin' in over the door sill and through the floor cracks, so fast it drove us all to take refuge on the second floor o' the hotel . . ."

Violet's brothers and father went for the last pieces of pie, glued to the cowboy's words, and Mrs. Edwards busied herself in the kitchen. Angela felt so wonderfully at home, soaking up the love and tender affections of this family, which made her miss anew her little sisters.

The sun was setting outside the window, and Mr. Edwards had sent word to George via little Henry that she was having supper and would be home late, so there was no rush for her to leave. Leaving was the last thing she wanted to do right now.

"What happened next?" Henry asked Tate.

The cowboy leaned toward the boys, across the table, with wide, concentrated eyes. "We looked outta the window, and there in the street men, women, and young'uns were afloat upon the wreckage, driftin' they knew not where, safe they knew not how long, shriekin' for aid no one could lend. Dumb beasts and fowls drifted by us, their cries risin' shrill above the wind—cattle bawlin', horses neighin', chickens cluckin' madly. It seemed the end of the world—at least of our little corner of it. But the buildin' withstood the strong current . . ."

Her heart warred within her once more as she sat there, catching glimpses of Brett's radiant face. Politely he listened to Tate's tale, but she knew he kept looking her way, hoping to catch her eye. His nearness was beginning to unsettle her, as were the tumultuous feelings she felt about him. He'd shown such calmness and courage in the face of terrible danger. Taking matters in hand, he'd managed to think quickly and get them all to safety—using wild horses that had never been ridden before.

Angela still couldn't believe how Brett had managed to calm the frantic animals. And convinced them to allow humans to get on their backs without throwing them off. She'd heard the Edwardses express utter astonishment over Brett's gift with those horses, and even Violet's brothers were enamored with their new hero, Brett Hendricks.

But as much as Angela admired Brett for the way he'd reacted in the midst of fire, she still couldn't erase the possessed look he'd shown that day when he killed those snakes. She wanted with all her heart to believe Brett was a good man, a tender man who would always show her the kindness and consideration he'd shown today. She'd hoped to forget him, but now she knew he was so entwined in her heart, extricating him would be agony.

Admit it, Angela. You're in love with him. Madly, truly, deeply. She shivered as if a cold breeze danced across her neck. You can't love him. You musn't. He's a wild horse, unpredictable, untamable. And what about your music? What about your dream?

Her love for music suddenly felt like a curse to her rather than a gift. She recalled a passage in the little book George had lent her. At the end of the story, Christian concluded that the common gifts to man were so great, it was sinful to desire "uncommon abilities from the Divinity." Longing to play the violin became a curse to him, and his pursuit of his dream caused him utter pain and despair. His next words felt branded in her heart with a hot iron: *"The man who stands in the beams of the sun is scorched by them."*

Is that what would happen to her, should she chase after her dream to be a great violinist? By longing for fame and approval and adoration on the stage, was she destined to be scorched?

Angela felt overwhelmed with sadness. Perhaps their ordeal in the clutches of the fire had seared her mind.

Why couldn't she be like most other women? Be content to be a wife and mother? Was that so bad?

She looked at Ginny Edwards, who stood humming as she stacked dishes in the wash basin, a wistful smile on her face. Mr. Edwards adored his family, and he'd been so relieved when they arrived in town with his family delivered from the fire, he'd wrapped his wife up in his arms and kissed her with such passion that Angela had flushed with embarrassment and turned away. Violet had laughed at Angela's reaction and ran to her parents and threw her arms around them. Envy had pierced Angela's heart in that moment, making her wish she would have reason to throw her arms around her mamá and papá like that.

Since she'd arrived in Greeley, she'd seen happy families. Families who loved one another, stuck together through difficult trials and seasons, and treated one another with the greatest respect and kindness. The Fosters, The Edwardses ... and George—all showed her what true love and devotion looked like.

Was it so hard to believe she could find happiness like this? Find a gentle, loving man like Logan Foster or Ed Edwards or George Fisk? Was she willing to take a chance on Brett?

Tate had finished his story, and while he sipped his coffee, he and Violet chatted quietly. If Angela wasn't mistaken, the lanky cowboy seemed just as enamored of Violet as she was of him. Mr. Edwards had excused himself, and the boys had run off somewhere, leaving the two cowboys at the table with Angela and Violet. Brett seemed lost in his thoughts, staring out the large window at the purple-tinted sky.

Would Violet be content marrying a cowboy? Tate's uneducated speech didn't seem to dampen her interest in him. Angela had been taught the importance of a proper education and of marrying a man of her "station." Her papá had been relentless in pushing her and her siblings to academic excellence, expected them all to learn more than spelling and counting. To keep a proper home, he'd drilled into her, you need to handle money and make wise decisions in running a household. The wives in Mulberry Bend purchased all the family's goods and staples, bartered and bargained over purchases with salesmen. They were well read and well informed of the goings-on about town and the country.

Still, all that education was for one purpose — to create a wife a man could control, who would obey his every order and fulfill his every whim.

But a woman who loved her husband would want to please him. Just as I want so much to please Brett and see his love for me well up in his eyes.

Yet, how much did they really have in common? She could hardly picture them sitting around a fire discussing Handel's sonatas or Paganini's caprices. And how much interest would she find in his tales of chasing cows and breaking horses? She feared that the passion she felt for Brett was only physical — and that he only wanted her because he thought her beautiful. *Mamá was beautiful once too — before she became a battered and defeated wife.*

"Wanna get some fresh air?"

Brett's voice startled her. She turned to him, and his smile snagged her like a skirt hem on a floorboard nail.

Flustered, she said, "Are . . . you and Mr. Roberts staying in town tonight? I mean, don't you need to get back to the ranch—?"

"Doc Tuttle's invited us to hole up at his house," Brett said. "We stopped by his office in town after seein' to the horses."

"Yep, Brett promised to tell 'im the harrowin' tale of the escape from the Island Grove Park Fire of 1877," Tate said, giving Violet a flirty wink.

Violet narrowed her eyes, incredulous. "That fire already has a name?"

"Does now," Tate said with a hearty laugh. "Generations from now'll be tellin' the story of brave Brett Hendricks—"

Brett stood to his feet, shaking his head. Tufts of bark-brown hair fell into his amused eyes. "Not if I c'n help it," he said. "Come," he told Angela, holding out his hand, "let's git away from the tall-tale teller."

Angela smiled but was taken aback by his gesture. How forward of him to expect her to take his hand—here, in front of Violet and her family.

"Come on," Brett repeated, "I ain't gonna bite."

Violet erupted in giggles as Tate shook his head, averting his eyes so Angela couldn't see the mirth he was trying to hide. Her friend waved a hand at her, as if pushing her along.

With a sigh, Angela gave in, and Brett nearly pulled her to the front door. She startled as he stepped outside onto the porch with her in tow, then closed the door behind them. The porch lay recessed in darkness as the night closed in around them. The warm air was filled with crickets chirping.

Her heart beat so hard, her chest hurt. "I don't know if this—"

Before she could finish her thought, Brett's lips were on hers, warm and wet and needy.

Stunned, she froze in place, and he took her in his arms. Without thinking, she pulled from him and turned to run down the stairs. How dare he kiss her in public, on Violet's front porch, for all to see?

She skipped down the steps, but Brett threw out an arm and hooked her at the waist. With a strong sweep, he lifted her off her feet. She spun into his steely embrace, and he crushed her to his chest. She could barely breathe as his warm skin melted against hers.

"Whoa," he whispered hot into her ear. "Why're ya runnin' off?" He trailed light kisses along her neck.

Unable to resist, she threw back her head, aching for more. A moan slipped from her throat. The touch of his wet lips and tongue behind her ear sent her wild with desire, and her body burned for him, for his hands to touch her all over. She hated her thoughts, her need for him. But she was helpless, like a cornered horse in a pen, as Brett coaxed her back into the darkest corner of the porch and found her lips with his own.

His mouth moved frantically all over hers, but not with force. They seemed to seek her, to beg for her to answer, and gladly she did. Her mouth opened in response, like a flower under the warmth of the sun, and her tongue entwined with his as he cradled her face in his hands and pulled her close, as if yearning to draw the love from her heart and into his own.

He fingered the buttons on her blouse, and before she knew what he was doing, her shoulder was exposed. His mouth fell on her skin hungrily as his hands slid down and covered her breasts.

A riffle of heat enflamed her, hotter than the fire that had simmered around her on the prairie. And while her mind protested in shock at his bold and brash action, her body went wild at the feel of his fingers playing with her nipples. Once more she tossed her head back and moaned, unable to resist, squirming under his touch as he pushed her hard against the wall of the house. With his body pressed against her, she felt his hardness and gasped—more at her wanton desire for him than at the shock of feeling him hot against her skirt.

This was wrong, so wrong. What was he doing?

She gritted her teeth and pushed him back. He tripped up on a board and righted himself, questioning her with his eyes. In the dim light coming from the lamps in the living room, she saw his face and it frightened her.

His eyes were hard and distant, causing an icy coldness to wash over her. Gone was the tender look and easy smile. Then his face loosened into a pained look.

"Angela, I'm sorry," he said, his words rushed. He put out his hands, palms up in apology. He took a step back, and she eased her way around him to the porch steps. "I didn't mean to . . . I mean, all I wanted to do was kiss ya. I'd been longin' to kiss ya again, ever since that day—"

"So you took what you wanted?"

Brett gave a pathetic grin. "I kinda thought it was what ya wanted too." He dropped his gaze to the ground.

Angela fumed, more angry at herself than at him. She was as much at fault by succumbing to his advances. She glanced through the window into Violet's house. Thankfully the room seemed vacated. The street was quiet, and no one was about.

"Maybe the women you're used to don't have qualms about throwing themselves into your arms—"

"Qualms?"

"Objection. Scruples."

Brett blew out a breath, the hurt in his eyes unmistakable. "I'm not around women all that much. Look," he said, "I . . . I just had to kiss ya. To show ya how I feel 'bout you. Ever since ya left Foster's ranch, I've been missin' ya every second o' the day. I thought you'd gone back to New York. So when I saw ya in the park, on the ground . . ."

Angela ignored his defeated look. "It's improper. You took advantage of me." A burst of anger laced her words, surprising her. "Just like a man. You're no different." Her head filled with pictures of her papá striking her mamá. She winced at the memory of the sound of his hand slapping her face.

She stormed down the stairs and hurried along the walkway. Brett ran up to her and kept pace at her side. "Where're ya goin'?"

"To George's. Please tell Violet I wasn't feeling well." She threw the words at him, her heart tumbling with her confused feelings. Didn't she want him to hold her and kiss her? Why then was she being so mean to him? She knew he cared for her; he wasn't toying with her.

But he pushed himself on you. He didn't first ask if he could kiss you. And you saw his eyes—that look. He was like a wolf in sheep's clothing. And that wolf hiding there, behind his eyes, scared her to her bones.

"Will ya trust me?" She heard Brett's words ricochet in her head. No, she couldn't. She hardly knew him. He lived in the lawless West, a cowboy who answered to no one but himself.

He took her arm lightly, but she pulled away. Tears threatened to push out of her eyes. "Please, let me go."

He dropped his arm and stopped walking as she rushed ahead. She didn't dare look back. But she knew he wasn't chasing after her. All she could hear were her slippers slapping against the dirt street as she hurried toward George's house, a sky full of stars overhead, the clouds that had dumped rain nowhere to be seen.

The acrid smell of fire lingered on the air, and Angela thought of the way the wildfire had raced across the dry grass and burnt it to charred stubble. The heat of her passion for Brett had done the same across her heart, leaving it scorched and raw. She wondered if it would ever heal.

Chapter 32

"THOUGHT MEBBE YOU'D LIKE A swig o' this."

Brett turned at Roberts's quiet voice. The buster held out a small tin flask that gleamed in the soft moonlight. Whiskey—just the thing to ease his throbbing head and hurting heart.

Nodding his thanks, Brett took it and said, "Where'd you git that?"

"Always have it tucked into ma belt."

Brett leaned against the back wall of Tuttle's house, a wool blanket wrapped around his shoulders, and let the smooth whiskey glide down his throat as he stared up at the night sky peppered with stars. He wished he had a whole bottle of the stuff to snuff out the awful feelings that rattled around inside him like a bucket of rocks on a three-wheeled wagon.

All he'd wanted to do was show Angela how he felt. And he'd let things spin out of control. Again. He'd been so stirred by his hunger for her that he'd forgotten her proper upbringing. A gal like her needed time and plenty of courting. He'd tried so hard to show her his good qualities, and in one moment all his hard effort to earn her trust had been squashed. He felt like a cockroach crushed under her foot. He doubted she'd ever speak to him again.

"So . . . uh, what's the story with you an' Angela?" Roberts asked, squatting on the spongy green grass that Tuttle watered each day to keep all nice in the hot weather. "You two know each other afore joinin' Foster's outfit?"

Brett's gaze lit on the tiny room in the next yard. Blinds covered the windows, and 'airy a hint of light seeped out. Angela was probably asleep in her bed. The picture of her that flitted in his head—of her in her nightdress, something soft and cottony and thin hugging her curves—heated his blood. He could hardly think of her without his body flaming with desire.

But that's what got ya into trouble tonight. You could do with a dunk in the river.

He flung away the image and turned to look at Roberts, who had lit a cigarette and was taking a long draw.

"We met here, come to think of it. In this here yard." He nodded at the little shack. "She's staying next door with an ol' fella that makes fiddles."

Roberts nodded. "Violet was tellin' me how the two of 'em play music. They'll be entertainin' at Foster's party Saturday."

Brett's brows rose. He hadn't known she'd be there, back at the ranch. Maybe he'd get a chance to apologize. *But what's the use? She jus' don't feel the way you do. And she deserves better—ya keep forgettin' that.*

"Ya seem sweet on 'er in a big way," Roberts said with a grin. "But Violet told me she's plannin' on going back to New York right after the party. Now that she has her fancy fiddle."

Brett's chest felt like someone had punched him hard. He knew Angela was set on going home. Her ma was in the hospital. *And she has those big dreams of playin' her music in a fancy performance hall.* He'd been a fool thinking he could convince her to stay in Colorado. There was nothing for her here.

"Well, I saw the way you were lookin' at Violet. She caught yer fancy?"

Roberts nodded, a thoughtful look on his face, like someone had asked him to add up a bunch of big numbers in his head. "I like her fine. She's spunky and fun—just my type. And I like her family. 'Sides, her pa's a builder in town. Mebbe he c'n rustle up some work for me."

Brett laughed heartily. "Listen to ya. Ya got all the angles worked out." He shook his head. "Ya think she'd go fer a crusty cowboy like yourself?"

"Why the heck not?" He smoothed out the baggy clothes Edwards had given him to wear. "I clean up as good as any other fella. All a gal really wants is for a fella to take a bath from time to time, be a good provider, and shower 'er with a lot of affection and purty dresses."

"Oh, is that right?" Brett said, amused at Roberts's serious manner.

Presently, a pale yellow light spilled from one of the windows in Fisk's house. The fiddle-maker was probably having trouble sleeping too, Brett reckoned. He didn't know the hour, but dawn was but a few shakes away. Like him, Roberts had trouble bedding under a roof. They probably would've slept better if they'd hauled the blankets outside and lain out under the stars on the squishy grass.

Brett hadn't even tried to get any shut-eye—not with his mind replaying his kisses and the way Angela had moaned under his touch. The way she'd pressed against him, begging for more, told him she'd wanted him. He knew he'd let his wild side take over, but how could a fella resist her soft, creamy skin and those scrumptious lips? He doubted any man with a healthy appetite for a gal could rein in such a craving. Was she so ignorant to think a respectable fella would be able to?

"I've been thinkin' 'bout those fellas at the roundup—from the Flying Y Ranch." Roberts stood and paced, the cigarette dangling from the side of his mouth.

The faces of those punchers were crisp in Brett's mind. He'd almost forgotten about them.

"Chances are Orlander'll be at that party," Roberts added.

His words made Brett straighten and push off from the house. He walked over to his pal, who was looking at some sculpture of an eagle sticking up in a patch of flowers next to Fisk's house.

Brett kept his voice low, not wanting the fiddle-maker to hear them through the partially opened window.

"Ya think there'll be trouble?" Brett asked.

"Those two at the roundup—they were keen t' find ya. A rancher like Orlander—he ain't gonna send his cowboys on the scout for someone 'less'n that someone had done somethin' bad."

Brett could tell Roberts had spent a bit of time pondering this. And he was right.

"Mebbe it'd be best if'n ya didn't go to the party," Roberts said, turning to look at him.

Brett thought a moment, then answered, "Naw, I ain't gonna hide. If Orlander means to settle a score, I'd as soon face him there as elsewhere."

Quiet settled thick around them in the cool air. Brett wrapped the blanket tighter around him, but he shivered anyway.

"Ya think he's dead—the rancher's kid?" Roberts asked.

Brett drew in a long breath and held it awhile before blowing it out. "That's what I'm afeared of. I shot at 'im over my shoulder, and the dust was too thick to see what I hit. But the kid and his pals stopped chasin' me right after."

"I heard tell that kid is all Orlander's got. That whole ranch—thousands of acres and as many head of cattle—all goin' to the kid. A rich fella like that, losin' his only son . . ." Roberts's words ran out, as if he knew he'd said too much.

Brett handed him back the empty flask. "Yep," he said, kicking at the ground. "I reckon Orlander is plenty mad." A scowl twisted his face. "But I'm not sorry—not one bit. I'd do it again, if'n I had to."

Out of the corner of his eye, he saw Roberts nod. "Well, I'll keep an eye out fer trouble at the party. I reckon we should be able to see it comin' a long stretch away."

"More'n likely," Brett said. "I'm appreciatin' of your help. Not many good fellas like you, Tate."

Roberts snorted at the compliment. He looked up into the sky. "Mornin's not long off. May as well try to git a little bit o' shut-eye before collectin' them horses."

Brett chuckled. "It may take some coaxin' to git 'em out of that nice, cozy barn with all that fluffy straw and those fat flakes of hay. Prob'ly so spoilt now, they'll dig in and put up a fuss 'bout leavin'."

Roberts laughed. "They'll do whatever yer Injun pony tells 'em."

"Ain't that the truth," Brett said, thinking on how Kotoo had kept the herd calm and led 'em through the fire to the river. How she'd kept Angela safe on her back. He hoped Sarah Banks would be at that party, so he could tell her the tale and thank her again. Though, he had a hunch she already knew plenty about the fire.

He threw another glance at the little shack behind Fisk's house. It sat dark and lonely back there. He wondered if he'd see Angela in the morning. The thought both excited and worried him. Would she even speak to him? Better if he gave her time to cool down before he tried to talk to her again. He and Roberts could slip out and head to the livery at first light. Saturday was two days away. While the thought of having to wait that long agonized him, it was probably for the best.

Why did he harbor such a foolish hope that she cared a whit about him? What did it matter? After the party, she'd be on the next train home. *Unless, somehow, by some miracle, you c'n convince her to stay.*

He snorted as he followed Roberts back into Tuttle's house. *Fat chance, Cowboy. You'd have better luck lassoing the moon.*

Angela gripped the teacup so hard, she thought she might shatter it. Despite the warm shawl around her shoulders, she shook as if chilled.

She couldn't believe what Brett had said. He'd killed someone? A rancher's son? And he'd do it again if he had the chance?

She could hardly swallow past the lump of shock and terror in her throat. If she'd had any last vestige of affection for Brett Hendricks, it was gone now. How on earth had she succumbed to his wily ways? He was a true cad—a criminal! And a man was after him, possibly with intent to kill him.

She knew the moment she'd arrived in Greeley and saw those cowboys at the hitching post that she was entering a lawless, dangerous world. Fine for someone like Violet, who lived in town, sheltered from the madness of the West by a protective and moral father. But the idea that a young unmarried woman could come to such a place and live in security was foolhardy and unconscionable. She'd be safer under her father's roof than here. At least the men she knew in her neighborhood, however domineering, weren't murderers!

Managing to set down the teacup without dropping it, Angela huffed in frustration and heartache. She began pacing the living room, careful to keep quiet and not wake George. She'd come into the house to get a cup of tea when she'd tired of flopping like a fish in her bed, sleep eluding her. And then, when she sat in his big padded chair, she'd heard voices outside. When she realized it was Brett, she'd inched close to the window. Yes, it was rude to eavesdrop, but she couldn't help herself. She wanted to hear what he might say about her to his friend. But she hadn't imagined . . .

Brett shot someone — some rancher's only son. And he was glad he had. Her head whirled in confusion. She had been so wrong about him. And he'd fooled her into thinking he was a respectable, honest man. What an idiot she'd been.

She thought about the letter George had handed her when she'd hurried from Brett's arms back to his house. Her aunt had wired her the money to pay for her return train trip. She urged Angela to come home, saying that Mamá was now out of the hospital. Zia Sofia was spending each day helping with Rosalia and Maria, as Mamá was still weak and tired easily. And Papá and Bartolomeo were readying to leave on a business trip — to Italy, for three months! While the thought gladdened her — for Mamá would be safe from his brutality should he leave — it meant her mamá would have to take care of all the household duties and chores. How would she even carry the trash down the flights of stairs to the incinerator in the basement? Her aunt had her own life to live. It would be wrong to expect her to stay all that time — it was Angela's responsibility to care for her mamá.

It was settled. She would take the first train to Denver come Monday morning. That would give her Sunday to attend church, rest from the party, then spend some time with George and Violet before leaving the West for good. While she would miss her new friends, her life was in New York. Her family needed her. *At least with Papá gone, I can stay in the apartment awhile. And maybe, just maybe, the philharmonic committee will consent to letting me audition again.* While Angela knew it was a silly hope, she was determined to hold her chin high and not let doubt crumble her nerve. One way or another, she would support herself by playing music. She had to. Any other life would be misery.

A peek out the window assured her Brett and Tate had gone back inside Dr. Tuttle's house. If Brett was still awake, she couldn't tell, as the windows were dark. She let herself—just for a few seconds—recall the way Brett's lips had felt on her neck, reliving the ecstatic feeling she'd reveled in when his hands slid over her skin.

Tears of disappointment filled her eyes. She'd wanted so much to believe in him. To believe he truly loved her. To believe he was a kind, gentle man capable of love.

How wrong she'd been.

Chapter 33

THE LIVELY SOUNDS OF THE party preparations drifted up the stairs of the ranch house to the familiar family room, where Angela sat by the window, tuning her violin. *My violin.*

George had surprised her yesterday afternoon, as they readied to leave for the rehearsal at the Opera House. He'd laid the open case on the table by the door, where she couldn't miss it. She recognized it immediately—the unique patterns of wood grain and the etched ebony pegs George had painstakingly detailed for her. When she'd lifted it from the case, George's smile spread from ear to ear. With a nod of encouragement, she'd picked up the bow and drew out a long high D note. The sublime timbre of the string resonated in a shimmer of sound around them, thick and intoxicating, musical nectar of the gods.

Without a doubt, this was her instrument—it would speak to her heart and sing out the music bubbling up from the caverns of her soul. It would speak the volumes of words she could not utter, and the music enticed from its heart would heal her own. Of these truths she had no doubt. She imagined this violin would be her closest companion, now and for years to come. And she so needed the soothing comfort it provided her, especially now.

Guests would begin to arrive shortly, and a few who'd come from far away were already settled into rooms in the big house, freshening up or napping before the festivities began. George was downstairs chatting with Violet, Daisy, and Rebecca, who'd come with Angela and George in the lovely carriage he'd leased for the weekend. Mrs. Edwards, such a wonderful seamstress, had worked magic on one of her own beautiful silk gowns and fitted it to Angela's thinner frame. Layered with crinkling petticoats underneath, the deep-gold gown accented her brown eyes—or so Violet insisted while having her try on the many stylish shoes she had in her closet. Long lacy white gloves and a beaded reticule completed her attire, making her feel elegant and much the lady of fashion—something she rarely felt and hadn't expected she'd feel in a small town in Colorado.

Riding over from Greeley, the carriage reminded her of those she'd been in at Central Park with her aunt, and though she'd engaged in the light and happy banter as they traveled along the bumpy, rocky road, her thoughts wandered lost. As much as she tried to push Brett Hendricks from her mind and heart, she found herself circling back to him, as if he were around every corner, pleading with her with those pained and needy eyes.

She wished Brett wasn't going to be at the party; he'd be a distraction she could ill afford. Adeline Foster had put months of work into this party, and Angela would not let her down by allowing her performance to suffer. While the pieces they planned to play weren't difficult, they required keen concentration so she didn't miss her entrances.

Yesterday's rehearsal had gone beautifully, and the music had erased all her heartache while she played. The magical feeling she reveled in as part of a quintet only reinforced her determination to become part of a symphony orchestra. How wonderful it would be to sit in a chair on a stage surrounded by fifty or more stellar musicians, the strains of her music weaving with that of all the others to make an exquisite tapestry of sound. She'd experienced such divine delight as a member of an audience, in a darkened auditorium, sitting next to her aunt and listening to Eugenia Pappenheim play. But she imagined that joy would pale in the light of the thrill she'd feel creating part of the music itself.

And while tonight's performance couldn't compare to those held in the New York symphony hall, it still required her professional demeanor. If Brett came into the room, she would ignore him and immerse herself in her music. And when they were finished, she'd keep by Violet's side, or George's, the rest of the evening, until it was time to leave. With sixty or more guests, surely she could avoid Brett Hendricks.

The door to the room flew open, and Angela, startled, jumped to her feet.

"Oh, there you are, darling!" Adeline, her hair pinned with a riot of thick curls topped with a slender diamond-studded tiara, came flouncing into the room in a gorgeous green silk gown with gathered sleeves and a V-neckline. A string of pearls graced her neck. "Have you gone into hiding?"

"Why, no. I'd planned to practice a bit before the party began. I hope that's not rude of me. Do you need my help?"

Adeline giggled and waved her gloved hand jangling with silver bracelets in the air as if shooing flies. "Oh, darling, of course not! The girls have been asking for you, but I told them they'll see you downstairs. Oh! Is this your new violin? George was telling us about it. Are you sure you don't want to come downstairs and meet some of the guests?"

Angela had seen the way Adeline spoke when excited, but the rancher's wife could now hardly catch a breath between sentences. Her powdered cheeks glowed with excitement as she waved a fan in frantic motion in front of her face, causing her lilac-scented perfume to tickle Angela's nose.

"I'll . . . be down shortly," she told Adeline, sensing her hostess's eagerness to show off her "favorite" violinist. Angela had overheard Adeline gushing about her to someone in the foyer when they'd arrived.

Adeline took a few steps into the room and lowered her voice with lashes aflutter. "And your cowboy is outside, waiting."

Angela stiffened. Brett, here? Asking for her? No doubt the perplexed and horrified look on her face is what made Adeline laugh mischievously and flap her fan even harder. *She must mean Brett,* Angela thought, recalling the way the matchmaking Southerner had teased her about him when she'd stayed here.

"Wh-what do you mean—he's waiting?"

Adeline giggled again and came up to Angela, looking her over. "You look like an absolute peach, darling. And that lovely dress is sure to set his itty bitty heart racin'."

"I don't—" she began to protest, but Adeline laid a hand on her arm.

"Remember what I said? That there's no better love than from a cowboy with a true and loyal heart?"

Angela's stomach soured, wishing Adeline would stop talking about love and cowboys. She'd had enough of cowboys to last a lifetime. She just wanted to play the pieces the quintet had prepared and pack for the trip home.

"Is he . . . downstairs?" All the more reason to hide up here and stall her entrance into the great room, where the guests would be milling and where the quintet's chairs and music stands were set up on the raised dais festooned with drapes of gold-trimmed cloth Adeline had had built for the occasion.

"Oh no, darling. The cowboys will be invited in later, after the guests have all arrived and mingled. Canapes and fine wine would be . . . wasted on those with unrefined tastes." She frowned, her arm still resting on Angela's. "You seem so upset. Is there something you need to talk about? George tells me you're still planning on leaving our wonderful state of Colorado to go back to the big, noisy, crowded city."

"It's not as awful as all that," Angela said, reacting to the look of distaste on Adeline's face. "But, yes, I'm leaving Monday. My mamá is home from the hospital, and she needs me."

Adeline's fan flapped again, blowing another burst of perfume into Angela's face. "Oh, surely there must be others who can tend to your mother. You have your own life to lead, darling. *Your* dreams. *Your* music. If you return to New York, you'll never know what you missed."

Angela looked at her in confusion. "Missed?"

Adeline sighed, and her body seemed to sag with disappointment. "Oh, Angela. Love, darling. Love." She said the words pointedly, as if each one were a nail she was hammering into Angela's heart.

A retort sat on Angela's tongue. Surely love could be found just as easily in New York as in Greeley, Colorado—if love were something Angela actually wanted right now. But she was already tired of this conversation. And she didn't want in any way to spoil Adeline's special night, so she mustered a warm, agreeable smile.

Adeline, not one to miss a hint, sighed again. "Twenty minutes. I'll have Clementine come fetch you when it's time."

"Thank you," Angela said, grateful that Adeline dropped the subject of love. *But what did she mean by "he's waiting"?* No doubt this was merely Adeline's way of getting Angela to seek him out, the rancher's wife so determined that Angela fall for a cowboy. *Maybe she merely wants to sway you to stay in Greeley so you can keep giving the girls violin lessons.* That was more likely the reason for Adeline's persuasive discourse.

After Adeline bounced out of the room, melancholy sat heavy on Angela's shoulders. Muffled dialogue and laughter seeped through the floorboards, and Angela felt her loneliness swell like a wave that crashed against the seawall of her heart.

Letting her mind empty of words, she again picked up her violin and bow and put the instrument to her chin. With her eyes closed, the poignant melody of the old Scottish folk song George had taught her swirled in her head. She lowered the bow onto the strings and let her fingers move of their own accord.

Why this particular melody haunted her, she couldn't say. It was as if it were composed of a thousand grains of sadness, and with each note she played, the more that sadness was drawn out of her, the way a poultice pulled heat from a fever. And like a fever, each note pained her with tiny pinpricks. Still, she played on, unable to stop either the notes from spilling out or her longing for Brett Hendricks from pouring into the empty space it carved into her heart.

Just as he had weeks ago—or was it a lifetime ago?—he stood out of sight below the upper window behind the house, listening to the fiddle music coming out the window. The sounds of carriage wheels rolling across the driveway and slate tiles, as well as the noisy activity of ranch hands at their chores around him and animals lowing, neighing, and clucking clogged the air, yet through it all, Angela's playing, alone, reached his ears.

Most of the other punchers were in the bunkhouse, getting ready for the big party—slicking their hair and moustaches with wax and putting on their best bibs and tuckers. After he and Roberts had driven their little herd of horses back to the ranch yesterday— much to Foster's surprise and relief over their safe return—Foster had given them both a bit of spending money and use of a wagon to go to town to buy some new duds for the party.

Brett's ears had gone hot when Roberts blathered how Brett'd gotten the folks safely back to town just in the nick of time, for the other buster had done as much or better to that end. And Brett told the rancher just so, though Roberts shook his head, being contrary.

But the good that came of it, aside from the pleasant satisfaction that they'd all come through the fire unscathed, was that Brett now had the means to wear something other than his tattered or threadbare riding clothes. Dressed in a soft gray chambray shirt and jeans, blue suspenders, and a pair of short black boots, he almost felt like a gentleman. He just wished Angela would think of him as such. How in blazes could he win her heart? It seemed a lost cause, and watching her play her fiddle all night was sure to make that ache in his heart grow to the size and hardness of a pumpkin.

He and Roberts had left at dawn to make their purchases, making it back to the ranch by midday, and Brett hadn't seen Angela—not that morning or since he'd come back from his shopping spree. But Miz Foster had stopped him with his arm full of duds from the mercantile when he stepped from the wagon over by the horse barn nigh lunchtime today. "That gal you're sweet on— she'll be here soon."

How in the world did Miz Foster know his feelings? Or was she just assuming, after that day he'd gone with Angela and Foster's girls to pick berries? *Or mebbe Angela said somethin' to her.*

He'd known women like Foster's missus, matching folks up, all a-titter with gossip about fellas and their courting ways. He reckoned women like Miz Foster had a lot of time on their hands, and maybe being stuck on a ranch away from town left them little else to do besides gossip and match-make.

Brett stood under a big tree with thick bare branches, the crisp fall day shining that thin sideways light that Brett loved, especially in the late afternoon. Smells from the big house drifted on the air—juicy meats and fruit pies and a whole tangle of mouthwatering vittles cooking in the kitchen. He thought about Roberts's warning—that Orlander might show up, on the scout for him. But he didn't care. He only had one thing on his mind, and that was Angela. She was dead set on leaving Monday. And he was dead set on stopping her.

His body slumped heavily against the tree trunk, and he closed his eyes and listened. After a moment his pulse started to race, as the familiar sad melody snaked in through his ears. There was something about that tune. She'd played it before—he was sure of it. Then he recalled that night he'd woke at Tuttle's house, feeling all twitchy when the fiddle playing floated in through the open window. It was making him feel the same way now. Like he wanted to bolt. Like a scared horse or a spooked jackrabbit.

What was wrong with him? Music never rattled him like this—and not something as sweet and sorrowful as what Angela was playing. And why would she be playing that? *Mebbe she's moonin' fer ya the way you're moonin' fer her.* He snorted. *More like she's missin' her home and her ma.*

He squinched his eyes to hear better over the hollering of some of the ranch hands doing their last chores of the evening around the barn.

The tune Angela played sounded like something a ma would sing to her babe —

Suddenly a voice sang in his head. A gal's soft and gentle voice. A voice he recognized but couldn't place. He strained to listen — to the words behind the music Angela played. He was slapped hard by a clear, bright memory.

> "The water is wide
> I can't cross o'er
> Neither have I wings to fly
> Give me a boat that can carry two
> And both shall row, my love and I . . ."

He saw a gal hovering over him, her sparkling eyes full of love, wheat-colored hair waterfalling over her shoulders. He was lying on a bed, staring at her, adoring her. Love so painful poured out of him; he couldn't take his eyes off her bright-green ones that shone in the light of the oil lamp on the nearby table. She reached down and stroked his cheek. Her singing melted his heart and made him feel safe, so safe. He couldn't move, could barely breathe.

> "A ship there is and she sails the sea
> She's loaded deep as deep can be
> But not so deep as the love I'm in
> I know not if I sink or swim . . ."

Sitting stock-still under the massive branches of the tree, he swiped at his face, and his fingers came away wet. He opened his eyes. Tears? He shot a glance up to the window. The music had stopped. His blood surged in his ears as he hurried over to the side of the house and looked up, hoping to catch sight of her. But he couldn't get the angle right. He had to hear more, to know who that woman was in his mind. To know why she looked at him like that. And why did Angela's playing make him feel so weepy?

He squatted on the ground and cradled his head in his hands, trying to swallow back the wad of hurt stuck there. With his eyes shut, he searched for that face, and then he found it, lantern light making her hair shimmer, like she was some angel.

"Oh love be handsome and love be kind
Gay as a jewel when first it is new
But love grows old and waxes cold
And fades away like the morning dew . . ."

Just then, the head yanked back, and the gal screamed—a piercing, terrified scream. Then he screamed—a high-pitched wail that filled the dark room. The lantern toppled, and hungry tongues of fire raced across floorboards, eating up the oil.

Brett sucked in a breath as shock rippled through his veins at the sight of his pa's giant scowling face glowering at his. Behind his pa, he saw her struggle to her feet, her hand inching up the side of her head, blood pouring from a gash above her ear.

Smoke filled the room, and Brett coughed, choking. Heavy footsteps ran across wooden floorboards, the sound fading as Brett wailed and wailed, staring at his ma, who lay up against the wall, stunned, blood dripping down her face.

He was thrown into that vision Sarah Banks had given him. He thought he'd seen Angela hurt. Thought it was he that'd struck her.

But it wasn't Angela—it was his ma, when she'd been oh so young and purty. Her light-brown hair looked dark in the smoky room, drenched with blood. And his pa had left her to burn with her babe, running to save his own hide.

A flood of tears streamed down Brett's face. He hardly felt them or his wet skin. Or his shirt wet around his neck. He watched as his ma scooped him up from his little bed—some kind of crib with sides on it—and kept up her singing, even though she stumbled and reeled from the blow. Flames danced around them, but she plunged headlong into them. Brett saw them eat at her hair and nightdress, and she pulled him hard against her chest, protecting him as she crashed through the house that bucked and groaned around them, fiery boards dropping from the roof and sparks raining on her head.

He peeked out from the swaddling blanket, staring at the house coming down atop them. But still she sang, meaning to comfort him, to keep him from wailing in fear.

Somehow, they got outside, out of the heat and into a cold night. A thin layer of snow lay on the ground, glistening bright orange as the reflection of the flames caught in the crystals of ice.

His ma dropped him and fell into the snow and rolled. The tongues of flame on her dress snuffed out, and the stench of burnt skin and hair filled his nose. He was cold and wet and started up crying again, but she gathered him into her arms once more. Her voice shook, packed full of fear and hurt and misery—he heard it so clearly in his head—as she sang one more verse.

"Must I go bound while you go free?
Must I love a man who doesn't love me?
Must I be born with so little art
As to love a man who'll break my heart?"

Brett fell back against the tree, feeling as if someone had drained every drop of blood from his body. Rough bark dug into his spine as he sat there, unable to move, staring at the gloaming light settling over the ranch house.

As the memory slipped from his grasp, it left him with a heavy sadness. He'd all but forgotten his ma and how purty she once was. The years right before his pa killed her, she'd lost all joy. She'd looked as if all the life had been sucked out of her, and that twinkle in her eyes had been snuffed out and replaced with a dull glaze that looked beyond this world. Her hair that had shone lost its sheen and lay pinned up tight against her head, as if those pins were all that held her together.

And while her empty eyes never entreated him, through all those years they'd suffered the slings of hate from his pa, he knew the burden had rested upon him and him alone to protect her. And he'd done nothing. Nothing at all. He'd cowered in corners and stuffed his pillow over his head to smother her cries. Even when he'd grown near as tall as his pa, he hadn't done a damned thing. The one time he dared to yell at his pa to stop, the beast had roared up and smashed Brett so hard upside his head, Brett had been knocked out into the next day.

Rage smoldered anew in his gut, but more from his failure than his hate for his pa. He replayed in his mind that last argument with his pa, when Brett had thrown his few belongings into a sack and told his pa just where he could go as Brett stormed to the door. His pa had yelled, "Go on, then. Git! An' don't show yer hide 'round here no more."

As his pa threw every dirty name at him that he could think of in his whiskey-soused head, Brett had caught sight of his ma hunched over the tiny kitchen table, her head in her hands. That look she gave him when she lifted her head burned like a hot brand once more. She'd urged him with her eyes to leave, to flee. *"Just go, Brett. Go. Save yourself while you can."*

She'd always wanted the best life for him—a life she couldn't give him. When he'd told her of his dream to be a cowboy and one day own his own horse ranch, she'd smiled and said, "Don't let anything stand in the way of your dream. No one and nothing. You hear me, Brett?" He'd been maybe ten or eleven, back when things weren't so bad. Back before his pa's drinking and womanizing got out of hand. *Back when she still clung to her thin thread of a dream.*

A dream of a happy life, a happy family. A dream you shattered by walkin' out.

Brett buried his head in his hands again, thinking he'd best just leave the ranch, fetch Kotoo and ride off somewhere, bed out under the stars at night and chew up some miles during the day, get even farther away from Texas, his past. *From Angela.* Leave all those stupid dreams behind to rot in the dust of the prairie.

Just run, he told himself, the thought tempting him like a meaty haunch of deer meat dangling from a tree in front of a hungry grizzly.

Run.

As if the very word set fire to his feet, he jumped up, wiping his sleeve across his wet face, intent on heading back to the bunkhouse to fetch his bedroll and war bag.

But the sight meeting his eyes made him freeze in place.

Angela stood in the back doorway, framed by the light spilling out of the house—looking every bit like that angel he saw in his memory of his ma.

His thoughts turned into a mush of confusion as he watched her come toward him, in a gorgeous dress, her silky black hair swept up onto her head, white gloves riding up to her bare elbows, the skin of her upper arms creamy and soft in the light splattering on her from the open door.

"Brett?"

He knew he looked ragged, with red-rimmed eyes and cheeks blotchy from rubbing. He wanted to pull his hat down so she couldn't see him, see his shame that he was sure was written all over his face. He felt as brittle as a sheet of ice crusting over a pond the first night of winter.

"What're ya doin' out here?" he asked her bitterly, not meeting her eyes, wishing for the first time that she'd go and leave him be.

"I . . . I was going to ask you the same thing. I wanted to get some fresh air, before I was called to play . . ."

Her words trailing off made him lift his head. She stood a few feet away, a frown deep-set on her dazzling face. Those full pouty lips set his heart aching anew. Her beauty hurt his eyes.

"What's wrong, Brett. Are you unwell?"

A grunt of self-reproach blurted out of him. He shook his head, unable to form any words that made a lick of sense.

"Jus' go, Angela. There's no cure for what's ailin' me." *And runnin' won't help neither—ya know that.*

He suddenly thought of the Cheyenne woman's pronouncements. His mouth dropped open as his mind pieced together a jumbled puzzle. The meaning was now clear as a glass window pane. Clear as snowmelt running over rocks on a crisp spring day. An urgency filled his blood—a need to understand.

"What is it?" Angela asked, laying her hand gently on his arm.

He breathed in the dizzying scent of her, his mind reeling, her nearness both comforting and agonizing. "She . . . she said, 'Look for the calm water. The song will lead you out.'" He searched Angela's confused face, wanting so much for her to understand what he finally understood.

"What are you talking about? Who said?"

"Sarah Banks, the Injun woman. She said, 'When the fire rages, look for the calm water. You will hear the song . . .'" He heard her strong voice in his head. *"There is a way out. You don't have to burn in the flames."*

He could kick himself for his stupidity. She wasn't talking about the brushfire that had trapped 'em at the fairgrounds. Not at all. Sure, Kotoo was the calm in the midst of the fire, and the pony'd led them out. He thought the calm water was the Platte, but that's not what she was talking about—not at all.

A grin rose on his face, pushing up the sides of his mouth and forcing out the shame that had presently been drowning him.

He stared hard into her eyes. "What was that tune ya was playin' up there?" He tipped his head up toward the window.

She swallowed, and her creamy throat glistened. Longing swelled and crashed over him.

"It's a Scottish folk song that George taught me. It's called 'The Water Is Wide.'" She looked at him, more with curiosity than alarm, her hand still on his arm. Her touch electrified him, but he couldn't think what that might mean. He had to figure this out. Maybe she could help him understand what it was he needed to know.

Before he could stop himself, the words poured out of his mouth. "When I was sixteen, I walked out on my ma. My pa beat her all the time, and I never stood up to him." His throat choked up with emotion, but he pressed on. He had to tell her. She needed to know.

She was the way out of the fire, out of the burning house of his soul.

He felt as if he were back in his ma's arms as she stumbled through the crashing, burning timbers of their shack, singing that song to him, her dress afire.

"I ran that day, and I been runnin' ever since. I cain't stop runnin'." Like a wildfire's been on my tail, chasin' me down, followin' me everywhere.

He took hold of her, gently, his hands on her bare forearms. He thought she'd bolt or protest, but she kept staring at him with that perplexed look.

"Doncha see?" he said. "That song ya played. Yer music . . ." There *was* a way out. Angela was the way out. Is that what Sarah'd meant?

He recalled Sarah's smile, that knowing smile. Like she'd known all along that he'd figure this out. He suddenly wondered if she was here, at the party. Surely Foster would've invited her. He had to talk to her. She could tell him. Tell him if there was hope for him. Any hope at all . . .

Someone called from the house. Brett turned. The violin maker stood in the doorway, waving an arm. "Angela!" he called out. "We're about to begin."

Angela met Brett's eyes, a brief glance. He saw so much there tangled up in confusion. Judgment, desire, hurt, anger. But he had no time to untangle another knot. *One at a time.*

"I—I have to go," she said.

He nodded and dropped his arms to his side. Her words slapped with the sting of finality. She wasn't talking just about now. She was talking about forever.

Desperation rose up into the back of his throat, tasting rancid. He swallowed it back down. A sense of danger and foreboding lassoed his gut. He knew he had one chance, just this one night, to convince Angela to stay. But he couldn't try until he knew for sure he'd found a way out of the flames.

And if he did, then he wouldn't have to run any longer.

Chapter 34

PHINEAS FRYE PACED NERVOUSLY BEHIND the long rough-planked bunkhouse, throwing an occasional peek around the corner. Isaiah Cummings stood talking to Orlander back a ways under a clump of trees near a corral. Phineas couldn't hear the two talking, but Boss was giving some instructions.

Presently, the Mexican named Marino and Big Bill Studley came rushing over to the shadows of the eaves. Phineas figured they'd tucked the wagon out of sight after tying up the horses. When they'd arrived at the fork that split off the road to Foster's ranch, Boss'd told 'em to circle around to the back, then meet 'em where them two punchers said.

But the two cowboys hadn't shown yet. Phineas worried they'd forgot. Or maybe something happened to them and they couldn't get here. Then he reckoned it wouldn't be hard for Boss to find out who this "Bronco" Brett Hendricks was. All he'd have to do was ask around. Phineas figured he could recognize the cowboy himself, but he didn't want to tell Boss. Phineas was hoping he'd catch sight of the fella first, so's to warn him about Orlander.

He thought on that look Boss had on his face when they'd stopped in the road. Hate twisted his features into a mess of lines, and his words had been spiked with poison. He knew Orlander wouldn't leave until Brett Hendricks was full of lead.

Fancy music drifted on the air, along with the smells of meat and bread and pies coming from the big kitchen round back of the ranch house. His mouth watered, imagining all them platters of food. He'd eaten some jerky and hard tack when they'd set out, and that's all he managed to grab when Boss announced it was time to go. They'd ridden hard and fast from Denver, following the fancy carriage Orlander rode in, all by himself. Miz Orlander had bowed out, said she was in no mood for a party, from what Phineas heard. She spent her days sitting by Wade's bed and nights crying. They'd hoped Wade would have gotten better by now, but he was the same. Those legs of his weren't never gonna work, and that was the God's honest truth.

From around that corner, Phineas could see all the bustle, with what looked like servants coming in and out, wearing black suits, and carriages arriving, one after the other, pulling up to the front of the big house.

A sinking feeling made Phineas slump against the siding. This was wrong, all wrong. Orlander should give the fella a chance to tell his side—not just shoot him dead.

"Hey," Cummings shot out in a loud whisper, waving him over with his hand. Phineas and the two other punchers went to him as Orlander, in his party duds, walked back up to the ranch house.

"Boss is goin' inside. We're to wait a half hour—no longer. If'n those two cowboys don't show, this is what he wants us to do . . ."

Phineas listened only partly while Cummings laid out the plan. Marino, in his sombrero, nodded, his smile showing half his teeth missing. Phineas had heard tell of this Mexican with the fast draw and a heart as black as pitch. Orlander had hired him special. Studley was a bear with a cadaverous face and could beat anyone in an arm-wrestling match. The cowboy's arms were as thick as lodge poles. He was the one Boss sent to break up fights atwixt his punchers. When anyone saw Big Bill coming, they shut right up, and fists dropped as fast as rocks skittering down a well.

Just then, the sound of boot steps on hard ground made them all turn around.

The cowboys they'd been waiting on were behind the bunkhouse. Their faces had lost the swell and purple from the roughing up they'd suffered, and Phineas took a good, hard look at them to fix their features in his head.

"There ya are," Cummings said, striding over to 'em, the rest of the group following.

"Told ya we'd be here," the tall, lanky fella said with a sneer. "We wanna see Hendricks get his due."

"But how're ya gonna get him to come outside? Orlander wants to do this quiet —"

"He won't s'pect a thing," the short one said, his beady eyes no longer swollen like plums.

"I wanna talk to yer boss," the other said. Phineas recalled his name — Handy. Ned Handy. The name seemed to fit.

"He's already inside," Cummings told him. "Look, this here's Marino and Big Bear Studley. Once ya git Hendricks to come outside, git him over to these trees here. This is where these fellas'll be waitin'. Boss wants Hendricks tied and gagged so's we can git him away from the house. No one'll be the wiser."

Phineas added with warning in his voice, "Orlander wants t' deal with Hendricks all hisself. He don't want 'im hurt."

Cummings glared at Phineas, chewing his lip. Phineas stared back, hoping his true feelings wouldn't leak out. Good thing it was too dark for Cummings to see his hands shaking.

"I gotta visit some bushes," Phineas said. "I'll go around the back of the house, keep my eye out in case Hendricks slips out."

Cummings's eyes narrowed even more. He was all business. "Alright." He turned back to Handy and his pal. "Git goin'. I'll git inside and sneak a look at who all's there. Keep an eye out fer any trouble."

The two cowboys nodded and headed for the bunkhouse. What their plan was, Phineas had 'airy a clue. But he figured they'd find a way to get Hendricks outside. And once he was outside, he was as good as dead.

I gotta get inside and find Hendricks. I gotta warn him. Maybe he could hide somewheres till the party's over. Or git someone to help 'im slip away without Boss noticin'.

Phineas scowled and fisted his hands as he left the men in the shadows of the trees and headed for the brush behind the house. Orlander had always been a right fair man. And Phineas understood him being angry and wanting revenge. But Boss didn't know the truth of it—that Wade was to blame, and the pain his kid was suffering was of his own making.

Phineas wished he'd come clean and told Orlander the truth. But he hadn't. And he prob'ly wouldn'ta believed ya anyhow. A man so torn up with grief like that needs t' find someone to blame.

He stopped and squatted behind some bushes at the back of the house. The pretty music was louder here. He imagined all those dolled-up guests drinking wine out of crystal glasses and eating piles of food laid out on big tables covered with starched white tablecloths. He'd never been to a party—not the likes of this one. Miz Orlander threw parties like that, from time to time. He doubted he'd ever get asked to one. Logan Foster had invited all his cowboys to the festivities. That was right nice of him. *Maybe I c'n git in with Foster's outfit.*

He reckoned, after tonight, there was no way on God's green earth he could keep on at the Flying Y Ranch. He just couldn't fathom it.

The knot in his gut tightened like a noose around a rustler's neck. He looked up and nudged his hat back. The moon and stars above shone bright on a cloudless cool night. A perfect night for a fancy party, he thought. Not the kind of night a fella expects to be shot dead.

Angela's eyes wandered from her sheet music as she bowed her violin. Quiet discourse carried on around them, but most of the guests' eyes were on the musicians—she supposed there were at least fifty in attendance at Mr. Foster's birthday.

Adeline stood nearby, her fan fluttering, smiling in approval and occasionally making excited remarks to those who sidled up to her and complimented her on the delightful party. Her husband made his rounds, greeting guests, chatting with them and thanking them for coming. For all the protesting Adeline claimed he'd done about her party plans, he strutted about like a happy peacock, proud of his ranch and family, and deservedly so. Mrs. Annie Green sat stiffly in a chair at one of the tables, her eyes fixated on their playing. Other guests talked around her, and her head bobbed with an occasional assent to a question asked of her. Angela never imagined there were so many of high-society tucked away in the tiny towns of the West.

What an exquisite party it was. Angela knew Adeline had been planning this for months. The house was decorated with streamers that hung from the walls and rafters and staircase, and a full staff of uniformed waiters served hors d'oeuvres and flutes of champagne and white wine. Angela had never seen so much food for so small a number of people, and the imported English serving dishes sizzled and steamed and bubbled with casseroles and cobblers and soups. Breads of all shapes and colors overflowed baskets at the end of the long table, and Angela longed to taste some of these Southern delights Adeline had told her about.

The two little girls sat like princesses at one of the small ribbon-festooned round tables arranged in front of the dais, their eyes riveted on the quintet. She saw the same surprise and delight that she must have expressed the first time she'd heard the philharmonic. She hoped Maddy and Clem would have a new, better appreciation for their violin lessons after this. *Though, now Adeline will be pressuring George once more to come teach them—once I'm gone.*

The thought of her impending departure dampened her spirits and compounded the heaviness she felt in her heart. And the confusion. Seeing Brett so distraught had stunned her. She hadn't expected to stumble upon him back behind the house. She'd had no doubt he'd been crying, and crying hard. Something she'd never seen a man do. Beneath all Brett's bluster was a sensitive man who seemed to harbor much hurt. And then he'd smiled and turned suddenly excited. She didn't understand a word of what he told her, but she knew it had something to do with the folk song she'd played earlier. Perhaps he'd recognized it from his childhood.

But what was all that about the music leading him out from the fire? About some woman named Sarah? Angela had no idea, but he'd become intense, urgent. She wished she could have heard his explanation. But now that would have to wait.

As would the more important explanation—why he'd shot at a man . . . and why he'd do so again if he'd had the chance. As kind and sensitive and handsome as Brett was, she could not—*must not*—forget he was a deplorable man who lacked morals. He might claim a belief in the Almighty and worship under the stars on the open range, but he thought nothing of marring a woman's reputation or shooting at someone who'd wronged him. She'd seen the way he lost his temper, let rage overtake him. He was little different from Papá. *And he carries a gun.*

And while Greeley might be a small shoal of God-fearing families intent on living good Christian lives, it was a tiny island in the lawless frontier. A rickety wooden fence erected around the town couldn't keep out the wild of the West. Brett was cut from this cloth. He could no easier change into a refined, honorable man than a wild horse could be truly tamed. Whom was she kidding?

She shook loose her wandering thoughts and gave full attention to her playing. Violet cast her curious looks between her flute passages. That is, between glancing over at the open double doors to the great room. Angela guessed she was hoping to catch sight of Tate Roberts. Maybe a rough-edged uneducated cowboy suited Violet just fine, but Angela just couldn't trust that Brett could ever love her the way she longed and needed to be loved.

She lost herself in her music, feeling each note feed and nourish her soul. A sigh of contentment slipped out of her as the strains of strings and flute blended together in perfect harmony. Daisy and Rebecca, while far from professional, did a wonderful job with their parts. George played his violin with gusto as they worked through the allegro movement, a smile beaming. It made Angela's heart glad to see him venture out of his grief and enjoying life. She knew it wouldn't completely erase his sense of loss, but George spoke truth when he told her music was a healer. She hoped it would heal all her hurts one day.

As they bowed the last few notes of the sonata, Angela noticed Violet's face light up. A glance across the room showed Brett, Tate, and a young redheaded teenager enter through a door behind the buffet table. Brett's gaze went right to her, regarding her steadily, and then he searched the room, as if looking for someone.

Applause broke out, and Violet nudged Angela to stand. The members of the quintet nodded their thanks, and George then motioned for them to sit and begin the next piece. Seeing Brett in the brightly lit room in his clean, pressed clothes, his auburn hair smoothed back and hatless, made her breath catch. He seemed more handsome than ever. But she knew what lay beneath his chiseled looks and muscular body. She just had to stop trying to make excuses for him.

For, that was just what her mamá had done for years, whenever Papá struck her or exploded into one of his loud tirades that all their neighbors could hear. Her mamá always had an explanation for his outburst. *"Your papá is tired. He's overworked. He's worried about the business. He's had a hard day . . ."* The excuses were as numerous as the stars in the sky. But there was no excusing violent behavior—not ever. If a man could shoot and even kill another without remorse, he'd think little of slapping or beating his wife.

You're too forgiving. And too weak. Just like Mamá. And if you don't want to end up like her, you'll put Brett Hendricks out of your mind forever. Just focus on your music, chase after your dream, and get on that train Monday morning.

LeRoy grinned as he watched Gennie, sitting so purty and listening to the music. She sipped at her iced drink and tapped a slippered foot in time with the music. When she felt his eyes on her, she looked up and over her shoulder, and he gave her a wink as he stood behind her chair, watching all the goings-on with the eye of a hawk. Folks all dandied up were socializing and eating tidbits of food off tiny plates that servants in stiff black suits offered them.

"Don't you want to sit with me?" Gennie's playful eyes nudged him, and he wished he could join her. But his ma had said some things on the way over in the wagon that gave him pause. *Particularly when she'd asked, "Did ya bring your pistol?"* She'd said it in her irritating matter-of-fact manner—which told LeRoy that question was more loaded than his gun.

He spotted his ma across the big room, over by a table chock-full of fancy glasses filled with bubbly liquid he guessed was champagne. He'd tasted the stuff once but didn't cotton to all those bubbles going up his nose. He wasn't much of a drinker anyways. His ma was talking to Foster, nodding and smiling at some tale he was bandying about. But when she saw LeRoy studying her, she shot him back a warning with her eyes. When they'd been welcomed into the gaily lit house and stepped into the foyer, his ma had whispered to him, "Go find that cowboy I gave that mare to—Brett Hendricks. He's gonna need your help tonight."

LeRoy leaned down and nuzzled against Gennie's ear, suddenly wishing he'd left her at home. But she'd wanted to come, and seeing as how she'd spent all those years alone in the mountains with only a wolf-dog for company, he would never think to dissuade her from a chance to get out of her ranch clothes and into something frilly with all those petticoats. Besides, his ma voiced no objections to Gennie's attendance. If some trouble was coming down the pipe, his ma didn't afear for Gennie's safety.

"Darlin', I'd like nothin' better'n to sit by yer side. But there's some fellas I need to say hello to. I'll be right back." She shot him one of her sweet smiles that made him want to scoop her up and plant kisses all over her mouth. Then she went back to tapping her foot and listening to the music.

Brett Hendricks had just walked into the room, with two punchers at his side. LeRoy recalled seeing those two at the corral the day they'd brought in the horses. The young skinny kid stood wide-eyed taking in the festivities. The other cast an interested glance at the musicians on the little stage. Hendricks's friends hung back as a few other cowboys ambled into the room, all looking like ducks out of water in their spiffy duds and slicked-back hair.

LeRoy figured they felt naked without their hats. He knew he did, but Miz Foster had insisted on a no-hat rule for the evening. Might just as well have told her guests to take off their boots. A cowboy's hat was his most cherished and useful piece of clothing. Not only did it protect his head from hot and wet weather, it sometimes served as a drinking cup or a pail to cart water to put out a fire. It was often a pillow on hard ground and a signal flag to warn the approach of danger. A head without a hat just felt plum naked.

Hendricks seemed to be searching for someone, but when he caught LeRoy's eye, he came toward him. LeRoy met him halfway, by the swinging door that led into the kitchen.

The buster had an excited look about him. He stuck out his hand for LeRoy to shake, saying, "You're Sarah Banks's son—ain't that right?"

LeRoy nodded. "How's that mare workin' out?"

Hendricks whistled and smoothed his hair. "She's a fine horse. I still don't git why she gave 'er to me, but I'm mighty grateful. That mare got us through the fire t'other day—calm as all git-out. We had to break through to the river, and I was with some town folks ain't never rode before."

When LeRoy had smelled fire two days ago, he'd ridden fast to the river just north of their ranch, where he saw the wildfire streaking across the prairie. He'd meant to turn back and head to town to help, but then the clouds had bust loose and dumped rain in sheets for miles around. Wet smoke and ash had soaked the air. He later heard the fairgrounds had been charred to cinders.

"Glad t' hear y'all got out safe." He took an immediate liking to Hendricks. He knew this fella had to be something special for his ma to do what she did.

Hendricks chewed his lip, lost in some thought. "I was wonderin' if'n yer ma was here. I'd like to —"

The cowboy's face drained of blood. His hands fell to his sides. LeRoy turned his head and looked to where Hendricks's gaze had swiveled to. Two fellas, obviously cowboys, stood back in shadows behind the long trestle food tables. Presently, one other eased into view near them, with a cruel and humorless mouth. They had trouble written all over them.

"Who're they?" LeRoy asked, his fingers drifting down to his Colt at his side, hidden under his dressy coat.

Hendricks spoke through a pinched mouth. "Ned Handy's that tall one yonder. Fella next ta him is Rufus Shore. Don't know t'other one. They got mixed up in a rustlin' outfit, and Foster'd set them afoot. Why in tarnation would they show their faces here?"

"'Cause they got some trouble planned." LeRoy nodded his head toward Hendricks's two pals, who were leaning against the wall near the main entry, eating food from plates they held in their hands. "Might be a good idea t' let yer pals know. And yer boss."

LeRoy looked back at his ma. Logan Foster was still chatting her up, and a few old ladies had joined them by the drinks table. His ma was chuckling at something the rancher said, paying no mind to the unsettling developments. The appearance of those cowboys at the rancher's birthday party could mean only one thing, from what

LeRoy could figure—they wanted payback. Which meant Foster—and maybe his family—were in danger. So what was his ma up to?

Phineas had planned to sneak into the house through the kitchen, but when he saw Cummings join up with those two punchers and slip inside through a back room window, he had to follow.

His knees had shook as he clambered up and over the sill moments after he watched their shadows move silently through what looked to be a bedroom and out the door to a brightly lit hallway. A streak of light splashed across the floor, and Phineas inched quiet as a mouse behind them. But instead of following the three, he went left down the hall and found himself in a part of the ranch house that lay in darkness.

He could hear music seeping through the walls, so he edged along past closed doors until he came to a parlor. A few older folks all gussied up in stylish clothes, sitting in stuffed chairs, gave him a polite hello as Phineas nodded at them and smiled for all the world like he had business being there—though for the life of him he couldn't think of an excuse to give 'em if they asked.

His heart beat hard against his ribs as he took stealthy steps past them and stopped in the doorway at the end of the room. Before him a grand party was underway, maybe fifty people all gussied, eating and talking and listening to folks playing some kind of lively music the likes of which Phineas had never heard before.

It didn't take him but a second to spot Orlander. The rancher stood by the little stage in brown trousers, a silk vest, and a long-tailed coat that Phineas knew concealed his long-barreled Colt. He was pretending to enjoy the music, but Phineas could tell he kept one eye on Cummings, who was now standing behind some tables alongside those two disgruntled punchers.

Phineas had tucked his own revolver he'd kept from the war into the back of his trousers, and it sat like a lump of hard coal against his spine. He nervously scouted the room. So where was this fella Hendricks? And how in blazes did those punchers think they could lure him outside? Maybe Cummings would go up to him and tell him he wanted to show him something. *Or maybe he'd be foolish and push the nozzle of his gun up against the buster's back and tell 'im to start walkin'.* But that wasn't likely. Too risky.

Suddenly, the music stopped, and a bright sound of metal against glass rang out. Phineas saw a young heavy-set woman in a blue dress poofed up with a bunch of petticoats step up onto the stage, her head bobbing with a hundred blond curls. She was clanging a glass with a spoon.

"Foster and I are soooo overjoyed to have you here to celebrate his fiftieth birthday. Logan, darling, come, come!" She waved a gloved hand toward a fella Phineas reckoned was the rich, famous rancher Logan Foster. The fella grinned and headed over to her, followed by an Injun woman in a buckskin skirt and white button blouse. Two silver-streaked black braids draped over her shoulders. Just as the rancher got to his wife's side, Phineas saw Cummings's face blanch and his mouth twist into a scowl.

Two young cowboys were headed straight for Cummings. Phineas reached his hand around his back and grabbed his gun, then dropped to a crouch. He was maybe forty feet from Cummings, but he could get a bead on him if he had to. He just knew one of them fellas was Brett Hendricks.

Chapter 35

BRETT'S PULSE RUSHED LIKE WATER in his ears. Handy and Shore had a lot of nerve stepping foot into Foster's house—especially at a time like this. Whatever they meant to do, it involved hurting a lot of people and causing Logan Foster as much anguish as possible.

Brett knew they had a beef against Foster. But he also recalled the venomous threat Handy had given Brett and Roberts for exposing their rustling activities. Nothing but bad was gonna come out of this, and Brett knew Roberts had the same idea—get those two outside and away from Foster and his family.

He was glad he'd listened to his gut about bringing his gun. He'd hoped he wouldn't need to use it. But he reckoned it was a fool's hope. *Jus' keep Angela safe. Whatever happens.* The thought of Angela getting hurt stirred up all those old feelings of protection and fury. Never again would he let some scum of the earth hurt someone Brett loved.

"I came was hopin' you'd come over here," Handy said with a nasty sneer when Brett and Roberts walked up to him and Shore and stared hard into their faces.

"What d'ya reckon you're doin' here? Ya got a lot of nerve," Roberts ground out in a quiet breath. "Foster'll have yer hide."

Brett caught a look at the cowboy standing off to the side, behind Shore. The crusty fella with a fat gut, thick black hair, and a red-streaked beard looked to be about forty, and he regarded Brett with glassy, empty dark eyes. This close, Brett recognized him, and then recalled where he'd seen him. All the air whooshed out of his lungs.

Orlander's man. That's why Handy and Shore are here—to deliver me on a stake to Orlander.

Brett laid a hand on Roberts's wrist. The Missourian turned and questioned Brett with his steel-cold eyes.

"Let me handle this, Tate," Brett said. "Jus' . . . go and keep Archie outta trouble."

Roberts's steely gaze told Brett—and the three scoundrels watching him—that he had no intention of leaving Brett's side.

Handy's eyes narrowed to slits. "Listen, Roberts. As much as I'd like to give ya what ya deserve, I got somethin' to say to Hendricks here—in private. So, skedaddle."

Roberts didn't move.

Orlander's man pushed up against Brett, and Brett felt the hard metal of a gun's muzzle press against his coat at his ribs. He stiffened.

"Outside, Hendricks," the puncher said with a bitter grin." Ya don't want ta cause a commotion in the middle of this here nice party—with all these nice people havin' such a good time."

Brett looked over at Angela sitting on the little stage. She was smiling and listening to Miz Foster ramble on about her wonderful husband.

Brett turned back to the fella at his side. He said in a low voice, "Jus' take it easy, fella. I'll head over to that door yonder"—he pointed at a side entrance to the big room — "and you c'n follow me out to the road."

"I got a better idea," the fella said, while Handy and Shore nervously watched the room, their hands twitchy at their sides. "Let's you 'n' me slip back into the kitchen."

Brett shrugged. "Fine. Let's go." He shot Roberts a warning. *Don't follow us.* He'd leave Roberts to deal with Handy and Shore. If those two thought they'd get away scot-free after helping Orlander's man, they were sorely mistaken. Brett wondered if Lambert was somewhere in the room. If he caught sight of those two, they'd never make it three feet.

Just then, a fella with a balding head in a dirt-brown coat yelled from across the room.

"Cummings! You hold it right there!" His voice had a heavy Texan twang.

Orlander's man spun around but kept the gun jammed up against Brett's ribs. "Frye," he muttered, equal parts shock and outrage.

The balding man brandished a gun, and party guests screamed and scrambled away from tables. Logan Foster, standing on the platform, swung around, scowling.

"Who in tarnation are you — ?"

"Stop that man!" the gun-toting fella yelled, pointing at Cummings, who clenched Brett's arm tighter.

Through the noise of chairs clattering and women shrieking — Miz Foster's voice the loudest and most hysterical — Brett heard the whistle of a bullet. An explosion of splinters rained down on his head when the bullet hit the rafter above him.

Cummings yanked Brett and practically threw him into the kitchen after kicking open the swinging door. The folks cooking and washing dishes screamed and ran pell-mell for the back door, vacating the kitchen. Brett twisted sharply and wrenched free of Cummings's grasp, then smashed his first into the fella's cheek.

With a *woof,* Cummings careened sideways into the wall as he pulled out his revolver. Pans hanging on the wall crashed to the floor.

Brett lunged and tackled him as screams erupted around him. The fat old puncher struggled to get purchase with his feet as Brett plowed into him, head aimed at the fella's bulging gut. Cummings's gun clattered along the floorboards when Brett laid him flat.

A gunshot fired in the room behind him. Brett's rage roiled like lava, but he swallowed it down and grabbed the gun tucked against the wall between some cabinets. A memory of Cummings's heartless and lustful expression flitted into Brett's mind. He'd stood by and grinned while his boss's kid tried to ravage that Mexican girl. Cummings had been one of the cowboys that had chased him into the desert, fired at him.

Brett kicked Cummings in the chest as hard as he could. The cowboy grunted in pain and tried to push up to stand.

Footsteps sounding behind Brett made him turn his head. Archie Halloran came tumbling into the kitchen, then skidded to a stop, his eyes wide.

"Brett! You're alright." He swiped at hand across his forehead, staring at Cummings moaning on the floor. "Things are going crazy in there!"

"Hold this," Brett said, handing him Cummings's pistol. "If he even moves a pinky, shoot 'im."

Brett saw the terror in Archie's eyes, but he knew the tenderfoot could handle it. "I know ya can't aim well, but this fella's big and close. Even if ya aim fer the wall, you're bound t' hit 'im in some part of his body."

Archie gulped and cradled the gun in both hands. Brett gave him a pat on the shoulder and rushed back out into the great room. His gaze swept the scene.

Roberts was embroiled in fisticuffs with Handy. LeRoy Banks had Rufus Shore by the arm and was dragging him toward the stage, which presently was a jumble of overturned chairs and music stands. Logan Foster crouched by the stage, his gun at the ready, his head swiveling around, watching for the next sign of trouble.

Brett searched the room until he found Angela. She was huddled with George and the other musicians—and a dozen other guests—in the corner behind the stage, nowhere near the doors leading out. He didn't see Miz Foster or her girls. *Good. Mebbe she got 'em out.*

But where was the balding fella in the brown coat that had fired the first shot? And who was he? Why'd he call Cummings out? Was he one of Orlander's men?

Just then Ned Handy yelled out and pointed at Brett. "That's him. That's Hendricks!"

Roberts smacked Handy's temple with the butt of his Colt, and Handy slumped, his head flopping to the side. He slid to the floor.

The doors to the great room flew open. Two big fellas rushed in—one a Mexican wearing a sombrero and gray poncho and the other a huge lumbering ox—their pistols on the draw. The room echoed with high-pitched screams as they slid to a stop and looked for someone.

Brett's eyes followed theirs and set upon one of Foster's guests standing with a defiant look by the food table. He was about the same age as the rancher, all spraddled out in fine party clothes, and he glared at Brett as he stood at the kitchen door. The fella then pulled a gun from the side of his trousers and aimed it at him.

Shocked, Brett barely flinched in time as another bullet whizzed past his ear. He dove to the floor and heard Angela scream. He strained to see across the room. Foster spun around and stared at his guest, flustered in confusion.

"Horace . . . ?"

The man ignored Foster. He aimed again as the two big fellas that'd just burst in took up positions behind overturned tables.

Crimany, this'll be a bloodbath soon enough.

Roberts landed a punch to Handy's kidney as LeRoy Banks tripped up Ned Shore, who planted his face on the floor. Sarah Banks stood over both, a pearl-handled revolver held in steady aim at the two now sitting doubled over.

Freed up, Roberts and LeRoy ran toward Foster. Lead flew through the air as the rancher ducked. The bullets weren't for him.

Roberts crashed over tables and chairs, silver utensils scattering and dishes shattering. He stumbled and fell, then got to his feet and found himself facing the Mexican.

The ugly fella smiled, half his teeth missing, as he set a bead on Roberts. Brett cursed and rushed headlong to stop him, but he was too far away. No time to shoot him either.

Another bullet exploded. The floorboard in front of Brett splintered and threw wood chunks into his eyes as he dove again, this time behind a giant potted plant.

Suddenly Brett saw movement in the corner, behind the Mexican. A big black object smashed down on the Mexican's head just as the scoundrel looked about to shoot. It was some kind of music case, like Angela owned, only bigger. One of the musicians stood behind the fella as his knees crumpled and he collapsed sideways.

Violet! Brett couldn't believe his eyes. The purty young gal had walloped the giant of a fella and knocked him out plum cold, a smug smile on her face as she looked down him sprawled at her dainty shoes.

Roberts could hardly believe his eyes either. He flashed a grateful smile at Violet, then spun around to grab the other burly fella. But LeRoy was already on the bear, a knife at his throat. He stood limp in LeRoy's arms, his beady eyes flashing with fear.

Two other of Foster's punchers had grabbed the finely dressed man by the arms, forcing the gun to fall from his hand. Another puncher picked up the weapon and then searched him for more.

Brett listened to the sound of quiet sink into the room. Voices hushed. Logan Foster got up out of his crouch and straightened, smoothing out his party clothes and twiddling his moustache. A heavy snort blew out his nose as he strode over to the man Brett had no doubt was Orlander.

It dawned on Brett—this whole shenanigans was about *him*. About what he'd done. About Orlander's kid. He'd thought he'd outrun all his troubles, but here they were, dragging behind him, the way they always did.

He stood and came out from behind the plant, then walked into the middle of the room and stopped. He set his face and waited.

Orlander scowled in disgust, mean spite in his eyes, flinging the cowboys' hands off him. Then he pulled himself tall and looked Foster in the eye. The two men faced off inches apart, glowering at the other.

"Horace Orlander, ya wanna tell me why ya brought yer scalawags here to shoot up my party?" Foster spit out.

The room got quieter than the grave. Orlander pursed his lips, then said in a trembling voice, "I didn't have no intention of ruinin' yer party. I jus' want to see justice done for ma boy."

Foster waited. Brett noticed Angela standing with her arm around the violin maker, watching and listening. His heart ached, longing for her, for her arms around him. What would happen now was anyone's guess. But Brett had a terrible sinking feeling that once Orlander told his tale—which would surely be a passel of lies—there'd be no hope that Angela would ever speak to him again. Who would believe a poor, homeless cowboy over a rich and powerful rancher? No one.

"I'm takin' yer fella there with me." He pointed at Brett.

Foster's brows narrowed. "Why? So's you c'n put a bullet through his head?"

Orlander exploded and got up in Foster's face. "He shot my boy."

Foster frowned. "Wade's dead?"

Orlander scowled, his hands fisted on his hips. "As good as."

Brett swallowed past the rock lodged in his throat. Clearly these two men were friends and cut of the same cloth. Hopelessness sought to suck him under.

A roomful of guests and servants stared at the two men. Sarah Banks stood at the back, her gun still aimed at the two rustlers. She looked straight at Brett, but not with pity. *She knows the truth of what happened. She gave ya that horse because ya done the right thing.*

Her look swept away his glum feelings and shot courage into him. He took steps toward Orlander. Foster cocked his head and studied Brett. "Whatta ya got ta say 'bout this?"

"I done nothin' wrong," Brett answered, glaring at Orlander.

The rancher detonated at Brett's words, lunging with hands outstretched for Brett's throat. "I'll kill ya! I'll kill ya!"

"Whoa," Foster said, grabbing hold of Orlander's shoulder and yanking him back hard. Orlander slapped Foster away, venom in his eyes.

"Stop protectin' him, Logan. He picked a fight with Wade, and then shot at him, no warnin' at all. Yer man's a killer."

"An' so ya brought these scamps with ya, to do yer dirty work?" Foster gestured to the bear of a man that LeRoy had a knifepoint and the Mexican that was groaning woozy on the floor at Roberts's feet. Brett met Roberts's eyes, and the cowboy's mouth quirked up into a grin. *He told me he'd have my back.* Roberts was as good a friend as Brett'd ever had. But nothing Roberts or the Cheyenne woman said could be of help. It was just Orlander's word against his own. That Cummings fella—he'd lied to his boss, covering for the kid. *Well, no surprise there.*

He turned and looked at LeRoy Banks, wondering at the satisfied smile on his face. And there was his ma, standing over Handy and Shore as calm as day, as if watching chickens setting on their eggs, a young, purty gal standing guard with her. Brett reckoned the gal to be LeRoy's wife. He might even have said they looked downright gleeful at this messy turn of events.

Some cowboys itched for a fight, but LeRoy and his ma were different. They'd risked their lives for him, jumping into the fight. This was all about honor for them.

He grunted at the word. What kind of honor did he really have? Even if he saved every gal in the world from the likes of Orlander's kid, it would never ransom the guilt he felt over leaving his ma in the clutches of that monster. No God in heaven, nor any human, could forgive him for his cowardly, selfish action that day. That song Angela played may have brought him a moment of peace, but it was like pouring whiskey on a gangrene leg. It couldn't save him. *It led ya out of the fire but dumped ya into the fryin' pan.*

Chapter 36

ANGELA LEANED AGAINST GEORGE, WHO held her close and stroked her hair. The room around them was in shambles, and her head reeled with the flurry of violence that had erupted around her. Streamers hung limply from the rafters and lay trampled on the floor. The beautifully decorated tables were strewn all over, and the chairs and music stands sat in a jumble on the dais. Food smeared the polished and varnished wood flooring that only ten minutes earlier had reflected back the shiny, happy faces of Adeline's dinner guests. At least she and the other musicians had kept enough wits about themselves to stash their instruments in the trunk behind the dais that had housed all the linens.

She shook from head to toe, glad Adeline had managed to escape with her girls. They were probably hiding under a bed upstairs somewhere. Never, in all her wildest imaginings, would she have expected a gunfight to break out at Logan Foster's birthday party.

So much for the West being gentrified, she thought with consternation. The sooner she fled back to New York, the better. Though there were perils there as well, at least they were ones she could anticipate and avoid. Those dark alleys and neighborhoods where the criminal element of society took advantage of unsuspecting passersby were pockets of danger. But here, in the West, danger was everywhere. There was no place safe—from snakes, from the harsh elements, from unprincipled men. Guns or fists seemed to be the answer to every problem.

The guests around her seemed just as flustered and distraught—especially the old ladies on the opera board. A gentleman leaned over Lavenia McConnoly, who'd managed to find an unbroken chair to collapse into. He spoke consolingly while Arta Pilsbury dabbed a handkerchief along Lavenia's brow.

Thick tension choked the room as Mr. Foster stood and argued with the rancher called Orlander. This was the man Brett and Tate had been discussing outside the window the other night. Tate had been right—the rancher wanted Brett dead for shooting his son.

She thanked God that no one had been shot, and that this angry rancher had been apprehended. But while it appeared that Mr. Foster was doing his best to protect Brett, she imagined that once the law got involved, there'd be no hope for Brett. Would he be hung? She had no idea what justice looked like in Colorado, but she'd heard stories. Terrible ones.

Her heart wrenched with misery and disappointment. Despite it all, she loved him. Loved him wildly and deeply. She couldn't help it or sway her feelings. No reasoning of her mind could squelch the passion pouring from her heart. Just looking at Brett—standing there, facing these accusations with dignity and calm—made her love him even more.

But she loved a criminal, an outlaw. If he didn't hang, he'd probably go to jail. And if by some miracle he walked away from this crime a free man, how could she ever believe he could be the kind of husband she needed and desired? How could she trust he wouldn't turn on her, hurt her? She couldn't. All of this — *this awful mess* — was because Brett Hendricks had picked a fight and lost his temper. *If he can blow up and shoot a gun at some cowboy, who's to say he won't shoot you — or your children?*

"I wanna hear Hendricks's side," Mr. Foster said after a long pause. He turned to Brett. "Son, why doncha tell what happened." He shot the other rancher a stern look. "And don't ya interrupt."

Mr. Orlander took a step back, his hands on his hips, and huffed. Mr. Foster looked at Brett, encouraging him to speak with a nod of his head. Brett let out a long breath and looked over at the Indian woman who was holding a gun over two men on the floor. Angela wondered who she was and why she doing that. She guessed the young man holding a knife at the throat of that huge frightening man was the woman's son. Were they Brett's friends? Why were they at the party?

Angela saw the Indian woman nod at Brett. He stood tall and looked directly at Mr. Foster. Violet mumbled beside her. "I don't believe a word of it." Angela turned and saw the angry expression on Violet's face. She whispered to Angela, "A man who risks his life to save strangers from a fire isn't the kind to go around shooting at folks for no reason."

Violet seemed about to say more, working up into a speech, but Brett started speaking. Violet clamped shut her mouth and noticed Tate Roberts smiling over at her. Her cheeks flushed, and she lowered her eyes. Angela could almost see the electricity spark between the two.

Violet's words spun like wheels in Angela's head. Brett was an enigma. Her papá was a selfish, mean, insensitive man. He never showed the kindness and sacrifice Brett showed again and again. Nor the tenderness and humility that often slipped out of Brett at the most unexpected times. Wasn't there a difference — between a man who cared not at all about the women he hurt and a man who struggled with his temper but whose heart was soft?

Brett's voice pulled her attention to his face. His jaw was set, and his eyes were dark even in the light of the many bright lanterns hanging from the rafters.

He cleared his throat. "After the contest, I was headin' to fetch my horse at the barn. That's when I saw yer son." He chewed his lip, then continued, his voice strong and sure. "He was attemptin' to rape a young Mexican gal—"

Orlander threw his hands up and yelled, "Liar! You're makin' this up!"

"Hear 'im out!" Mr. Foster demanded, blocking the other man with his arm, to keep him from jumping on Brett. Brett stood, unflustered, unblinking. "Go on, son," Foster told him.

"I . . . uh . . . interrupted yer son. Well, I punched 'im—I'll admit it. But he had it comin'.'"

Mr. Orlander's face was nearly purple with rage. Mr. Foster grabbed the rancher, who started to lunge at Brett. Angela thought Orlander might drop dead of a heart attack right where he stood.

"I helped the gal get away, and then fetched ma horse. But then I saw yer kid and his pals runnin' after me, yellin'. So I took off, and they soon chased after me."

Mr. Orlander was shaking his head in a furious manner. George made a noise of irritation. His sympathetic gaze told her he believed Brett's story and didn't like the angry rancher one bit.

"I rode hard, headin' north, but a fierce wind kicked up. I couldn't see for all the dust, but I heard 'em ridin' after me. When they caught up, I stopped. They tol' me to git down off ma horse, and they held their guns on me. So I got down." He looked Mr. Orlander in the eye. "But jus' as I made to git off ma horse, yer kid shot me in the leg."

Orlander screeched. "I heard enough!" He got up into Brett's face, Mr. Foster trying unsuccessfully to pull him back. "You're a lyin' son of a snake, and I'll see ya dead—"

"He's tellin' the truth. The whole truth!"

Everyone turned at the sound of the loud, gravelly voice coming from an alcove off to Angela's left. A large balding man in a long brown coat came striding toward the center of the room, a deep frown etched on his bearded face.

"Frye!" Mr. Orlander said in a growl. "What do ya think you're doin', ya stinkin' traitor? Ya just 'bout got Cummings killed. And mebbe ya did. I don't see him anywheres."

Just then a young skinny cowboy no more than sixteen came through the kitchen door, dragging a short, fat cowboy with a dark-red beard and bushy brows behind him at the end of a rope. The man's hands were tied behind him, and he looked angry enough to strangle someone.

"Is this who you're lookin' fer?" the young man asked in a high, squeaky voice.

"Cummings!" Orlander said, his visage one of utter disappointment and chastisement.

"Them two—they were the ones chased me, along with yer kid," Brett told Orlander. But he studied the one called Frye. No doubt Brett, like everyone else in the room, was wondering why the man was speaking up on Brett's behalf.

Frye stopped in front of Orlander, blocking him from Brett. "I didn't speak up—on account o' Wade being hurt like he was. But I'm speakin' up now, Boss. This here buster—he did right. Yer son"—he sucked in a breath and straightened tall—"is a piece o' dirt. More times'n I c'n count, he's taken advantage of defenseless women." He scowled at the other cowboy called Cummings. "I tried to look t'other way. But it's wrong—there ain't no two ways 'bout it. 'N' while I 'preciate my job and all the consideration ya shown me all these years, I cain't, in good conscience before the Good Lord, keep ma trap shut no longer." He took in a deep breath and added. "That's the God's honest truth."

He looked over with sheepish eyes at Brett. "I'm sorry, Hendricks. I shoulda tol' Boss the truth. I feared for my job. 'N' that weren't right o' me. I shoulda spoke up years ago, when that kid started in on his bad behavior. Maybe a good whippin' woulda taught 'im a lesson and spared some o' those women he mistreated."

Orlander stood aghast, his mouth open wide, like a fish out of water. He looked at the other cowboy, whose twisted features attested to the truth of Mr. Frye's words.

But Angela was also aghast. Like the rancher, she'd been quick to judge Brett, to believe he'd so easily shot a man. But he was the one who'd been shot. Dr. Tuttle had found Brett nearly dead and nursed him back to health. She felt ashamed for jumping to conclusions, for letting her fear turn Brett into her papá. *He's nothing like Papá.*

Her heart ached with love for Brett as he stood there, a grateful smile on his face as he listened to Mr. Frye talk.

"An' it weren't this fella here that shot first. After Wade shot 'im in the leg, he got back on 'is horse. The dust was so thick, ya couldn't see a derned thing. Hendricks fired off a couple o' blind shots—so's he could git away—an' I'd'a done the same. One o' them bullets grazed Wade's horse, and it reared up and tossed 'im into some rocks. That's how come he hurt 'is back."

Orlander snorted air out of his nose like a horse, but Angela noted the defeat on his features. In a strange way, she felt sorry for him. How awful it must have been for him to hear the truth about his son. But that in no way excused his violent actions.

Her shoulders slumped in relief as Foster's cowboys took Orlander's three gunmen in hand, after getting them to their feet, and escorted them out the double doors that led to the foyer. No doubt Mr. Foster would inform the sheriff of what had transpired.

Logan Foster put his arm around Brett and said something to him, a smile on his face. Brett's knotted features softened at his words, and he cast a glance at Angela that made her body shiver. It was a look of love so tender and needy, so utterly reckless with desire, she could hardly take a breath.

Her urgent need to flee Colorado and this wild Western town melted like snow under a hot sun. Brett's need and the adoration in his eyes for her was like that sun—hot, oppressive, relentless.

Seeing the way Brett stood up to that rancher—proud of the way he'd protected that woman—swept away the last shreds of fear she had for this rough-and-tumble cowboy. She knew now, with a certainty, that she would always be safe in his arms.

Logan Foster patted Brett on the back. "I hope you'll stay on with ma outfit, son. You're a fine buster—the best I ever seen—and a man o' honor. I see a big future for ya with the Foster Cattle Company."

Brett felt warm all over as the rancher's words sank deep inside him—words he'd always wished his pa would've said to him but never had. All those hateful feelings he'd carried for his pa melted away under Foster's proud and approving gaze. He reckoned then and there that some men weren't deserving of respect—they never earn none. And scoundrels like his pa could never be happy because they only lived to please themselves. Brett expected that as his pa rotted in jail, the scalawag only had himself to blame for his miserable life. His pa was to be pitied, not hated.

Brett looked over at Roberts, who smiled back, a grin that stretched the limits of his cheeks. Brett wasn't sure whether that smile was prompted by Brett slipping from the Devil's grasp or Violet's quick thinking with that hard fiddle case that had saved Roberts's life. Or both.

Just then, Brett caught a flash of movement out of the corner of his eye.

Orlander leapt at Roberts, and before the cowboy could react, the rancher snatched the pistol from Roberts's dangling hand, knocking him off-kilter.

Orlander spun, roaring in rage, swinging the gun around to face Brett, only a few feet from his face.

Brett froze, feeling Foster stiffen beside him. His mouth soured as his stomach flopped, his eyes locked on Orlander's thumb cocking the trigger.

Foster tried to push Brett aside in a flash of desperation, but Brett grabbed the rancher and swung him behind him, blocking him from the bullet about to come his way.

Just as Orlander made to fire, a blast of gunpowder erupted by Brett's ear. Orlander yowled as the gun he gripped flew like a startled bird out of his hand. Blood squirted from the hand Orlander cradled as he dropped hard to his knees. The pistol slapped the floorboards and slid a dozen feet to a stop at the fiddle-maker's shiny black shoes. Fisk stared at it as if it were a dead rat.

All eyes swiveled around to see Archie Halloran—the kid who couldn't hit a cow in the middle of a stampede—holding Brett's own long-barreled Colt, smoke twirling from the muzzle. Archie's hand shook like a dried-up leaf clinging to a tree in a gusty wind, his eyes as wide as saucers.

Roberts took Orlander by the arm and yanked him to his feet. The rancher stood, hunched over, hugging his shot hand to his chest, blood soaking into his starched white shirt, a dark-red bloom spreading across his chest. The fella's face was pale and stricken with a look Brett couldn't suss out. It almost looked like remorse.

Foster seethed, his face almost purple with rage. But instead of chewing out Orlander, he turned and walked over to Archie, shaking his head. With his thumb and pointer finger, he plucked the Colt out of Archie's hand—all eyes fixed in shock upon the tenderfoot who had just saved Brett's life—especially the punchers, who knew Archie's lack of aptitude for hitting a target.

Foster gave the kid a nod of approval, a grin tugging at the sides of his mouth, before he turned back to deal with Orlander. Brett shook his head, still unable to believe what'd just happened.

"Archie, I'm astonished at how you managed t' knock that gun outta Orlander's hand," Brett said, patting the shook-up tenderfoot on the shoulder. "Not many cowboys c'n hit a mark like that on a quick draw."

Archie's face turned blotchy with embarrassment. "I . . . I was aimin' fer 'is chest."

The downtrodden look on Archie's face made Brett chuckle. The other cowboys in the room burst out laughing and called out Archie's name with whoops and hollers. Archie's eyes lit up with a crooked grin. The kid sure had gumption.

Brett looked around him at Foster's disheveled guests and the tore-up room. The whole crowd of about fifty had relieved smiles on their faces, but the one that grabbed his attention was Sarah Banks's. She nodded her head thoughtfully at him, then her eyes fixed on something behind him. Brett turned and saw Mack Lambert stomping into the room, his thick black hair flying and a look of utter confusion on his face. Foster's foreman stopped short and took in the room, ill at ease in his fancy suit, the coat looking like it pinched his massive shoulders.

"What in tarnation happened here? I thought y'all were havin' a party, not a saloon brawl."

Foster grunted good-naturedly. "If'n ya'd got here on time, ya wouldn't'a missed all the fun."

Lambert snorted. He muttered beside Brett, "I couldn't find a suit that fit." He lifted his head and called over to Foster. "Reckon I didn't need t' go t' all that trouble gettin' dressed in all this fumadiddle fer yer party after all." He added, "I shore hope y'all saved me some food."

Laughter rippled across the room again. Brett looked over at Angela. Her face gleamed like an angel's. All he wanted in that moment was to pull her into her arms. But her smile gave him hope that he just might get that chance — another chance.

An old woman in a big blue dress that hardly restrained her ample bosom was wrapping Orlander's hand as he sat on the polished pine floor. Tate hovered close by, but it was clear all the steam had gone out of the rancher. Funny, Brett didn't feel any malice toward him. Just a peculiar sense of sadness. The fella loved his son — that counted for something. For a lot, in Brett's book. His own pa wouldn't have cared a whit if Brett had got hurt.

The rancher looked up at Brett, his eyes teary. Then the rich and successful owner of the Flying Y Cattle Company broke apart. Loud sobs burst from his chest, and as he shook up and down, his head dropped into his hands, the room got deathly quiet — a kind of respectful silence.

Lambert sidled up to Brett with a puzzled look on his face. "Ain't that Horace Orlander?" When Brett nodded, his eyes glued on the rancher, stunned at seeing the man cry, Lambert whistled low. "Last time I'll be late for a party — you c'n be sure o' that."

"I understand this is yours," Foster said, coming up to Brett and holding out the gun, his features quiet and solemn. "I'm s'prised ya trusted that tenderfoot, but he shore proved his mettle tonight."

Lambert's eyes went wide. "What? That green kid did somethin' heroic? Won't no one tell me what's goin' on?"

Foster said, "I gotta go find Adeline. I'm sure she's crying in her pillow over all this mess." His serious expression turned amused. "I doubt she'll believe me when I tell 'er this was the best birthday I ever had—but it's the God's honest truth." He laid a hand on Brett's shoulder. "You c'n fill 'im in—but first, tell ever'one to gather in the parlor yonder. I reckon folks could use a stiff drink—or some coffee, if'n whiskey ain't their fancy."

Brett gave a nod, and Foster hurried out of the room. Angela came over to Brett, and while he ached to hold her, there was something pressing on his heart. He asked Angela if she and Violet would herd the guests into the parlor, and maybe ask the folks in the kitchen—if they'd come back—to fix some coffee.

"I gotta do somethin' first," he told her, when she questioned him with her eyes. "I'll be in presently." She nodded, those smiling lips beckoning him, but then she turned and set about the task.

Brett heaved a sigh and coaxed his feet to move. A heaviness sat on his shoulders—maybe from all the fighting and gunplay. Or maybe because some of Orlander's sadness triggered so much of his own. He imagined the rancher was suffering from regrets—something Brett knew plenty about. And then some.

Tate Roberts was leading Orlander out of the room, three other punchers flanking him, like they'd rounded up a calf that had torn away from the bunch and were now dragging it back to the pen.

"Hold up," Brett said. Roberts and the others stopped. Orlander's narrowed eyes locked on Brett's. The fella looked weary and defeated, as if all the life had seeped out of him.

Brett faced Orlander, but kept out of arm's reach—just for good measure. He cleared his throat, and Brett saw a barely perceptible flinch on Orlander's face.

"I jus' want to say I'm sorry 'bout yer son. It was never my intention to hurt him bad. I only wanted to help the gal git free. An', I s'pose, teach Wade a lesson." He recalled that was the name Foster'd mentioned. "As far as I'm concerned, the matter's over. Jus' go home and love yer son."

His words hung in the air between them. A long shaky breath slipped from the rancher's mouth. "I'm the one shoulda taught 'im his lessons. I knew he . . . was a domineerin', headstrong boy. It's my fault."

Tears filled the wells of the rancher's eyes. The other punchers stood, unmoving. Roberts watched Brett, his grip loosening on Orlander's arm.

"I . . . I'm sorry, Hendricks. Right sorry. An' I'm much obliged for your kindness." The rancher's voice was rough with emotion, and he swiped an arm across his eyes.

Brett glanced down the hall, through the foyer to the open front doors. Some of Foster's cowboys aimed pistols at Orlander's three accomplices, who stood on the steps with their hands tied behind them.

Brett looked at Orlander. "If'n ya promise to take those scoundrels with ya and keep 'em outta trouble, we'll untie 'em and let 'em go."

Orlander nodded. Brett looked at Roberts, who gave him a grin of approval, then left the cowboys to go find Angela.

When he walked into the big parlor, Miz Foster was there, rushing around like a mother hen, pouring coffee into cups from a big silver pot. Two of the servant gals passed out slices of cake on little white plates. The ladies took up the chairs, and more had been brought into the room. The male folk stood crowded behind the ladies, drinking coffee and whiskey and talking quietly. Sarah Banks and LeRoy and his gal stood by the hearth, and a newly lit fire crackled and spit as flames danced, throwing a warm glow of light onto all the faces. Angela stood by a table, opening up her fiddle case.

Miz Foster gave a little speech, chattering faster than a chickadee being chased by a fox, waving a fan, her round face looking hot and flustered. Foster and his cowboys gathered in the wide doorway, and Brett caught sight of Orlander's puncher, Frye, hanging back behind them. A cowboy with no place to go.

Brett had been there plenty of times. *And he's afoot cuz of you.*

Then Miz Foster said, "I've asked Angela Bellini to play us something on her violin"—she threw a Brett a sly-looking smile— "to help . . . ameliorate the night's tumultuous and unexpected turn of events . . ."

Amelio-what? Brett shook his head, chuckling to himself, his eyes trained on Angela. A strand of long hair had slipped from her head and tickled her ear. He wanted to push it back and run his fingers down her cheek, feel her tremble in his arms again the way she'd done the other night.

His body erupted in a hot passionate need for her—a need so strong he could barely stay still on his feet. But he reined those feelings into a tight corral, then locked the gate. Keeping a polite distance from her was torment. He wanted to blurt out his love and his need, and declare his eternal devotion to her, but this wasn't the time or place. Would he have that chance? He had to get to her, talk to her privately, before she slipped off into the night and out of his grasp.

Chapter 37

ANGELA PICKED UP THE BOW, then positioned her beautiful violin under her chin. Violet sat in a big upholstered wingback chair by the heavy damask drapes and gave her an encouraging smile. George, behind her, closed his eyes, preparing to listen to the music about to fill the room. The eyes of dozens of people—wealthy townspeople and ranchers and cowboys—watched her expectantly. But none more so than Brett.

Angela swallowed. She knew just what to play.

Adeline nodded at her to begin, curls bouncing around her face. The room fell utterly quiet. Angela's nervousness drifted away as she pulled the bow across the strings. Warm, rich tones spilled from her violin, like honey, saturating the room with the gentle, simple melody. George's lips curled into a smile in immediate recognition, but Angela didn't dare look over at Brett.

After the quintet's last rehearsal the day before, Angela had asked George about this Scottish folk song he'd taught her. He'd pulled a book from a shelf in his library and showed her the poem that had inspired the song. It made her think of the characters in that little book George had lent her, *Only a Fiddler*, and particularly about Christian, who'd never seen his dreams come to fruition, and who lost his true love, Naomi. Why George had given her such a sad book to read, she didn't know. But the story now wove into the notes she drew from the strings, and her heart ached over a lost life, a lost love, a lost chance.

The song's lyrics were sad as well. About love's disappointment—how, at first, love proved kind and bright and full of hope. But then it waxed cold and faded like morning dew.

The song's words embodied all her deepest fears. They told her that if she loved another, it would only lead to disappointment. That one day she would be old, alone, and lonely, lamenting her bad choices and lost chances.

Yet, as she played, the music transcended the words, soaring above her, like a bird escaping from a raging wildfire below her.

The notes held power in them—and healing. She knew then that the power was in her hands, in her heart. She had a choice— she wasn't bound by the words. She could escape on the wings of her music—escape the prison she'd lived in all these years. A prison of her own making.

Strangely, she felt awash with peace and an abiding sense that she could make Greeley her home. All that awaited her back in New York was disappointment, denigration, and despair. Yes, her mamá needed love and support, but she had family and community surrounding her. Her mamá needed to find her own strength to stand on her feet. If she didn't want to tolerate her husband's mean treatment, she would need to speak up or walk out. Angela couldn't do that for her.

She was stung by the realization that she had been enforcing her mamá's weakness, by cowering alongside her instead of standing up to Papá's temper. That was her prison. And it was her choice to wallow in it or soar above it.

What had begun as a sorrowful tune now skipped around the room like water babbling brightly over rocks. The slow, dark melody had changed into a lively, uplifting, hope-inspiring jig that caused her listeners to straighten with surprised looks and begin tapping their feet.

Violet excitedly jumped out of her chair and found her flute. Soon, her high dulcet tones joined with Angela's in delectable harmony as she stood at her side. Angela's smile made her cheeks hurt as she bowed with the greatest enthusiasm, reveling in the way her heart kept soaring and soaring, their notes entwining and resonating layers of rich harmonics.

But it wasn't just the music and the surprising freedom she felt that made joy fill her to overflowing. It was the look on Brett's face as he watched her play. He was utterly transformed in her eyes.

Brett thought his heart had stopped. When Angela played those first notes, he froze. So many feelings tumbled like rocks inside him, he feared an avalanche would bury him. He stood, unable to move a muscle, as heard his ma's voice singing in his head and felt the age-old guilt and anger rise in his gut. The sad, sorrowful sound of the fiddle near broke his heart. He felt as if he were far away, watching himself as he stood in the house that day he left, looking at his ma sitting at the kitchen table, tears shining on her cheeks. He recalled the hopeless feeling he'd had when he slammed the door behind him, leaving her to his pa's abuse.

Sarah Banks's words played again in his head, now so clear to him. He couldn't change the past, couldn't make a different choice. The fire of his shame had charred him to the core. *"But you don't have to burn in the flames. There is a way out. When a fire races across the prairie, it burns the grass to stubble. It is not a bad thing. From the ashes, new grass sprouts. New life begins. It must be."*

It must be . . . Brett understood that now. The fire served a purpose—to burn away all the ugly stuff growing like mold inside him. But at some point, the fire petered out. Rainclouds dumped water, and plants grew out of the blackened ground. A fresh start.

Then the song had changed. Angela's face had gone from serious to practically gleeful. And with each new lively note her fiddle sang out, Brett's spirit lifted a little higher. And soon, he felt it soar like a bird to the heavens, freer than he'd ever felt, like he'd been locked in a cage all his life, and Angela had the key.

It wasn't just the song or the way she played her music. It was Angela's heart. He felt it now, as if it were beating in his own chest. As if the song she played was *his* song—*their* song. A song that could smother any fire except the one he wanted to keep smoldering in his heart—this fierce love her felt for her. He never wanted to put that out, and, if truth be told, he knew nothing on God's green earth could ever put out the love coursing through his veins right at that moment.

He had a temper—that was certain. He often acted impulsively, without thinking. He sometimes let his anger take over. He'd shot at a few fellas and punched twice that number.

But that don't make ya a killer. It merely means ya have passion, that ya care for others. That you have love in yer heart—like yer ma had. An' that's not a bad thing, not somethin' to be afraid of.

He would declare his love for Angela, and he would do whatever it took to convince her he could be her protector. He'd learned from horses how trust was something earned, something that took time. He couldn't expect her to lose all that fear inside of a week—fear that her pa had instilled in her. It might take years, but what did he care? He would take all the time needed to win her trust. Even if it meant chasing her to New York.

Brett watched, enchanted by the truths ringing clear in his head and by Angela's beauty. In the glow of the lamps and firelight, she was breathtaking. He let his eyes roam over every inch of her, his hunger for her gnawing at him. Her skin looked milky and smooth, and her black hair shone like obsidian rock. He thought he'd explode with all the things he wanted to tell her.

He might not have the book learning she had, and he couldn't speak proper either, but he knew they were meant for each other. He believed with all his heart that God had saved him in the desert and brought him to Tuttle's house so he'd meet her. So he'd hear her music. So he'd be freed of this weight he'd been dragging behind him for years. Free to love.

Brett let his mind empty and just listened as Angela played the last bouncy notes, Violet blowing her flute with gusto alongside her. When that last long note faded away, everyone in the room clapped and cheered, and the two gals gave a little bow.

Brett glanced over at Sarah Banks and caught her studying him. He got the feeling she had something more to say to him. He wasn't sure, though, if he wanted to hear it.

With everyone praising the two gals, like hens pouncing on a bug, Brett hung back, his heart pounding, waiting for a chance to get Angela alone. One by one, Foster's guests drifted into other rooms, and the cowboys and some of the other men stepped outside to smoke and drink under the stars. Then Brett saw that puncher Frye looking to slip away unnoticed.

He figured the fella to be nearing forty. Punching cattle was a hard life, and not many cowboys lasted up to the age of this fella. Brett figured with all the times he himself had been thrown off a horse, been tripped up, been stepped on by a cow, slept on rock-hard ground, got bit by snakes and bugs and other critters, he'd never make it to forty on the open range.

That longing for a ranch grew bigger and more desirous with every new ache and pain. If only he could see that dream come true. If only he could provide for Angela the way he longed to. Maybe, if he stayed on with Foster, he'd eventually work up to foreman. Make enough to at least buy a little place on a piece of water.

He called Frye over. The cowboy caught Brett's wave and headed to him.

Up close, Brett made out a scar running under Frye's right eye. Frye rubbed his part-bald head.

"Where ya headed?" Brett asked him.

Frye shrugged. "I'll find me a place." He huffed. "I rode ma horse over here, but I'm guessin' my boss took it back to Denver with the others." He made a face. "*Former* boss."

Brett noticed Foster looking his way and nodded him over. Before Brett could bring up the idea, Foster spoke in that low, big voice of his. "That took a lot o' guts to speak out like ya did. Seein' as you're presently out of a job, would ya like to work for me? I'd be right proud to have a fella of your integrity in ma outfit."

The cowboy's face filled with a mix of relief and gratitude. "Thank you. Ya got winter work?"

"Always plenty to do round here. What c'n ya do?"

"Pretty much everythin'. My back's not as good as it used ta be, but I c'n still work cattle out on the range."

Foster held out his hand. "Consider yerself hired. What's yer Christian name?"

Frye shook the boss's hand. "Phineas. Phineas Prescott Frye." He gave a shrug. "Jus' call me Frye."

Brett put out his hand for Frye to shake. "I'm in yer debt, friend."

Frye shrugged again, the matter closed. But Brett would never forget it. "I'll show ya around, git ya set up in the bunkhouse. But . . . uh . . . I got a few things to do afore that."

Foster waved him off with a wink. "Go talk ta yer gal. I'll git Frye introduced to the other cowboys."

Brett felt his neck go red. He's jus' as much a matchmaker as 'is wife.

The rancher patted him hard on the shoulder. "Hurry up, now. Don't keep 'er waitin'. Gals always want a fella to show up when they're expected."

Frye grinned along with Foster, then the two turned and strode over to the door leading outside, chatting amiably.

Brett looked over at Angela. She'd put her fiddle away. Violet gave her a hug, then hurried over to where Tate Roberts was standing by the fireplace, watching her with a crooked smile on his face.

Maybe love was in the air. Brett sorely hoped so.

"Would ya like to take a stroll under the stars?" Brett asked, his voice hesitant. If she didn't know him better, she'd think he was shy. But she imagined that after the way she'd reacted to his kiss the other night, he was downright terrified.

She didn't blame him. She felt such a fool, the way she'd acted. It was her fault, really. She'd been so swept up in the passion she felt for him, she'd practically ravaged him.

She giggled at her thoughts.

"What?" he asked, standing erect beside her, polite and unbearably handsome. He rubbed a hand over his clean-shaved chin. "Did I forget a spot when I shaved?"

She thought his smile would be the death of her. That smile made his hazel eyes sparkle. She saw so much in them—mirth, joy, teasing, silliness. Love.

Definitely love.

Oh my Lord, I truly am head over heels with this cowboy. Heaven help me.

"Penny for yer thoughts."

"I think not," she teased, hardly able to gather her wits about her. She entwined her arm around his, and his eyes opened wide in surprise. She demurely looked at him from under her lashes. "Mr. Hendricks, I'd be pleased to take a stroll with you under the stars."

Violet and Tate stood in front of the fireplace, the flames flickering light over their clothes and faces. The two were oblivious to Angela and Brett, engaged in quiet, intimate conversation. If Violet didn't seem to think loving a cowboy was a mistake, then maybe . . .

Brett was quiet by her side as they walked through the foyer to the front yard. The cool fall air took her breath away, and she dropped her head back to gaze at the thousands of shimmering stars that floated in the sea of night.

Brett untwined his arm from hers and let his hand slide down to grasp her fingers. His skin was warm and rough, and his hand was big and enclosed hers entirely. When he played with her fingers, a rush of heat ran through her body, and her knees grew wobbly.

"C'n ya smell it?"

She kept her gaze upward, distracted by his fingers stroking the back of her hand. His touch was oh so gentle, it tantalized her. "Smell what?" She identified the pungent fragrance of sage and other desert plants, the horses and hay. She breathed deep, relishing these scents she'd come to love—so fresh and alive. Not like the acrid and metallic odors of the city.

"Snow's comin'. Tonight, mebbe in the mornin'."

She looked at him. "Truly? The sky is so clear. How can you tell?"

He turned to face her, his eyes searching hers—the way he often did, as if looking for something he'd lost. Looking for her. She had been lost, but he'd found her. Found her heart.

"Honey, ya oughta know by now—we cowboys are good at predictin'. We seen enough weather to know when a storm is comin' or rain, even a flood."

This time when he called her *honey*, it sent a thrill through her. "What else can you predict?" she asked, blood rushing through her veins. She thought her heart was thumping so loud, he'd surely hear it.

Brett let go of her hand and stroked her cheek, then let his hand drop to her neck. She shivered, holding in the moan aching to slip out of her mouth. She wanted to melt into him, until they was no space between them.

"Well . . ." he said, his eyes dropping from her face down to his hand trailing along her shoulder. A muscle twitched along his sculpted jaw. "I predict some right happy times ahead for a young and purty fiddle player."

She gasped as he put his mouth to her ear. He breathed against her, his lips trembling. But he didn't kiss her. She didn't dare move for fear of falling. She was already falling—falling hard. But she hoped Brett would catch her before she hit the ground.

"Is . . . is that right, Mr. Hendricks?" she said, barely squeezing the words out. "And . . . why . . . why would you predict such a happy life?"

She yearned to hear him say it. He didn't disappoint.

"Because ya got a cowboy that loves ya. And he plans to spend the rest of his life showin' ya just how much," he whispered in her ear.

She pulled back and met eyes that overflowed with love. He was inches from her face, his lips almost on hers. She couldn't utter a word, and her mouth fell open. He licked his lips as if getting ready to taste her, and she thought she would swoon. He was torturing her.

"And since . . . uh . . . this cowboy is so crazy in love with ya, do ya think it'd be all right if'n he kissed ya?" He added, "I don't want to appear overbearin' or demandin'."

Angela's heart pulsed in her throat. Somehow, she managed to answer him. "I believe I . . . I'll allow it—just this once, mind you." She lifted her chin and gave him a stern look, but he merely grinned and took her head in his hands and kissed her—deeply and sweetly and gently. She collapsed into his muscular arms that enwrapped her, but just as she pressed into him for more, he pulled back.

"What?" she asked, flustered and hot, even with a biting wind nipping at her neck. Why had he stopped? She wanted to kiss him all night, even forever.

Brett raked a hand through his thick chestnut hair. "Ya said jus' once. That was a bit more'n once."

"Was it?" she asked, putting her hand on the back of his head and pulling him toward her. "I couldn't tell." Her lips landed on his, and she kissed them playfully. Brett groaned and threw back his head, his hands gliding up and down her sides. "Maybe we . . . ought to try it again. I'll pay better attention this time," she assured him.

Brett laughed, his lips working their way down her throat. Angela's longing for him exploded like a wildfire, racing over her skin hot and unstoppable. But this time she let the fire rage, knowing she would come through unscathed, unburned. Just as

Brett had led her through the flames at the fairgrounds. Led her to cool, soothing water. A way out of danger. To safety.

His lips came back to her mouth—hot and needy and moist. She couldn't get enough of his mouth and his teasing tongue. After minutes of excruciating delight, he stepped back and took her hands in his.

"How was that, Miss Bellini?" he asked, his face flushed and his body taut, like a wildcat ready to pounce. The air around them pickled with electricity, just like on the day of the fire. "Did that kiss suit yer fancy?"

Angela laughed. "It suited me just fine." She added, staring deep into those gorgeous eyes, "*You* suit me just fine."

Brett's smile widened until his whole face was alight with joy. "Angela Bellini, if ya don't stay and marry me, I'll come chasin' after ya. I aim to make you ma wife."

Angela heart soared. She couldn't believe her ears. Or her feelings. He was asking her to marry him . . .

Before coming out West, she'd decided she'd probably never marry. What man would marry a woman who wanted more than anything to play music? A fear tickled her neck.

"If I marry you, Brett Hendricks, would you expect me to give up my music? Relegate me to the kitchen to cook?"

"Relegate? What's that?" His face held a stricken look. "I would never want ya ta give up yer music. That's who ya are. You gotta chase yer dreams. Ain't it yer dream ta play on the big stage, in the big city? In front of hundreds o' folks?"

"It is. Was," she said, wrapping her arms around her chest, feeling suddenly cold. Would she be giving up her dream if she married Brett and stayed in Colorado? Couldn't she make hers a Colorado Dream and find joy in playing for a few appreciative people? She knew her dream had been fashioned more from a need to be loved and approved than from a desire for fame and recognition. It was a flawed dream, a mistaken dream. This—this cowboy—was her real dream come true.

She reached up and rested a hand on Brett's cheek. He turned and kissed her hand, taking it in his own.

"I don't want ya to give up yer dream," he said, clearly meaning every word. She was amazed. She never thought she'd hear any man say such a thing to her.

"What about a family? Do you want children?" she asked him.

He blinked. "I . . . I never thought that far ahead. I didn't reckon I'd ever find a gal ta love. I wasn't expectin' to fall for ya, Angela. I didn't mean to. But I couldn't help myself."

She laughed at his serious explanation. Before she could respond, he said quickly, "If'n ya want kids, that's fine by me. I'd like ta wait until I saved some money afore we married, so's I could buy ya a house. But if'n ya don't want kids—If ya jus' wanna play your fid—yer *violin*—then I'd be jus' as happy. Ya got a gift. Ya cain't give that up—never. It'd be wrong."

His sincerity was undeniable, his affection genuine. How could she doubt him? How could she say no to a man who loved her truly and deeply for who she was? Her music had brought them together, healed both their hearts, entwined them in love. No, she couldn't see him ever demanding that she give up playing. Her songs were his songs.

"So," he said, shifting nervously on his feet, squeezing her hands. "Ya got an answer fer me?"

She couldn't help but smile. His face, even in the half-moon's light, was flushed red. He looked like a schoolboy waiting miserably to learn if he'd flunked a test. She'd put him out of his misery.

"Yes," she said, waiting for him to respond.

"Yes, you'll marry me?"

She nodded, a laugh bursting out at his shock.

He rubbed his jaw. "Well, I'll be . . ." He shook his head. "I . . . I plum run outta words ta say how I feel."

Angela took his hands and draped his arms around her neck. "Then just kiss me, Brett. Like you mean it this time."

He laughed—a big hearty laugh. Then he said, "With pleasure, honey. A whole lot of pleasure."

His sparkling eyes danced in the moonlight as he pulled her tight against him and kissed her, feeling his love pour into her like a roaring waterfall. She had no doubt he meant it.

Chapter 38

ADELINE TAPPED A SPOON AGAINST her glass as she stood at the end of the long trestle table, the chandelier overhead flickering with a dozen tiny flames that made the crystal glasses and china plates sparkle. The dining room was replete with decorations for the Thanksgiving holiday: chains of large orange and yellow maple leaves draped the walls, and a large overflowing horn of plenty sat on a table in the corner, filled with colorful gourds and dried sunflowers and nuts.

A cheery fire snapped and crackled in the hearth, adding to the warmth and glow at this joyous occasion. Angela couldn't imagine being any happier than she felt at this moment.

The eyes of Adeline's twenty elegantly dressed guests gave her full attention, and Angela listened as her hostess and friend cleared her throat.

"My dear, honored guests. I am sooo overjoyed to have you join Logan and me, and our precious girls"—she tipped her head at Madeline and Clementine, who sat poised and mannerly in their beautiful chiffon dresses, their hair coiffed in curls and looking so much like their mother—"to celebrate the end of harvest and to give thanks to the Lord for all our many blessings . . ."

As Adeline gushed about all the things she was grateful for, Angela set eyes on her gorgeous fiancé, who looked itchy and uncomfortable in his three-piece wool suit. He'd complained earlier in the day that he wished he didn't have to dress up, when she saw him by the barn, getting ready to wash up for the extravagant dinner Adeline was preparing. But ever since the disastrous birthday party more than a month ago, Adeline was determined to make this Thanksgiving party the most memorable in her family's—and perhaps the West's—history. So Brett was willing to suffer for a good cause.

It seemed the rancher's wife would get her wish. Surrounded by close friends and family, Adeline beamed as she spoke, the intoxicating aroma of turkey and yams and freshly baked bread steaming from the imported chafing dishes covering nearly every inch of the table.

Brett sat, listening attentively to his hostess, looking every bit the gentleman—as did Tate Roberts and Mack Lambert. A stranger would never know these men were cowboys who spent more time in the saddle than on the ground, slept on a blanket in thunderstorms on the dirt, or risked their lives day in and out to move thousands of temperamental, dangerous animals across hundreds of miles of perilous desert.

Since she'd come to Colorado, her impression of cowboys had greatly changed. She'd thought such men slackers, unprincipled, uncouth, and disrespectful. But since she'd come to know well Logan Foster and some of his "punchers," as he referred to them, she realized how wrong she'd been. Now she understood why George had so highly praised and defended the life of a cowboy when she'd first arrived in Greeley. She'd been shocked by his words, for she had just met the abrasive and cocky Brett Hendricks, and he embodied—or so it had seemed—everything she loathed in a man. How wrong she been with that first impression.

Brett must have felt her eyes upon him, for he turned ever so slightly and snagged her gaze, the corner of his mouth lifting into a grin. Every time he smiled at her, a delightful warmth spread over her, like a comforting blanket. As she passed her days at the ranch, teaching the girls violin and Italian cooking, while waiting eagerly for her Christmas wedding, she and Brett strolled along the river in the evenings, after he finished his ranch work. Sometimes he took her riding—often putting her up on Kotoo, his beautiful mare, instead of Nicker. Brett had assured her it was too late in the season to worry about rattlesnakes, but he indulged her by keeping their rides confined to the cool, damp banks of the river, where crisp fall breezes puckered the surface of water and shimmering blue dragonflies hovered over clumps of cattails.

And when Angela wasn't busy helping around the ranch house, Adeline engaged her relentlessly in the planning of her wedding, as if Angela were her own daughter about to be wed. Though Brett had expressed hope that they could have a small ceremony, with just a handful of friends, Adeline wouldn't hear of it. But Brett good-naturedly shrugged when Adeline dragged him and Angela into the parlor to lay out her strategy for an unprecedented Christmas wedding that would be the talk of Colorado. How could they so disappoint the woman who had played a hand in bringing the two of them together?

Adeline insisted on hiring her favorite seamstress, who lived in Fort Collins—a young woman named Grace Cunningham—to make Angela's wedding dress, and the two of them had taken a day trip, accompanied by Brett and Tate and Violet, to the sweet little town nestled along the Cache la Poudre River. Angela had taken an instant liking to Grace and had been surprised to learn she and her husband, Monty, were close friends with LeRoy Banks and his family.

Her eyes lighted on LeRoy and Gennie. No one could miss the love that passed between the two. She looked around the table—at George, Sarah Banks, Dr. Tuttle, the ladies from the opera board, Violet, Clem and Maddy, and a dozen other friends of the Fosters. Angela felt so at home, so content. She couldn't wait to introduce her mamá and aunt and sisters to these wonderful, special people. Perhaps when they came out for the wedding, they'd consider staying and making a life in Colorado.

She planned to do all she could to convince them, which included introducing her mamá to a few Italian transplants who'd come from Mulberry Bend and were now living in Greeley. With her papá and brother now living in Italy, with no plans to return to America, there was no reason for her family to stay in New York—not reason enough, Angela thought. Here, her family could create a new life, a new dream—just as she had done.

Her aunt had hinted at Papa's reason for leaving New York. He could no longer hold his head up in a community that whispered about his mistreatment of his family. Many in Mulberry Bend had witnessed him pushing Mamá down the El Train stairs. The thought of never seeing her papá again saddened her only a little—mostly for what had never been rather than what she'd lost. Would he someday feel remorse for all the hurt he'd meted out to his family? She didn't know, but she hoped so. While forgiveness was difficult to summon, she knew in time she'd find it in her heart to forgive her papá. She needed to—to come to peace with her past.

Adeline turned to her husband after finishing her long oratory and asked him to say grace. When the amens died out around the table, the guests chatted boisterously as they passed the platters around and dug into the food, which was delectable and beautifully prepared by a staff of cooks. Angela, though, had slipped into the kitchen earlier in the day to prepare a special Italian holiday dessert—a new favorite of George's.

"Well, this is a lovely dinner," George said, at her side. "Much less . . . exciting than Logan's birthday party." He added with a smile and nudge, "Though, I'd go through all that mayhem again just to hear you play that piece the way you did that evening. Exquisite, simply exquisite. You played as if the melody welled up from the very depth of your soul."

"You chose the right violin for me," she told him. "I'll cherish it forever." And the fact that he'd hardly charged her half of what it was worth. When she'd protested, he would hear none of it. Her heart swelled with affection for the sweet violin maker. If not for him, she would never have come to Greeley—or stayed long enough to fall in love with a cowboy.

He smiled and slathered butter on a chunk of dark bread. "And I'll get to hear you play it for years to come. I can't tell you, my dear, how happy I am that you'll be staying in Greeley. You will stay, won't you?"

"I don't know where we'll end up. Brett plans to keep working for Mr. Foster, but we can't stay on the ranch forever."

George's face hinted at a secret. Angela knew him too well.

"What?" she asked. "Is there something you know that you're not telling me?"

"Have you tasted this bread?" he said, changing the subject. "It's . . ."

Logan Foster got to his feet, and the guests quieted and gave him full attention. "I have a few happy announcements I'd like ta share with y'all. Brett, Angela—would ya come 'ere for a moment?"

Angela exchanged a curious look with Brett. Whatever Mr. Foster planned to say seemed to be a surprise to him as well. Angela supposed the rancher intended to share the news of their upcoming wedding with those guests who hadn't yet heard.

Brett got up from his chair and walked to the end of the table, where he took Angela's hand in his when she came up beside him. Her heart beat fast as he squeezed her fingers and whispered softly in her ear, "I love ya, Angela."

He never seemed to grow tired of saying those words to her, and she never tired of hearing them. He was just as amazed that they'd fallen in love as she was. Funny though—none of their friends seemed amazed at all. They expressed the sentiment that the two of them were more than well suited—they were a match in every way.

Logan Foster cleared his throat and stroked his trim moustache, looking at Brett and Angela. "It always brings me—'n' the missus— great joy to see young folks fall in love. Life in the West is no picnic—unless o' course yer talkin' 'bout one beset by ants 'n' wildfire." That earned him a few chuckles. "With what-all we face out here in Colorado—blizzards 'n' droughts 'n' locusts 'n' floods 'n' such—without someone to love ya by yer side, standin' faithfully with ya, keepin' ya warm nights—well, it makes it a rough road. Love has a way o' smoothin' it out. And it's my hope 'n' deep desire that you two will enjoy many years o' love and happiness—"

"And have lots of children," George chimed, eliciting a smattering of lighthearted laughter.

"So," Logan continued, his brows furrowing in seriousness, "while the missus and I have enjoyed havin' ya both here at the ranch, ya won't be here much longer. We'll miss ya, but we hope ya won't forgit us."

In the silence that ensured at his strange pronouncement, Angela looked at Brett. His face showed the same confusion she felt — but worse. He looked upset. Surely Mr. Foster wasn't firing him.

"Logan, don't torment the poor lovebirds!" Adeline said, tugging at his coat. His serious expression then turned mischievous, and Adeline smacked his arm with her fan.

Logan laid a hand on Brett's shoulder, giving him a big smile as he pulled an envelope from his vest pocket.

"I told you a while back that I'd pay you 'n' Roberts fightin' wages for helpin' stop them rustlers." He nodded his head at Tate. "Already done paid yer pal there. This here's your share."

He handed the envelope to Brett, who took it with a look of gratitude. "But there's somethin' more in there."

Brett waited for Logan to say more, but the rancher gestured for Brett to open the envelope. As he did so, Logan looked at the guests at his table, who hung on his words.

"Horace Orlander — the owner o' the Flying Y Ranch — sent a letter of apology for his . . . behavior at ma birthday party. I know y'all feel as bad as I do 'bout his son, Wade. He loves his son dearly, and because of . . . a misunderstandin', he acted as he did. I cain't blame 'im fer what he did. I know what it's like to love a child so much it nearly breaks yer heart." He looked at his two girls, who were paying more attention to the bubbling pies being set on the table than their father's words. "And in a show of quality, Horace wanted ta give Brett a little somethin' in compensation. Fer the trouble he caused. And to thank Brett for teachin' 'im a lesson in honor." He looked at Brett. "It takes a heap o' courage to stand up and do right. Not tolerate bad behavior. It takes a man, a real cowboy, ta do what ya done, Brett. Ya deserve this."

Angela choked up at hearing the rancher's words. Brett looked stunned as he stood, unmoving, the envelope fisted in his hand. He turned to Angela, and she urged him with her eyes to open it.

Orlander sent an apology? Brett flashed on his pa, who was rotting in a Texas jail, trying to imagine hearing an apology come from those lips. He reckoned that was something he'd never hear. Even though Orlander had tried to kill him, Brett understood his rage and need for revenge. The fella'd just been misinformed, that's all. The rancher was probably decent, all in all, his only failing in loving his son too much. *That sure beat a pa that loved his son not at all.*

Brett figured he'd read Orlander's letter later. He wasn't all that good with the written word, and all of Foster's guests were looking at him. It made him twitchy, and what with being trussed up like a turkey in this suit, his feet were halfway out the door ahead of him. But he'd be rude if he didn't comply with Foster's request.

He opened the envelope and saw a bunch of money pinned together, a fifty-dollar bill on the outside. Brett gulped. Just that one bill was more than a month's wages. He fished out the piece of paper behind the money.

At first, when he unfolded the slip of paper, he was perplexed. It wasn't a letter. It was a ledger of some kind, with some numbers on it. The heading at the top said, "Bank of Denver City." Then it hit him. He'd seen the like before. His pa used to get these slips after brokering the cattle to the shipping yards. It was a bank check, signed by someone at the bottom and stamped with an official-looking seal. His eyes locked on the amount. He wasn't sure what all those zeros meant, but it was a whole lot of money. His money?

He looked at Foster, whose big grin answered him. "Enough there ta buy yerself that ranch. I cain't think of no one better to break and train horses than you, Hendricks. Sarah Banks knows of a place ya might like ta buy. Talk ta her."

Brett's head swam. A ranch? His ranch? He looked down at the slip of paper again. Blood thumped in his ears, and he swallowed back the raw emotion seeking to undo him. A warm hand took his, and he turned and saw Angela's face — his angel. Her eyes regarded him with love and pride. He never imagined, in any of his dreams for his life, that he'd be standing next to such a fetching, amazing gal — one soon to be his wife. And that he'd have enough money to buy that ranch. To raise horses and train them and sell them. And to build a fine house — a house where he and Angela could happily live out their days on the Front Range. He'd been fretting so, about how he'd be able to make a life with her. Now . . .

His heart swelled with gratitude. Gratitude for so many things. He'd felt so lost and alone for so long. He'd thought if he kept running, he'd someday stop hurting. Stop feeling the guilt and the shame for his past. But he'd been wrong, oh so wrong. Running wasn't the answer. He'd needed to go through the fire and let it burn him to cinders. That was the only way he could start over. A new beginning, Sarah Banks had said. *"It's not a bad thing,"* she'd added.

A grin spread across his face. *No, not a bad thing at all.*

He drew Angela into his arms, and she laid her head on his shoulder, her soft cheek against his skin, wet. He pulled back and saw tears glistening in her eyes. But they were tears of joy. The only kind of tears he ever wanted to see trickle down those rosy cheeks.

Music played in his head — Angela's sweet fiddling. He hoped she'd play for him every night. Music that would heal their hearts and wrap them up in joy. She'd been worried that he'd want her to quit playing. But he was flabbergasted to hear it. "You could no more quit playin' yer fiddle than I could quit breakin' broncos." He was glad to hear she'd joined the Greeley Orchestra. He pictured sitting in the audience with her up on a stage, looking up adoringly at her as she enchanted one and all with her playing—like she'd done the night of Foster's birthday party. He'd be nothing but proud.

Chairs scraped and guests got to their feet. Roberts and Violet came up to him and Angela. His pal shook his hand, grinning. "I happy fer ya, Brett. I bet one day yer horse ranch'll be famous the world over."

Brett chuckled. Others came over to congratulate him and Angela. He shared a few words and laughs with Lambert, noting the big cowboy wasn't wearing that same troublesome suit that had made him late for the last dinner party. Doc Tuttle practically talked Brett's ear off with all his excitement over their getting hitched. Brett could hardly keep up with all the well-wishing and pleasantries thrown at him.

As the guests left the dining room and Miz Foster's servants began clearing the table, Sarah Banks came up to them. She gave Angela a hug and a big toothy smile, then looked deep into Brett's eyes. He felt a mite squirmy, hoping she wasn't about to hint at some new danger soon to vex him. But she eased his mind.

"When Lucas Rawlings met Emma," she said, glancing back and forth between him and Angela, "he wasn't sure if his feelin's were true. If he could risk hurtin' his heart again. Risk lovin' another woman." She grunted, a smile on her face like she was remembering back over the years. "I told him what I want to tell you. 'When two people are meant for each other, their hearts will sing together. The sky will embrace them, and the stars will shine ever brighter.' When I look at ya two, I hear your heart song, beating loud like a drum. I hear music stronger than any Indian medicine. Music that heals. Music that speaks."

She turned and looked directly at Angela, whose mouth had dropped open — that mouth that Brett couldn't seem to stop kissing at every chance. "Listen to it, to the music, Angela. Let it heal your heart. Let this cowboy" — she poked Brett in the side — "love ya. For he surely will, to the end of his days."

Angela sighed with a tremble that Brett felt through his own chest.

Then Sarah Banks looked at Brett and said, "I'm glad you aim to start a horse ranch. My old, tired bones are complainin' more an' more ever' day. Eli's up and married, living in Fort Collins. LeRoy and Gennie are helpin' with the horses, but they won't stay forever. I been hopin' someone — the right someone — might go chasin' down those wild herds so's I don't have to. When ya find some time, after the wedding, I'd like to show ya some land I know about. A perfect spread, just south of Greeley, east, along part of the Platte. Has a pretty little house on it already. The owners up and left for Oregon last month. LeRoy and I can teach ya all ya need to know about breeding and selling horses. Bustin' them? — ya do that better'n anyone in the territory." She winked and said, "But I can teach you a few Cheyenne tricks I bet ya don't know."

Brett shook his head, feeling overwhelmed. Every secret dream he'd held close to his heart was coming true. A whole avalanche of blessings he didn't deserve. "I'd be much obliged fer any help ya c'n give me. Any advice."

Sarah chucked — a big hearty chuckle. "Best advice? Love your gal with all your heart, an' do right by 'er. The rest'll fall in place, like pebbles settlin' to the bottom of a still pond."

Brett pulled Angela close, his arm around her waist. He gave her a squeeze, and she squealed and pushed at him playfully. "That's jus' what I plan to do, Miz Banks. Thank you — for everythin'."

Sarah merely nodded, turned, and went to join LeRoy and Gennie by the warming fire, leaving Brett alone with Angela. Conversation drifted to his ears as he took her hand and led her out of the dining room and over to a quiet, dark corner of the big living room. Brett stopped in front of the large glass window that looked out over the prairie. The night spread like a black blanket punched with holes that firelight peeked through. So many feelings clogged his throat, he couldn't think of a thing to say. But Angela didn't seem to need any words from him. She looked up at him, her eyes moist with tears, her lips curled up in that smile he loved to see.

What else could he do but kiss her?

Angela drowned in Brett's kiss, then resurfaced, catching her breath as if she'd been underwater for an eternity. And that's how she felt, in a way. That she'd been drowning, flailing in a tumultuous sea, with no sight of land. She'd longed for love, and when it didn't seem possible she'd ever find it, she'd buried herself in her music. Music became her solace, her closest companion. Music comforted her, cheered her, healed her heart. Where words failed, music spoke.

And her music had spoken to Brett—it had drawn him to her, like a moth to flame. But instead of burning him, they'd burned together in these coals they couldn't escape. Coals that incinerated their fears and pain and hurt. What Sarah Banks said was so true—their hearts sang together. Together they would create a new song, many songs. Songs of love and promise. Songs of comfort and joy.

She and Brett would see all their dreams come true. All their Colorado Dreams.

Angela threw her arms around Brett's neck, and to her surprise, he swung her around and swooped her up into his arms. She exploded in laughter as he carried her to the door leading to the wide and wild outdoors—the desert prairie that spread out for endless miles in all directions. A place that had once frightened her but now she could call home.

"Where are you taking me?" she asked, giggling as she looked into his eyes so full of love and playfulness.

"I ain't got a clue." He stopped and planted a kiss on her forehead. "Will ya trust me?"

She gave him his answer—a long, deep kiss that left her head swooning and yearning for more.

The End

NOTE FROM THE AUTHOR

MANY THANKS, ONCE AGAIN, TO Peggy Ford, director of the Greeley Museum. She spent hours with my husband and me last year, telling us stories of Greeley's past, about the founding colonists and some of the colorful people who played interesting roles in the history of this town. The museum's exhibit featured history on a violin maker named George Fisk. Many of the facts of his life come alive in *Colorado Dream*, and his story was the spark for my novel. When I heard how people came from all over the world to buy a violin from the "Stradivarius of the West," I instantly imagined a young woman in the East, who longed to play in a symphony but lacked both a proper instrument and the support of her family.

Then, while my husband and I were having dinner in the downtown area—where thirty years ago he'd once played jazz gigs while attending UNC, we met a cowboy who was world famous for breaking wild horses. As he told us his tale, I pictured my young violin player meeting a wild cowboy on the run, with a wild, untamable heart. I thought of how soothing music can be, and then pictured this cowboy always restless, yearning for peace but unable to find it—until he heard her play the violin.

And that's how *Colorado Dream* began to form. While the rest of the characters in the novel—except the colorful Annie Green (who penned the song lyrics noted at the beginning of *Colorado Promise*)—are figments of my imagination, I did my best to capture the type of people who lived in Greeley in those days.

After our visit to Greeley, we then drove north to Laramie, and while visiting this unique town with a strange history, we took the tour of the Wyoming Territorial Prison. When I learned that women also were incarcerated there, and that more than 25% of the prisoners escaped, I had an avalanche of ideas for future books.

So next year, watch for the release of the next books in The Front Range Series, set in Laramie, Wyoming.

I pored through more than a dozen books on the lives of cowboys and the early days of cattle ranching in order to bring color and accuracy to my novel. Some of the events, characters, and even dialogue have been borrowed faithfully from accounts by punchers that lived in the 1870s. I feel it's my duty to not only tell a wonderful, engaging story but to also be as historically accurate as I can. And while fiction writers use license to expand on the truth or even fabricate outright fantasy, I do my best to convey the flavor and description of Colorado in the 1870s to the best of my ability. Any errors in accuracy are mine—either through lack of knowledge or deliberate tampering.

I'm ever grateful to all my fans for their support, wonderful comments and reviews, and encouraging words. If you enjoy my novels, please tell your friends, leave reviews on Amazon, and join my Street Team! If you join my mailing list, you'll get free books and sneak peeks. You can even suggest characters and plots for me to include in future novels! I write for you!

—Charlene Whitman, October 2016

ABOUT THE AUTHOR

CHARLENE WHITMAN SPENT MANY YEARS living on Colorado's Front Range. She grew up riding and raising horses, and loves to read, write, and hike the mountains. She attended Colorado State University in Fort Collins as an English major. She has two daughters and is married to George "Dix" Whitman, her love of thirty years.

If you enjoyed this book . . . One of the nicest ways to say "thank you" to an author is to leave a favorable review online. I would be appreciative if you would take a moment to do so! Thanks so much!

Comments? Questions? I love hearing from my readers, so feel free to contact me via my Facebook page: Charlene Whitman, Author, or e-mail me at charlwhitman@gmail.com.

If you've missed the other novels in The Front Range Series, *Colorado Promise* or *Colorado Hope,* you can get your paperback or Kindle copy on Amazon.com

Be sure to join Charlene Whitman's readers' list to get free books, special offers, giveaways, and sneak peeks of chapters and covers.

Sign up at www.charlenewhitman.com!

Here's a sneak peek at *Wild Secret, Wild Longing*—a long novella that tells the story of LeRoy finding love in the wilds of the Rocky Mountains …

Chapter 1

October 7, 1876

BRIGHT LAUGHTER TUMBLED THROUGH THE heavy oak doors behind LeRoy Banks as he shouldered his way out of the stiflingly warm lodge. A cool breeze tickled his face, and the sweat on his brow swiftly dried as he stood in the late afternoon glare of sunlight that splattered golden patches across the brown grass of the pastures sprawling up into the foothills west of Whitcomb's ranch.

He walked over to the hitching post, undoing the top buttons of his stiffly starched white shirt, and breathed like a man freed of chains. But it wasn't just the collar that had been constricting his throat. He knew that for a fact, but what he didn't know was how to sort through the feelings rippling through his heart.

He wasn't one to take a deep dive into such things, but this uneasiness tugged on him with the relentlessness of a green horse fixing to break through a makeshift pen. It made his feet twitchy.

His gaze came to rest on the herd of horses grazing lazily afar, and he listened to the comforting snuffling and flicks of their tails. Blankets of droning insects shimmered in the light, and heavy dark clouds sagged over the peaks of the mountains, whispering of snow.

Horses, he knew. A wild, terrified mustang confined within fences for the first time in his life LeRoy understood. One look into the eyes of a wild creature displaced and fearful of his future and LeRoy knew just what the animal was feeling. And he knew exactly what to do to help the horse work through that fear and come to trust. Not just trust, either, but also to find his joyful place living among his two-legged brothers.

LeRoy let loose a sigh and gripped the splintered railing, thinking of his brother, Eli, and the way his eyes had shone like crystals as he recited his vows to his new bride, Clare McKay. LeRoy's heart beat in happiness for Eli, and as he'd stood by his brother's side and watched them be pronounced man and wife by the preacher, he couldn't recall a happier moment in his life. But as the exuberant pair stepped down from the festooned platform to be congratulated by the dozens of guests, LeRoy had felt a strange and disturbing sadness threaten to dampen his joy.

Why this sadness in the midst of such a happy occasion? LeRoy wished he knew.

The loud eruption of fiddle music caused him to swivel back around.

"There you are," Eli said, waving at LeRoy, Clare hanging on his arm like a new permanent appendage. LeRoy chuckled as they pushed the doors wide and strode over to him. Eli, all dressed up in such finery, with his boots polished to a spit-shine that almost hurt LeRoy's eyes—he was quite a sight. LeRoy doubted he'd ever see his younger brother in attire like this ever again. With his wheat-straw hair slicked back and his face scrubbed and shaved nearly raw, Eli reminded LeRoy of a newly shorn sheep—one that wouldn't stay all clean and purty for long.

"What're ya doin' outside? We're about to start dancin'," Clare chided him, narrowing her eyes playfully at him. "And ya did promise me you'd do a reel with me."

"That I did," LeRoy said, giving Clare a smile that acknowledged she'd caught her quarry. He marveled at the intricate beadwork along the neckline of her floor-length wedding dress— tiny creamy pearls. Now that he had a chance to see the bride up close, he noted the hand-stitching rivaled anything he'd seen in the Cheyenne ceremonial garb his ma kept in her cedar chest.

"Grace make you that dress?"

Clare beamed and sashayed from side to side, making the layers of petticoats flounce against her dainty little shoes. Shoes like nothing feisty Clare McKay ever wore. She and Eli sure looked like porcelain dolls, all gussied up like that. They shoulda listened to his suggestion to get married on their horses, all roped and tied up, like they'd just lassoed each other. They hadn't much liked his idea, go figure.

Clare bounced on her toes, her face alight with joy. "She did. Just like she promised. Made it exactly like the picture too. She's some amazin' seamstress."

LeRoy merely nodded. Eli punched his shoulder. "Maybe she'll make one for your bride someday."

A laugh caught in LeRoy's throat. He pushed words past it. "Don't hold your breath, Brother. I ain't fixin' to get hitched anytime soon."

"Why not?" Clare asked. She pursed her lips and stared LeRoy down.

"My, you're being personal, Mrs. Banks," Eli said, his eyes dancing with mirth despite the scowl on his face. "My brother's just waitin' for the right woman to come along. Ain't that right, LeRoy?"

Clare rolled her eyes. "Huh. We'll be waitin' until the snow melts atop the Rockies," she said, her tone chastising. "I introduced you to Shannon—ya didn't like her?" she asked LeRoy with a raised eyebrow. "She's every bit as good a rider as I am. Well, nearly—"

Eli playfully tugged Clare's arm, tipping his head at the lodge. "Clare, leave him be. Your sister ain't but sixteen. That makes LeRoy nearly ten years older."

"So? What's wrong with that?" She frowned at Eli, who tugged her a few steps toward the doors. Music drifted to their ears—a rousing tune of fiddles, bass, and washboard, and the accompanying stomping of dozens of boots on the wood-plank floorboards.

"Honey, don't you wanna dance?" Eli asked her. "All the guests are gonna be wonderin' where we went—"

"Oh, let 'em wonder." She turned and pinned her eyes on LeRoy. "I'm serious, LeRoy. You need a wife. It'll do ya some good."

The laugh that had snagged in LeRoy's chest now burst out. He shook his head. "Clare, I do love you. You're . . . something."

"Somethin' else, for sure," Eli said, giving LeRoy a surrendering shrug and that crooked smile of his.

"And I love ya too, LeRoy," Clare told him, finally giving in to Eli's urging and letting herself be dragged toward the doors. She waggled a finger at him with a giggle. "But I won't brook rude behavior at my wedding. So c'mon back inside and give me that dance ya promised."

"Will do, ma'am," LeRoy said, touching the brim of his hat, still chuckling as Eli pulled his beautiful headstrong wife back inside Whitcomb's lodge.

He caught a glimpse of his ma through the open doors of the big log house, her dark braided hair shining under all the many flickering Chinese lanterns strung along the rafters. She was chatting with Lucas Rawlings—LeRoy's closest friend—but she suddenly turned and saw LeRoy, and fell silent upon seeing him.

LeRoy grunted. As if he could hide his inner turmoil from a Cheyenne medicine woman who knew him better than he knew hisself.

He had a sudden urge to head over to the bunkhouse to find a piece of quiet. He'd been living this past month among Whitcomb's ranch hands, helping the rich rancher break the wild mustangs he and Eli had run down the mountain that day they'd gone after those two outlaws—the last of the Dutton gang. What a day that had been—cornering that varmint Wymore after he shot dead Monty's lying snake of a wife, and watching him get trampled underfoot by the stampeding herd. Finding the other outlaw nearly dead, the cabin ablaze. Monty gone after Grace, who'd fallen with her baby off the cliff.

LeRoy shook his head and blew out a breath. That had been more'n enough excitement to last out the year. He was grateful for the predictable daily routine of working the horses, and although he considered Whitcomb's men plenty amicable, he tended to keep to hisself. It took some adjusting—living with a dozen men in one room, with all their snores and stench. Some were plenty rough around the edges, and a few took issue with LeRoy's Indian blood and made snide remarks, but Whitcomb brooked neither drunkenness nor tomfoolerly, and so any scuffling and contentions were soon snuffed out.

With Lucas married and living in his own cabin north of the Poudre, and Eli setting up a homestead in Fort Collins so Clare could be close to her family, LeRoy's ma was all alone at their ranch north of Greeley. Despite her protestations that she was managing just fine—and enjoying some real peace and quiet for the first time in years—he worried about her. Well, he'd be back home in a few weeks, with some right fine mustang mares in tow to add to their breeding stock. The railroad might be replacing the stagecoach, but folks always needed horses. His ma would stay busy. And maybe that'd keep her from prying the lid off his inner rumblings.

Through the large window, LeRoy watched Clare entwine arms with Eli and lead him out on the sawdust-strewn dance floor. Clare was the perfect match for Eli. No doubt about it. His brother was lucky to have found her. LeRoy couldn't imagine Eli marrying some quiet, demure girl who never spoke her mind. Eli needed the challenge of a wild filly, one who had no intention of being broken or trained. Or tamed. She was a handful, but exactly what Eli loved about her.

He thought about Shannon, Clare's sister—the sweet little redhead with the freckles spattered across her nose. Sure, she'd make some man a great wife. A nice-looking gal, hard-working, plenty capable from what LeRoy could tell. But . . .

But what? Sure, he wanted to marry—someday. Or did he? There were plenty of moments when the longing struck him, when a twinge of loneliness reared up like a feisty stallion. But although he'd met plenty of eligible girls over the years, none had lit a spark in his heart—not like the way Clare did to Eli. Did he even want that?

Maybe he was too used to being alone. He liked his independence, and like some old man, he had his ways of doing things. He preferred his own company to any other's. The idea of giving up his freedom to be with a woman—every day, year after year—didn't sit easy in him. Having to change his ways, getting nagged, pressured to speak his mind when he liked to keep his thoughts to hisself . . .

He thought about Lucas and the stormy day he'd brought Emma to the ranch on his horse. She'd been thrown from her mare and knocked out, and Lucas had laid her down in the barn and tended to her. LeRoy well knew Lucas's story—how he'd lost his wife and baby in childbirth two years earlier. Last thing on Lucas's mind was falling back in love. But he had—and he'd fallen hard. LeRoy had thought the upper-class spoiled Easterner would be the last woman to turn his friend's head, but he was wrong. And Emma had truly surprised LeRoy. She took to the West like a hog to mud, and now the two were expecting a baby and couldn't be happier.

Despite all this, LeRoy had seen his share of miserable married men—if the truth be told. Plenty of 'em. More unhappy than happy—men who seemed to rue the day they'd spoken their vows before God and man. LeRoy didn't take vows lightly, as some did. When—if—he ever married, he'd have to be sure. He wanted the kind of love his parents had had. A love that nothing could destroy.

Their love had withstood the hardest trials anyone could possibly face—a white man marrying a Cheyenne woman in a fierce season of hatred and killing and distrust. Over the years to come, their love had survived the massacres and broken treaties and relocation of his ma's tribe to Oklahoma. Instead of leaving with her people—her parents and brothers and sisters—she'd stayed in Colorado Territory with his pa and worked the ranch. LeRoy knew how much that loss pained her, though she rarely spoke of the past. Sarah Banks was not one to wallow in memory or sadness. She was busy getting about living.

A wave of sadness washed over LeRoy at the thought of his pa. His chest tightened, and his breathing grew labored. Pressure built behind his eyes, making him suddenly realize the source of his pestering unease.

His pa should have been here to witness Eli's wedding. His absence was what LeRoy was feeling. An absence that loomed large, making LeRoy wonder if his pa's spirit was present. He looked around, then felt a little silly thinking his pa might make some kind of appearance. Despite his ma's firm assurances that the deceased John Banks was closely watching the goings-on of his two sons, LeRoy had never sensed anything akin to what his ma often seemed to. LeRoy chuckled. Maybe his ma only said that to him and Eli over the years as a way to scare them out of misbehavior.

Guilt welled up when he realized he'd never once thought of his pa this day. Or much at all in recent months. LeRoy did a quick calculation in his mind. Fourteen years. He'd been twelve when his pa was thrown off that horse and smacked his head against the fencepost. Died instantly. Eli had been ten.

The memory of that day engulfed him in a dark cloud of pain and hurt. Pain he'd squelched in his heart over and over for years until it lodged like a hard pebble in his chest. But presently it had grown again to the size of a boulder, threatening to force LeRoy to his knees.

He shambled over to the lodge and leaned against the warm wood log siding, trying to calm his racing heart. Then, a hand touched his arm, startling him. He jerked his head up and met his ma's searching dark eyes.

He straightened, and his breath suddenly calmed. He breathed in deep and managed a smile.

His ma turned her head and watched the festivities through the window. Her silver-streaked black braids lay down her back, and her Cheyenne features seemed magnified by the soft deerskin ceremonial dress she wore and the strands of colorful beads hanging from her neck. The strains of lively music tickled the air, and the foot stomping of those dancing shuddered the porch floorboards under LeRoy's feet.

Without looking at him, she said, "Now that Clare's takin' care of Eli, he's not your responsibility any longer." Her voice was quiet, thoughtful. She tipped her head and smiled, watching Eli and Clare dance. She wrested her gaze and turned to him. "Now it is time for you to make your own path for your life."

A chill danced across LeRoy's neck as a breeze kicked up. Cool, rarified mountain air drifted down and filled the valley. He smelled the river not far away, and a hint of snow. Had she known what his pa used to say to him before he died? She must have, for why would she have spoken of caring for Eli? *"It's your job to look after your little brother. To set an example. Teach him to be honest and honorable and upstanding. If anything should ever happen to me . . ."*

LeRoy heard the words as if his pa were speaking into his ear. He closed his eyes, remembering the sound of his pa's warm, deep voice calming his anxious heart.

"He loved you so much," his ma said, an unusual surge of emotion lacing her words.

LeRoy studied her face, but she was practiced at keeping so many of her secrets well hidden. He said nothing, just swallowed and nodded.

Her smile was wistful. She ran her hand through his hair, the way she used to when he was a boy. She hadn't done that in a long time, and it was strangely soothing. "You are so much like him." Her eyes glistened as they regarded him steadily. "He would have been so proud of you."

LeRoy didn't know how to answer her. He swallowed back tears and nodded, turned his head and stared into the hills. Sunlight crawled along the ground as the sun slid west toward the snowy peaks. Clouds bunched like thick cotton batting along the horizon to the north.

After silence settled into the cracks between them, she cleared her throat. "Well, they're gonna be cuttin' the cake shortly. Wouldn't want to miss out on that."

"Ma," he said, turning abruptly to look at her. "How . . . why did you marry Pa? Why not someone from your tribe?"

Sarah chuckled, her face softening and the years of hard lines falling away. "Your grandfather was some mad, I can tell you that. But he knew John was a good man, had a good heart." She studied LeRoy's face, and it made him squirm. He just knew she was going to give him an earful about finding a wife and soon.

"LeRoy, when you love someone, it doesn't matter what anyone else thinks. It doesn't matter if the whole world is against you. Together you find strength to face all the trials life throws at you. You are more than two." She grew thoughtful a moment, then took his hands. "Your grandpa—your pa's dad—used to preach in Evans. You prob'ly don't remember him, but before he died, we used to haul you and Eli to his church on Sundays. When John first took me to meet him and your Grandma Banks, I was a mite anxious—"

LeRoy's eyebrows rose. "You, anxious?"

His ma smacked his arm and scowled. LeRoy hobbled his lip. He knew better than to tease when she was working up to her own version of a Sunday sermon.

She turned from him and watched the horses. "Your grandpa, being a man of faith, was wont to quote Scripture, and he looked at your pa and me and told us we'd face a lot of tribulation if we married. But the Good Book says love conquers all. And more importantly, that perfect love casts out fear. 'He that feareth is not made perfect in love.'"

His ma sighed. "Your grandpa was right, LeRoy. When you finally give you whole heart to someone, you'll understand."

"But . . ." LeRoy pushed the words out past the lump in his throat. "If you love someone that much, you know you're gonna hurt when you lose them." His pa's face filled his mind, followed by the image of his ma's grieving body hunched over his grave. Suddenly LeRoy saw him so clearly—the pale-green eyes and bushy eyebrows, the light-brown hair tucked under his wide-brimmed hat, trailing down to his shoulders, his encouraging smile and voice as warm as a lazy summer day. This time LeRoy couldn't hold back the tears. They dribbled onto his face, and he quickly swiped them away.

"We all lose everyone we love . . . someday," his ma said quietly, smoothing out her deerskin skirt. "Does that mean we should hide in a cave and never take the chance our heart will be broken? LeRoy," she said, her firm tone making him look at her, "this life is a brief passage, a stopping point on the way to *Ma'heo'o* and *Seana*, where all who have died reunite."

She looked up into the sky as if seeing the path among the stars the Cheyenne believed all spirits traversed after death. But LeRoy wasn't sure what he believed with his feet mired in the mud of two worlds—the white man's and the red man's. Most of the time he felt he didn't fit in either.

His ma sighed wistfully. "If you love, you will know pain and loss. But if you never love, you will never be whole. Your longing will grow like a prickly bush and pierce your heart."

"I like being alone—"

"Pshaa!" His ma puckered her face. "It's the men who say that who least mean it. It's not good for a man to be alone. You seen 'em—those old crotchety geezers who never had a wife. You want to end up like one of them? With a shriveled-up heart and an ornery personality?" She snorted and took his hand. Her earlier tenderness disappeared like a ripple on a lake. "You're smart not to rush into marrying. But don't let your fear hold you back. Listen to your heart, my *ka'éškone*. It will tell you when the time to love has arrived." She added with narrowed eyes, "It may be sooner than you think —"

Suddenly an eruption of horse squeals shattered the afternoon calm. Across the pasture dozens of mustangs reared and screamed as they bolted in all directions.

"What the . . . ?" LeRoy took off running toward the split-rail fencing, the sound of animals in pain stabbing his heart. He glanced back upon hearing men's shouting. A half dozen of Whitcomb's ranch hands raced behind him. LeRoy hoped a few had grabbed their guns. They'd seen mountain lion sign just last week, and LeRoy had spotted tracks up on the southwestern ridge, near the river. But it wasn't like a cat to come this close to so many folks, and not in daylight. Or in the fall, when game was plentiful in the mountains.

Plowing through the knee-high grass of the unfenced pasture tired him quickly, and he nearly busted the buttons on his snug shirt, breathing as hard as he was. Now that most of the horses had hightailed it to the farthest corners of the fence, LeRoy could see unobstructed to the back fence line, maybe fifty yards yonder. And what he saw caused a burst of rage and anguish to race through his veins.

Three horses struggled on the ground, kicking legs in the throes of death. Their mournful screams of pain wrenched LeRoy's heart as his keen eyes took in every inch of the land spread out before him. Behind the fence to the west, the hogbacks rose up steep and melted into thick conifer forest swallowed in darkness cast by the web of overhead branches. Two other horses pranced in place, turning tight frantic circles, blood streaming down their necks and flanks, their eyes wide with terror.

Men shouted behind him, then a rifle sounded. LeRoy heard the whistle of two shots—likely .44 gauge—zip past his ear. He wheeled around and saw Whitcomb's son, Andy, level a rifle at the woods.

LeRoy leaped over the fence, his heart hammering his ribs. He moved cautiously among the injured and dying horses. They hardly noticed him in all their fear. Now, close enough to see the wide gashes streaking down their necks, LeRoy knew what had attacked.

Vóhp-áhtse-náhkohe. Grizzly.

"There!" someone called out. LeRoy turned as another two shots thundered in the air. He saw where the man was pointing, and now LeRoy spotted the creature too.

"Don't let it get away!" Andy yelled, then screamed out a string of cuss words. "It's got one of the mares!" Another rifle shot sliced through the air. This one sounded like a Big Fifty—a Sharps buffalo gun.

Cursing that he was without a gun, and wearing all this finery that was soon to be blood-soaked, LeRoy stood and watched Whitcomb's men scramble over the back fence and head into the trees. The grizzly lifted his head as if a thousand rounds of bullets couldn't concern him in the least, then left off dragging his quarry and ambled into the shadows of the woods, which swallowed his massive bulk.

LeRoy started humming softly and took slow steps toward the mustang with a white blaze down her bark-brown head. She eyed him wildly and reared up as if to pound him into the ground. Then she dropped her front legs and stepped in agitation akin to a tribal war dance.

"Whoa, whoa," he said quietly, then resumed his humming. Finally he was able to lay a hand on her neck. The other horse near her calmed a bit in response.

"What're ya doin' in there? Fool Injun!"

"You wanna git yerself kilt?"

LeRoy ignored the men standing back from the fence glowering at him. He looked over at the three horses lying prone on the blood-splattered grass. Two were dead, their eyes open and glassy. The other lay panting with her stomach ripped open.

Andy merely stood at the fence, cussing with every foul word he could come up with.

LeRoy rested his hand on the horse's neck, kept up his humming. Out of the corner of his eye, he saw someone clamber over the fence and come toward him.

Lucas Rawlings.

His friend had doffed his hat and party coat, and his sleeves were rolled up. He carried his vet bag in one hand and a Colt pistol in the other.

Lucas blew out a hard breath as he stopped ten feet from LeRoy and assessed the situation. LeRoy saw the heartache in Lucas's eyes. Lucas loved horses more than anyone LeRoy had ever known, and that was saying a lot. So he knew what the man was feeling when he lifted his gun with a pained frown on his face, took aim at the last living mare lying on the ground, and shot the suffering animal in the head. His aim was steady and true.

The mare's head thumped dead on the grass, and her legs stopped paddling. LeRoy swallowed.

"What do ya think?" he asked Lucas in an almost whisper, making Lucas pull his gaze away from the dead mare. LeRoy nodded for him to come over as he kept up the gentle patting and stroking of the mare's neck, saying soothing words to her.

Lucas looked her over, then glanced at the other injured horse. He took a slow walk around the both, and the men watching grew quiet. LeRoy spotted his ma hurrying across the pasture, carrying a satchel. Upon Lucas's arrival, the ranch hands climbed up on the fence to watch in silence. Further back, dozens of party guests stood in a crowd just off the porch. No doubt Whitcomb had told them to stay put. LeRoy grunted. He could just imagine what grief Eli was giving his host — and his new bride. He was sure Clare had Eli nailed to the floor by now with him doing his own brand of squealing. Eli was not one to stand back and let anyone else jump headfirst into danger. At least not without him by their side. But it wouldn't be proper for the groom to get all dirty and bloody on his wedding day, would it?

"That one's got some surface bruises and scratches," Lucas said, coming alongside LeRoy and rubbing a hand on the mare's rump. "More'n likely hurt when the horses panicked." He pulled a halter and lead rope out of his bag. "Let's get her back to the barn. She'll probably be fine once I stitch her up, although" — he took a good look at the exposed muscle in her shoulder without touching it — "that bear tore her somethin' deep. She may end up with a limp."

"She may be bad hurt, but at least she's got her life." LeRoy looked sorrowfully at the three dead horses and thought about the one the grizzly had hauled easily over the split-rail fence. He'd encountered grizzlies on occasion — thankfully never close up — and they were fearsome creatures. They could wrench off the side of a barn in one swoop. Plenty of tales were told about men who'd faced a grizzly and barely lived to tell about it. He hoped Whitcomb's men had killed this one, but it wasn't easily done. Some bears had dozens of bullets in their pelt and flesh and kept on going. And killing. And there were few things more dangerous than an injured and suffering grizzly.

LeRoy took the halter from Lucas and gently slipped it over the mare's head. With a quiet clucking, he got her to take a few steps. Lucas crouched down and took a jar from his bag.

"You go on ahead; I'll meet you at the barn." He dabbed some ointment on the other mare's leg. She stood still, eyeing Lucas suspiciously, but she gave no indication she was about to bolt.

Lucas added, "Tell Emma where I am. I disappeared on her, and she'll be worried."

See, pardner, that's what happens when you marry. You end up with someone worrying about you all the time. And ya gotta answer for everything you do.

LeRoy snorted as he led the mare back across the pasture at a slow walk, the scattered horses now taking a cautious step or two away from the fence. Calm once more drifted into the valley, as if the bear had never attacked.

LeRoy glanced back and saw men gathered along the back fence line. He made out Andy and two of the men who had gone off after the bear. He'd heard no more shots. Well, the bear was either dead or had run off. It could have been worse. LeRoy exhaled hard as his ma walked toward him. He stopped and looked at the deerskin satchel she held out to him. It was one of her medicine pouches. Why was she giving this to him?

"You want me to give this to Lucas?" He figured she had some special ointments or tinctures in here. Maybe something to calm the horses. Not like Lucas needed anything though. He kept his own medical bag well stocked. And the barn had all the typical ranch supplies—for both animal and human injuries and illnesses.

"No," she said, an intense look flaring in her eyes.

LeRoy's nerves jangled. His pulse quickened, and he swallowed hard. He knew just what that look meant. It was the same look she'd given him and Eli the night those murderous ranchers had attacked them and ended up dead—when she put the everlasting powder on them to prepare them for battle. And it was the same look as when she'd told them to go to Fort Collins to offer to help Sheriff Eph Love track those outlaws. She urged them to be careful, that blood was going to spill.

"What is it, Ma?" LeRoy asked on papery thin breath. He gripped tight the lead rope as she handed him the satchel. He really didn't want to hear her answer.

"It's not for Lucas. It's for you." She added solemnly, "You're going to need it."

All LeRoy could do was nod.

Want to read more?
Buy *Wild Secret, Wild Longing* at Amazon.com.

CPSIA information can be obtained
at www.ICGtesting.com
Printed in the USA
LVOW08s1748160217
524502LV00004B/958/P